GRAVE

Book Three of *The Queen of the Dead*

MICHELLE SAGARA

DAW BOOKS, INC.
DONALD A. WOLLHEIM, FOUNDER
375 Hudson Street, New York, NY 10014

ELIZABETH R. WOLLHEIM
SHEILA E. GILBERT
PUBLISHERS
http://www.dawbooks.com

First Paperback Printing, February 2018

1 2 3 4 5 6 7 8 9

DAW TRADEMARK REGISTERED
U.S. PAT. AND TM. OFF. AND FOREIGN COUNTRIES
—MARCA REGISTRADA
HECHO EN U.S.A.

PRINTED IN THE U.S.A.

This is for Jane Fletcher.

She made school as sane and bearable as it could possibly be for my son when it was absolutely essential, and I can truly say that he is as much a product of her guidance and leadership as he is of mine.

No matter how difficult things were, he knew that he could go to Ms Fletcher, talk to her, be heard. He knew that ultimately, at the top of the chain, there was both accountability and trust. She made school feel safe.

And that is so very, very rare.

ACKNOWLEDGMENTS

I feel, as of late, that my acknowledgements are a frantic, grovelling, thank you to people who have had to endure my flailing and my optimistic sense of my own abilities. And they are.

Grave is the third and final novel in a trilogy that has seen more revisions, more "throw away two-thirds of the book" author angst than *any* other series I have ever worked on. This was enormously hard on me—but that almost goes without saying. No one expects someone to toss out their year's worth of work multiple times and be overjoyed to do so, given that they've got to start again at ground zero. I mean page one.

Terry, as always, read every word as it was written. All four times. He probably heard all the whining more often as well. And he reminded me that making a mistake does not equal total permanent failure. Which, as things wore on, became unfortunately necessary.

But people who are not in publishing seldom see the effect it has on the publishers, the editors. It knocks books out of schedule, which means the entire schedule has to be reshuffled. It makes it harder to gain any reader traction, because of the gaps and uncertainties in the publication timing. It is . . . bad.

And throughout this, I have to say, if my editor was furious—and seriously, human, she must have had those days—she kept it entirely away from me. If she had a dart-board with my picture on it, I would accept it as no more than my due. My managing editor, Joshua Starr, has been unfailingly polite, helpful, and almost instant in answering my frantic emails. No, polite is the wrong word. He actually sounds cheerful most days, as if he enjoys dealing with people like me who are, let's face it, not making his job any easier.

Cliff Nielsen's art for the cover of the third book is perfect, and I felt blessed by it, which again has nothing to do with me, the writer, but is the first thing most people will see of the book.

And of course, if the book falls short, if there are problems with it, it is, in fact, on me, and not on the people who did so much to guide it to your hands.

NATHAN

THE QUEEN'S MEDITATION CHAMBERS ARE large. The ceilings are high enough you can't see them if you don't crane your neck. Looking up is a lot like falling; Nathan avoids it out of habit. The dead don't fall—even when that's what they want. They can jump off a cliff or the roof of a building and hang there, ignored by gravity. They've got no weight.

The Queen is not dead. She burns with life. She is luminous, beautiful; if the dead aren't careful, they are struck dumb at the sight of her. She doesn't know what she looks like in the eyes of the dead; she can't see herself the way the dead do. She's therefore incredibly impatient. She takes a dim view of disobedience.

She is the only law the dead know.

The Queen walks to the center of the round chamber. Elaborate chairs dot the circumference of the smooth, rising walls; there are cabinets with cut-glass doors that catch light and reflect it. Books line the shelves; books lie face-up across the various tables situated between the chairs. She touches none of them. Instead, she positions herself in the center of a large engraved circle. The perimeter of that circle contains runes or glyphs that Nathan would have found fascinating while alive. He barely sees them, now.

The Queen is not wearing her full court dress. She doesn't need it. If she wore sweats and sneakers, it wouldn't matter. People here aren't bowing or scraping at her dress. Nathan understands that bowing and scraping—when too obsequious—annoys the Queen. He doesn't do it.

But he doesn't speak, either, unless spoken to. He doesn't crack a joke. He doesn't ask her how her day went. Mostly, he doesn't want to know. And there are reasons for that.

She gestures. She doesn't speak. Or rather, she doesn't speak to Nathan; she can choose who, among the dead, hear her voice.

Four of the dead do.

They come to her as she stands, flowing through the walls as if the chamber were a vast, unmarked clock face; they trace the path from the quarter marks of time—twelve, three, six, nine—as they approach. Nathan closes his eyes, but it doesn't help. He can still see their faces. He can see their expressions.

There are two girls and two boys. They are all Nathan's age—or they were, when they died. Left to themselves, the dead tend to wear the clothing they spent their last living minutes in. But the dead in the citadel are not left to their own devices. They wear what the Queen dictates. Today—or tonight—they are wearing loose, flowing robes. The robes are a pale, luminescent gray, as is everything else about them.

They walk with a quiet, hopeless dignity. One of the girls struggles; he can see the strain in the lines of her mouth, the narrowing of her eyes. But he can't see it in the steps she is forced to take. She understands what is going to happen to her here. He wonders if the other three do. He can't ask. Literally. His mouth doesn't move.

That's probably for the best. Nathan is not a screamer. He's not a cryer. But the urge—the sudden, visceral urge—to do both is strong.

He understood, as he followed the Queen to this chamber, that she meant to "clothe you in life," a fancy way of saying "build you a body." He understood that all of the Queen's power is derived from the dead—and that the city itself is home to many of them. More come every day; overpopulation isn't an issue when your citizens can't eat, can't work, and don't particularly need a place to live.

He did not put the three things together. The building of a body. The power necessary. The source of that power.

She means to honor him. He knows this. He knows that this is how she sees what she is doing as she waits implacably for the drifting dead to reach her until she is the heart of their formation. Nathan can see her through the transparency of their bodies. No surprise, there; he can see her through the solid stone of her citadel's many walls.

She knows. She turns to him, smiling, her expression radiant. She looks—for just that moment—like a sixteen-year-old girl, not the ancient ruler of a dead city. The four surround her now. They reach out—to each other—and clasp hands.

They are already dead. So is Nathan. But he feels their fear; it's like a mirror of his own. He doesn't need to breathe—but even if he did, he wouldn't. She raises her arm, then raises her face, exposing the perfect line of a throat that clearly never sees sunlight. Her hair, loose, trails down her back, straight and unconfined. It is the only thing about her that reminds him of Emma.

No, that's not true. The Queen of the Dead reminds Nathan of Emma because she is, at this moment, everything that Emma *isn't*. Emma would never surround herself with unwilling victims. Emma would never reach out with her graceful, slender hands and *bury* them in the chests of the two young women, reaching for the hearts that they don't actually have anymore.

Nathan wants to scream. He wants to shout. He wants to beg the Queen to *stop*. To tell her that he'll take being dead—being invisibly, unreachably dead—because no form of life, no form of actual body, could be worth the cost.

The dead girls throw back their heads, just as the Queen did, but for vastly different reasons. Nathan can see only their profiles; their mouths are open in the silent scream that Nathan is certain shapes his own. When the Queen retracts her hands, the girls come with them, as if their bodies were made of cloth and she has yanked them out of shape. That cloth is like silk or satin; it has a sheen that catches light, implies color.

It doesn't look human anymore. But Nathan knows, watching, that it is. The Queen is radiant with color as she shifts in place. She turns to face Nathan, and as she does, she reaches out again for the center of two hearts. The two boys. They're braced for it; unlike the one girl, they don't struggle at all. Their eyes are wide, rounded; they watch the Queen—just as Nathan does. Like moths to flame.

She unravels them as well. Her arms are cocooned with glowing light; it's almost painful to look at. Nathan understands that the dead are there, exposed, rendered both helpless and potent; she has taken whatever they have left to give.

And she uses it now, as he watches. She works those strands of colored, brilliant light, as if weaving a basket or a wire dummy. He can almost hear the voices of the four as she does; they are weeping. They are so close to her, so close to the warmth of the light she sheds—and it makes no difference. Nathan wonders, then, if she can hear them at all.

But she must, because she can hear him. She looks at him now, as she shuffles threads, joining them, binding them, making their weave tighter and tighter until they seem solid to the eye. She then looks at her work with the critical eye of an artist. Her gaze pins Nathan and leaves him, over and over again.

Nathan has no idea how much time passes. No one comes to these chambers but the Queen. No one interrupts her when she works here. And she works now. She works, her brow furrowed, her eyes narrowed; she works until sweat beads her forehead and small strands of pale hair cling to it.

All the while, the voices of the four thrum; they have a pulse and a beat, an ebb and a flow, that are synchronized almost exactly with the work she does. It is the chamber music of hell.

Nathan, like anyone else alive—or, rather, anyone who was once alive—has no memory of being born. He has dim memories of childhood, and he believes some of them occurred when he was three—but he's aware that he might be wrong, even if they *are* his memories. He tries to sort through them now, as the Queen continues to sculpt: to shear off pale flesh from cheekbones, to elongate neck, to narrow the lines of chest, arms, hands.

When she is finished, it is the hands of her masterpiece she holds. "Nathan," she says, her voice softer than he has ever heard it, "come to me."

Like the single girl, he hesitates. He knows the hesitation could be deadly, but at this point, he almost welcomes it. He can *still* hear dim, attenuated voices, and he understands that they are part of the finished form.

It looks like Nathan, to his own eyes: like Nathan, but stark naked. He can't see the flaws. He knows they're there, but he can't see them for the light she still radiates. If he could plug his ears, he might even feel awe or gratitude. He can't.

Oh, he can lift hands to ears, but it does no good. His ears aren't actual, physical ears. His hands block no sound.

"Nathan."

He walks. He walks toward where the Queen clasps the hands of her empty, shining creation. He notes that the eyes—the body's eyes—are closed and wonders whether his eyelashes were ever that long. It's an absurd thought.

Absurd is better than horror.

He is not terrified of the Queen as he approaches her; horror and terror are different. But he understands, as she waits, why someone would run away from her no matter how much she loved them.

Nathan doesn't love her. If he had a choice, there is almost nowhere else he wouldn't be.

"Give me your hand," the Queen says.

He doesn't think; his hand is in hers before the echoes of her words die. Her palm is warm. It reminds him of Emma.

Emma is a Necromancer.

He didn't understand why Chase was so angry at Emma. He couldn't understand what Chase feared. No one who knew Emma could be afraid of her. They might be afraid of losing her—and the love she offers so steadily—but that was never Chase's concern.

He understands now. Emma glows with the same

interior fire that burns at the heart of the Queen. Emma has as much power as the Queen of the Dead. Emma could—if she knew how—do exactly what the Queen has done today.

Emma would never do it. He knows. But he wonders what anyone could do to stop her if she did.

"Close your eyes, Nathan."

He does. He doesn't tell her that it makes no difference. She doesn't plunge her hand into his chest. She doesn't yank his heart out and stretch it into filaments. She doesn't destroy him for the raw materials she needs to create anything else. But he wonders, now, whether everything in her world—the citadel, the streets, the buildings that line them—was made the same way.

The warmth of her hand becomes heat, and the heat becomes pain. It is not a pain he associates with burning—he's burned himself before. It's not a pain he associates with physical injury. It's not localized. It's not confined to the hand she grips.

It travels through him. It curls up inside of him, as if he had swallowed it whole. It has no way to escape him; he has no way to set it free. Some small part of him thinks: It's better than feeling nothing.

He expects to be swallowed in a similar way; he's not. She attaches herself to him in a hundred little ways—in a thousand. As she does, the cold recedes. There's nothing sexual about her touch. Nothing predatory. She is alarmingly gentle.

It's the gentleness that almost does him in. If he couldn't hear the dim, distant voices of the others, he would surrender himself entirely into this woman's keeping. He is *so* tired. And he is warm. He almost believes he has finally come to a place of rest.

But the voices don't stop. They're quiet. They're dim. But they're inside him now. Or he's inside them. He opens his eyes. He blinks. The Queen withdraws the hands that held his—and they are his hands, now. The voices weep to let her go; they can't cling. Nathan could—but he doesn't. He has that choice.

He is standing before her. He's naked. He should feel embarrassed, but he doesn't; she recreated his entire body.

There's no part of it she hasn't seen and no part of it she hasn't already touched.

"There is a robe on the far wall," the Queen says. "Take it and leave. Someone will be waiting to lead you to your rooms. You will require rooms, now; you will require food."

He doesn't ask her about sleep. He doesn't ask her about anything. He knows he should make some show of gratitude, but he can't quite force his knees to bend because he doesn't feel any. If he works—and he does—he can keep the horror from his expression. More than that isn't in him.

And he knows that there will be a bill for this, down the road. The Queen's generosity is never a gift. He is afraid that the bill won't be presented to him.

He puts on the robe and turns, once again, to face the Queen; she is standing, arms wrapped around her upper body, in the center of the circle. He looks away immediately. It is not—it is never—safe to see the Queen's pain, and it is evident now; she is a confused, lost girl, her fragility both her armor and her weapon. If he were a different man, he would go to her; he would slide an awkward arm around her shoulder; he would offer her comfort.

He doesn't. He knows there's no comfort she'll take from him. There is only one person she wants.

And that person has devoted himself to her death.

Nathan doesn't remember being born. He will never forget being reborn.

REYNA

REYNA LIVES WITH THE DEAD.
This wasn't always true.

As a child, living on the edge of villages, and once or twice, larger towns, she spent her days helping her mother in her various gardens, and helping her uncles when they went on errands for her mother. When she was eight, she took care of Helmi, her squalling, infant sister. From time to time, she played with other children, but in truth, not often; strangers always made her mother nervous.

Reyna has lived with the dead since she was just shy of thirteen. The dead don't frighten her. They can't do anything on their own. The scariest person Reyna knows is alive.

Reyna's mother is frowning at her over a circle etched in chalk. Reyna drew that circle. It's not good enough for her mother. Nothing is ever good enough for her mother. But the floors are rough here; it's hard to draw straight lines — or solid, curved lines — with chunks of chalk. Chalk is *not* to be wasted. Nothing is to be wasted. Reyna understands why.

She makes no excuses because she's learned, with time,

that no excuse satisfies her mother and the attempt to offer one darkens a mood that is never bright to begin with. The circles are anchors. Without anchors, searching for the dead is not safe.

If she's to leave this house before sunset, these circles have to be exact. Her mother will settle for nothing less. Reyna works with deliberate care, even if her hands are shaking. If she makes mistakes, she will have to do it all over again—and that will take too long, always too long.

While she works, her mother talks about the only thing that matters to her: the dead. The dead who are lost. "It's cold," her mother says. "It's cold, where she is."

Reyna doesn't ask who. She knows. Somewhere— nowhere close to the village in which they've lived for almost a full year—someone died. Death didn't free her. She is trapped somewhere cold. She's afraid. The dead are almost always afraid.

"Did you see her?" she asks her mother.

Her mother shakes her head.

Reyna is surprised.

"She's not close enough for me. You're going to have to do it." It's said so grudgingly, it stings. Reyna swallows back-talk. Beneath her mother's words is the acknowledgment of the uncomfortable truth between them: Reyna's gift is more powerful than her mother's. Of course her mother's not happy about it.

But she has to be worthy of that power. "Can't you use the lantern?" she asks.

Her mother snorts. "We don't use it unless we have no other choice."

Daring more, Reyna says, "If you let me use it—"

"No. Not yet. You're not old enough yet."

But she *is* old enough to sit in a circle for hours, walking a path toward a stranger who died somewhere cold. Reyna doesn't say this. She tries not to resent it. Instead, she draws and redraws and tries to do it quickly.

Reyna has a secret.

It's never wise to keep secrets from her mother or the rest of her family—and it's *always* hard to keep them when Helmi is underfoot. But more than half of Reyna's life is a secret now; she's had practice. She knows when to speak, and she knows how to say very little. She knows how to let people fill in the silences and the spaces between words on their own.

And *this* secret is not a guilty secret. This is not a secret she keeps primarily out of fear, the way her mother keeps secrets from every stranger, every neighbor, everyone who might—just might—become a friend, otherwise. She keeps it because it is *hers* and it has nothing to do with the dead, nothing to do with the life the magar forces her family to lead.

This secret is about life. It's about living. It fills all the spaces that have existed as empty gaps and insecurities for as long as Reyna can remember. It is about love. Reyna's love. And the fact that Reyna is loved.

She feels she has never been loved before now. She has certainly never loved this way before. When she is with Eric, she never thinks about the dead. When she is with Eric, she isn't confined by circles of chalk and stories of death and loss. She barely thinks about the future. She wants every minute in his company she can get—because every minute is precious, and they seem to fly by, hours becoming minutes and minutes, seconds, until it's time to return to the darkness and the secrecy.

Reyna lives with the dead—but she's not dead yet, and she wants, she desperately wants, to *live*.

Reyna knows when Eric became so important to her.

She doesn't understand how it happened—but she thinks about it because it gives her joy. She thinks about every moment, from the first meeting to the last, every awkward word; she thinks about the fear of speaking, and the fear of touching, and the fear of being sent away. All of it—the anticipation, the insecurity, the hesitance—is part of the perfect story, because she knows how it ends. She loves the ending, so she has to love the beginning.

They talk about it in snatches at the end of the day or before the day starts; they have only stolen moments. Eric is the smith's son, and he is expected to work. They talk about the first time they met. They talk about how they saw each other. Reyna could listen to Eric talk about it all day, every day.

But she knows the important moment, for her, was his laughter. It was so open, so loud, so low, so instant—and so unguarded. He was laughing *at* her. That should have ended things right there. It had before. But his voice was so—so *joyful*. As though he had swallowed life and her part in it, and he had to let the happiness out somehow. There was no laughter like that in Reyna's life.

There was barely any *life* in her life.

Shade dappled Eric's face and hid the color of hers; even the birds fell silent. She can close her eyes and see Eric so clearly she could spend all day with her eyes closed. She can remember her own laughter, welling up in response to his, as if the sheer sound of him had opened a dialogue in a language she didn't know, until that moment, was her mother tongue.

"Reyna, *pay attention*."

Reyna opens her eyes. This is the wrong thing to do. She can see the crimped, weathered lines of her mother's face— her mother, who is just past forty and looks as though she's already at the end of her life. Age has withered her skin, and the pinched frown lines around her lips, eyes, and forehead are so different from the lines that transform Eric's face when he laughs.

If there is joy in this room, her mother will hunt it down and kill it.

"What are you *thinking*?" her mother demands.

Reyna doesn't tell. She grabs her joy and she holds it close and tight in the cage of her body, because if her mother finds it, she will take it away. She exhales and tries to wipe the vestiges of a smile from her own face. She is not supposed to be thinking of Eric, or of life with Eric.

She is not supposed to be thinking of life at all.

∽⚬✕⚬∽

Reyna's mother only has eyes for dead people. Reyna remembers wishing, as a child, that she were dead—because then, her mother would come for *her*. Then, she would be the only person her mother could see. She would have all of her mother's attention.

The closest she ever comes is during lessons like these, but there's nothing unconditional about her mother's attention. She sits in judgment. She waits to criticize. Nothing Reyna says will be a good enough reason to wait. Reyna says nothing. She tries to focus. If she does what her mother wants done *quickly*, she will be able to see Eric.

Reyna listens. Eric's constant presence doesn't make her deaf; the reminder of life doesn't inure her to death. She understands the desire for home, for a place to belong. The dead trapped here don't have that, because no matter what they were in life, life has moved past them. The only people they can talk to are people like Reyna and her mother. Reyna doesn't understand why she can see the dead. She doesn't understand why her mother can. She knows it's a gift.

But tonight, it feels like a burden or a curse. Tonight, Eric will be waiting. If she could *explain*, it would help. She can't. If her mother is wrong about Eric—and her mother absolutely is—she's not wrong about villagers. People fear what they don't understand.

Then let me tell them. Let me explain *it.*

What will you tell them? That you can speak with the dead? That there are dead who are trapped here? They already have ghost stories, girl. Stories of the vengeful dead are not going to make us welcome.

But the dead aren't vengeful. Mostly.

No. The dead are people who have become invisible. But the invisibility is necessary. No one wants to let go.

Reyna thinks of the lingering dead who were killed in anger, or for greed.

Even hatred is a form of attachment, her mother said. She tries to remember this, but it's hard. She is not full of hatred, now; she is overwhelmed by love, and yes—she wants to hold on to it. There is so much that is hard and difficult and fearful, holding on to things that give joy makes sense. It makes all the sense in the world.

In the distance, Reyna hears weeping. She opens her eyes; her mother's are closed, her mother's brow furrowed in the etched lines of concentration.

*   *   *

Reyna has always been powerful. It is her mother's pride—but also, Reyna knows, her mother's fear. The only thing her mother has is her role as magar. Take that away, and what defines her? Nothing. When Reyna was younger, she attempted to hide her power, to ease her mother's fear. It didn't work, and her mother didn't appreciate it. Reyna's power has only served to increase her mother's expectations and the harshness of her mother's lessons.

Helmi, Reyna's surviving youngest sister, takes lessons that are far less harsh, far kinder. Helmi, however, is too young to show even the traces of the power that came to Reyna when she was twelve or thirteen. Reyna can't remember her mother ever being as kind to her oldest daughter as she is to her youngest.

It's not a gift, Reyna thinks. She wants to tell her sister that. It's *not* a gift. It's just another way to fail. But maybe Helmi will be free of the curse. Helmi will be allowed to have friends, or maybe even fall in love. Helmi won't have to be magar.

Helmi won't hear the weeping.

It draws Reyna; it pulls at her while she sits in the confines of the circle she etched in such broad strokes. Safe in the circle, Reyna lets herself be pulled into the pit of another person's pain. Walking this path is hard. It's not like the first dead girl she met; that had been an accident.

She'd been working in the new field. The sky had been blue and the earth, brown; in the distance, trees blurred the horizon. Talking to the stranger had been natural, a part of the day.

Talking to this stranger is not. The circle defines the landscape, as Reyna sits at its center. There is no natural sky, no natural gardens, no trees; there are no people and no possibility of people. Reyna goes to the dead girl, but she walks the magar's road to do it.

She thinks the weeping voice belongs to a girl, possibly a young woman. The road takes the shape of the dead girl's memory. Reyna looks for some sign of her mother, but her mother is not present; Reyna is walking the narrow road alone.

There are trees in the distance, shadowed and gray. The

magar has warned Reyna, many, many times, not to add color or substance to the world she sees while she sits in the heart of the circle. The circle is supposed to be both guide and anchor. It is a reminder of the life that exists outside the world of the dead. But it's hard not to add traces of color to what she sees, to give strength to the echoes of another's memories. She does it without thinking, as she walks. It's easier not to do it when it's night, because at night, there is very little color.

The path is familiar; Reyna realizes this only as she draws close to the voice itself. It's the path Reyna walks to see Eric. She is glad her mother has not yet found the girl; it gives Reyna time to let the natural landscape of the dead reassert itself. She stands very still until she no longer recognizes the turn of the road, the rise and the fall of the gently sloped land, the shape of the trees. She no longer hears the brook passing yards from her closed eyes.

She no longer feels the touch of Eric's lips or hands.

Instead, she feels cold. It is bone-numbing. She no longer sees earth, but something that looks whiter and softer. It covers branches, flecks bark, hides the rounded gnarl of tree roots entirely. It is hard to see past it. It is not hard to listen.

She walks across the ground, leaving no tracks; this is not reality. It once was, for the girl who is now dead. The cabin, such as it is, is covered in white. There are shutters; she can see their shape in outline. They're closed. So is the door. Neither matters. Reyna was no part of the girl's death. No part of death at all. Memories don't, and can't, contain her.

The girl is huddled in the corner of the room farthest from the shuttered windows. She is sitting in the dark—and it is dark here. There is a fireplace; it contains ash. There's no wood beside it. It is so cold in this room, breath is visible. She died here. She died alone.

There is a table in this room. Three chairs. A fireplace. There are plates on the table. Cups that look like tin. There is a door that leads to another room. Reyna skirts around the weeping girl and looks in. One large bed. One fire grate. One small table that contains shut drawers and the remnants of a melted candle.

This is where the girl died, but she didn't live alone. Reyna drifts back through the door and comes to stand a few yards away from the girl herself. This has always been the hardest part of the job for Reyna. The dead don't always pay attention to the living because they're so caught up in their own final moments. If she knew the girl's name, it would be easier. The dead often respond to their names.

She doesn't. The girl—and probably her family—died on the outskirts of an entirely different village.

Reyna tries anyway. But the girl can't hear her because her own pain, her own fear, is too loud. It has to be. If it weren't, she wouldn't be trapped here.

Reyna exhales. She then reaches out to touch the girl's shoulder.

In the heart of the circle in a distant, darkened room, Reyna flinches. The cold eats sensation in her palms, but not quickly enough: It *hurts*. She has to push past the cold—and quickly—or her arm will be numb for a day.

The dead are not meant to speak with the living. It's a natural law. The cold is a reminder, a sign that means: Stay out. But it's a thin sheet of ice. When one knows how to stand on it, it breaks. Beneath that ice, beneath the overwhelming cold, there is heat and warmth, a reminder that the dead come from the living.

The girl's eyes widen. She lifts her head, tightening her arms around her knees as she meets Reyna's eyes. Reyna doesn't know what the girl sees; what Reyna sees is a gaunt face, hollow eyes, pale, sunless skin. A threadbare dress, too large for the girl who inhabits it. The girl died when she wasn't much younger than Reyna. Or older. With the dead, it's hard to tell.

They don't age when dead.

"Who are you?" The girl asks. She lets go of her knees and rises. To Reyna's surprise, the girl is—was—taller.

Reyna doesn't give her name to strangers, even dead ones. "I've come to find you."

"Have you found my father? Is my father—"

"Your father," Reyna replies, "is waiting for you."

"How did you get here? With all the snow—" The girl shakes her head. "It's been snowing so long. You can always hear the wind screaming, just outside. We ran out of firewood."

And food, Reyna thinks, but doesn't say it out loud. She holds onto the girl, and the girl doesn't seem to notice; she walks, quickly, to the door. It opens for her, because it is not a door in a real house; it is the memory of a house. Just as the girl herself is the memory of a life.

The door opens into a howling snarl of wind and ice and snow. The girl struggles to close it. Reyna feels the undercurrents of her fear; it is so strong, it pulls her under. If the door is left open, they'll both die.

She shakes the fear out, almost literally. This death is *not* her death. She is not dead. The girl is—and doesn't realize it. She's caught in the moment of fear; it's all she can see. That and Reyna. Reyna takes shallow breaths. Her mother still hasn't found them, but she's closer, now.

There's only one certain way to break the dead out of the trap they've built for themselves—and it does take power. But it takes the power they carry within them. Reyna looks at the door. She looks at the room, and the empty fireplace, the empty table. To lead the girl out of this nightmare, she will have to alter what the girl perceives.

Fear is hard to shift. Reyna thinks, again, of Eric. She wants to be in his arms; instead, she is holding the remnants of a terrified girl, and she knows, looking at her, that there will be no time for Eric this evening. There might be no time in the morning, either, before the day's chores truly start. She swallows.

She swallows and accepts it. Yes, her mother could—and will—find this girl. She won't find her as quickly as Reyna because she's never been as sensitive. But even if she does find her, Reyna's not certain her mother could do what needs to be done. The winter and the isolation are both so strong it's hard to think of the circle and the summer that she left hours ago. And it has been hours.

"The snow will stop soon," she tells the girl. She takes a chair—an empty chair. "I brought food—it's cold, I'm sorry."

"The snow will never stop."

"The snow stopped long enough for me to make my way here," Reyna points out.

"Did—did my father send you?"

"Your father wasn't in any shape to travel," she replies,

completely truthfully. If the girl's father left the house during this storm, he didn't survive it. Reyna's certain he couldn't see three feet in front of his face. He might have gone out, turned back, and been unable to find his way home. "I came instead."

Lying to the dead is tricky. Reyna thinks of it as telling them a story. It's a story they need to hear. It has to be believable, because if they believe it, they can step outside of the fear. Fear is a story, like any other story. Change the story a bit, and the ending shifts with it. The ending the girl faced was death—either by freezing or starvation. Reyna can't tell which, and it doesn't matter. She needs to shift the ending enough that the girl can leave the house. If she leaves the house, she should be able to see where she has to go.

That's the way it always works. It's no wonder her mother's not as good at it—comfort has never been one of her mother's strengths.

"If you're not hungry, I'll take the food with us. You'll need a coat," she adds.

The girl stares at the food; it's dried meat, hard cheese. There's nothing fresher than that. Her hesitation wars with her hunger—she doesn't get many visitors, and she's wary of strangers, here. But she's desperate. Sometimes that helps Reyna break people free of the spaces they create for themselves—and sometimes it makes things almost impossible.

The girl shakes her head; Reyna puts the food away. She does so deliberately, carefully; she takes no short-cuts. To be here at all, she's lost the evening with Eric, and if she's lost that, she might as well do *something* right. As she carefully slides meat and cheese back into the pack she's carrying, she concentrates on the weather. The howl of wind recedes; again, it's slow. She sits it out, waiting. She almost offers to build a fire, but she thinks that would be too much.

It's enough to still the storm. It's enough to stop the snow.

The minute her mother arrives, she knows; her mother remains invisible, watching. Reyna feels her fists clench; she feels her throat dry. It is always this way. She tries to focus on the poor, trapped girl, instead. When it's been quiet for long enough, she rises and walks to the door; the girl follows.

The wind begins to howl again, and Reyna says, "It's quieter, but we're not clear yet." She goes back to the table, knowing that this will happen again. No matter how quiet the cabin is, approaching the door brings the storm. Opening the door is death.

She doesn't tell the girl that leaving it shut was death, anyway. She works, and she waits. She offers the girl food each time they retreat from the door. The third time, the girl's shoulders slump, and she nods. She handles the plates; she tries to be host to a guest. When she begins to eat, Reyna thinks it is almost over.

She's wrong.

Five hours later—five actual hours—Reyna has fought the wind to a standstill. The girl has eaten. She has eaten everything. The fabric of her hunger is woven from memory, but when she has finished, she lets it go. She knows she is no longer hungry, because when she was alive, she wouldn't have been. It's enough of a change that she can—barely—believe that the storm that consumed her family will end.

She lets Reyna open the door. She has dressed, now, for a long trek in the bitter cold; she is prepared to step outside of her home. This should be enough.

It isn't. They can barely get the door open. It's almost as if the house itself has been buried. Reyna doesn't understand snow very well; she half suspects that the monstrous amount of it is also part of the girl's fear. She could make the snow vanish; she suspects she's skilled enough to do that. But the snow is just another wall, and if the wall isn't carefully deconstructed, the girl might never see beyond it; she'll build it again and again and again.

And so Reyna spends hours digging a path through the snow. It makes her arms and shoulders ache; she is so tired by the end of it she wants to crawl back into the imaginary house, into the imaginary bed—there's room enough for three—and sleep. There's a danger in that. Reyna almost made that mistake once.

She has never repeated it.

The girl, on the other hand, doesn't tire. She digs, and the memory of desperation lends her a strength the living don't possess. This could be another trap—a different one—if

Reyna weren't by her side; the girl might spend eternity digging and never look up to see sky. It was evening when Reyna arrived; it is not evening now. She knows it is not night in the world beyond her circle. She can hear bird song and argument in the distance; she can hear crickets and the buzzing of dragonflies and other insects. She can hear the sounds of Helmi.

Helmi knows better than to interrupt Reyna or the magar when they stand, or sit in their circles.

Mother, she thinks, *where are you*? There is no answer, of course. This is a test. Another test. And Reyna knows what she must do to pass it. She must dig, as the girl is digging. She must become part of the girl's cage, the girl's fantasy. She must become enough a part of it that she can find the door and open it.

Find it too soon, open it too soon, and the girl will slip free of Reyna, not the cage; she will retreat, restructuring memory, and cloak herself once again in her uninterruptible fear. There *must* be another way. But if Reyna tries to make one today, she will fail.

So she talks while she digs. She talks about Eric.

The girl actually smiles. It's a shy smile, as if she's not quite used to talking to other people—and given the situation, she might not be. But she asks about Eric, about his father, about the village, as if she's hungry for news. And as Reyna is just digging, and she's tired, and she wants to stop and rest, she answers. Talking about Eric gives her energy. Talking about love makes the cold seem warmer, as if it could melt the snow just by existing.

Hearing the girl's tentative questions makes her seem like a real girl to Reyna. A living girl. Someone who has known loneliness and the fear of rejection, someone who can appreciate the gift that love *is*. Answering them—answering makes her seem almost like a friend. Reyna doesn't have a lot of friends. Living the life she lives, and moving from year to year, makes friendship impossible. She can't talk about what she does. She can't share it. She knew, before she could talk, that she was, and would remain, an outsider.

But the truth is, she doesn't want that. She's never wanted that.

What she wants is Eric. She wants to be loved, not feared.

She wants to be understood. She wants to stand up and shout the truth to the world: She is here to *help people*. She is here to help the people that most people can't even *see*. She almost says as much to the girl, who is one of those people.

But the girl is talking about her father, now. He hunts and traps. She is talking about her mother, who died when she was very young, in a winter like this one. She is talking about her own dreams—of love and freedom and, most of all, summer. Summer, when the snow melts and the world is warm, and standing outside of four walls won't kill.

Her dreams are smaller than Reyna's, but she glows with them, and as she speaks, the tunnel through the snow expands; the digging quickens. She works—as all the dead do—without being aware of the work itself; by speaking of the things that she anticipates, the girl is pulling herself out of the hard shell of her fear. As she does, the tunnel lengthens.

The color of the sky shifts. The snow doesn't so much melt as vanish. The girl stops, midsentence, her mouth hanging open as if she's forgotten she was speaking. And she has. She is staring ahead of her, her eyes wide and unblinking. There is a look on her face that is almost painful; Reyna can't describe it. She struggles to find words for it, but the ones she comes up with don't work: love, desire, peace.

Reyna's mother says the dead don't cry.

She's wrong.

"What do you see?" Reyna asks. Her mother will be angry about it later—and her mother's anger never goes away—but she feels the sudden, visceral need to know.

The girl doesn't hear her. Reyna is holding her, and Reyna's hands tighten—just as they once did around her mother's skirts. "What do you see?" she asks again.

The girl whispers a word in a language Reyna doesn't understand. She's never had that happen to her before. She has always understood the dead, no matter where she finds them. They speak the same language. "I don't understand."

The girl then looks away from whatever it is she sees. "You can't see it?" she asks.

Reyna shakes her head.

The girl's tears fall again; she looks—with pity—at Reyna. As if it is Reyna who is trapped, or Reyna who is blind. "It is everything I ever needed."

"*What* is?"

The girl lifts her arm. Points. Frowns. "You helped me to come here. My father is waiting. And my mother. My mother." She looks down at her hand; Reyna is holding it. Reyna has been holding onto the girl for the entire, long night. "Close your eyes," the dead girl whispers.

Reyna does.

Eyes closed, for one long minute, she can see what waits for the dead. It is . . . like light. But not visual light; it's the essence of what light offers: illumination, vision, beauty. It is *home*. It is *warmth*. It is a place—at last, after so much struggle and fear and resentment—to *belong*. She cannot describe it because it isn't something that can be seen, even if she sees something; it is something that is felt. Here, all anger, all rage, all fear, all ambition, can and must at last be set aside.

She understands, then, why it is forbidden to look. If it did not remind her so much of what she feels for Eric, she is certain she would walk by the girl's side until there was no turning back.

And that she wouldn't regret it.

"There's no rain coming," her mother says, as Reyna works.

Reyna knows. The stream is so low in the bed beside the ring tree. This is not the first year the rains have been sparse. There is water, of course, for their own gardens. There will always be water for their gardens. But her mother doesn't like to use their gifts that way, even if it keeps them fed.

The villagers will notice.

The villagers, who know that there's been so little rain. Rumors will start. And eventually, someone will say, "They're stealing the rain!" It's not true, of course. It's never been true. If Reyna's mother weren't so afraid of people, she could make it rain for the whole village, and then, they'd be welcome. They'd be heroes.

But she doesn't. The only time Reyna was foolish enough to ask *why*, her mother slapped her. Her mother, bent and wiry, has a temper, but she almost never *hits* her children, not with her hands; she uses words for that.

"The power does not come out of nowhere!"

No, of course not. It comes from the dead. "If we're

finding them *anyway*," Reyna countered, "they don't *need* that power. The only reason they have it at all is to help us search for them and free them. Once they're free of this world and their pain, why *shouldn't* we use that power to help the living?"

"Because that is where it would start," her mother replied grimly. "And it would not end there. It never does."

"And how would it end?" Reyna demanded. "If we only want to help people—living or dead—why is that bad?"

"Why do you want to help the living?"

"What?"

"Why do you want to help them?"

"Because then *we* won't be hated. Then we can *stay*!"

And her mother shook her head and said, again, No.

EMMA

SNOW CLUNG RANDOMLY to highway signs along the 401, obscuring letters or numbers designed to mark the way. White borders absorbed white clumps; no one unfamiliar with the signs could be expected to read them.

No one tried, anyway. Amy was driving, and Amy knew where they were going. It was a comfort, to leave the driving to Amy—the only comfort in this small space.

Michael was on the right-hand side of the SUV's bench, head pressed against the window, chin tucked toward his chest. His eyes were closed, but he wasn't sleeping; his hand was running rhythmically across Petal's head. Petal, in theory seated in the middle of the bench, was actually sprawled across both it and the two passengers on either side of him.

Allison had his back end, which meant the stub of his tail as well as his damp paws. She didn't lean against the window; her head was tilted back, her neck almost rounding as she rested the weight of her head against the top of the seat. Her eyes were closed. It was dark in the car. Dark enough that her pallor shouldn't have been visible—but her expression suggested the absence of color; her lips were almost as pale as the rest of her skin. Her glasses, flecked first with snow and then with the water snow became, rested at a slight tilt across the bridge of her nose.

Emma was certain she was thinking about Toby, her baby brother. Toby, who was in the hospital, in the ICU, hooked up to god only knows how many machines, courtesy of a gun; it had been hours. Toby had been fine at dinner. He'd been his usual, annoying younger brother self until people broke into the house, looking for Allison.

Allison had escaped. Chase had made her leave.

Emma didn't know what to say to her. Allison hadn't shot her brother. But it was Ally the attackers had been after. Had there been no Necromancers—and no necromantic best friend—there would have been no break-in and no guns. Had Allison refused to get caught up in the lives of the dead, she'd be doing her homework or reading her latest amazing book.

Instead, she was on the run, trapped in a car with Amy Snitman, who had always made her feel uncomfortable, driving away from a brother who might die at any minute, instead of running in a frenzy of worry and fear toward him.

Ally couldn't phone. She couldn't ask how her brother was doing. She couldn't go home; if she did, it was only a matter of time before Necromancers once again descended on her home and family.

The only person who could feed Emma and her friends information about Toby was Emma's father, who happened to be dead. He'd promised to keep an eye out, to report any changes in Toby's condition. Emma didn't know if his absence—so far—was a good sign.

She wanted to believe it was, but she couldn't force those words out of her mouth. She wanted to comfort her best friend, but she didn't have anything to offer. If it weren't for Emma, if it weren't for that friendship, there would have been no home invasion. Toby would never have been shot.

Emma wondered if this awkwardness, this desire to help mixed with the certainty that *nothing* would be helpful, was natural; she felt like a failure of a friend. Was this how Ally had felt in the months after Nathan's death? Wanting to help, but awkward with uncertainty about how?

And the truth was, nothing had been certain to help Emma, then. Minute to minute, what Emma wanted or needed from her friends had changed. What she'd wanted was to have Nathan back. She couldn't have that. Some days, she'd wanted to go to the places she and Nathan had gone together, and some—she wanted to avoid them because all she could *see* there was loss and absence.

What had kept her sane? What had kept her *here*, as far as grief's gravity allowed that? The answer was contained in this car. Michael. Allison. Petal. Even, in her fashion, Amy. Amy could understand the theory of grief and loss, but Amy had never been big on sympathy—she considered it too close to pity, and no one who liked having a social life, however stunted, pitied Amy Snitman.

Had she cried on their shoulders?

No. Because she was a Hall, and Halls don't cry. Even at funerals.

What, then? She glanced out the window at snow that was almost horizontal, turning the question over and over in the terrible silence of the car. She almost asked Amy about her current rival in school, just to have that silence filled. But she realized that Amy, tight-lipped and active, wasn't in that much better a place than any of the rest of them, which was unsettling.

What had these friends given her, when she thought there was nothing of value that the universe could, anymore? She thought, although it was uncomfortable. Emma had always been taught, in subtle ways, that every request for help—or time, or attention—put pressure on another person. Asking was forcing someone else to say No, and given how much Emma hated saying No herself, asking for things became, as she grew up, a social crime.

She glanced at Amy's grim profile.

Amy asked—if by "ask" one meant demanded—for things all the time, but Emma didn't hate it, or her, most days. On the other hand, hating Amy would almost be like hating rain or snow. Amy didn't need anything to be Amy. Or rather, she didn't need anything from anyone else.

And that was beside the point. Emma looked at the rest of her friends in the mirror and understood what they had given her, in lieu of obvious, superhuman comfort. They had needed her. Even when she was at her worst, when she'd felt so empty she thought she'd crumble into dust and ash just trying to take a step forward, they'd needed her. They reminded her that she was necessary, even without Nathan. There was still an Emma-shaped space in the universe that had to be filled.

She would have said they'd asked for nothing. And, in words, they hadn't. Words weren't necessary to walk Michael to school. Words weren't necessary to walk and feed her dog. Words were definitely superfluous when listening to Allison talk about the most amazing book she had just read.

They hadn't asked.

They had assumed. No—that was the wrong word. They had *trusted* her. She had needed that silent trust. She still needed it. It didn't make her happy the way Nathan's presence—and silence, and speech, and actions—had. It merely reminded her, constantly, that she was still Emma Hall, even without Nathan. That even when she felt, when she utterly believed, that she would face the rest of the future alone, she was not, in fact, alone.

Emma Hall had been raised to ask for nothing; to be independent, to take care of her own needs without expecting anyone else to leap in and do it for her. She inhaled.

"Problem?" Amy asked.

Exhaled. This was not a discussion she wanted to have with Amy in the car. But Amy was in the car, regardless; if it weren't for Amy, they might still be huddling in Eric's house, numb with terror or grief. Silence was cowardice.

"I'm grateful," she forced herself to say. "I'm grateful that I have friends like you."

Amy had that "water is wet" expression. Allison, however, opened her eyes and lifted her head, meeting Emma's gaze in the mirror.

"Don't start apologizing," Ally said. "I won't be able to deal with it tonight."

"Emma always apologizes," Michael pointed out. His eyes were still closed, his cheek still pressed against the cold glass window.

"I didn't apologize to Nick after I dropped a book on his head."

"I would cut you from all my social circles if you did," Amy said. Michael did not respond. "But Allison is right—it takes a *lot* of patience to listen to you apologize for everything, and my patience is nonexistent right now. You were saying?"

Allison grimaced in the mirror, although it was brief.

"Even when things are crazy—or disastrous—you've always reminded me that I—I have something to give. Something of value." She hesitated.

Allison didn't. "You always did."

Emma shook her head, lifting one hand, a gesture that meant she had to continue now, or she would lose the thin thread of courage that kept the words coming. "When Nathan died, I thought the world had ended. Or that it *should*."

Michael opened his eyes; he was watchful now, although he could enter a conversation with his eyes closed.

"The world didn't end, of course. What I feel—what I felt—didn't change the rest of the world. Only me. I forgot. I forgot what it was like to be Emma Hall, on her own. And I didn't really want to remember. If I couldn't *feel* Nathan's loss, I felt as if I'd be saying he never mattered.

"But you needed me to be what I'd been. You knew me before Nathan. You knew me during. And you knew me after." She exhaled again. "I'm not sure I can do this without you. I know it's selfish. I know—"

"No apologies, remember?" Amy cut in.

Emma swallowed. "I don't know what's going to happen. But I'm grateful that you're here to face it with me. I don't think I could do it without you."

"Do what?" Michael asked.

"Find the Queen of the Dead," she replied, after a long pause.

"How are we going to find her?"

Allison said nothing, but she met Emma's steady gaze in the mirror. She even smiled, although as smiles went, it was terrible.

"That's the question," Amy said. "I'm personally less concerned with the question of finding her and more concerned with the question of how we handle her once we do. I don't suppose any of your invisible dead people have wandered into my car?"

"Without your permission?"

That dragged a brief laugh out of Amy. "We need to ask them what the odds of being discovered are. There are five or six places we can run to, if we have to—but that's not going to last if they're smart."

More silence. It was Allison who said, "We can ask Merrick Longland."

"I wouldn't trust a *word* that fell out of his mouth," was Amy's heated reply. She had not forgotten Longland's actions at her party. She had not forgotten what he'd done to her brother, Skip. "Even if we could, I'd just as soon not owe him anything."

"I don't have that luxury," Allison said, her voice thin and slightly shaky. "He saved my life."

"I haven't noticed that fact softening Chase's attitude toward him."

"Allison isn't Chase," Michael said.

"Thank god."

The snow let up forty-five minutes from Amy's destination, but by that point, it was irrelevant. Plows had come through what passed for main roads; they had also carved ditches out of the smaller side roads. The sides of those ditches were taller than Amy's SUV in places.

The moon was out, the sky was clear, and the snow reflected enough light that the sparsely placed street lights were enough to see by. Amy's winterized cottage was not so much a cottage as a very large, modernized house; they had their own generator somewhere on the property. They clearly had someone who maintained at least the drives. Driving to the garage was almost easier here than it was after a snow dump in the city.

"What?" Amy said, as they exited the car. "I phoned ahead and asked Bronte to take the snow blower for a spin."

That wasn't all she'd asked the unknown person to do; there was food in the fridge, and the wood stove was both full and burning. Also, coffee, which Amy decided she needed. One glance at Michael, and she added hot chocolate to the impromptu menu while they waited for the second car to arrive.

Amy wanted to place bets on how many people would be in it when it did.

Eric, Chase, Ernest, and Longland were in the other car. Although he'd been cleaned up, Chase looked as though he'd been at the bottom of a game-deciding Hollywood tackle, where all the other players had also been given knives. He had not killed Longland. Longland had not killed him. Both of these statements hung in the air like unfinished sentences.

Longland, however, had saved Allison's life. For his own reasons, of course, which were almost entirely selfish—but they didn't matter. In the end, without his intervention, Ally would be dead. The thought made Emma forget to breathe for one long minute; when she exhaled, she exhaled white mist. Allison, shivering, was on the steps waiting for Amy to fish a key out of her purse.

Michael was tromping in circles in snow, one of which was rottweiler shaped, when the second car pulled up. Eric was behind the wheel. Ernest was beside him. Chase and Longland occupied the back seat, and both still appeared to be in one piece; neither looked best-pleased with the company, and they exited the car, putting anyone still standing outside between them.

Longland stayed close to Emma. Amy opened the door and ushered everyone inside; Longland, as he entered, was pale. He stared at Emma in a way that made her distinctly uncomfortable. He knew it and attempted to look elsewhere, but his gaze kept returning to her, and it stayed anchored there until she glanced in his direction.

Chase, for his part, went to Allison as if to ascertain that she was still breathing. He kept himself between Allison and pretty much everyone else, the exception being Michael and Petal. He didn't particularly care if Longland attached himself to Emma, because he didn't particularly care if Emma survived.

Emma, the Necromancer.

Amy immediately continued her stage directions once coats, boots, and other outerwear had been removed. She had already chosen the rooms in which her guests would stay and led them there, catching Michael's arm when he failed to follow immediately. She deposited Longland in the room between Ernest's and Eric's; Chase was, she told Eric, his problem. She commandeered the room her parents occupied when they were here and let Allison and Emma share a room across the hall; Michael was one door to their right. Petal, like Chase, was not Amy's problem.

Chase sourly noted the parallels between the designations.

"I should probably apologize," Amy told him, no hint of regret in her voice. "Petal actually *listens*. I am going to make coffee. I will also make hot chocolate for those who don't drink coffee." She then turned and marched down the hall to the stairs.

Chase, Eric, and Ernest did not join them in the kitchen. They risked the wrath of Amy by poking around the rooms in the house, and Emma privately thought Amy was right: there was no possible way Necromancers had come *here* first. Chase, between clenched teeth, pointed out that they were not attempting to destroy Necromantic foci, but Ernest cleared his throat. Loudly.

"With your permission," he said, "we would like to be more proactive in rudimentary defenses on the perimeter of your property. Or," he added, as Amy opened her mouth, "your house and the road that leads to it."

Amy nodded.

Chase said nothing, loudly. He could be sarcastic without saying a word.

"How likely is it we'll be followed?" She didn't ask Ernest. She asked Longland.

"The Necromancers with whom I arrived are dead." He hesitated. "It is possible—probable—that they were not the only knights sent. Emma is powerful."

"You didn't consider her a power the first time you met her."

"I did not see her then as I see her now."

"Neither will the Queen."

Longland nodded. "But the Queen's knights are not her only servants. She can, on occasion, send the dead to do her bidding; they are not capable of interacting with the mortal world—but they can observe and report directly to her almost instantly. None of the dead could fail to see the power Emma has."

"She could always use a phone." Amy folded her arms.

"She is not conversant with modern amenities, by her own choice. It is the only advantage the hunters have. Change, when it has come to the court, comes slowly through the knights. Had you joined us, your knowledge of things modern would inform both you and the service you offered; had your service—in pursuit of the Queen's goals, of course—been successful, she would review the mechanisms behind that success."

"Emma would not have survived to join the court," a new voice said. Emma turned toward Margaret Henney, who entered the conversation in a way that made the air cold. She was dead. She had been dead the first time Emma had laid eyes on her. She could make herself visible to the living, with Emma's help.

With Emma's unconscious help.

"Oh?" Amy said.

"She is too powerful. Had she been willing to learn what the Queen could teach, the Queen would have discovered this. Merrick is right: The dead see her just as clearly as they see the Queen; to our eyes, she looks almost the same. The Queen would have come to understand this within a handful of years—perhaps less. She would not have suffered Emma to live."

"How, exactly, do you know all of this?"

Margaret frowned and turned to Emma. Emma said nothing, but she clasped cold hands behind her back.

"I was a Necromancer, of course."

"Not a terribly impressive one," Longland added, with cool derision.

"Not terribly impressive to the Queen, no. It was only very briefly my life's ambition to be so. What I know of the Queen's court is not current, but the Queen was conservative, in her fashion. She did not value change for its own sake. Between my death and yours, how much did the composition of her inner court change?" The question was clearly rhetorical.

Merrick did not appreciate it. He glanced once at Emma. Emma, however, nodded.

"I am no longer her servant."

"No. Are you mine?"

Everyone but Petal fell silent.

Watching his expression, Emma wondered if Longland had truly served anyone but himself. She had seen similar expressions in Grade Seven and Grade Eight. Fear, humiliation, desperation, the need to be seen as belonging. She'd often envied adults like her parents who didn't seem to have any of the same emotions.

". . . Yes," he finally replied.

"Then please answer Margaret's questions."

"Is Margaret yours?"

Emma started to say no.

Margaret, however, said, "Yes. Until the door opens and I can leave this place, I serve Emma."

"Just in case there's any doubt," Chase said, "no one else here is bending a knee. We don't serve Necromancers."

Longland ignored Chase. Margaret apparently ignored him as well; she turned a severe glare on Ernest, who was leaning against the nearest wall looking even older than he usually did.

"Chase," he said, "we're doing a perimeter sweep." When Chase opened his mouth, he added, "Now."

Longland, however, continued to speak to Margaret—as if the rest of the living were of no concern. "Two of the Queen's knights—from your era—have died. Three, if you count me."

"And the citadel?" the older woman asked.

"There is one new wing, a small one."

"The city?"

"It has not changed."

Emma cleared her throat. "What is the city of the dead like?"

"It is not a city as you would understand it. None of the living occupy its buildings, although there are completed buildings. At some point, we believe the Queen intended her city to be occupied. The logistics were difficult. Food, in particular. She did not complete the city she had planned. Half of the streets are bare outlines formed of cobbles and forgotten intent. The dead wander there in numbers."

At the tightening of Emma's expression, Longland shrugged and looked away. "They have no power. Those that remain are not worth harvesting; the novices practice binding on them. You would not enjoy the city of the dead."

Amy glanced at the door. "We don't have our hunters. I think we should try to get some sleep; we can make plans over breakfast." No one in the hall mistook the suggestion as anything other than it was: a command. Amy was the closest thing they had to a queen, here.

"I want to know why you kissed me." Allison Simner squared her shoulders, lifted her chin, and spoke as forcefully as she could, given the subject matter. If the statement — which had started life as a shaky, confused question — sounded well-practiced, it's because it was.

"That was better," Emma told her best friend. "But you dropped the last two syllables."

Allison's shoulders were already bunched up so tightly they were practically at the level of her ears.

"Are you sure you have to ask? I mean — the answer seems pretty obvious."

Allison turned from the mirror, in which she'd been practicing the "right" expression. It was a small mirror, given that it belonged in Amy's family's cottage. "Why do you think Chase kissed me?"

Emma shook her head. "Because he *wanted* to?" When Allison failed to reply, she added, "He's Chase. He pretty much does what he wants. There is no way he would kiss Amy."

"But kissing Amy at least makes *sense*."

"If you're Chase?"

That pulled a smile out of Allison. "I guess it would be suicidal."

"Good point. Now it makes me wonder why he hasn't. It's Chase, after all."

Allison's smile became a laugh — the first of the day. The first, Emma thought, of two days.

Petal chose that moment to push the bedroom door open. It wasn't completely closed. He headed straight to where Emma sat, cross-legged, on the bed, jumped up, and made himself at home. But the blankets were wrong, the bedsprings were wrong, the bed was the wrong shape; the only thing that was right about this particular room, in dog terms, was that Emma was somehow in it.

For a rottweiler, he could make himself appear smaller

and vastly more pathetic without apparent effort. He did have his leash attached by the mouth—at least until he dropped it in Emma's lap.

"Not now, Petal," she told him, setting the leash to one side before he dropped his head on it. "Sorry," she added, to her best friend.

Allison had been in Emma's life since before Petal came to join it. She shrugged off the interruption. "He wants to go for a walk."

"And I want to avoid a lecture." Emma scratched behind Petal's ears. "Eric's so tense the air is practically bouncing off him. I can pretty much imagine what he'd say if I told him I wanted to take the dog for a walk."

"The dog has to pee sometime." Allison glanced at Petal, and added, in a more dire tone, "Or some*where*."

This was absolutely true.

"I'll come with you."

Emma's face remained expressionless. If her first impulse was to avoid a lecture—and, sadly, it was—it was only because she'd refused to think about Chase and his possible reaction to Petal's needs. Chase wasn't tense the way Eric was—but he had a much shorter fuse and a much blacker temper. He had kissed her best friend. He clearly—to anyone whose first name wasn't Allison and whose last name wasn't Simner—loved her. And his love came with a stack of resentment for Emma, whose existence endangered her.

It had endangered them all.

Chase confused Allison. Emma had spent an hour listening to that confusion and the worry it caused; she offered advice only when Ally specifically requested it. Allison never talked romantically about boys; romantic boys were exotic creatures that other people had to deal with. They existed between the covers of books and on various screens. If she daydreamed about them, she kept it secret from even her best friend. Boys seldom gave Allison a second glance.

Confused or not, there were certain things that Allison was never going to willingly accept.

Emma knew that on any other day, in any other place, Allison would have kept her confusion to herself. But sharing it was better than the only other alternatives. She could talk about what had happened when she and Chase had faced off against two Necromancers without immediate backup. She could talk about the fact that she had escaped Toronto without talking to her parents, and her parents were probably frozen with terror. Or she could talk about her younger brother, Toby. Toby, who'd been shot, and now lay hooked up to hospital machinery of various types, in a city they had fled. They had no idea whether or not Toby would survive.

He might already be dead.

Emma and her best friend had grabbed onto Chase as a safe subject. Safe, in this case, was still dicey. Emma looked out the window. Allison's face was pale in reflection.

"If," Allison said, proving that all the work to remain expressionless was pointless, "you're worried about what Chase will say, don't."

Petal liked snow. He liked going for walks. Being outdoors while Emma carried her end of the lead had pulled out his internal puppy. Allison's presence confirmed for the rott-weiler that *some* things were still normal.

Emma avoided the ravine in the winter, at least while walking her dog; he therefore bounded from tree to tree, practically dragging his tongue behind him. Given the utter absence of cars or pedestrians, she was tempted to let him off the lead. Instead, she gave it its maximum play.

She looked, as she always did, for her father; he wasn't here.

Neither was Nathan.

Nathan's death had been—until this past week—the worst thing that had ever happened to Emma. Worse—and she thought it with guilt—than her father's death half a lifetime ago. She cut one sharp, cold breath. Her eight-year-old self would never have agreed.

But her seventeen-year-old self had had time and distance. She had had her mother, her friends, school life, and her dog. Life's friction had dulled the edges of that pain until it no longer cut her anytime she returned to it. She could think of her dad now and remember the *good* things. The funny parts. The comforting bits. She could even remember the anger she sometimes felt.

Thinking about Nathan was still too painful.

For a brief couple of weeks, it hadn't been—because he'd been beside her. He'd been dead, yes—but death hadn't been the impersonal, silent wall at which she grieved. He had come back. He'd come back to her.

He'd come back to her at the command of the Queen of the Dead—and he'd left the same way. If he'd been like Longland—dead, but in possession of a body—he'd still be here. He might hear the Queen screaming orders at him in the distance, but he wouldn't have to obey.

"Em?"

Emma forced herself to smile.

Allison's exhale was just this side of a snort. "You know I hate the fake smile."

Emma shrugged. "Sometimes I'm better at making it look like a real one." She shook her head. "Look at the two of us—we're both having boyfriend trouble."

"Only one of us is having boyfriend trouble," Allison replied. "I don't *have* a boyfriend."

"That's harsh," the non-boyfriend said, as he stepped around the trunk of a not particularly large tree.

NATHAN

NATHAN DOESN'T SEE THE QUEEN for three days. He has his own rooms. They are not small, but they're not modern; he's not given a computer or a phone or a television. The rooms seem to have materialized from the pages of a stuffy Victorian novel or a Hollywood set. The bed, in particular. It has *curtains*.

Nathan can't actually tell what color they are, beyond dark. He understands that he is meant to sleep in the bed. His body theoretically requires sleep now. The problem is, Nathan doesn't. There's a disconnect. He lies down anyway. He lies down after changing into what might pass for pajamas. He closes his eyes. It makes no difference. He is not asleep, and he will not sleep. He won't dream.

He won't have nightmares. But if he refuses to lie down, if he refuses to *try*, he weakens. It's not exhaustion, not exactly—but it's what exhaustion would be if he were standing to one side of himself and looking in from the outside. His body requires sleep.

In the silence, though, it's hardest. When he is still, when he is not in constant motion, he can hear the voices of the dead. He thinks of them as his dead, because they're part of him; they surround him with their cold, their lack of life. He hears their muted whispers. They are not angry at him. He's not certain they're aware of him at all; he's not certain they're aware of each other.

The first night, he tries to speak with them. To speak to them. Mostly, he apologizes. He wants them to understand that he didn't ask for this, didn't choose it. That's guilt talking, and if Nathan's not Emma or his mother, it still keeps him going for at least an hour.

No one replies. Or perhaps they do: They cry. They plead. He can't make out most of the words, but he doesn't need them. They could be speaking binary and he'd still understand the meaning.

If he's moving, he can ignore the voices. They're so quiet that it's only in silence that they can be heard at all. But the body itself won't keep moving; it collapses in inconvenient ways, as if it's run a race that he somehow missed.

This is not living.

Maybe if he'd been dead for long enough, it might seem similar. He kind of doubts it—but sometimes the dead notice him, and they stare at him with a blank, silent *envy*. As if they can no longer tell that he's dead.

The living look at him differently. Or maybe he's over-thinking because the living can see him now. He's not a mute, invisible spectator. He's a mute, visible one. The Necromancers of the Queen's court don't expect a lot of talk from the dead—even the resurrected. That's what they call Nathan: resurrected.

If they die in service to the Queen, they, too, will be able to escape death.

He doesn't tell them that there is no escape.

Nathan needs to eat. He needs food the way he needs sleep. He gets hungry, but the sensation is faint, and he doesn't, for the first day and a half, identify the fuzzy feeling *as* hunger. Food, however, is delivered to his rooms. The young woman who delivers the food is silent; Nathan thanks her, and she looks straight through him. Given that she *can* see him, he finds this surprising.

But she's dressed in a uniform that would be at home in the same universe the rooms are. And she's followed by a ghost. This shouldn't surprise him. It does, but it shouldn't. The Queen can't keep tabs on the living the way she can on the dead—and the dead, absent bodies, can't perform the menial tasks a living Queen requires. Even if they have bodies, they'd probably be terrible cooks.

So the girl in the uniform is either a Necromancer in training or a regular person who works for the Queen. But a regular person wouldn't be dragging a ghost behind her. The young girl grimaces as Nathan thanks the servant.

He frowns.

The girl sticks her tongue out. "I'm not with her," she tells him.

Nathan almost asks the child if the servant can see her. He doesn't.

"You're not very smart," the child continues. "I'm just keeping an eye on you. For the Queen."

Because he isn't certain that the servant isn't a Necromancer, he doesn't say anything. The dead child leaves with the servant.

He eats. He doesn't taste food. He is aware of the difference between textures, but everything about the experience is bland. He doesn't feel full when he stops. He has no desire to continue.

If he needs food, he probably needs water more. He doesn't feel thirst, but he drinks. He's never liked the taste of alcohol of any stripe—and he's clearly been given wine, judging by the shade of gray in the glass—but in this, being dead is helpful. Wine has no taste, either.

He does bleed. He's apparently gotten used to walking through walls, and that doesn't work so well with a body. Gravity works far better than it did a few days ago, as well. He would have said that no one gets used to being dead, but he would have been wrong.

He doesn't feel attached to his body. He feels it as if it were a straitjacket. He has to learn its rules and its requirements, but they come to him secondhand, through observation and effort. He makes the effort. If the Queen is absent from the throne room, her presence is felt everywhere in the long halls; she casts a shadow the size of the citadel.

He doesn't ask to leave it. He doesn't ask for anything. Learning how to mimic life takes up most of his time. He does learn. He can read; there are books in his rooms. They're old, so he assumes they're musty; his sense of smell is—like everything else—poor. But he can read the words themselves. Reading was never one of his big hobbies. But as he becomes accustomed to the daily routine of life among the living, his fear and uncertainty gives way to boredom.

It is when he's reading that the young girl returns, peering through the door without actually fully entering the room itself. She watches him. He ignores her. It takes a bit of effort; there's something about her that is loud, even in the silence.

"What's it like?" she finally says. Her head, from the neck and shoulders, is now fully in the room. The rest of her is on the other side of the door.

Nathan knows what she's asking. "Same as being dead but less convenient."

The child frowns. "Really?"

Nathan's aware that she could be the equivalent of a hundred years old, by now; her appearance gives no indication of how long she's been dead, given the Queen's preferred style of dress. The dead wear what she wants.

The girl sidles her way into the room and sits. She sits in midair. "That's not how it's supposed to work," she tells him, folding her arms.

"Oh?" Nathan sets the book aside. He's seen Allison do this a hundred times over the years when dealing with Toby, her perpetual annoyance-in-residence. Except that Toby's not in residence anymore.

"You're supposed to be alive again."

"Do I *look* alive to you?"

The girl frowns. " . . . No. But she says you're alive now."

He doesn't ask who. "I don't understand how I can look alive to her—she's the *Queen*. Of the Dead."

The child shrugs. "She's always seen what she wants to see. It used to make our mother *so* angry."

If Nathan weren't already caught in the perpetual chill of the dead, he'd freeze. "Your mother?"

She nods. "It's funny. She *has* our mother's temper, but

she *hated* it in our mother. Why are you staring? She's alive—she had to be born *somehow*."

"You're—you're her sister."

"Yes."

"Her—her baby sister."

"I'm older than you are."

"How are we counting, exactly?"

She snorts. She is the only dead person Nathan's met who doesn't seem terrified of the Queen.

"Why don't you have a body?" he asks, before he can catch the words and reel them back.

"Because Eric's not here."

This makes about as much sense as half of what falls out of the mouths of children who look her age. "Eric can't give you a body."

"No. But she's saving her power. She said. And then she made *you* one. She's made bodies for her knights. Just not *me*."

"Why?"

"Because she doesn't want to worry about me dying."

This makes about as much sense to Nathan as anything else the Queen has done.

The girl is not impressed. "I'm already dead," she points out.

"Duh."

"So she doesn't have to worry that anything worse will happen. If she resurrects me, someone could kill me."

"And then you'd be dead again. You wouldn't be any farther behind."

"No." The child is quiet for a long moment, and then she says, almost conspiratorially, "But I'd be *away* from her. It would be harder for her to find me."

"It would be easy for her to find you."

"How?"

"How does she find any of the rest of us?"

"She binds *you*."

"But not you."

"No. *I'm* her sister." Just in case he is stupid, she adds, "*I'm* important to her. She trusts *me*."

And not any of the rest of the dead. Nathan doesn't bother to put this into words. He tries to find the little girl charming. "She didn't kill you."

"Are you stupid?"

"Sometimes."

The girl snorts. "No. Other people did—but she found them. You're probably walking on some of them," she adds.

"I can't hear them, if I am."

"No. I can't hear them either. But she says she does. She hears them everywhere." The girl shrugs. "She hates them, you know."

"And the rest of the dead?"

"What about them?"

"Does she hate them, too?"

"Probably not. It's because of the dead that she can build. The dead give her life. The dead," she adds, "give you life."

"This isn't life." Nathan lifts an arm. Flexes his fingers. Lowers his hand. "It probably only looks like life if you're living."

"So . . . why did she resurrect you?"

"She didn't tell you?"

"No."

"She didn't tell me either. And I'm not her sister. I couldn't ask."

The girl unfolds her legs; she doesn't bother to actually stand on the ground. If what she said is true, Nathan doesn't blame her. "Everyone's afraid of my sister but me."

"You have to admit she's pretty intimidating."

The girl shrugs. She shrugs a lot. She walks around the room as if inspecting it. She even puts her hand through Nathan's book. If she weren't dead, she would seem like a normal, bored child. Nathan doesn't believe it, although he tries.

"So," she says. "You have a girl?"

"I thought you said she didn't tell you."

The girl's smile is bright and feckless. "I lied." She reaches out experimentally and puts her hand through his right arm, which happens to be closest. He feels a wave of expanding cold at her touch, but it's not centralized.

"I don't have a girl. I don't have anything anymore. I have a cemetery plot. My real body is probably ash."

"Didn't the Queen tell you that love is eternal?"

Nathan is getting tired of the girl. "What about yours?" he counters.

"My what?"

"Your love. Did you never love anyone when you were alive?"

She stills.

"Is your love eternal? Have you found the people you loved? Do you talk to them, spend time with them, comfort them? They should all be dead, right? They should all be here somewhere."

He realizes he should shut up. Her eyes are like glass.

"They're not all here," she says, in a voice that no longer suits her body. For a moment her face ripples. Literally ripples—a reminder, if needed, that the bodies of the dead have an elasticity that the living don't. He looks, briefly, at his hands, and he shudders. "Some of them escaped, before the end. We're not like the rest of you. We're not stupid about death. Even if we have no power or light of our own.

"Some of us took too long to die." Her face has hardened. She looks like every demon spawn in every bad Hollywood horror movie Nathan's ever watched.

He doesn't step back. "You took too long to die."

"I almost didn't die. If I hadn't bled to death, she would have saved me. I would be here in the flesh. If I'd stayed quiet. Stayed hidden. If I'd made no noise. I was younger, then. I was afraid. So they found me.

"By the time she did find me, it was too late. You can see the door, can't you?"

Nathan has whiplash.

"It's closed. It was never closed before my sister."

The words sink in slowly. He knew the truth. Of course he did. But he's never heard it stated this way. "The Queen closed the door."

The girl nods. "She closed it so the dead couldn't leave. And she's never going to open it, either." She folds her arms and waits. Nathan's not sure what she's waiting for. "You're not very smart."

"No. Not usually."

The girl's eyes widen. She laughs. Her laughter is high and thin and as childlike as she looks. "You won't like it here," she says, with a touch of innocent malice. "But I'll like it. You can tell me about love."

Nathan's ambitions—in life *or* death—have never included long discussions about the nature of love with someone who died too young to experience it.

"But not now. I have to go."

"Where?"

"To find Eric."

CHAPTER ONE

ALLISON'S FACE WAS ALREADY RED from the cold. She told herself it couldn't get any redder.

Petal headed over to Chase and sniffed around him as if he were a tree. He didn't, however, mark him as if he were one.

"What," he asked, with his friendly, easy smile, "do you think you're doing?"

"Taking the dog for a walk," Allison replied, before Emma could. "Unless you'd like to have him pee in *your* room."

Chase wasn't biting. "He's an old, half-deaf dog. You're thinking he's much protection?"

"I'm thinking we don't need a lot of protection, at the moment. We're in the middle of literal nowhere, and we don't intend to stay."

Emma had been silent throughout. She remained silent, although she pulled the lead in when Petal wandered away from a person who wasn't offering to feed him. Chase didn't add criticism, which was theoretically helpful; he didn't add anything, which was awkward.

"I should head back," Emma predictably said.

Allison would have grabbed her hand if it had been closer. "You're not going back to the house by yourself."

"I'm going back to the cottage with Petal. If Chase is here, you'll be fine."

"It's not—" *me I'm worried about.*

"Ally, I'll be fine. You'll be fine?"

"She will."

"You," Emma said to Chase, "can barely speak without offending half the school. I'd just as soon let Ally speak for herself."

Chase's brows rose, the left one over a distinctly sallow eye. He'd survived two Necromancers—but not easily and not without injury. Allison could forget this when he was snarling at her best friend. Or, to be fair to Chase, at everyone. It was harder to ignore it now.

"I'll be—I'll be fine," she said.

"I'll make hot chocolate."

Chase said nothing. Neither did Allison; Emma felt like a traitor for ignoring her expression, which spoke the volumes she wasn't. But she knew Chase would never hurt Allison. And she knew Allison was, if not openly interested, fascinated by *his* interest. And intimidated by it.

Allison was a person who struggled, always, to live up to her promises. To live up to herself. There was no context for living up to someone else's inexplicable interest in her. Emma had seen Allison be nervous before, but not like this.

People were shallow. Emma herself was willing to admit she spent at least half her waking life—if not more—in the social shallows of the pool, with no regrets. She liked to look at attractive guys. Or she had, before Nathan.

That was as far as she wanted to take this thought. Allison didn't really understand shallows; she treated all of life as if it were the deep end. She jumped in only when she was certain she could swim—and jumping in for a dive when there was only a foot or two of water could be a disaster. But if you were drowning in the deep end, Allison *could* swim. She could lend you the hand you needed to drag yourself out.

"I have something on my face?"

"Too much of a chin, given the way you're sticking it out

there," Emma replied. "I know I'm usurping your role here, but—I'll kill you if anything happens to her on your watch."

"Emma . . ."

"Sorry," she told her best friend, without meaning it. "Come on, Petal. I think Michael may have a Milk-Bone or two."

Allison would have followed Emma, but Chase stepped into the footprints her retreat had made. "She shouldn't be out here on her own."

"She's the only one they probably won't kill on sight, and we're in the middle of nowhere. I wouldn't let her go if I thought there was a real danger." He glanced once over his shoulder. "We're less than half a mile from the house; I think she can make it back without getting lost or freezing."

Since Allison was far more likely to get lost—mostly by not paying attention to the outer world—she said nothing. The nothing was painful and awkward, and she knew she should fill it. But she almost resented the fact that Chase looked so comfortable with the silence. He was grinning. At least, it looked as though he was grinning to Allison—but maybe she was seeing things in the dark; when she thought of him, it was that grin she could see.

And she could pretty much see it these days with her eyes closed.

"If we were in a different country," Chase said, relenting, "I could give you a gun and teach you how to use it." As an opener, it was almost what she'd come to expect from Chase, and she found herself relaxing.

"You're sure Emma will be okay?"

"We can follow her—at a distance—if you want. I just wanted to talk to you."

"You didn't much look like you wanted to talk to anyone."

He grinned—this one definitely wasn't her imagination. "I decided not to start a land war in Russia." The grin faded. "I'm trying to remember that Longland saved your life. I hate that he had to do it."

She looked down at her feet. Looked up again. "I'll apologize if you want, but I'm not sorry I didn't run."

"Apparently, neither am I. Angry, maybe. Sorry? No."

His hands found his pockets and bunched in them. "I didn't give you the knife and tell you to kill someone with it."

She was silent.

"I didn't give you the knife to tell you to *threaten* to kill someone, either—with your training, that's just handing the knife to someone who'll kill you."

"I know." She exhaled. "I made it to the fence. I could have made it through."

Chase nodded. He took a hand out of a pocket to run it through what remained of his very red hair. "Believe it or not, I didn't come here to lecture you."

"No?"

"No—that part happens automatically. It would have been worse if I hadn't done the perimeter sweep. We're clear," he added. "I did salt the earth a bit here and there."

"Is it going to cause problems in actual cottage season?" Allison asked, cringing.

"I'm not spending the evening worrying about Amy's parents' reaction."

"I was worrying about Amy's reaction."

"Not spending the evening worrying about that either. I'll admit it's more practical, though."

"What are you spending the evening doing?"

He exhaled a plume of mist at a speed that suggested annoyance. Chase's temper didn't faze her. Other things about him did. "Thanking you." This was not what she'd expected—but Chase was never what she expected.

"Thanking me?"

"For the whole sticking around because you thought you could somehow save my life thing."

"Really?"

"No—it was stupid. I'm trying to be gracious. It's hard work, and I'm not seeing a lot of reward-for-effort."

Allison laughed.

His smile deepened, but it shifted. "Thank you for surviving. I mean that one."

"Still looks like you're having to work at it."

He laughed. The line of his shoulders became less rigid, and he looked—for just that moment—younger. Because he did, Allison took courage in her hands and clung to it for dear life. She stopped walking, drew clear, cold air into her lungs, and expelled it. With words.

"Chase—I want to ask you something."

He nodded. He didn't even look wary.

"When we were—when the Necromancers were coming for us and you—when you—" Holding on to courage, on the other hand, meant she let an hour of practice—much of it in front of a mirror—evade her.

"Yes?"

"We were—I was—it was after—"

He laughed again. It was louder.

"You're not being helpful."

"I have a reputation to consider. And given that I'm wearing one of Eric's hideous jackets, I have to work harder at it."

"It's too dark to see the jacket."

"Are you kidding? Look at this collar."

She did. As far as Allison was concerned, it was a thick, black jacket with studs. She didn't know enough about current fashion in any era that wasn't the tail end of the eighteen hundreds to have an opinion one way or the other. But it didn't look ridiculous on Chase—certainly not as ridiculous as it had on either her or Michael.

She slid her hands into her pockets, missing both Emma and Petal. Looking at her feet, which were mostly buried under snow, she tried again. She wasn't always good at finding the right words until long after she needed them—usually when she was on the way home and the opportunity to say them was long past. But she wasn't going home any time soon. "I want to know why you kissed me."

He didn't miss a beat. "I didn't have enough time for anything else."

Eyes widening, she looked up at him.

He laughed. "That's not how you make fists," he told her, reaching for her hands. "You'll only break a finger or two if you actually connect with anything."

"I wasn't trying to—"

"Thumbs on the outside." His hands, gloveless, were pocket-warm. She could feel their heat as he gently but deliberately uncurled her fingers. "And never, ever go into a fight biting your lip." He didn't let go of her hands.

She was aware of the difference in their heights, of the different textures of their skin—his was callused and rough; she was aware of the difference in their clothing, their attitude, and their lives. But mostly, she was aware of just how close he was standing. She wanted to pull her hands back. And she wanted to leave them in Chase's forever—as if she could extend the confusion of the moment, holding it for eternity.

"Do you really have to ask?"

She nodded. Having forced the words out of her mouth—and they were even the right words—she had none left; they were lost to a breathlessness that she would have said wasn't in her.

"Why? Is it really impossible to believe I'd want to kiss you?"

She closed her eyes. "No one else does. Except Petal, and while I love that dog, I could do without the dog-breath and slobber." It was embarrassing to admit this. "Have you actually looked at me?"

"A lot, actually."

"And I have a pretty face?"

"Pardon?"

"That's what they tell you. 'Such a pretty face.' It's like a consolation prize."

"I don't know," he said. She couldn't tell what he was thinking. But he released her hands and raised his to her cheeks, lifting her head gently. He met her eyes; she wasn't certain he was actually looking at anything else. Her eyes, on the other hand, were firmly behind her glasses. "Well, no. I wouldn't say you have a pretty face. But it's the face I want to look at. You understand that I don't care what anyone else thinks of you, right?"

Allison exhaled slowly. "What if I do?"

He grinned; his smile was much closer to her, now. "You're part of that 'anyone else.' I don't care what you think of you, either." His thumbs stroked her cheeks. "Why do you think people obsess about their looks?"

Allison shrugged.

"My guess?" He continued when she failed to answer. "They want to be attractive. They want to stand out."

Allison nodded, because that made sense. She was having difficulty, at the moment, making sense of anything.

"So, looks exist to grab the wandering attention. But once you've got it, what then?"

She really hadn't thought that far, because the first part of the equation had always been beyond her. "Chase—"

"Then it's all down to you. Who you are. What you want. What you demand. What you give."

"But it's not."

"Oh?"

"It's not just about the mythical 'you'—it's about what your friends will think. It's about what other people think of you for having an ugly girlfriend."

His hands froze. "What did you say?" His voice changed. It had become softer and much, much quieter. It was also more intimidating.

"It's about what other people think of you for having an ugly girlfriend."

He shook his head in exaggerated mock sorrow. "And there's that word again."

She closed her eyes. "Chase—I see myself fairly clearly. I don't lie to myself except in daydreams."

"We'll talk about daydreams in a minute," he replied. "Right now, we're talking about me."

She opened her eyes.

"I've been a student in your school. I hate it. I think it's a waste of time. I feel like I'm surrounded by idiot children who think they're almost-adults. Some of them think they're tough. It's not worth the time to set them straight. You expect me to care what they think of me?"

She couldn't shake her head, because Chase was still bracketing her face with his hands.

"Right. No. Who else does that leave? Let me tell you: It leaves only you. Other people are allowed to be idiots. I don't like it; Eric says I can't school them. Fine. But you? No. You don't get to be that stupid. Not when you're around me. So: You never, ever get to use the world 'ugly' again."

"She can if she's describing you."

Chase cursed. He didn't lower his hands. He did lift his

head. "If she uses it at all, she'll use it the wrong way. It's why I didn't make exceptions, even for you. What do you want, Eric?"

"The old man wants a report on your portion of the perimeter sweep. He'd probably like it sometime tonight."

Allison could hear Eric's voice; she couldn't hear his footsteps. There was too much noise on the inside of her head. That and embarrassment. She pulled away from Chase, and he let her go.

"And Emma's probably worried about Allison, judging by her expression."

"If she were worried, she wouldn't have left her."

"Not that kind of worry, idiot. We might have a problem."

Everything about Chase changed at Eric's tone. Allison started to turn toward the cottage. Chase caught her shoulders. "We're only finished with this for now," he said, voice low.

Given Amy's suggestion that everyone get some sleep, Allison was surprised to see the fire in the fireplace to one side of the entrance hall. Michael and Emma sat side by side in exactly the wrong type of silence. Allison's glasses had become opaque enough that she couldn't make out their expressions.

Hot chocolate was, in fact, in cups on a tray on a low table beside Michael; he had a mug in his right hand and a lapful of mournful, sighing rottweiler. Petal and Emma looked up when Allison entered the room; Michael didn't. Firelight added color to his face and his almost vacant stare.

Allison sat beside him.

Michael, staring into the fire, said, "Emma's dad came."

Allison froze. After a long, silent moment, she rose and moved so she could stretch her hands out in front of the fire; she was cold. She was so cold.

"Toby is alive. Mr. Hall said he hasn't woken up yet. Your parents are at the hospital. So are the police." He spoke the words carefully, as if from a list. It probably was. Michael was not generally the person sent to convey important emotional information. Allison wasn't surprised when Michael started to cry. The tears were like an afterthought on his face; they didn't change his expression.

Emma slid an arm around his shoulder. "Thank you, Michael."

"I want to be able to help," he continued, still staring at the burning logs. "But there's nothing I can do."

"That more or less describes me," Allison told him. "I don't know how to fight. I don't know how to defend myself against people who do. I don't know how to stop the Queen of the Dead, and most of the people who might know are dead. Only Emma can see them.

"Do you want to go home?"

Michael shook his head. "I want to be *at* home. But I'm worried about Emma." He paused, and then added, "I'm worried about you."

It was never helpful to lie to Michael. "I'm not worried about me," she replied. "I'm terrified for Toby." Looking up at the ceiling, she added, "If I get him back, I will never, ever threaten to strangle him again."

Michael said, "Yes. You will."

She laughed. It hurt. "Yes, you're right. I probably will."

"But he knows you don't mean it." He paused. "Amy had an argument with her dad. On the phone."

"Her dad is a far braver man than I am. What about?"

"I only heard Amy's part. She's angry because her father doesn't trust her. But," he added, frowning, his face falling into more familiar lines of confusion, "she doesn't trust him enough to tell him the truth, either."

"She trusts him to be himself. But there's no way he's going to think that Amy is better prepared, more knowledgeable, or more competent than he is. It's just the way parents are. Except your mom," she added quickly.

Petal whined and looked hopeful. Allison took a deep, deep breath and held it, trying not to think about her baby brother. The last time she'd seen him—at dinner—she'd threatened to upend her plate over his head. He'd laughed. She wanted to ask where he'd been shot. She wanted to know what his injuries were. But her mouth was too dry, and she couldn't find the words for it.

Emma's eyes were red.

Allison found space on the couch between the arm and Emma and put an arm around her best friend's shoulder. She didn't tell her that everything was okay; it wasn't. They both knew it. She didn't tell her that things would *be* okay, because at this exact moment, she couldn't see how that would ever happen again.

She settled for a silence that contained them both: the arm across Emma's shoulder a bridge, a connection that said, *I'm here.* Or, in this case, *we're in this together.*

Amy joined them. Amy never looked frightened or uncertain; when she was upset, she looked angry. She was clearly upset now. "I swear, I am going to disown my father."

"He called you again?" Emma asked, voice strained.

Amy's lip curled. "I called him. Don't ask." She exhaled. "He threatened to call the police to drag us all home."

"Wow, he really *is* worried. He's going to being paying for that for—"

"The rest of his natural life," was Amy's furious response.

"You think he'll do it?"

"I wouldn't bet against it yet. He's—"

"Angry?"

"Enraged."

"At *you*?"

Amy snorted. "No—I'm just collateral damage. He doesn't understand the situation, and I can't explain it. This is not improving his mood any." She glared at the phone in her hand.

"He knows what happened to my brother?" Allison asked.

"I doubt it. I certainly didn't tell him."

"He's not a complete idiot. Do you think Skip talked?"

Amy's teeth snapped shut as the glare she was aiming at her phone sharpened. "I will *kill* him."

"If he did?"

"No," Amy snapped at Michael. "Just on general principle."

All in all, it was better to have Amy's restless anger aimed at someone who was in a different city. Amy was a lot like her father in that way. Allison had always envied her lack of fear and her ferocious self-confidence. Nothing that had happened in the past month had changed that. Her envy for Skip, however, had taken a nosedive and didn't look to be coming back, ever.

Emma stiffened beneath Allison's arm. Emma, always much more socially adept, could feign both delight and ease when she felt neither, and her expression, while a little more alert, gave nothing away. But her shoulders were tense, her neck, stiffer.

"Ally," she said.

They all turned to face her.

"Get Chase and Eric."

"Ernest, too?"

She nodded.

Michael was the only person present who asked, "Why?"

"I think—I think we're going to have visitors."

CHAPTER
TWO

A LLISON LEFT THE LIVING ROOM before Emma had finished answering Michael's hushed question.

"Is Longland necessary as well?" Amy asked.

"If he's not part of this? Yes. But—I'm not certain he's not." Emma didn't look at Amy as she spoke. "So wait until Chase gets here and take him with you if you're going to find him." Amy didn't reply; that didn't bother Emma. Amy pretty much did what she felt was the right thing to do in any given situation, and anyone else's opinion was—unless asked for—superfluous.

"Emma?" Michael said, his voice closer than Amy's. "What are you looking at?"

"A dead child," she replied.

The child was between the ages of eight and ten, to Emma's eye; it was hard to tell because her expression was at odds with her age: It felt cold and ancient. Framed by dark hair that trailed down the side of her face in ringlets—with ribbons, no less—her skin was pale; she wore clothing that would have looked at home on the set of a period piece in which the director was not concerned with accuracy.

She should have looked cute. She didn't. Her smile—and she did smile—was slow to come, and when it did, it hardened an expression that hadn't been youthful to begin with.

"There really isn't much point in calling everyone to you," she told Emma. "They'll just die more quickly. But Eric *is* here, isn't he?" She paused and looked around the room, her snub nose wrinkling in disdain. It was the first expression that somehow matched her apparent age.

"Emma?" Michael asked.

Emma knew she could make ghosts visible by touching them. She *so* did not want to touch this one. She opened her mouth to say as much.

"Your companion's not a Necromancer," the girl said. There was a hint of question in the words, none of it friendly.

"No."

"And the loud girl?"

"No."

"The fat one?"

Emma folded her arms and stood. For a moment, she felt as if she were eight years old again, the desire to say, *you take that back right now* was so visceral.

"Do they serve you?"

"They're my friends."

The child snorted, and this sound also aligned with her apparent age. "You're a Necromancer. You don't *have* any friends." But she frowned for a moment, her forehead creasing. "You *are* a Necromancer, right?"

"That's not what I call myself, no."

"She is," Margaret Henney said.

Emma turned. So did Michael. Petal was too busy starving-to-death to do more than lift his head.

The girl's eyes widened. "Margaret."

"Helmi," Margaret replied. She turned to Emma. "We need to move, Emma. We need to move quickly."

"It won't help," Helmi said, staring first at Margaret and then—to Emma's surprise—at Michael. "They'll be here soon." She sauntered over to the fireplace and then turned to look at Michael again, her brow creased in faint confusion.

"What have you done?" Margaret demanded, in her most intimidating angry school teacher voice. Clearly, that voice was only effective on people who had lives to lose.

"The Queen ordered me to find Eric," she replied. "If I were you, I'd run. She won't be happy to see you."

"She's coming in person?" Margaret's voice was a bare whisper.

"Who knows? She told me to find him. I found him."

Michael rose as well. "Margaret, what should we do?"

"Gather anything you absolutely need right now. We may not have time to come back for it."

"Tell him to wait," Helmi demanded.

Neither Margaret nor Emma appeared to have heard her.

"Tell him to wait," the girl said again, "and maybe I'll help you."

"Michael. Wait," Emma said.

"Emma, dear, we really don't have time for this. I've spoken to Ernest, but if Helmi is here, the Queen—or her knights—will follow. We need to be away before they arrive."

Michael froze in the doorway. He turned back, his eyes darting between Emma and Margaret. Helmi's forehead creased; she looked at Michael and watched as he stood, indecisive, in the door.

"Ask him," Helmi told Emma, in the same imperious tone. "Ask him why he can see Margaret but not me."

"I can answer that," Emma said. "And I will. But let Michael go and get his stuff. Sorry, Michael."

Michael shot through the door and bounded up the stairs. He didn't weigh much, but he had never had a light step; he sounded like panicked thunder.

"Margaret can make herself visible to the living if she wants."

Helmi's small hands found her hips and rested there, in fists. She clearly did not believe a word Emma was saying. Emma would have found this annoying in other circumstances—no one liked being called a liar, even silently—but the air was getting colder by the second.

"And how exactly can she do that?" The child's voice dripped condescension.

"Emma is not precisely accurate. I can't," Margaret said, surrendering. The look she sent in Emma's direction, though brief, was pointed. She did not approve of any conversation with this particular dead person. "Not on my own."

Helmi turned to Emma, then. "She's yours?"

Emma said, "No."

But Margaret said, "Yes."

"Which one is it?" Helmi's fists tightened.

"I am not bound to Emma the way the dead are bound to Necromancers," Margaret said. "But I serve her while I have any choice or any say in the matter."

"*Why*?" The mask was off the child's face; the anger, the pain, the sense of betrayal were entirely exposed. It made her look younger. It made her look, for a moment, the age she had been when she died.

"Look at her," Margaret said.

"I *am*."

"What do you see, Helmi?"

"You know what I see. It's what *you* see."

"No," was Margaret's surprisingly gentle reply. "It's not. Emma is not using my power. I am indirectly using hers."

The words made some sort of sense to the Queen's younger sister; they appeared to make more sense to her than they had made—and did make—to Emma.

"There is no point demanding explanations from Emma—she doesn't have them."

"She—she's giving *you* power?"

"Yes. She broke the binding that held me to Longland. She didn't realize what she was doing, at the time. Nor did I. But I understood it afterward, in a way that Emma cannot. I am dead. She is alive."

"Is this true?" Helmi asked. She asked it of Emma; her voice had dropped until it was almost a whisper. Her hands were bunched in her skirts, as if anchored there.

Once again, it was Margaret who answered. "I don't like to do it—but the choice is mine. If I leave, she can't force me to return if I have no desire to do so. If I choose to remain unseen by the living, she does not force me to appear. I am here because . . ." Her voice trailed off.

Helmi's glare had slackened, her narrowed eyes losing

the sharp points of their edges as they shifted position. "Can they—can they touch you?"

Margaret shook her head. "What Emma gives is not what the Queen of the Dead gives. She cannot make me more than I am; she gives me the ability to be *all* that I am."

"How?"

"Helmi—"

"Tell me *how*," she said, voice low enough it sounded like an adult voice. Margaret appeared to be thinking; Helmi was not patient.

As Michael came thundering down the steps, Helmi turned to Emma. "Is it true," she asked, in the same low, intense voice, "that you opened the door?"

Emma saw some of Longland in this dead child. "Yes."

"How?"

Emma glanced at Margaret. Margaret did not come to her rescue. "I'm sorry," she said, the intense irritation at the girl's attitude evaporating, "but I don't know. The dead came to me, and they gave me permission to use their power to open the door. I needed all of it. I could only barely move the door, and it took pretty much everything they had."

"And that's enough of that," Eric said. He had entered the room; Allison was behind him.

Helmi turned to face him. If Emma expected triumph or sneering, Helmi ran counter to expectation. "Do you know what she did?" She was, on the other hand, still demanding.

"Yes. And I know she won't survive to do it again if they find her."

"Tell me."

"We don't have *time*, Helmi. If you've told her—or her knights—where we are, we need to move."

"If you don't answer, I'll just follow you until I know where you're going and tell her the new location. I don't *have* to tell her anything if I don't want to. You should know that well enough by now. If I told her everything, you'd never have escaped in the first place." She folded her arms.

Emma turned to Eric. "You recognize her?"

He didn't answer the question. To Emma, he said, "Allison and Amy are ready. It's just you and Petal."

"Is it true? Can she follow us and return to tell the Queen where we are?"

"Not as easily—"

"Yes," Helmi said. "It used to be harder. I've had practice. I've had nothing but practice." The words were laced with bitterness and resentment.

To Emma, Eric said, "Yes, she can follow us. She can leave for the City of the Dead and return almost instantly to the location she left from. But it is not trivial for the dead to navigate among the living; there are memories of streets and roads and fields and ancient homesteads that seem just as real to the dead as the streets you walk every day to get to school do to you. If there were a Necromancer here, he could build a kind of circuit that would serve as a beacon to her, but there isn't one."

"Longland is here," Helmi replied.

"Longland," Eric snapped back, "is dead. The dead—no matter what they were in life—can't *be* Necromancers. He might look alive to you, but he's just as dead as we are."

"But the Queen says—"

"The Queen has said many, *many*, things. You never used to believe most of them. Why have you started now?"

Emma understood why. It was always easy to believe the things you wanted to believe, because they gave you hope.

Helmi started to shout back, but no words came out. After a brittle and unexpected pause, she said, "So, Nathan was right."

"What did you say?" Emma found herself across the room and in arm's reach of the child before she could think about moving.

This did not terrify the child. "So you do know Nathan."

"I know Nathan."

The intake of breath in the room—and just outside of it—was sharp enough to cut. Of course it was. Only Emma— and the rest of the dead—could hear Nathan's name until Emma spoke it.

"Nathan is in the citadel. But don't worry—you'll be there soon."

"Emma," Eric said. He might have said more, but Amy

appeared with Chase and Longland; Ernest was nowhere in sight. Amy was dressed for winter: coat, boots, scarf; her gloves were in her hands, her earmuffs looped over her right arm. "We have to leave. We have to leave *now*."

Longland's curt, sharp curse could be heard over Eric's steadier voice.

"Merrick Longland," the girl said, turning only her head toward him.

"Lady Helmi," he replied. He astonished everyone in the room by bowing. Even Emma. Only Helmi seemed to expect this as her due.

"Why are you here?" she asked.

"I was captured in a failed attempt to assassinate the red-haired boy and his companion." He spoke smoothly and without inflection, separating himself from Amy. Chase stood between Longland and everyone else, knives in hand. He was angry.

"You haven't escaped."

"I haven't had time, Lady. We have only just arrived. And I did not think that escape in this empty wasteland would be helpful to our cause. I have no transport. I was not allowed to return to my dwelling; I have no mirror and no easy method of communication. But I am the Queen's, and bound to her; I trusted she would find me."

Helmi snorted. "She hasn't. Well, not yet."

"May I ask why you are here, Lady?"

"She sent me. She *asked* me to come."

"To what end?"

"To find Eric. She knows where I am now, and her knights are coming."

Allison caught Chase by the elbow and held on with white-knuckled hands. Chase didn't take his eyes off Longland, so he couldn't see Ally's expression. But he didn't stab Longland or slit his throat. Emma wasn't certain how she felt about that, either.

"Ernest has the car ready," Margaret said.

"Michael, Ally, Amy," Emma said. "Go."

"I've got my car running," Amy added. "But I think we're *all* supposed to leave that way. Now," she added.

Helmi stared at all of them.

"I assume Margaret can follow on her own."

"And Longland?"

"Leave him here," Amy said.

"No." Everyone looked to Emma, who added, "Michael, can you grab Petal, too?"

"Em, if the Queen can track Longland—"

"But she didn't. She tracked Helmi."

"Who?"

"The dead child."

"Fine. We *all* leave," Amy said, folding her arms. "Don't even think of staying behind."

The hall was a flurry of coats and boots and too many people in too small a space.

"The road isn't safe," Helmi said, watching them all. She seemed almost surprised at the words that had escaped her small mouth, but she didn't withdraw them; she stared at Emma.

Everyone who could hear her stopped moving. Everyone who couldn't noticed the lack of motion. Amy, who *was* worried, compressed her lips. "Emma."

Emma then turned to Helmi. Swallowing because her throat was dry in a way that couldn't be blamed on cold winter air alone, Emma held out her left hand. Helmi stared at it as if it were a dead fish. But she also stared at it as if she were starving, and the fish wasn't dead enough to be poisonous. She reached out and placed her right hand in Emma's left. Emma felt instant, searing cold. It was far, far worse than touching Mark had been.

But Helmi's eyes—Helmi's dead, oddly colorless eyes—widened and blazed with light. For a brief instant, her eyes looked almost brown, almost living. Ribbons fell out of her hair, and ringlets fell with them; the hair itself straightened into a fine, waving fall around her shoulders and back.

She looked up. The dead didn't cry; Helmi's eyes seemed filmed with tears she couldn't, therefore, shed. "It hurts," she whispered.

Emma's brows folded together; she tried to withdraw her hand, but the girl tightened her hold on it. "I'm sorry—it's never hurt anyone else—"

Helmi shook her head. Her clothing went the way of her

hair, falling into something simpler and baggier, the sleeves too long and rolled up at the wrists. Her feet were bare. Her eyes were bruised.

"Helmi," Margaret said, voice sharp.

Emma shook her head. "Let her be, Margaret."

"Helmi is older than any of the dead you have ever met," Margaret countered, once again using the angry teacher voice. "She has perfect control of her appearance; she can take on the face and the features she chooses, down to the last detail. It is not *necessary* that she show you—"

"Please. Let it go."

Blood trickled from the corner of Helmi's lips; those lips had swollen. The whole of the left side of her face had become bruised; the blood that fell from her mouth began to almost pour. None of it touched Emma; none of it reached the floor. Emma looked.

Looked, and stopped. She was staring at a livid, gaping wound in the child's chest. No, not one—three. She dragged her gaze away and was not surprised to see a fourth wound, across the child's throat.

"*Helmi.*"

Emma was not afraid for anyone in the room but Michael, oddly enough. Michael and Allison. They could see Helmi, because she held Helmi's hand. What she had, by holding that hand, agreed to bear witness to, they might also witness. Helmi was not kind.

"This is how you died," Emma told the dead girl. Her voice was steady, because Helmi *was* already dead. Knowing how she'd died might make Emma ill—but it changed precisely nothing. Helmi had been killed. Had Helmi died of—of scarlet fever instead, she would still be dead.

Still trapped here, where all memory seemed, at the moment, to be pain.

"Em," Ally said. "What are you talking about?"

Emma started. Blinked. Helmi once again looked like an eight-year-old child. Her hair was long and wavy, her dress, simple. But the blood and the bruising were gone. "You didn't—you didn't see her—"

"We can see her fine," Amy said.

For one long moment, Emma felt the edge of an absurd gratitude: Helmi had, at least, spared her friends. They weren't Necromancers. It wasn't their job to see the dead. *And is it mine?* She wondered. She set that aside. "Thank you," she told the dead child. "These are my friends. And this," she added, looking at the living, "is Helmi."

Helmi's frown softened, although it still hugged most of her mouth.

"I died."

"I know. And now I know how. Why were you killed?"

"Because my mother told me to hide, and I hid, but I could hear the screams and the shouting, and everything took too long," Helmi said. "So I came out of hiding too early. They thought we were witches. Or demons. Or something."

"You weren't."

"No. My mother was always afraid that that's exactly how we would die. It wasn't the first time it had happened to our people; it wasn't the last. Can you understand what that's like?"

Emma was silent for one long beat. "No, not really. No one has murdered my parents. I have no siblings — but my father died when I was eight, and my mother has never remarried. I have friends. Some of them are with me. No one was hunting them, either."

Amy said, "My great-grandfather almost died. Because he was Jewish. But — I'm like Emma. I've *personally* had a safe life. Both of my parents are still alive. I have a stupid older brother. The only person who's ever threatened him is me."

Helmi looked up, but this time, her gaze passed over Emma's right shoulder. In theory she was looking at the upper corner of the large room; in fact, she was looking at a very closed window. Or door. Emma knew.

"How did Nathan die?"

It had not been long enough that the question didn't cut. Given everything else that had happened since his death, Emma thought it should have been. But maybe there was no *long enough* at the end of which Emma Hall could calmly and objectively contemplate Nathan's death and what it meant for the rest of her life.

"He was in a car accident. He was hit by a drunk driver."

Helmi waited.

"I didn't tell him to hide." Helmi's dead eyes were almost alive as they once again returned to Emma's face. "You can't hide from life. He was in his car. He was on his way to meet me."

"What did you do to the driver?"

Emma blinked.

"Is the driver still alive?"

"Yes, the driver survived. He can't walk properly."

"Why did you leave him alive?"

"Kid," Amy said, "you're creeping the rest of us out."

Helmi's eyes didn't even flicker in Amy's direction.

Emma exhaled slowly. In her darkest dreams, the driver had not survived. He had groveled. He had begged for both forgiveness and mercy. His pleas had hit the wall of Emma's endless grief and rage. She shook her head, mute, and struggled to find her voice. "The reason," she said slowly, "that it's called an accident is because it wasn't deliberate. Your wounds—your death—was no accident."

"Do you think the men who killed me deserved to die?"

"Yes."

"Even if you *know* what waits for them at the end of their life?"

Silence. Profound and utter silence. Emma felt as if she had run a marathon.

Helmi turned then. She faced Longland, who was white and stiff; to Emma's eyes, he looked almost corpselike in the stillness. "You killed people. Deliberately. Does Emma know how many?"

Longland didn't answer. But his fingers curled until both of his hands were fists. He was, Emma thought, afraid. He was afraid of every word that was now leaving Helmi's little mouth.

"I don't need to know how many," Emma said. "I have no doubt at all that while alive, he was a murderer."

"And now that he's dead, it doesn't matter?" she folded her arms. The look she gave Longland was withering.

Longland waited in silence, and the silence was cold. Did it not matter? Honestly? Toby was fighting *for his life* in the hospital because Longland, the substitute teacher, had had access to all of the student records—and therefore, their home addresses. If Toby died, his death could be laid in part at Longland's feet. Had she forgotten that?

"Does he deserve peace, Emma Hall?"

She looked at Longland, at his hands, bunched in fists, at the expression that was taking hold of the rest of his face. He knew her answer. He knew the only answer anyone reasonable had to offer. He had threatened to kill *Allison*. He had threatened the life of an *infant*. Without the unexpected intervention of a four-year-old boy, Emma was certain that he would have killed them both.

And Chase. Michael. Amy and her brother. Eric. Ernest would have survived, because he wasn't stupid enough to come out of hiding unless there was *some* chance. Emma would have survived—possibly—because she was a Necromancer, and Necromancers were the only people the Queen acknowledged *as* people.

She glanced at Allison, mute now, as the reality of Longland's actions once again took root. It was Ally who would suffer.

Who was already suffering.

This wasn't a decision that Emma could make on her own. She almost asked Ally for input or opinion. And Allison was not her best friend for nothing.

"You've already answered the question," Ally said quietly. "If you want *my* opinion, you already know it."

Emma felt her shoulders tighten.

"But I'm not God. If my brother—if Toby—" She faltered. She couldn't say the verb. Emma would never have demanded it. "I will hate Longland for the rest of my life."

"And you'll want him to suffer," Helmi said.

"Yes, I'll want him to suffer—but I'll want him to suffer what *I* suffer, and he *can't*. I don't think he's ever loved anyone. I don't think he's ever been responsible for anyone *else*. Maybe I could make him feel pain. Maybe. But *not* the pain I'll feel."

"But he'll feel pain forever if he can't leave," Helmi pointed out. "Maybe it's not the same pain. But it's as close as you'll get."

Allison's jaw hung slightly open for another long pause. Emma thought Eric was about to speak; Chase certainly wasn't, although he was staring at Emma's best friend, as if something about his own life hung on her answer. And maybe it did.

"It's not up to me." Ally punted. But then, because she was Ally, she added, "And maybe that's *why* it's not up to me—or to any of us. We shouldn't judge—and we always do. What I know is this: Longland won't be the only person suffering. My grandfather died. He's trapped here, just as Longland is. And my grandfather was not a murderer or worse."

Helmi frowned. "It doesn't matter what you think, anyway. You're not a Necromancer. Emma, what do you think men like Longland deserve? What do the people who murdered me deserve?"

Helmi waited. Emma understood that to Helmi, the response was critical, and Emma had never liked making instant, enormously important decisions—not when she *knew* beforehand what their weight was.

"Sometimes," she finally said, "We get what we don't deserve. And that cuts both ways."

"Pardon?"

"I can't—I literally can't—judge Merrick Longland. I didn't live his life. I wouldn't, from what little I know of it, *want* to live his life. And Helmi? He saved my best friend's life. If he hadn't been there, Allison would be dead."

This didn't seem to mean much to the dead child. The angry dead child. "He was powerful."

Emma nodded.

"And respected."

"Not by me."

Helmi said, "So that's your answer?"

"It's *my* answer, yes. Ask someone else in the room, and you might get a different one. I can't answer *for* people. I can't answer for—for society. I didn't demand an—an exit interview—when I asked the dead gathered nearest the door for their help—and their power—in prying it *open*. I didn't ask if they were murderers. I didn't ask if they were monsters. I didn't deem them worthy or unworthy. I knew—and they knew—that if I succeeded, they would finally go to the place they've been looking at since they became aware of their deaths.

"I needed to open that door, and they needed to leave." She exhaled. "Look, Helmi—if, to reach the land of peace and love and belonging, we have to be worthy, I'm not sure *any* of us would ever be allowed through that door."

Helmi said nothing. It wasn't enough.

Emma tried again. "What Longland deserves—no, let me try that again. What I think he deserves doesn't matter. Maybe, if he had lived in a world where there was no hatred and no fear and no pain, he wouldn't even *be* the Longland we both know. What I know is that Merrick Longland will never cause that kind of pain again—if he leaves.

"Right now, he *could*, because he has a body again, thanks to his Queen. But it's no longer what he wants. He wants what the dead want."

"Em," Ally said, "I think Ernest is going to die of apoplexy any second now."

"If Ernest doesn't, *I* will," Amy added. "And I'm not going alone."

Emma apologized. Sort of. "I have one question for you, Helmi."

"I don't have to answer it."

"No. I can't force you. But it's the same question. Does he deserve peace?"

"You already said he doesn't."

"I said I don't think he does—but I also said it's irrelevant."

Helmi nodded.

"Would you keep the door closed so that he would never, ever know the peace he doesn't deserve?"

Helmi didn't answer.

But Emma, continuing in that vein, said, "Is this part of the reason the Queen won't let any of the dead leave?"

CHAPTER
THREE

"THEY KILLED US," Helmi said, after a pause in which the air in the room dropped in temperature. "They killed everyone she had ever loved."

"You've already said that."

Helmi's brows rose.

Chase, who had been rigidly silent, said, "Your sister killed everyone I loved. She killed them *in front of me*. She *made me watch*. She even killed our dog."

"What had you done to her?"

"Nothing. I knew nothing—at all—about Necromancers or the Queen of the Dead until that day. Nothing. I have no idea if our ancestors somehow crossed paths with her—she didn't say. I asked. I asked *why*. I asked what we'd *done*. Do you know what she said?" His voice was low.

Helmi looked down at her hands. No, at her hand; at the hand that held Emma's. The dead didn't cry. Helmi was not, therefore, crying. But it seemed to Emma that she would. And she was eight.

"Chase—"

Helmi lifted her free hand and reached up to cover Emma's mouth. She shook her head; her hair was a spill down her back, her expression ancient. "I understood why she killed the villagers. She killed Eric's father. She killed Paul—and he was already sickened by everything the adults were doing. He didn't *want* to be there. He couldn't—" She shook her head. "I understood. I even understood why—in the moment—she slammed the door shut. She didn't want the rest of us to desert her—and she knew we would. We were dead.

"She was never very strong. She was just powerful."

Helmi looked at Chase.

Chase didn't blink. His knuckles were white; his eyes were narrow, his lips as pale as the rest of his skin. "She'd kill everyone Emma has ever loved, given half a chance—at this point, she'll probably kill Emma. If Longland doesn't deserve to pass on, your sister deserves a permanent hell of her own."

Helmi said, quietly, "Is that not where she's already living?"

And Emma understood all of the questions, then. All of them. "You love your sister."

"Yes. And I hate what she's made of herself. I *can* judge her. But it's not in my hands, and it never was."

"She's in pain."

"She's nothing *but* pain. She can't let go of it because it defines her. Without it, what does she have?"

"What do you want, Helmi?"

"I'm dead," Helmi replied.

"No kidding," Amy said. Her arms were folded tightly, her expression about as friendly as Chase's. Then again, Amy's father had been shot, as well.

"Helmi, it is time to let go of Emma's hand."

For the first time that evening, Helmi hesitated in the way Emma associated with the young. "It's warm," she said to Margaret.

"It is not warm for *Emma*," Margaret replied, radiating chilly disapproval.

"No?" Helmi looked up at Emma.

"It's—it's okay," Emma heard herself say. And then, because Michael was there, "The dead are a bit cold to touch, so I can't do it forever. You just said that the roads aren't safe?" Helmi was staring at their hands. Her gaze traveled up Emma's arm to her face and then shied away, for reasons that weren't clear to Emma. "The roads aren't safe. That's probably where the gate will open."

For one long moment, no one spoke. They had gathered their belongings in haste; they had every intention of piling into the two cars and gunning for a different destination.

"Why the road?" Amy demanded. She was the first to speak, which wasn't surprising.

"Because people who are trying to escape will probably drive." Helmi's expression shifted. "I've never driven. I've seen cars. I'm not sure you'll be able to escape by car; they'll be waiting for you. The gate is being conjured on the road near this house."

"By Necromancers."

"By the Queen's knights, yes."

"You told them where we are?" Longland demanded; his voice was both deeper and harsher than Amy's, his fear more palpable.

"I was sent to find Eric. They know that Eric is here."

"And Emma?" He said. "Did you tell them that Emma is here?"

"I didn't know her name." Helmi continued to stare at Emma, at the hand that momentarily bound them. "My sister knows that Eric isn't alone. I told her that there were hunters here."

Longland cursed.

"Well, there *are*. I wasn't lying. And I'm not lying about the road, either. They'll start at the road."

No one liked their chances of escaping on foot, either. A ripple went through the gathering as everyone silently considered their options. In the city, escaping on foot opened a range of other options. There were subways, yards, friendly houses or buildings, shopping malls or strips. Here, there was a lot of snow. The neighbors weren't close—and no one suggested neighbors. Well, no one but Chase, who asked.

"The cottages here are mostly winterized," Amy had replied. "I have no idea if people will be in them or not at this time of year. Probably not, given it's not a weekend—but if they are . . ." she let the words trail off. Everyone heard the "people will die" anyway.

"I'll tell Ernest." Margaret vanished to do just that.

Chase leaned against the nearest wall and cursed. His attention was divided between Helmi and Longland. Longland and Helmi, however, were now regarding each other with disdain, dislike, suspicion.

"Why are you telling them this?" he demanded.

Helmi's hand tightened again; Emma returned the grip while she could still feel hers, as Helmi turned her back on Longland. This did not please the former Necromancer. "You want to see Nathan, right?"

"Yes."

"He's in the citadel."

"I don't know what—or where—that is."

"It's the Queen's home in the City of the Dead."

"You cannot trust—" Longland began.

"And she can trust *you*?" Helmi snapped. " 'But I am the Queen's, bound to her; I trusted she would find me.' " Her mimicry was savage and exact.

Longland was not impressed. The demeanor of respect—of obsequiousness—vanished as he looked down a very fine nose at a much younger girl. "Emma opened the door. She opened the way. Some of the dead are free and forever beyond the Queen's reach for the first time in their existence. She didn't do it for power. She didn't do it for status. I *do not* understand why she did it—and I don't care."

"You *have* a body," Helmi continued. "I have *nothing*."

"*You* have freedom—which is more than any of the rest of the dead have in the City. You can come and go as you please. You are the only person the Queen can command who has any choice in the matter."

"Yes. But you have *something*. If you're telling Emma that she can trust *you* because of what she did, why are you telling her she can't trust *me*? I've been dead longer than any of you." Her hand tightened. Emma did her best not to wince.

"Because you're the Queen's *sister*!"

"And I'm *still* dead. I'm *still* trapped here. I might be one of her family. She might profess to love me. But in the end, I suffer the same fate as the people she hated."

"You don't. You've never served as a source of power. You've never been forced to take the form or shape of furniture; you've never been a pillar or fuel to open a portal."

"She doesn't hate most of the people who have been used that way either. You served her, Longland. You obeyed her commands. You killed when she ordered it."

"You—" Longland's face flushed. "You did her bidding. You spied on *us*."

"Yes. She found you. She rescued you from the fate she suffered. And you would have happily killed her to take her place."

"Do you think Emma will *not*?"

"Emma will not take her place."

"Emma will kill her. She has no other choice."

Emma cleared her throat.

Longland and Helmi turned toward her.

"Well?" Helmi demanded. "Are you going to kill her?" She settled one fist on her hip, looking like a miniature Amy. She almost pulled her other hand free—but to do it, she would have had to let go of Emma. Her eyes narrowed. "You haven't even thought about it."

Had she?

No. Not really. She glanced at Chase, saw a flicker of contempt, and saw Allison turn toward him before he could open his mouth. Had she really thought that they could somehow neutralize the Queen of the Dead in a way that didn't kill her?

Or had she just assumed that somehow Chase would do it? Or Eric? Or Ernest? Someone who *had* killed Necromancers in the past? Had she assumed she could somehow leave it in Longland's hands?

"There is no way," Longland said, in a far less heated voice, "that you will escape this if the Queen of the Dead is still alive."

"Did you want to kill her just to—"

"I never wanted to kill her," he replied, before she could even finish her sentence. "She was the only one who saw potential in me. The only person, ever. She taught me everything I know. She gave me power I had never had; she gave me a home and food and an education."

"Why did the other Necromancers want to kill her, then? Didn't she give them the same thing?"

"Had you arrived in our city, Emma, she would have offered you what she once offered me, yes. But, like the Necromancers of very recent vintage, you have had no experience of privation, starvation, disease. You have lost no one to war or famine. Your entire experience is far, far freer than the life a Necromancer knows.

"It is always about context. In her early years, she gathered those with similar potential. Some of them already had status or wealth, if not respect." He hesitated, and added, "Historically. She had stopped gathering those when I was found; they were costly and ambitious. They understood her roots, and they despised them; they did not feel her fit to rule, or at least, not as fit as they would be. They are gone," he added.

"They are not," Helmi replied. "She is never safe from the machinations of the Court."

"She is *always* safe! There are things she has not, and will never, teach *us*."

Helmi's shoulders slumped. "She teaches you all the things she taught herself. She withholds only the things she was taught before she became Queen." She turned to look up at Emma. "He's right. You won't ever be free while my sister lives."

Emma had to retrieve her hand to put on her boots and her coat; she had to ask Allison for help to deal with buttons, zippers, laces, her hand was so numb. Helmi hovered by her side, her luminescent eyes a contrast to the rest of her pallor; she seemed shadowed and defeated. And she did so as an eight-year-old girl. Emma knew she wasn't eight in any real sense of the word, but it was hard to hold on to that knowledge.

Margaret walked through the closed door. "Ernest is in the car."

Amy immediately opened the door and walked into the winter night, clearly staking out her territory as the other driver.

"Has Ernest seen—"

"No. But I have. Helmi is correct. The gateway is not yet operational, but it will be soon. I could not approach closely enough to determine which of the Necromancers are present; there appear to be two." She glanced at Helmi, and added, "The only one of the dead who could approach them and be guaranteed either freedom or safety is the one who stands by your side. No Necromancer would be foolish enough to touch or bind her where the Queen has not."

"Emma," Helmi whispered. Emma automatically bent her head to bring her right ear closer to the girl. "Bind me."

Longland's eyes should have fallen out of their sockets. Margaret's surprise was less obvious.

"I can't," Emma said quietly. "I don't know how."

It was Helmi's turn to looked shocked. "What do you mean, you *don't know how*?"

"She means," a familiar voice said, "exactly what she says."

The dead young girl turned to face the magar.

Helmi left Emma's side in a heartbreaking rush of arms and fast limbs, as if she had forgotten that the dead didn't actually need to run. As if—and this was worse—she had forgotten that the dead couldn't touch anything, not even each other.

Only when she was inches away from the magar did she come to a sudden stop, lowering her open arms, closing herself off.

"I am not her magar," the older woman said.

"You must have taught her *something*."

"No. Her life has done that, and better than I could. She cannot bind you. It's possible that Margaret or Longland could teach her, indirectly, what she would need to know— but not in time, Helmi. Even if she could do as you have asked, what use would it be to her?"

"Not *her*. Me. *Me*. She *has* Margaret. Margaret is bound to her."

The magar looked at Emma. "And how do you hold Margaret?" Which was the question Emma was expecting.

"I don't know. Maybe Margaret can answer."

If Margaret could, she didn't.

"What will you do now, Emma?"

That was the question, wasn't it? Emma looked to Michael and Allison. "We can't stay here. If we hit the road quickly enough, we'll be able to escape, at least for a short while—but we can't spend forever on the run. We can't go home if—if she hasn't been—been stopped."

Margaret nodded. "She cannot be stopped from Canada."

"Can she be stopped from anywhere in the world that isn't her citadel?"

"I don't think so, dear," Margaret replied.

"No," Longland said.

"No," Helmi whispered. The words overlapped, adding texture and certainty to the discussion.

"Is she coming, now?"

Helmi shook her head. "If there were more Necromancers, if she hadn't lost so many knights, she might take the risk. The Queen of the Dead is safe in her citadel. She won't leave it—"

"She's left it before," Chase cut in. Something in his voice caused Allison to raise a hand; it hovered a foot from his arm, as if she wanted to touch him to offer comfort and realized just how little that comfort would mean. Emma was surprised when he caught her hand in one of his.

"She won't leave if she doesn't feel her safety is guaranteed. In the past, she might have come here. But with cars and phones and internet, she's no longer certain to have uninterrupted time. So much has changed, so quickly." She turned, again, to Emma.

Eric, silent until then, said, "She's safe in her citadel. No one can touch her there."

Helmi's expression hardened further, and given the death glares she'd leveled at Longland, that should have been impossible. She said nothing, waiting as all eyes fell on Eric.

"She has, three times in the history of the court, come close to death," Longland said, when Eric didn't speak. "Once, before the citadel was constructed. To construct the citadel was not the act of a month or even a year. It required power on a scale that she had never before used. It required a gathering of the dead that she had never attempted. I imagine," he continued, when Eric failed to interrupt him, "that what Emma gathered in order to open the exit was the only gathering that might come close. How long did that take?" It was a rhetorical question; he knew the answer.

Helmi said, "You have the lantern." She turned, then, to the magar and said, in a quieter voice, "You *gave* her the lantern."

"And will you accuse me of betrayal, who are dead—and trapped—as I am?"

"My sister wants the lantern."

"She always did. And think of what she might have built if she had claimed it." She turned to Eric. "You are too silent."

He exhaled. "I have an idea."

Helmi said, with scorn, "And we know where *your* ideas lead!"

"Helmi," her mother said.

Eric ignored the interruption. He looked to Emma. "No one *could* touch her in her citadel back then. But you weren't there. If you want—if you intend—to stop her, you'll have to go to her."

"How? I have no idea how to *reach* the citadel."

"The living need to eat. Very little grows in the citadel. There is some fertile land, but even that is only enough to feed a small family. She has to import food."

"Where does she get the money?" Michael asked. It was the first time he'd chosen to contribute throughout this lengthening emergency council.

"There is a long and complicated answer to that question. We can discuss it on the way."

"On the way to where?" Michael replied, an edge to the words. "Where are we going?"

"If you're willing to take the risk? The citadel."

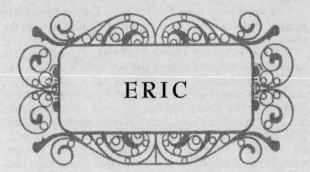

ERIC

ERIC HAS EXISTED FOR SO LONG he thinks he should be immune to pain, to fear. And perhaps he is; he is not afraid of Helmi. He is not afraid of Emma. He is not comfortable in the winter glare of the magar, but she never liked him, never accepted him.

And yet, for years, she has guided him. Years.

Longland is afraid of everything except Emma. Longland knows the fate of the dead who displease the Queen. So does Eric. But that fate might be peaceful, in the end. If he has no choice, he has no responsibilities—and he has shouldered responsibility, however imperfectly, since the moment he died. He is tired.

The magar offers no guidance. Her eyes—her dead eyes—burn with accusation and guilt. Eric wonders if his do the same. He is so tired.

"You want to return to the citadel," the magar says.

"No."

"There is a throne waiting for you. And a very lonely girl."

Chase curses, the sound familiar and almost comforting.

"You could have returned at any time," the magar continues.

Eric turns away from her. He turns toward Emma. He sees her as the dead see her. She is the brightest thing in the room, the warmest.

He came to kill her. He could not make himself do it. He had seen too much of Emma and her friends: Allison, Michael, the intimidating Amy Snitman. He couldn't imagine that Emma could become one of the Queen's knights. She might have the power, yes, but the potential didn't define her. If his target had been Amy? Maybe. Maybe Amy Snitman would be dead, and Eric would be in hiding, planning the deaths of Necromancers and longing for the moment when he might kill the Queen of the Dead and redeem himself at last—just as he's done for centuries.

On the night he made the decision not to kill Emma, Emma did not look like this. The seed of potential has grown, has flowered. The small light has become a miniature sun, a source of warmth. To the dead, there is very little difference between Emma Hall and the Queen.

As if she can hear the thought, Helmi lifts her hand. Emma's rises with it. "Can you kill my sister?" Helmi demands. "She loves you. Even after all this time, she loves you. She says love never dies."

"Love dies," Eric replies. He is not willing to have the rest of this discussion with Helmi. It's not a discussion to have with anyone who has spent centuries hating him, blaming him. Which is ironic, because Eric has spent those same centuries hating and blaming himself. Wishing, fervently, that he had never met Reyna. Wishing that he had never fallen in love and, failing that, that Reyna had never returned his love.

Love led them here. Endless pain. Endless regret. Endless guilt—a vortex that has destroyed not only Eric's existence but also the existence of every single person who has died since. It has been so long since he has seen Reyna. It has been so long since the girl he loved has existed in the eyes of the woman he has vowed to kill.

Every guardian has doubted that desire. Ernest doubted it—loudly—when they first met. But Ernest is not that young man; he is older, more fatherly, his fury burned to determined embers with the onset of age. He is so much younger than Eric.

Love dies. It's the answer he gave to Ernest, those many years ago. It's the answer he gave to Philip, the man who preceded him. It's the answer he's given to anyone who has known enough to ask. It's been a theoretical answer.

Eric is dead.

There is no action he can take against the Queen of the Dead on his own unless she desires it. She can immobilize him with a single word. All discussions about the nature of love, about his ability to kill the Queen, have been safely theoretical or philosophical. Until now. And now? Emma is here. The question is no longer theoretical.

Eric can return to the citadel at any time he chooses. But Emma and Chase can't. Emma doesn't even have the travel documents necessary to leave her own country, and Eric's not certain she'd survive the attempt if she did.

But if Helmi is right, if the Necromancers are truly coming in any force at all, there *is* a chance. There's a way. It's risky, and it means that Eric must return to face Reyna one last time.

"The magar is right. There is a place waiting for me in the citadel." He exhales and turns to Longland. Merrick Longland, the man he—and Chase—killed. "I have a plan."

NATHAN

NATHAN SPENDS HIS DAY READING, and when reading fails to keep his attention, he rises and heads to the door that separates his rooms from the rest of the citadel. He chafes at the clothing he's forced to wear because he's aware of every itchy thread; he feels the rough cloth and the edges of lace and wonders why a top-heavy wig hasn't been added to the almost comic assembly.

Being dead, it appears, is about discomfort and silence and boredom. And pain. Sleep still eludes him because he listens for the sounds of his body. Weeping is his heartbeat and his breath. He bleeds, and grows weak with lack of food or water. He will not, he is told, incubate many diseases.

Diseases are carried by the living. The only living person he regularly sees is the one who brings his food and leaves it in stiff silence.

Today, standing inside his door, he takes stock of the life he's been given. He considers the alternative. Being disembodied isn't pleasant, but there's freedom in it that being embodied doesn't have.

The door is heavy and opens outward; the hinges are on the exterior. The hinges are on the exterior of almost all doors in the citadel; only the doors to rooms the Queen occupies are normal.

No one moves in the hall facing the door, but the hall is not empty. Two of the dead stand at attention, framing the doorway. Nathan has been to London; he's aware that the dress guards at Buckingham palace will stand at attention as if they're carved statues. He doesn't expect the dead to notice him as he leaves—unless he has been ordered to remain in his room.

They make no sound; they make no movements. He nods at them anyway before he turns, arbitrarily, to the right and begins to walk. Other guards—dead guards—are standing immobile in the hall. They are furniture. They take no breaks.

Nathan wonders if they think. He wonders if they pass their hours and days trapped and encased with no escape; he wonders if they are still sane. And then, as he walks, he wonders whether the floors have ears or eyes or some way of seeing who passes above them and whether the walls are, like the guards, just more furnishings, but given no human shape.

He wonders, in short, if this is hell.

Helmi appears to his left in answer to the unasked question.

"Nathan," she says. "I need your help."

He continues to walk as she drifts by his side. He doesn't actually like her much, but she's company.

"What," he asks, voice tight with contained sarcasm, "could I possibly do to help you?"

"Emma is coming to save you, but she won't survive if you don't help."

Emma. Emma is coming here. The thought simultaneously fills Nathan with dread and desire. He holds up one hand. "Don't tell me this. Do not tell me another word." What he wants to ask, as well, is *when* and *where is she*. Those are the wrong questions. The answers are dangerous to know.

"You're worried about what you'll tell the Queen." It's not a question.

"Yes. If she asks—if she commands—I'll tell her everything." When Helmi fails to reply, he stops walking and turns to face her. "I *want* to know. I want to see Emma again. But—she can't come here. She'll die."

"Which is *why* I need your help. The citadel isn't the whole of the city. If the Queen and her court are distracted, Emma might be able to sneak in."

"How the hell do you sneak into a *flying city*?"

Helmi looks at Nathan as if he's too stupid to live. "You want me to answer *that* question, but nothing else?"

Put that way, she's right—and Nathan's not up to explaining that his question wasn't actually a question at all.

"The Queen hasn't summoned you today, and after I talk to her, I don't think she will. She'll be busy."

"Doing what?"

"Preparing," Helmi replies, with a hard, tight smile that is way too old for her face, "for Eric's return."

"Eric's coming?"

"Yes. Eric is finally coming home. If no one does anything too stupid, that's what will take up every single thought she has. We need you to run interference to make sure that the less-obsessed-with-Eric among the court don't call her attention to anything else. There might be people new to the court who would help with that, but I doubt it. They're not new enough not to be terrified of the Queen of the Dead."

"Neither am I."

"Does fear make you stupid?"

"Not exclusively."

Helmi says, "Well, save the rest of the stupidity for later. Follow me. Pay attention. You're only going to get one chance to get this right."

"But no pressure," Nathan replies. The irony is lost on Helmi. Then again, the citadel probably sucks the humor out of everyone who is forced to remain here.

CHAPTER
FOUR

THE SNOW WAS WARMER by far than the air above
it. Amy, who had abandoned the warmth of an idling,
large car, was exhaling what looked like steam. Eric and
Chase had led them to within a hundred yards of the road
nearest the cottage; given that they paused at even intervals
to do something to mark the path—and to check it for Necromantic traps—it took longer than the combination of distance and snow dictated. No one was warm. No one was
particularly happy, except possibly Petal.

Eric handed off the backpack he wore to Michael. Chase
continued to shoulder his. They had packed all of the food
that was easily portable, with can openers and the type of
throw-away dishes taken on camping trips. If they managed
to make it to the city, they wouldn't be dining with the
Queen; Longland had implied that food could quickly become the biggest problem they faced if they survived. That,
and water.

There was one permanent portal to the citadel, but it
wasn't in Canada. They'd be able to access it from the

citadel-side, but not easily, and the trip down might be one way. They would not have permission to be in another country, and they wouldn't have passports should that permission somehow be required. They would, on the other hand, speak the language.

Michael had asked how they would get home.

Ernest, however, declared that a non-problem. If they survived—if they somehow succeeded—he could arrange it with relatively little fuss. Emma wasn't certain she believed him. Michael needed details. Details were provided on the walk because the walk gave them time; Ernest would otherwise never have surrendered. He didn't *like* the plan, but he was confident that he could build the careful paperwork lies that would allow whoever survived to come back.

Whoever survived.

Petal was now Emma's biggest worry. It wasn't displacement worry, either; no one was safe. No one was guaranteed to survive. But every other living person present understood the rough, shaky plan that Eric had outlined. Some had greater belief in it than others. Petal, incapable of comprehension, was neutral.

He was not a poorly trained dog—Brendan Hall would never have allowed that, especially not for a rottweiler—but his hearing was not what it had once been, and his first tendency when going someplace new was to explore. Chase wanted to leave the dog, as he called Petal, behind.

Abandoning him here was almost certainly abandoning him to starvation and death. Emma's first suggestion—that Michael remain behind with Petal—was met with solid, logical resistance. Michael had not been affected by Longland's magic. Everyone else had. That resistance might—just might—save their lives if they somehow managed to arrive, as planned, at the citadel. Since the resistance had come from Michael, Emma swallowed and let it go. Allison would not remain behind either.

That left Amy.

Which meant Petal was either coming or being abandoned near a winter roadside.

"You understand what you're meant to do here?" Eric asked.

Chase nodded.

"Then Longland and I are heading back to the cottage. Wait. You'll know when it's safe. Helmi?"

"I don't have to leave yet. I'll come when you're closer." She glanced at Emma and at Emma's hands, now heavily mittened against the winter cold.

"Eric's plan will work," Helmi said, when time had passed. How much, Emma couldn't say. She didn't wear a watch, and the phone she used as a replacement was entrenched in a pocket she couldn't reach without removing her mittens.

"It doesn't make sense," Emma replied. Amy frowned but did not insist on being part of the conversation, which was good — Emma's hands still hadn't recovered from the previous one. "First of all, they knew we were here."

"They knew *you* were here," Helmi countered.

"Why wouldn't they hunt for me, then?"

"They can't afford to hunt and keep the portal open."

"That didn't stop them in Toronto."

"No. But in Toronto, you didn't have me. I have to go back to the citadel. I need to tell the Queen that Longland has Eric. The reason they've set up in the road is to catch you if some of you manage to leave by car. If she knows that Longland has Eric, she'll forget everything else — at least for a little while. She might tell her Necromancers to remain here to hunt the rest of you down. If she does, they'll be searching, but they'll start at the cottage, not the road.

"Even if they discover your trail here, it will end at the road. They're not going to guess that you went *to* the citadel.

"The portal itself will close. You could prevent that if you knew what you were doing; you probably can't on your own. Margaret will help you, so listen to her, and listen carefully. If you could bind me, I could do it."

"The Queen would know."

"No, she wouldn't. She doesn't own *me*." Helmi rolled her eyes before she continued what was, in essence, a lecture. "Let the portal collapse naturally — and step through before it vanishes. Don't worry about the portal after that. Worry about leaving the area you arrive in."

"What will happen to Eric?"

"Who knows? The most important thing you need to understand is that Eric's safety is guaranteed. No one else's is.

That's why we're doing it this way." She frowned at Emma's companions. "I think you should leave them behind."

"I know."

"But Margaret told me how they've helped, and maybe, in the end, you can't do this on your own. Just—don't fall apart if they die, okay? I have to leave. I'll come back again when it's safe for you to move."

Chase was not happy. No one was, but Chase was one of the few people present who could actually *do* something in the worst case scenario. He had an arm around Allison's shoulder because Allison was shivering. Allison had an arm around Michael's shoulder because Michael was doing the same; only Michael leaned into the offered support. Allison was too stiff.

She bit her lip; she bit her lip when she was nervous. Had she been inside, she would have cleaned her glasses, because she did that a lot as well. Chase wanted to send her somewhere else.

"Don't even think it," she whispered, her words visible as clouds of mist.

"I'm not. I'm thinking about what we do when we land. Or how we do it. Longland bothers me."

Allison said nothing.

"Just because he's dead, we're trusting that he's changed sides."

"He has," Emma said. "By default. He's dead."

"He—"

"And the only sides he now sees are the dead and the living. We're all eventually going to be on the side he's on now."

"Or we'll be fuel for the side we're not on now."

"Or that. I wouldn't trust him with my personal happiness; I think he still resents any happiness that isn't his own—and frankly, he's a person who believes 'smug' is the definition of happiness. Normally, I'd find it a bit sad. Right now I don't care. He won't turn us in, and he won't have us killed because dead, we're no use to him. We'd be just as helpless as he is."

Chase could see Emma in the light that reflected off the snow; she was straight, narrow; her profile implied an edge that he had never seen in her. He didn't threaten her; he didn't disagree with her. No point.

Instead, he leaned in toward Allison and whispered, "I suppose kissing you is out of the question?" Her outrage was warming. He was fairly certain she wouldn't slap him while she was holding on to Michael.

"It is absolutely out of the question," Amy replied.

Allison stuck her tongue out—at Chase; Amy snorted. Michael pointed out that public displays of affection made people uncomfortable. Chase considered asking him why but decided against it because he wasn't up to the convoluted logic that would likely follow; he was sure he would find it amusing, but given Amy's expression, it wouldn't be amusing enough.

"Chase," Emma said. Wrong tone of voice. He let his arm fall from Allison's shoulder, surprised at how the cold rushed in. "Helmi says there's trouble."

"Necromancer?"

"Just one. The portal's not activated yet, but Helmi says he's by the road."

"Does she think he's remaining to hunt the rest of us down?"

"She missed a small part of the conversation, but—yes."

He smiled. "Did she recognize him?"

"Her. Yes. I think she knows all of the Necromancers at court. She says the woman is young." There was a brief pause, which ended with Emma saying, "That is *not* our definition of young, Helmi. Sorry. She thinks she might be part of Margaret's cohort."

"Is Margaret here?"

"She is now," Margaret replied. "Before you ask, no, I am not going to be a useful source of information; I'll be seen. Helmi occupies a unique role at court; the same courtesy is not extended to anyone else. If I'm seen and Helmi is correct, I'm likely to be recognized. Who," she said, turning to face nothing, "is it?"

Chase didn't hear the answer. Margaret, apparently, did. She turned to Chase. "She was in the citadel when I arrived."

"Is she powerful?"

"Yes. She is not powerful enough to be a concern if she is unprepared. I think," she added, "that's unlikely."

"No kidding."

Allison caught his arm. "She might leave—"

"She might, yes. But if she leaves, she'll be on the other side of the portal when we arrive. We don't want to face her there if we can avoid it. And we can." He glanced at Ernest.

Ernest nodded.

Allison's sudden stiffness had nothing to do with the cold. They were facing possible—probable—death. It made no sense to worry about her anxiety and her fear. But he did. "I'm not going to alert them to our presence; I won't take her down before Eric and Longland are gone. How many Necromancers in total?"

"Three," Margaret said. She blanched. "One of them is older than Longland. The Queen has lost many of her powerful knights in recent weeks; Longland was a significant loss. The man he killed to save Allison was similarly costly. In my youth, she would not have risked the man who is here. Be careful, Chase. He is canny and sensitive, and he's clashed with hunters before."

And clearly, if he was standing here, the hunters were the ones who'd died.

Silence. Silence broken by Petal, by breathing, by movement across the icy surface of old snow. Silence broken, more definitively, by the sound of a car. Helmi appeared in front of Emma, a foot above the snow, her eyes almost level with Emma's. "They're all in the car," she said.

"Eric—"

"Is safe. They won't kill him. They won't dare. Alraed might consider taking Eric as hostage—but it's risky."

"Should we—"

Helmi shook her head, the edge of a smile adorning her lips. It was the type of smile that could almost draw blood; she looked, momentarily, like a vengeful demon. Whoever Alraed was, she didn't like him. "I told him the Queen knows he has Eric."

"If he bound you," Emma replied, "would that change things?"

"She'd kill him," Helmi said. "She'd kill him slowly and terribly. Binding the dead isn't trivial. And it's not instantaneous. He won't have the time. She wants to see Eric. She'll be waiting to meet him. If it takes too long for Eric to arrive, she'll come in person."

Silence. Fear. This plan seemed so slight, so fragile a strong breeze might break it, shattering all hope. Emma inhaled and exhaled, her breath a mist between their faces. "Does she have any friends?"

"The Queen?"

"Your sister, yes."

"Would *you* be friends with her?"

Emma thought of Nathan. Of Allison and Michael. And, yes, of Amy, the most terrifying of her friends. She had no answer to give, because everything in her screamed No. But she had hated Mark's mother until she had finally met her, too.

"She blames herself for my death," Helmi said.

"Do you?"

"Do you always ask so many questions?"

Emma shook her head. "Usually Michael does. But he can't see you right now."

"I do blame her for my death. But not completely." Helmi shook her head. Her hair moved as if it were real. "Our mother would have been so angry at her. Our mother *is* angry. She wanted to leave the village; there had been no rain. People were afraid.

"My sister wanted to stay. They argued. They argued for two days. In the end, my mother agreed. But she didn't know—we didn't know—why my sister thought it would be safe. My sister had already gathered the power of the dead she found. She had kept them bound to her instead of walking them to the door. She kept them hidden."

"Why?"

"Because she wanted to make it rain," Helmi replied. "I knew. I watched her practice with small patches of land, in secret. She thought if she could make it rain in the middle of the drought, the villagers would love her. They would be happy to have her there. She thought they would accept her, and if they did, we would be safe. And loved. And welcomed.

"That's why she had power when they came. She had more power than the magar. She used it—but not for rain." Helmi lifted her face, gazing to the left of Emma's shoulder—to the left, and up. "She told me she killed the villagers before they could kill her. Those deaths were messy, but they were fast.

"I wasn't there," Helmi added. "I didn't see it. I went where the dead go. But I couldn't leave. No one could leave. No one has been able to leave since the day Eric died."

REYNA

REYNA SCREAMS.

Reyna screams and screams and screams. There are no words embedded in the sounds because the screams are so visceral, so complete, she has no thought left to form them. She sees men, she sees clubs and torches and pitchforks and—yes—long knives. She sees the elderly, the aged who are not yet infirm, the men who, broad-shouldered and grim, have seen war and bandits and other deaths but have lived to father children of their own.

She sees the young men, men Eric's age. One is green-faced and shaking, but she doesn't remember his name; she doesn't remember the name of the father who stands, grim and proud, by his side.

She shouldn't see anything about them at all, because they're alive.

Her mother is not. Her mother was the first to die. Her uncle followed quickly, his raised arms meant to indicate that he meant no harm, that he was not a threat. Of course he wasn't. He wasn't armed. He had no power. He could not stand against the dozens assembled here. And Helmi is bleeding. Helmi, who might have survived had she stayed hidden. It is too much. It is *too much*.

Those deaths would make her weep. They would freeze her heart, her voice, her lungs.

But they are not real, not yet. Eric's death is real. Eric's blood is bright and dark and endless. Eric's eyes are fluttering, his chest is rising and falling far too quickly, far too shallowly; his skin is torn, his ribs broken; his lip is swollen because of his father's backhand. Eric is—Eric is—

Reyna screams in utter terror.

Eric is the only thing in Reyna's life that was about life and living. For Eric, she would have *saved* this village. For Eric, she had begged her mother. Defied her mother. Because her mother had wanted to leave. Her mother had wanted to leave a month ago, and Reyna had refused. Had refused to believe that her bitter, angry mother was *right*. Eric loves her. Eric's love was supposed to be the shield against the world. Eric's love was the promise of life—and his own people have destroyed it.

He will leave. He is leaving, even now, as she screams. All promise, all dream, all hope is a lie—a lie written now in blood, in a language too messy to read.

The end. The end. The end.

Rain falls, then. Lightning flashes. Thunder rumbles. The storm is her storm; it says—and does—what she cannot. If they want death, they'll have it. That is why they've come. To bring death. To end life. To end Reyna's life.

Let death take them instead. She doesn't need them here. She doesn't want them.

She looks up, and up again; rain washes blood from her hands, from her lap; she takes Eric's body into her arms, and bends, and kisses his open mouth. There is no response. She screams his name. *Eric! Eric!* Two beats, over and over. He has always answered her before.

He does not answer her now.

He is gone.

"How could you kill your own son?" she demands of the blacksmith. But the blacksmith, like Eric, will never answer that question; he lies face down in dirt that is rapidly becoming mud.

No, no, no. Eric. *Eric*. She gestures and the rain stops. The lightning stops. Silence falls instead, a blanket, a shroud. She *will not* gift the village and its fields with rain. Not now. Not *ever*.

He is still here. He is still here, somewhere. He has not left, might not leave. She has seen and spoken to so many of the dead. She has seen the door, the window, the exit to which they must all walk, in the end. She knows where the dead go when they accept the fact of death.

She rises. She rises and gently rolls Eric's corpse off her lap. She glances, once, at her mother, grimaces, and turns away. Her mother is dead. Her mother has no voice; her hands will never rise again, to either strike or caress. Her voice, her harsh, judgmental voice, is gone to silence, and Reyna will not call it back.

Reyna has always lived with death. She has accepted the wanderers and the lost; she has dedicated most of her childhood to finding and freeing them. But she has wanted life. *This* life.

Eric loves her. She loves Eric. Love is meant to last a lifetime.

But the dead don't linger unless they are frightened or trapped. They don't stay. They don't *want* to stay. Once they know they're dead, they leave. It's just a second stage of abandonment. She *believes* Eric loves her. She believes he will want to stay. But he doesn't know that she can see him. He doesn't know that she can talk to him.

And he won't know if he sees the exit. He won't have any *reason* to stay.

Reyna knows.

She turns, walks into the home that will never be home again, and finds chalk. In a darkened room, she draws her circle, thinking that one day—one day—she will have one of stone, a place where she might sit and search as if it were both her duty and her right.

She does not cry as she works. Tears will smudge the circle. Tears will destroy the chalk. Her mother's harsh and angry voice reverberates in memory, and this time, Reyna listens. She will take what she needs, now. She is the last of her family. She is magar.

But she does not have the lantern. She does not have the

light. Her mother would not pass it on to the daughter who was—and is—far more powerful than she. Reyna doesn't *need* it, to be magar. The lantern would make things easier, but in the end, it is up to Reyna. All she needs now, she has.

A circle. Chalk. Knowledge.

She has walked the path to the shining, brilliant warmth that is the promise at the end of life and death, and she will walk it now. She will walk it, she will reach it, and she will close it so that the dead cannot leave. Because otherwise, Eric might leave. He doesn't *know*. Eric might leave before she can find him.

They'll understand, surely. The dead will understand. And she will let them go when she has finally found Eric. But she needs the *time* because she does not have the lantern. And the dead are forever. A year or two won't harm them at all.

CHAPTER
FIVE

"YOU KNEW HE WAS DEAD, RIGHT? You're a Necromancer."

Emma said nothing. She didn't want everyone else to hear. But Helmi prodded and prodded until she spoke. "No. I didn't know until I spoke with Longland."

"You're not very bright."

Broken, iced snow cracked beneath Emma's boots; it sounded like glass. She froze, aware that no steps could be silent, here. "No, Helmi. I'm not very bright. This is still new to me. Margaret won't teach me anything—don't make that face, it's rude. I thought your mother might, but we've had *no time*."

"My mother gave you what she could," Helmi replied. Her tone was grudging. "I'd teach you if I knew anything. I only know how to draw circles."

This sounded like a non sequitur.

"Circles are for containment," Helmi continued, correctly interpreting Emma's silence. "When you go to find the dead, you sit in a circle. You have to draw the circle, unless you have a stone one. The Queen has one," she added. "I can show you how to draw a circle." Her expression grew remote and thoughtful. "Or I could show you where the Queen's is."

Emma's eyes widened.

"I don't mean right now," Helmi said. "I mean later."

"We're supposed to *avoid* the Queen."

"Not forever." The subject was clearly distasteful, and she dropped it. "Circles are supposed to keep you safe."

"How?"

The child's lips compressed. "I don't know. I died when I was eight. I can tell you how to draw a circle. I can't tell you why it works. But the circle is the way you root yourself in the world when you go looking for the dead."

The younger man in the distance waited until Longland disappeared. He then turned to the older one.

"Be right back," Helmi said, and she vanished.

Chase didn't return.

Instead, Eric's car did. They could see headlights in the distance, moving up and down as if the driver were drunk. But no: It was the road. The roads were thick with flattened snow, thick and uneven.

They hid behind trees, keeping trunks between the road and their bodies. It was almost impossible to believe that no one would see them, that no one would look. Helmi, watching, told Emma that there were four people in the car. Two Necromancers, two passengers. Eric was driving.

Longland was behind him, gun pointed at the back of his head.

Beside him, in the front passenger seat, a man—the Necromancer Helmi feared. To one side of Longland, a younger man.

"He's afraid," Helmi said, with obvious derision.

"He should be. Eric's probably killed a lot of Necromancers, in his time."

"Not enough of them," Helmi replied.

On the other side of the road, less hidden, was the woman. Chase would kill her. Emma's hands shook; she turned to Margaret, who shadowed Ernest. "Why did you stop?"

"Stop serving the Queen?"

Emma nodded.

"I met Ernest."

"Ernest talked you out of it?" Emma's words carried her disbelief. Ernest had certainly been keen to see Eric shoot Emma on an autumn lawn months ago.

"Not exactly, dear." A ghost of a smile—literal and figurative—moved Margaret's lips. "He tried to kill me."

"He failed?"

"He was using the wrong bullets at the time, if I recall correctly. Yes, he failed. The Queen was responsible for my death." She grimaced, recalling that death; she didn't offer details, and Emma would never ask. "I did not go willingly with the Queen's knights when they came to 'save' me. I didn't have your mother or your father; I didn't have your friends. And perhaps," she added, lifting her chin, "that was my choice. The friends, at least. I had no reason to trust people—but they had no reason to trust me, if I'm honest.

"I was trapped by life. I was doomed to serve the Queen; I was doomed to bind the dead and drain them of life and somehow keep myself alive. The schooling is both rigorous and treacherous; the peers—if you have them—are just as angry and just as untrusting. They understand survival of the fittest; they don't believe there is *any* strength in numbers. I could not leave the citadel; failure to comply or learn what was necessary would only harm me. I had always felt trapped by life. Ernest's intent—to kill me—was something I welcomed. It would have been a fast, relatively painless, death.

"I was perhaps five years older than you are now. I had burn scars up the inside of my left arm."

"The Queen?"

"No. Another student. He died. I do not believe I had ever been happy—it's hard to be objective. I meant to let Ernest kill me. Because I did, he didn't. I think he was confused—he was younger then, as well. He had lost much to Necromancers; he is like your Chase."

"So not mine."

"A figure of speech, dear. He thought it was a trick, of course. But I think he also knew it wasn't. We had no reason to trust each other. I was angry at the time. I didn't have the strength of will to end my own life, but it shouldn't have been necessary. Hunters kill us when we're weak. It's what they do. He was my only viable form of suicide." Her smile deepened. "I was so *angry* at him when he hesitated. It takes a very peculiar type of strength to hold still and wait for death; I was shaking. My partner, such as he was, was already dead.

"I believe I may have lost my temper, then. I may have shouted at him; I am not certain I remember the exact words, and even if I did, I would not repeat them. He was even more confused. I was already wounded," she added. "I fought until my partner died. Even then, I did not want to die and come face to face with the Queen. I knew what would happen after death."

"It happened anyway."

"Yes, dear, but later. By then I had truly earned her anger. I know very little of what occurred between my death and my meeting with you. Look at the road, Emma. It's starting." She turned to Ernest; he nodded.

Eric's car met road and stopped as it turned onto it. Four people got out; Eric was first, not last. He paused, gaze downcast. Longland looked, briefly, toward the trees. Emma held her breath, praying that Petal would remain quiet. No one spoke.

The air above the road, yards from where Eric now stood, began to shimmer.

Emma glanced at Allison and Amy; their eyes widened. What she saw, they could also see. Green light shot up from the snow-covered asphalt in two pillars; the pillars then bent toward each other, reaching and grasping at air until they met. When they did, they flared, in a green, twisting light that paled as it grew in brilliance until it was almost white.

The white light fell in a sheet from the height of what was now a very tall arch. At this distance, Emma could see only the shape of the portal; she couldn't see the dead who must be anchoring it. Her hands nonetheless became fists. She did not forget—could not forget—that people were its fuel.

She caught sight of the diminutive form of Helmi as Helmi joined the four. Longland stiffened; so did the older man. The younger did not, apparently, fear her, which made sense. Emma knew who she was but couldn't see beyond her apparent age; Helmi could irritate or annoy but not terrify. Not yet.

Helmi then vanished.

She reappeared by Emma's side. "Now," she said. "You won't have much time. Therese is holding the gate, but she's got no power. She's meant to come through it before she lets it go."

"If Chase kills her—"

"There's a bit of danger, yes. But the portals don't collapse instantly. If you have to, you can hold its shape long enough to get everyone else through—just listen to Margaret and do what she tells you to do. Are you really going to bring your dog?"

"I can't leave him here."

"We don't have a lot of dog food," Helmi said.

"I know." She swallowed. "Michael, can you hold on to Petal?"

Michael nodded and bent, hooking Petal to his leash. Petal was excited until he realized that Michael's hands were empty of everything but leash. No treats.

"Remember: When you get through, do *exactly* what I tell you to do."

"What happens to us if we're caught?"

"The Queen, in the end. You'll all die. Eric's job is to keep her distracted." This last was said sourly.

"Can he do it?"

"I don't know. She's been waiting for him for a long time. She'll probably be happy at first."

"And after?"

"She's pretty angry. It might get ugly." Helmi exhaled. "Why are you worried about Eric?"

"I don't want him to—"

"To what? Die? He can't. He's already dead."

Emma didn't ask what a bullet could to do to the body the Queen had created. She knew that the bodies bled. She knew that they could be injured. She had no idea what the person who inhabited the body would feel at the moment the body was destroyed. Nathan now had a body that was very much like Eric's. Or Longland's.

*   *   *

Emma watched as what she assumed was a woman joined the two men; it was hard, at this distance, to tell. None of them wore distinguishing clothing, and the woman was not short. Chase was not visible at this distance; she looked for him, holding her breath.

She saw Helmi instead. Helmi was seated, midair, ten feet from where the three Necromancers gathered, in full view of the portal. Her arms were by her sides, her palms pressed down into a nonexistent bench. She should not have been so remarkably clear, given the distance—but she was. She was the only person who was.

As Emma watched, forgetting, again, to breathe, Helmi lost substance. She didn't lose clarity, although at first that was Emma's assumption; she lost shape. The blurred outline of her body—with her ridiculous clothing and her ringlet hair—remained, but it lengthened, gaining height and width. Without thought, Emma took a step forward.

"Emma." Margaret's voice, while quiet, was harsh. Angry-teacher harsh. Emma stopped moving automatically. "Your father told you about the ancient dead, did he not? Helmi is among the oldest of those that remain trapped here. She is not being bound; she is asserting herself in a different way."

Assertion, as Margaret called it, was transformation, in Emma's vision. Amy cleared her throat; she was annoyed. The fact that Emma couldn't gift her with vision didn't appear to lighten Amy's mood. She did not like—had never liked—being left out.

As if viewed through a ground-glass lens, Helmi's new form sharpened and hardened, coming at last into a different focus. Her face was no longer the face of an eight-year-old child; it was a woman's face—she was ten or fifteen years older than Emma Hall or any of her friends. She wore a dress that would have been at home in an old James Bond movie and gloves that ended at her elbow.

Emma couldn't discern the neckline of the dress and didn't try.

"Would she have looked like that if she'd lived?"

"I highly doubt it." Margaret's voice was dry. "The Queen prefers her sister to look familiar. Her sister chooses to honor the Queen's preferences. Her normal appearance is generally advantageous—it makes her look harmless, and people tend to ignore her. But Alraed won't; she could regress to the form of an infant, and he would still understand the danger she poses.

"This is merely an act of petty malice on her part. She does not—and has never—cared for Necromancers."

"Why would she? She's dead."

"Once, she would have," Margaret replied, voice neutral. "Her own kin—" She stopped.

Emma turned toward the road again. Ernest moved forward, waving everyone else back, although no one but Emma had moved.

The three Necromancers turned their backs to the roadside that Emma and her friends were so timidly occupying. Chase was on the other side.

"Ernest, don't."

The old man—as Eric called him—now carried a gun in his right hand.

"He knows there are—or were—hunters here. He is not a fool. You won't be able to take him with the first shot. You are unlikely to get a second."

Ernest didn't appear to hear Margaret.

"The children will die."

That, on the other hand, caught his attention. Emma didn't even mind being referred to as a child, but it wasn't making Amy any happier. "What is she telling them?"

"I can't hear her. Nor can I approach in safety. Alraed might not recognize me, but Therese almost certainly will. If I'm seen, they'll know that something is afoot. They almost certainly know about you."

"Longland."

Ernest lengthened the distance between himself and the group. Margaret looked at his back. "He is fond of Chase," she told Emma quietly. "He was fond of every hunter he managed to save and train. His life—since before me—has been about killing and death. If the citadel falls, I don't know what he'll become."

"And you?"

"Free," Margaret replied. "You've seen it. You've seen what is waiting for us."

Emma swallowed and nodded.

One voice rose in the distance. "I said *find him*."

"That would be Alraed."

No voice rose in answer but Helmi's. "Shall I ask my sister?"

"The Queen will not care; this is beneath her now. She has what she desires." The words were carefully chosen, carefully spoken.

"She doesn't. Eric has agreed to return to her side—but he has not been seen and has not been recognized by her court. Will you deny him that legitimacy now? If he means, finally, to join her, killing the hunters will be trivial in the future. Will you risk two of her knights when she is almost at the pinnacle of her success?"

"She's good," Emma murmured. She had been afraid that Helmi would tell them where Chase was, and she felt guilty.

"She was always capable of engendering hatred and rage," Margaret replied.

"What else did she have? From everything you've said, the Necromancers weren't exactly friendly or kind."

"No. But perhaps they might have been, in different circumstances. We will not know; they are, now, what they are."

Lightning struck the road. The sky remained clear.

Helmi was unmoved, but the Necromancers who had been wavering were not; they fell to either side of the great crack that appeared beneath snow and asphalt. The ghost of the Queen's sister then unfolded her legs; she appeared to be stepping down from an invisible chair. She approached the fallen man; the woman was already rising, unsteadily, to her feet. She knelt; her hair covered her face as she bent her head.

"The two of you, go," Alraed said, his voice thunder to the brief flash of lightning. "I will find the hunter. Play witness to your Queen."

"Their Queen?" a new voice said. Emma recognized it instantly. The winter chill became absolute. Ernest froze. Margaret froze; silence robbed every element of the night of warmth. "*Their* Queen?"

The voice emanated from the portal. The Queen failed

to follow it. But Alraed turned to face her, and it was clear, as he fell to one knee, that he could see what Emma couldn't.

"My Queen," he said, his voice soft enough that it barely carried. That wouldn't have been enough for Amy—the only person Emma knew who could carry off this type of fury and make it look natural—and it wasn't, apparently, good enough for the Queen.

He knew it, too.

Helmi lost her adult look, becoming again the child the Queen recognized and preferred. She then vanished, to reappear seconds later by Emma's side. She looked worried, now.

Alraed lifted his face—only his face, he didn't rise—and said, "You have known for centuries how I feel about you, my Queen. I have—for centuries—endeavored to prove both my loyalty and my love. I have obeyed your commands. I have returned to your side, time and again. And I will return to your side now if that is your desire."

"It is."

"But it is difficult for me to watch him take his place at your side. Lord Eric is a *hunter*. He has killed my friends"— Helmi snorted in disgust—"and comrades. He has treated you as if you are an enemy. He is not worthy of you."

Helmi snorted again.

"Surely," the disembodied voice said, "that decision is mine, and mine alone, to make." But some of the anger had drained from the Queen's voice; it was cool now, but not icy.

"Of course, my Queen. I am being foolish. I am being . . . unworthy."

"You have never been unworthy," the Queen replied. "But I do not wish you to waste your time. We are preparing, and I want your counsel."

"My Queen." He bowed his head again, and this time he rose. Without a backward glance at the two Necromancers behind him, he strode into the portal.

"The stupid thing is, she believes him. He'd slit her throat if he thought he'd have any chance of surviving it."

"She understands jealousy and envy," Emma replied. "What he said is perfectly believable."

"It's not. If it weren't for her power, he'd find her contemptible. He already does." She glanced at Emma. "You thought I'd turn Chase in."

Emma closed her eyes and exhaled. "Yes. I'm sorry."

"I considered it. Sacrifice Chase, and the rest of you could all get through." Emma opened her eyes and saw that Helmi was looking down at her hand. At her palm, which was cupped and turned toward her.

"Thank you," Emma said, and meant it.

"I think like a Necromancer. I think too much like a Necromancer. It's not comfortable. Be ready. The minute the last Necromancer walks through the portal, you have to be there."

"The Queen is there. We can't walk through—"

"The Queen won't be there once Alraed joins her. She'll keep an eye on him. She might even attempt to offer him some sign of her renewed favor; the reasons he's given make sense to her. Eric *has* been killing her people." Helmi tilted her head to the side as she looked up at Emma. "Eric probably came here to kill you."

"He did. We don't talk about it much; it's in the past and it upsets Allison."

"But not you?"

"It doesn't quite feel real to me—and I guess I'd prefer not to think about it. Whatever might have happened, didn't. To be honest, I was more upset about my first meeting with your mother."

"She has that effect on people." Helmi looked up. "Go. Now."

Emma had seen a portal very like this before—on the night Allison had almost been killed. She'd never examined one closely. She approached it from what she assumed was behind, given the direction that Alraed had walked—but this ended up being a bad assumption. The portal had no front and back. From either side it opened into what appeared to be a large, plain room; the walls were lit with torches, and the light they cast was both gloomy and inadequate.

Emma couldn't see people.

She could, on the other hand, hear shouting. It wasn't close; it seemed to be receding. Random words caught her attention and faded as she clenched her hands in fists. She was shaking. It wasn't from the cold.

This was, she thought, the point of no return. She could enter the City of the Dead and leave her friends behind. They'd be safe without her. She glanced back, once. There was enough light in the room on the other side of this tall, standing rip in the air that the night seemed darker; she couldn't see her friends clearly.

"You want to leave them behind."

She could, on the other hand, hear Chase. He came from the other side of the road.

"I didn't think you were going to survive that," she said quietly. She lifted a hand; it hovered an inch above the surface of the portal.

"I had some concerns as well." His shrug was pure Chase. "You're changing the subject."

She was. She inhaled cold air, exhaled mist. She wanted her friends to be safe. "Would you stay with them?"

So did Chase. "I would—but she has Eric. I'm going." He hesitated. "Michael's not wrong. I don't know how he escaped Longland's original spell. Neither do Ernest or Margaret. But there's a decent chance he can do it again."

"Have you been there? To the City?"

Chase didn't answer. "I really wanted to hate you."

"I wasn't under the impression you were failing."

He chuckled. "Are you alive?"

"Point taken. If I leave—"

"I am not staying behind with angry Allison. I don't give a damn about Amy. But if you're going, you'd better decide quickly; Ernest's coming."

She wanted to leave them behind. That was the truth.

But she wanted them to come with her, and that was the truth as well. She balanced between two different types of guilt; she drew another breath. She needed her friends. She'd needed friends when her father had died, even if she hadn't really understood, at age eight, what death *meant*. She wasn't eight, now. She understood death: endless silence, endless absence, utter loss. But she'd needed her friends when Nathan had died, as well—she'd needed them more.

"I'm not you," she said quietly. "Sometimes I wish I were."

"You don't."

"I don't want—I don't want what happened *to* you. But if I were you, this would be easy."

"It's not worth it," he said, his voice so soft that she glanced to the side to look at his face. "I hated you because I love what Allison represents. But—without you, I would never have found it, never have recognized it. My life is all about loss. And fear. You don't get to be Chase Loern and have anything that you care about. I'm terrified that she'll die. Sometimes I can't breathe through the fear." He looked away. "Margaret said that you're not the Queen of the Dead because you have friends and family, and they survived. She doesn't think you can become the Queen—because of that. Maybe she's right."

"She's right," Allison said, taking the decision out of both of their hands. How long had they been talking? Emma hadn't even heard her approach, and it was impossible to walk quietly in this snow. "I think the portal's beginning to . . . fray."

It was.

Emma reached out to touch it and withdrew her hand, frowning. She walked past Allison, leaving her with Chase, and approached the portal's visible edge. Fraying was exactly the right description; she could almost see liminal threads as they lost cohesion and shape. Without thought, she caught those threads in a mittened hand. Nothing happened.

Her hands were already cold. Worse than cold. They ached. But she pulled off her mittens and shoved them in her pockets, thinking, absurdly, that she had no idea what the weather was like in the City of the Dead—as if this were a class trip or a not entirely welcome family vacation.

The air was bracing; she expected that.

The threads were like ice. She'd expected that as well but had hoped it would be different. They didn't pass through, or around, her exposed palm; she caught them. They began to glow.

Margaret appeared to her left. Helmi appeared to her right.

"What will she do with Eric?" Emma asked softly.

"Love him," Margaret replied.

"Does she even understand what that means?"

"No," Helmi said. "She can't hurt Eric."

"She can. She can turn him into another power generator."

"Do you think that's much worse than what he has now? After what you've said?"

Emma did. But she couldn't say why or how because she *wasn't* dead. She couldn't see the world as the dead did. "Will my father be able to find me?"

Helmi's jaw dropped. She turned to Margaret. "Is she for real?"

Margaret, however, said, "Yes, dear." To Helmi, she added, "Allison's younger brother is in the hospital, fighting for his life because of your sister's actions. Emma's father is the only information conduit they currently have."

"Did he—did he come out of hiding too early?"

Emma didn't understand the dead. She couldn't imagine that someone centuries old would think to ask that question—and in that tone of voice. She didn't know if death defined the dead in any way but state. Yet she heard the question clearly—and heard all that lay beneath it, and she thought that maybe the dead were not so easily changed as all that. She held out a hand not to the ancient, dead sister of the Queen of the Dead, but to the little girl who had been murdered by angry, terrified, villagers.

Helmi took it. And, oh, the *cold*. "You need both your hands," she said, but so quietly Emma almost missed it. Nor was Emma unkind enough to point out that Helmi was holding her hand regardless.

"I don't know what I'm doing with *one* hand," she told the girl. "But if I do end up needing two, I know you'll let go." She caught more of the threads, winding them, by simple motion, more tightly around her palm and her fingers. Cocoons in stories worked like this; the strands shimmered, impossibly delicate.

The more she gathered, the more slowly the portal frayed.

"Go through?" Chase asked.

Emma frowned. "Not yet. There's something—" She shook her head. "Don't let me fall?"

"What?"

She closed her eyes.

*   *   *

In the darkness, there was no road. In the darkness, there were people. In Amy's house, Longland had bound four; whoever had created this portal had bound two. They weren't like Margaret had been; they could see her. They could follow her with their eyes.

No, she thought, frowning; they weren't looking at her. They were looking at Helmi. Helmi, attached by the hand, was visible to Emma, even through closed eyes. Everything about the child was cast in sharp relief. The lines of her hair, her face, her hands and her clothing seemed harder, crisper. Light lent a glow to her eyes.

It was the light that drew the eyes of the two bound to the portal: a woman Margaret's age, with long, thick dread-locks that fell down her back and around her shoulders, and a prim man who appeared to be much older and paler.

They could neither move nor speak, but their gaze fell on Helmi.

"It's not me they're looking at," Helmi whispered. She lifted her face and looked up at Emma. Emma was surprised at how much her expression hurt. When Helmi spoke to Longland—or to Alraed—she looked older and harder and just . . . meaner. But right now, hand in Emma's, she looked as if she needed an anchor, a guardian. She was a child.

She had seen things no child, in any sane world, would *ever* have to see. She hadn't come to Emma seeking rescue, not really; she'd come to find Eric. Possibly to torment Eric, she seemed to dislike him so much.

But she *had* found Emma. She'd found Michael. She had overcome her reluctance and fear for long enough to take the hand Emma offered her. It was literal, yes, the offered hand—but it was also metaphorical, because life could be, and often was, both. Emma's hand was cold. Emma's *everything* was cold. But she made no move to free herself.

Instead, she lifted Helmi's hand.

"You have to move *quickly*," Helmi told her, looking at the two dead people who powered the portal. "They'll be pulled back. This was never meant to last."

Emma had once stood, lantern in hand, and asked the names of everyone who approached her. All were dead. But all were human. She didn't hold the lantern now, and she was afraid to do so, this close to the place where the Queen of the Dead had stood, commanding Alraed. She had no illusions: The Queen of the Dead had more power and far greater experience. Emma had power, but it was a power she didn't understand. She'd never sneered at good intentions—they were better by far than bad ones, in her opinion—but good intentions here wouldn't cut it.

And yet.

She couldn't give up on them. "Come with me," she said to Helmi, as if Helmi were actually eight, and lost.

She approached the woman first; the woman's dead eyes seemed to see her, although they didn't move. No chain bound her, not that Emma could see. Margaret and the others had been bound together, roped in necklace-thin golden light that connected them.

Helmi, however, said, "Their feet."

Emma knelt. Helmi was right; the binding that held these two in place was anchored, somehow, to the road itself. "Do portals always require an anchor?"

"Yes. Here the road is best. It's much harder to open a portal without that grounding. Longland could do it. Alraed *can*. But it's a huge outlay of power, and it leaves the Necromancer vulnerable should he be attacked."

"By hunters."

Helmi nodded. "Or by other Necromancers looking to rise in the ranks. There are other ways to anchor, but those aren't taught now. They were, once. After she almost died, my sister changed what she taught the Necromancers she gathered."

"I've always wondered how she could find us."

"But not how Eric could?"

"I don't think Eric does—I think your mother does. But I can't imagine your mother helping the Queen of the Dead." She hesitated and then said, "I need my hand back for a minute."

Helmi closed her eyes. Nodded. It took Emma a moment to untangle their fingers, because her hand was numb. The winter air felt warm in comparison, but only briefly. She reached for the delicate chains that bound the woman's ankle. They were much tighter than the chains that had bound Margaret—and they were colder.

She opened her eyes and crossed the road to examine the chains around the ankle of the man. They were just as tight. Nothing seemed to bind him to the woman across the stretch of the portal.

"Emma?" Ernest's voice reached Emma as if from a great remove. She shook her head.

"Emma," Margaret said, her voice much clearer. "If you do not leave soon, you will not be able to follow. There has been some confusion on the other side of the portal; I believe we can take advantage of that confusion—but we must do it *soon*."

Both the man and the woman appeared to be serving as support pillars; the portal stretched between their still, bound forms, rising in a half circle above them. That, too, was collapsing slowly.

Emma frowned, and then, bending until her face was almost touching the dirt covered, flattened snow, she found her way in: a single, slender chain that ran from ankle to road and vanished there. This was short enough it was hard to grasp, but she managed; she could find no other way to pull at the chains that seemed almost a part of their skin.

These chains cut into her fingers as she tugged at them, but as she did, they loosened, falling away from ankles to float almost freely in the air. The man blinked and looked down at her—he had to look down—as she rose. She ran across the road again, back to the woman, looping golden wire around her palm before she did.

The woman was bound to earth the same way the man was; Emma freed her in the same way. Neither moved from the position they'd occupied, but they did move; they seemed to inhale as they noticed their surroundings. They blinked. They turned toward her and toward Helmi.

"I'm Emma," she told them, voice shaking slightly. "Emma Hall. And I'm sorry, but I need your help."

CHAPTER
SIX

THE OLDER MAN SPOKE FIRST. "Where am I?" His accent was thick, but Emma recognized both the words and the confusion in the question.

"You're a couple of hours outside of Toronto. That's in Canada," she added, in case he didn't know. "It's winter." She wanted to ask him where he thought he was, or when he'd last been aware of his surroundings; she didn't. Instead, she turned to Margaret. Margaret spoke to the man quietly, as Emma turned her attention to the woman.

"What would you have of me?" The woman asked, her voice so worn and weary Emma's initial impulse was to say, *Nothing, you've done enough.* But it wasn't true; she wanted—she needed—something, and that something was not, in the end, different from what the Necromancers demanded.

"I need you to do what you've been doing until my friends and I can reach the—the City of the Dead."

"It is not someplace you want to be," the woman answered, with more force and less resignation. "You're not dead."

"I'm not, no."

"All that waits you there is death. It's where the dead go. It's where the dead *rot*." She looked up, past Emma's shoulder. Emma thought she would cry. Her lips twisted in a bitter grimace instead, which was better—but not by much. "I won't help you if it's my permission you require."

Margaret came to stand beside the woman. Her expression was frosty; she lost the carefully cultivated look of a matron as she regarded the woman. "She requires permission, but if you will not give it, you will not. Move."

"Margaret—"

"We *do not have time*, Emma. Short of agreeing to go with the Queen's knights, as she calls them, you will never reach the City of the Dead. And if you are accompanied by those knights, you will, in all likelihood, not survive an hour. Nothing you can do—nothing we can do—is effective against the Queen herself at this distance."

"I opened the door," Emma said quietly. "And I was nowhere near her at the time."

"Yes." Margaret's expression gentled. "But you could not *keep* it open. If you truly mean to free the dead, you must go to the Queen."

Emma looked at the glowing, slender chains around one palm. She reached out and offered her hand to Helmi again, and Helmi took it, even as Emma flinched at the cold.

"Eric will kill her," Chase said.

Margaret did not reply. The older man, however, said, "Ms. Henney is persuasive. I apologize for my disorientation. It is seldom that I both serve and am left to my own devices and my own form. We are here to anchor the portal. You can see it, yes?"

Emma nodded, throat dry, as Allison and Michael approached her. "You—you know what—what's done with your . . ." the words trailed off.

The man smiled at her gently—and as if she were four years old. *All of you look like babies to someone as old as me.* Who had said that? She thought it was Ally's grandfather but couldn't be certain; the voice was strong, but there was no accompanying image. Just her own sense of resentment at being treated like a child.

There was no resentment now. If someone arrived who

could take the burden of this fight from her hands, someone responsible and—yes—adult, she would hand it over gratefully.

And yet, here she was, all the responsible adults in her life hours away. Ernest was here—but Ernest wasn't a Necromancer. Whatever it was he intended Emma to do, he couldn't do it or he would have done it by now, and they wouldn't be here. She was holding the hand of a girl who had existed for far longer than she had, and people were looking to her for guidance or even orders.

Emma's desire in life had been—and still was—to play a supporting role. She could imagine herself as the second-in-command almost anywhere, tending to the details and supporting the person who could deal with the big picture and make the decisions. All of the decisions she felt competent to make were small: what to wear, what to do with her hair, what make-up to buy, what to cook or eat for dinner, what classes to take. Even the question of which university to attend had given her hives.

This? This was too much. It was too much for her.

And this man seemed to know it. His smile was kindly, but it wasn't exactly saturated in respect, and oddly enough, right at this very moment, she couldn't resent it at all.

"I'm terribly sorry," he said. "I didn't introduce myself. There hasn't been great call for good manners for a long time. My name is Marcel." He glanced at the woman, who glowered. But she looked at Helmi, at Helmi's hand, ensconced in Emma's, and her expression gradually softened.

"Name's Belinda. Friends called me Belle, back in the day." She extended a hand. Emma glanced down at Helmi, who looked mutinous. She then lifted the hand that was bound in their chains—it was the right hand, anyway.

Belinda took it firmly; when she'd been alive, she'd probably had a crusher handshake. Her hand was cold. Emma expected that. What she didn't expect was the way the handshake changed the woman's features. Her brows rose, her mouth dropped open. No words came out for what felt like too long.

"Do we have time for this?" Amy asked. She added, because she was Amy, "I'm Amy Snitman, Emma's friend. We're in a bit of a rush because that portal isn't going to last all night."

The woman's eyes opened further. "You—you can see me?"

Sarcasm flashed, briefly, across Amy's face. Amy was not part of the welcoming committee, anywhere, ever. She managed to rein it in and said, "When Emma holds your hand, the rest of us can see you. It's not good for Emma, though."

Belinda shook her head. "It's so *warm*." She proved she was more adult than Helmi; she released Emma's hand. "What do you want with that portal?" Some of the wonder was still contained in the hard edges of her very practical tone.

"We need—all of us—to get to the City of the Dead."

"You'll die."

"We might. But we're all going to die one day, anyway."

"Not the way she'll kill you. You want to kill her?"

"We want—" Emma exhaled. "*I* want to stop her. I've led a pretty easy life. I've never lived in a war zone. I've never lived on the streets. Almost all of the violence I've seen, I've seen at a safe remove."

"Almost?"

"Long story. I don't know if I *can* kill another human being. But if she's not stopped, she's the hell that everyone I love is going to. I don't care if she dies. What I want is for the dead to be able to leave this world."

"It's what the dead want, as well," Belinda said. "Fine. If I tell you I don't want to help you, will you force me?"

Emma shook her head. "But ... I have that luxury. Helmi is here. Margaret is here. They're willing to help even if you're not."

Helmi snorted. "She's testing you."

Emma nodded. "Wouldn't you, in her position?"

"Marcel isn't."

"Maybe he's just more trusting."

"Or more of a suck-up," Belinda snapped. Marcel didn't appear to be unduly upset by the insult.

"How can you help?" Emma asked.

"If it's true that we have choice," Marcel replied, "I believe that we can shift—slightly—the destination to which the portal will take you."

"I've arranged for a bit of distraction," Helmi told him.

"Yes. Perhaps our help is unnecessary or even unwelcome."

Emma shook her head. "Do you know the City?"

"I doubt I know it as well as the Queen's sister—but yes, I know it. The dead come to the City and not always because they are called. If they are wise, they avoid it, of course; some have even escaped it, once they've walked its streets. I was not so wise."

"Are you bound to the Queen?"

"No. And yes, the person who held my reins will know that I am gone. He will perhaps assume that I have finally been fully consumed. I cannot offer to take you somewhere safe; there is no safety in the City for the living."

"Or the dead," Emma murmured.

"Even so. But you must move quickly, as your friend says."

Margaret walked to where Belinda had been standing while she was bound. "Let me," she offered.

Belinda nodded. She came to stand by Emma's side, her hands behind her back. Yes, Emma thought, she was being tested. And yes, it made sense. Respect wasn't always given; sometimes it had to be earned. Belinda had no reason to trust anyone living who could actually see her—and many, many reasons not to.

Michael still held Petal's lead. Chase, red hair almost glowing with reflected light, joined them, as did Ernest. Amy stood slightly back, frowning, her arms folded.

"Where will the portal open?" Emma asked.

"There are buildings in the city itself that are no longer used—if they ever were. The dead don't need housing. The Queen did not pull those buildings down, and when she chooses to walk—to parade—in celebration, she orders the dead to fill the windows as she passes beneath them. That is where you will be going."

Emma repeated this for the benefit of the living. To Amy, she added, "Any last questions?"

"A lot. They'll have to wait."

Ernest went first, at Ernest's less than silent insistence. Chase followed, glancing once at Allison as if he were afraid to leave her behind. Maybe he was, but he was more afraid of what waited on the other side, because they couldn't *see* anything. Dim outlines and darkness, that was it.

She almost asked Marcel if the buildings were furnished,

but Chase cursed loudly enough to be heard. Emma stopped breathing until the cursing stopped; it was followed by the right type of silence.

Helmi let go of Emma's hand. "I'll meet you there," she said. "I don't like portals, and I don't use them."

"Belinda? Marcel?"

"We will follow you before the portal vanishes," Marcel replied. When Emma looked confused, he looked, pointedly, at her right hand.

Emma reached out—with her numb left hand—and placed it gently around Michael's shoulder. "Let's go," she said quietly.

"And get Nathan back?" Michael asked, as Petal sniffed the hem of his coat—where the pockets were.

She nodded.

Stepping through the portal was not at all like stepping through an open door, which was what Emma had been expecting. It was very much like entering an old train tunnel, but without concrete or plaster or rock for walls.

It was gray here, charcoal gray. There were hints of light, but like faint stars, they could only be seen in the corners of Emma's vision; they vanished when she turned to look.

"No wonder Helmi doesn't like portals," she said aloud.

"Helmi dislikes portals because she understands the perversion that creates them."

Emma was not surprised to see an ancient, rag-covered woman walking by her side. She carried a cane, although it wasn't necessary. Nothing about her appearance was necessary.

"Oh?"

"Do you think we traveled this way in my youth? We could have avoided a great deal of danger had we done so. Travel was not for the faint-hearted; it was for the desperate. And we so often were."

"Yet you're here."

"Yes, Emma, I am here. This is a space that the living do not own; they can use it only if they have the power of the dead to anchor them. It is a space we once reached without the need to physically enter it; a space we traversed to find the lost and bring them safely to their new home." She looked, briefly, to her left, somewhere above Emma's head. "It is how we found the dead we could not touch or reach. It's not what you did when you went to the boy in the fire. It's not what you did when you found Mark. Were you trained, you could have done either from the absolute safety of your own circle, your own home.

"This path is not bound to, or by, geography, because the dead aren't."

"Andrew and Mark were, though."

"They were trapped; they believed they were still alive. When I was magar, boys such as those would have been my responsibility. They were lost.

"Belinda and Marcel are not. They are not trapped in the moment of their death. They know where they must go — and know, as well, that they cannot. They should not be here. In my youth, in my life, they would not have been."

"Are you here to guide us?"

"You have your guide at the moment. I am not bound to you."

Marcel appeared by Emma's side, gazing about the gray and featureless landscape as if he were on a nature walk. Emma wondered what he could see because, clearly, he could see something. She didn't ask. Instead, gathering courage, she said, "Marcel, are you bound to me?"

His brows rose, but his smile was gentle. "You are definitely unlike other Necromancers I have known. Yes, Emma. At the moment, I am yours."

"I don't know how to let go," she confessed. "Binding is supposed to take hours. This didn't." She lifted the slender chains.

"Perhaps," he said, "it would be best — for me at least; I cannot speak for Belinda — if you continued to hold me. I do not believe that Necromancers are taught how to release the dead they control, but I could be wrong."

"You are not wrong," Margaret said. "Divesting oneself of power was not a concern. Gathering it was."

Petal whined. If everyone else found the nothingness of the landscape unsettling, Petal found it frightening. There was very little as pathetic as a frightened creature the size of a rottweiler. Emma would have distracted him with food, but food was in backpacks, and they would need to husband it. They had no idea where they were going and no idea whatsoever how long they would be there.

"Marcel?"

"Ah, apologies," the older man said. "It has been some time indeed since I've been free to wander." He coughed a little, which Emma understood to be a type of punctuation, and added, "My apologies if I stare."

"At what?"

"You, Emma Hall. When I'm this close, what I see in you is enough to blunt the hunger."

She didn't ask what hunger meant; she thought she knew. She had seen what lay beyond the closed door she had, with so much effort and so much support, opened briefly, and she had wanted it for herself: an end to grief, an end to loneliness, an end to the weight of responsibility.

She did not, at this moment, want that. She wanted life, because life was not only those things. The man beside her would never have that life again. Emma had mastered the art of small talk by learning to find almost anything superficially interesting. At the moment, that hard-won mastery deserted her; she had almost nothing to say.

But true to Hall upbringing, she felt slightly guilty about it. "Do you know very much about the Necromancer who bound you?"

Marcel was silent for one long minute. "Not directly, no. The Necromancers are not particularly interested in the dead as people; they are interested only in the power they can harvest. As a virtual slave, my interest in my master would be different: I want to pay attention and to understand them in the vain hope that that understanding will give me the key to avoid both abuse and punishment. But the knowledge the dead gain simply by being dead is about what you'd expect. You possibly know more about me now than the Necromancer did."

"I only know your name," Emma pointed out.

"Indeed."

"Do you know how much longer this is going to take?"

"I don't have the same sense of the passage of time as you do. The dead generally don't. It is perhaps one of the few mercies granted us in this world. I believe, however, that the passage through the portal is extended by geographic distance. It won't take as long to reach the destination as it would by boat or foot. Did you really open the door?"

"Not fully," she replied, "and not for long. And it took — it took hundreds of people's help."

"Dead people."

She nodded, and because there was no end to the walk in sight, she told him about Andrew Copis and the events that led to the opening of the door. She left out the lantern, because the magar remained by her other side.

When she had finished, he nodded gravely. "I believe," he said, "we are here." He glanced at the magar.

Belinda, walking slightly ahead, snorted. "You always talked like this?" she asked him.

"In English, yes. It was not my mother tongue."

"It would drive me crazy," Belinda told him. "We're here, girl. Time to go back to the real world."

The real world, as stated, was a dark, large room, but by the time Emma entered it, it was crowded. The dead didn't need space, but the living did, and they took up a lot of it.

It was cold, in this room. Almost as cold as it had been in Amy's cottage before the electric baseboards had been turned on. There wouldn't be any source of heat here, if Marcel was right. This room was part of a building designed and created only for display. She was a bit surprised that there was more than just facade, a stage prop that could be brought out and carted off based solely on need.

"There should be windows," Emma said, into the darkness.

Someone moved past her, and something moved into her legs, at almost the same time. Petal whined. Emma knelt and hugged him, scratching behind his ears. Petal wasn't much of a barker, unless he was at home. This wasn't his home, and he knew it.

This wasn't anyone's home. A wall of harsh light broke the darkness as Ernest pulled heavy curtains back.

"That's a pretty serious window," Amy said.

Given the size of the room, it was.

Ernest stepped back, lifting an arm. "If we're standing in the window, we can be seen." That stopped everyone, even Amy.

It didn't matter. One didn't have to stand in the window to see out. On the opposite side of what Emma assumed was street was a two-story building with long, tall windows. Two-story buildings seemed to go on in either direction, although to the left, they appeared to end in a corner. Individually, they weren't impressive, but they were of a kind; there were no odd houses, no notable differences in architecture.

It didn't matter; after the first glance, they became irrelevant.

Towering above them at a height that almost obscured all of the sky was a building that defied imagination. A Tolkien artist might have created it in concept sketches before someone had to draw and render it, or worse, create it from scratch. It was both wide and tall; it had one spire that rose, narrowing slowly as it gained height. Beneath that spire were towers, all of stone, and upon those towers, flags had been raised.

The dead couldn't raise flags—and couldn't lower them, either.

"Yes," Margaret said quietly, when words failed them all—even Amy. "That is the Citadel. In it, you will find the Queen of the Dead."

"If she believes Eric," Amy said into the pause that followed, "will she decide that it's the right time for a parade?"

It was a good question. And Helmi, who had not accompanied them on their long walk, was the one who answered it. "Yes." Emma reached out and offered Helmi a hand, which Helmi took with almost alarming speed. She then, to Emma's surprise, repeated the answer so that Amy could hear it.

"Which doesn't make this the ideal hiding spot."

"No. But it might help us, anyway."

"How, exactly?"

"If she believes Eric will finally stay with her forever, she'll do two things. First, she'll summon her Court."

"Which means that there won't be random Necromancers on alert anywhere else."

"They're always careful," Helmi replied. "They use the dead to spy on each other. The advantage of being dead—

and bound—the *only* advantage, is that the spies can't be killed. They can't be blinded, and they can't be bound by anyone else. The older Necromancers use this to intimidate the newer ones. Those that survive learn to overlook the presence of other people's dead." She hesitated, and then continued. "If the dead are left to spy—and they will be if Court is in session—they'll tell their masters what they've seen. They don't have any other functional choice."

"I can stop them," Emma said, with more confidence than she felt.

Helmi nodded. "But if you stop them, the Necromancers will know instantly. The Necromancers who used Belinda and Marcel to sustain the portal know that they've lost them both. They're not going to be particularly happy about it, either. If it was Alraed—"

"It was Alraed, at least for me," Belinda said.

"—his concern will be replacing them. He'd be sweating if Longland were still alive. With the absence of Longland, there's less to threaten him. Without Belinda, he's still powerful. He doesn't have the power of the Queen, but the Queen seldom kills her knights. She leaves them to kill each other.

"After she's enthroned Eric, after she's made a public display of both him and his love, she'll probably leave the Citadel to go on parade. In other circumstances, you might even like the parade—it's pure spectacle. She'll expect every attendant she has, every servant, every knight, and even the dead who personally serve her, to be lining these streets and filling these windows. During that time, the Citadel will be empty.

"That's when we need to make our move."

Chase and Ernest exchanged a glance. "How many of the dead are used as spies outside of the Citadel? How many could we expect to find in these houses?"

"Here?" Helmi shrugged. "None. I told you: no one lives here. The Necromancers, especially the youngest, live in the Citadel. It's where they train, eat, and sleep."

"Where does their food come from?"

"That," Helmi replied, "is a good question. It's not grown here. There are no farms in the city. There's a greenhouse in the Citadel, but it's not used for food."

"Food has to be brought here."

Helmi nodded. "Among the oldest of the Necromancers are those with less power and less ambition. They see to the Queen's finances and the necessities of the living—but they do it from the ground."

"Ground?"

Helmi frowned. "Ground." When this failed to sink in, she added, "We're in the air. The whole of the Citadel is a floating city. It is built on the dead, and of the dead—literally. There are very few structures here—including this one—that aren't composed entirely of people who were once like Belinda and Marcel."

"What do you mean?" Allison asked. She'd been silent since they'd entered the portal. "You don't mean we're standing *on* the dead?"

"I mean exactly that," Helmi replied; she looked annoyed. "You've seen—maybe you haven't. Emma has seen the shapes the dead can be forced to take. We only look human in our natural form—but we can be molded, blended or twisted into almost any shape. The beams beneath the floor; the planks beneath your feet; the stones in the street below. All of it. She built this city out of the dead."

REYNA

THE QUEEN IS WEEPING.

She has sent everyone—living or dead—from her chambers and has sealed herself in the large, stone room into which, over decades, she has carved a fitting circle for a Queen. It was meant to bring her power. And peace. No tears, no act of human rage, can break it. Nothing can be erased by the accidental brush of skirts, of feet. The circle is complete and whole.

There, on the northernmost edge of the circumference, wind, air: the symbol for breath and thought. Opposite it, the most complicated of the symbols, water, for life: for tears of both joy and despair. The latter, she has shed for centuries, an ocean's worth.

She cannot be seen to be weak. When she is weak, people attempt to take advantage of the weakness; they think her stupid or shallow or vain. And perhaps she is, in part, all of those things—but only in part.

She has no living family. Of the dead, only Helmi remains by her side; those she did not bind left her, sooner or later. She bound none of her family. None. Their power was not meant to be a weapon. It wasn't, in the end, meant to be a shelter either—she knows the lie in that belief. They died. She didn't.

Her mother left almost immediately, abandoning her to her dreams of safety and freedom in angry judgment. And what, in the end, was Reyna's crime?

She didn't die. The power that she'd used to survive was the power of the dead, yes. But what had the alternative been? To die, as her mother had died? To bleed out the rest of her short life without ever *knowing* life at all?

Yes, her mother says. Even though she's not here, Reyna can still hear the word. She has lived the whole of her life under the cloud of her mother's disapproval. She no longer expects that to change.

No one, in the end, stays by her side.

And she has wanted it. Once, when she was young, she had had a brief dream of life, of love. She had planned to have daughters, but her daughters would not be forced to become seekers, as she was. Her daughters would have the life that she herself had wanted so badly and was denied.

There are no daughters, for Reyna. No children. The only person she has ever wanted to create a family with is Eric. And Eric, like her mother, refused her. She offered him everything. She changed the world to bring him back to life. He is alive now only because she loved him so much she was willing to do anything for him.

Anything.

She stops weeping; she inhales several shaky breaths. Eric is finally returning. It doesn't matter why.

She dresses. She has help dressing; the youngest of the Necromancers—two boys, one girl—have been trained to assist her when she requires assistance. They are sullen, bruised children; the smaller of the boys has a discolored eye. They are not as graceful as they will no doubt become—if they survive.

She thinks about Eric as she is dressed. She thinks about Eric and the village in which she met him, about love and death and abandonment. She thinks that she is lying to herself; why he's returning does matter. She worries at it in stiff silence. She has called for a full meeting of the Court, and her own attendants must be given time to prepare themselves appropriately—but she wants to look her best.

Her best involves powders and starches and oil. Her best involves complicated, intricate dresses. Her best involves the crown that she wears only in the massive audience chambers—it is too heavy to wear at other times.

She has a similar crown for Eric, if he will wear it. He has never once taken his place at the throne by her side. She does not know whether he will take it now. This is not the first time he has been in her Citadel. But it is the first time he has agreed to the escort of her knights without killing some of them first.

Why? Why now?

This should be her moment of triumph. This should be a moment in which life—the desire for life—triumphs. But a single word inserts itself into the stream of her thoughts, like a large rock in a small stream.

Emma.

She feels as if she is falling, although the ground beneath her feet is solid. He has come home, yes—but is it a coincidence that he has come only at the appearance of this Emma, this stranger who she is now certain opened the door, however briefly?

She suspects that her mother has given Emma the single gift she had left to give. She did not pass it to her daughter; of course not. She passed it, in the end, to a stranger. A girl who would be here, helping her Queen dress, had it not been for . . . Eric.

How did he meet this Emma?

How did he meet her and fail to kill her? He has killed others before; some were younger than Emma, some a bit older. It makes no sense. What did he see in this girl? What did her mother see? She should have demanded more information from Nathan. She shouldn't have been content to let things slide. But she was, and now she is paying for it. She has all the time in the world—and so does Nathan, if she desires it.

But all the time in the world has become a very sudden now. This moment contains Eric. And she will face him without all the facts she suddenly feels she needs.

Reyna is afraid in the moment of her greatest happiness. She is afraid that he will not love her. That he might, instead, love someone else. That was her fear in the village, as well—but she never feared it when she was actually by his side. His smile, his focus, his dreams destroyed all but the shadow of fear.

He has not been with her for centuries, and that shadow is so strong it looks like night.

She will know. When she sees Eric, she will know.

CHAPTER
SEVEN

EMMA KNELT.
  Her knees had locked for three long breaths as Helmi's words sunk in. This was probably good; it prevented her from collapsing.

  In the graveyard in which Nathan's ashes were buried her dog had run across grass and inlaid stones. She hadn't thought twice about it. She herself, however, had never stepped directly upon the symbols of grief and memory that other families, other bereaved, had left.

  Even so, there was a layer of stone and earth over ash—or coffins. She would not, in a million years, have let her dog walk across corpses. She would never have walked across them herself.

  And yet, here she was, and the floor—which looked and felt like a normal floor—was composed of the dead. Not of corpses, not precisely; it was worse than that. She swallowed; her throat was dry in the cold air, and for just a moment, she wondered if she would ever feel warm again.

All of the dead she *could* see watched her: Helmi, Belinda, Marcel, and Margaret.

"Can you see them?" she asked, her voice almost inaudible to her own ears.

Everyone living looked at her then as well.

No one answered.

"Can you hear them?" she asked, her voice louder. Her hands were shaking, and not with cold, although Helmi's hand had numbed hers.

"Can you?" Helmi countered. She was the only person who spoke. The only dead person. Amy wanted to know what Emma was talking about.

Emma closed her eyes. She placed her free hand on the surface of the floor itself; the floors were cold, but not in the way that Helmi's hand was. She listened, but Amy's voice was too loud. That might have been a mercy in any other circumstance. Today Emma couldn't allow it.

"Amy," she said, eyes closed. "Give me a minute."

"To do what?"

"To listen to the dead."

Amy fell silent. Emma could imagine her expression.

Silence. The silence of the dead. The silence of the grave, which, no matter how personal the loss, was also unapproachable and impersonal: a fact of life. Death was. But as Emma listened, she could hear the attenuated, distant sound of weeping. There was more than one voice. There were no faces. Nor were there words. Not for the dead and not, at the moment, for Emma.

She pressed her hand into the floor; it fooled the senses. It was *floor*, with about as much give as any of the floors in her own home. For one long moment, Emma wanted to join the voices in their weeping and their grief.

That would help no one.

"What are you doing?" Ernest asked, taking over Amy's role.

"I'm trying to . . ." what? What exactly was she trying to do? "I'm trying to reach them."

"Reach *who*?"

"The dead, Ernest."

How had she reached them before? The lantern. She

almost lifted it—how, she wasn't certain—but stopped. She was in the Queen's city, and she felt certain that if the lantern were raised here, the Queen would know. Hiding would be impossible.

Without its light, what did she have? Had Mark been a part of the floor, she would never have heard him. She could never have spoken with him. Who spoke to the floor? Or the walls? Who expected them to weep?

Emma reached.

She heard Helmi's sharp intake of breath—a breath that was cosmetic in every way—but didn't look up. The floor's texture changed; it became disturbingly less floorlike beneath her rigid palm. The weeping grew louder, more distinct. Emma reached again, as she had once reached for the mother of a dead four-year-old boy.

This time, she felt pain, ice, and nausea. And the voice beneath her hand grew ever more distinct. The weeping stopped, shuddering to a halt the way weeping sometimes did. A disembodied voice asked, "Who's there?"

Hope was carried in the two words: hope and fear.

"Emma," Emma said. "Emma Hall. I'm—" Words failed her. What could she say? *You're part of the floor and I'm standing on you*? No. No, she couldn't say that. She had no idea how much awareness the dead had. When Margaret had been bound to a wall in the Snitman mansion, she had seen—and heard—nothing. Or so Emma had assumed.

She forced herself to work free of those assumptions now. The dead were like clay. They could be molded and shaped into any form; they could be forced to fill any function. Here they were the floors. The floors, the roof, anything else in this unfurnished room. They weren't the windows—their absence was—but they were probably the cobbled streets outside the windows, the facades of the architecturally uniform buildings, the *stairs*.

Anything but the food.

This was a type of slavery that Emma had never conceived of in her life, and she'd spent a unit in school studying slavery until it had become very difficult not to be sick to death of humanity.

"Emma?" The voice was quavery, but Emma thought a

young man spoke. Or perhaps a young woman. It was hard to tell, and at this particular moment, it was irrelevant.

She was sickened, yes. But that led to two places: despair, which she expected, and anger. She did not want to speak in anger now, not to this person, who didn't deserve it. Marcel had said the dead didn't really mark the passage of time the way they had when they were alive, and Emma fervently prayed that this was the truth.

"Yes. I'm Emma."

"Where are you?"

"I'm right—I'm right beside you. I'm holding your hand. Can you feel it?"

"I can—I can feel your hand. It's—it's so warm."

The dead always said that. To Emma, the floor was not as cold as Helmi. She didn't know why, and at this point, she didn't want to interrupt what little conversation there was to ask Margaret, who might be able to answer.

"Emma," Margaret said, speaking far more gently than she usually did. "I think I understand what you're attempting to do, but it is not wise. It is not yet time for it."

"And when *is* the time for it?" Emma asked, before she could stop herself.

"When the fall won't kill you or your friends."

This made no sense for one long minute, and during that minute, Emma willed herself to feel a stranger's hand, a stranger's fingers. She transferred part of her attention to Helmi, whose hand she did hold. The hands of the dead—even Nathan's—felt like hands with all the warmth sucked out. They had never felt like the flat, impersonal surface of the floor.

But these floors—if Helmi were right—weren't impersonal surfaces.

When the section of floor became a hand, she gripped it far more tightly than she had gripped the hand of anyone dead—except Nathan. And Nathan, she couldn't hold, in the end. She hadn't been prepared for the truth: The Queen had bound him, and the Queen could summon him, in an instant, across a geographical divide Emma could not easily traverse. Love didn't change that in the afterlife.

Love hadn't changed that in life, either.

Emma believed that love was eternal, that it could last

forever. It was a thin belief, tested and damaged by Nathan's death, and before that by her father's; she had come,
on dark days, to understand that the only eternity was
death. Death and its endless silence, endless absence.

And eternity was being played out here in gutting ways.
Emma wasn't always certain what she believed about the
afterlife—and in some ways, she still didn't know. But this?
This was hell. It wasn't the hell of demons or endless fire or
endless punishment, but it didn't have to be. Human beings
were perfectly capable of creating hell on earth. She just
hadn't expected that they could continue to do so when
their victims had died.

She meant to end it.

She meant to free the dead.

Thinking it, feeling the heat and the weight and the anger of it, she pulled on the hand she now grasped. She put
weight behind it because she had to. She imagined that this
was very like catching someone by the hand as they slipped
off a cliff. Her arm strained with the weight of a stranger,
and her hand locked with the visceral fear that if she could
not hold on, they would be lost forever.

It wasn't true. They would be *here*. She could find them
again.

But she didn't *believe* that, and she held on until she
thought her hand would snap off at the wrist, it was so frozen.
Held on to the falling weight, the weight of someone who
would be lost if she couldn't maintain her desperate grip.

Michael said, in the distance, "Emma, you're crying."

Was she? She couldn't feel tears on her face—but she
felt that particular thickness of throat that comes just before tears, when you're still trying to *talk*. She swallowed
and realized he was right. She was crying. But she forced
herself to speak, anyway. "Michael, what do you see?"

"It looks like you're trying to make a fist. But there's
something in the way."

"You can't—you can't see a hand?"

His silence went on a beat. "Maybe?" he finally said, his
tone doubtful. With Michael this actually meant uncertainty.

"You can see Helmi."

"Yes."

Emma found her voice after a long, thick pause. "I am holding someone's hand. I can't see them. I have no idea who they are. I just—I have their hand. It's like when someone's falling off a cliff or a building. I can't let go. But I can't—I can't pull them *up*. I'm not strong enough."

Michael was Michael. He trusted Emma enough that he was willing to try to help; trying sometimes paralyzed him. She almost told him, as he knelt beside her, that there wasn't anything he could do—but she didn't. Because as he reached for her hand, as he placed his *over* hers, interleaving their fingers, she felt *warmth*.

It was warmth she needed now. She closed her eyes briefly before tightening that hand and squeezing Michael's fingers. She didn't know what the dead person felt, if they felt anything at all. Maybe they were just too afraid of falling to have room for anything else. Michael was just afraid for Emma.

Petal nosed around them both; Emma opened her eyes to a face full of anxious rottweiler. The dog-breath she got anyway. But both seemed right, now. "Help me," she whispered to Michael. "Help me pull them up."

And he did.

Inch by inch, the hand that Emma had grasped so desperately became arm, wrist appearing first, and extending—agonizingly slowly—into elbow. She *pulled*, the force of her weight and Michael's almost knocking her off her knees.

"I can see an arm!" Michael said, loudly, in her ear. He had forgotten himself enough to speak loudly—his natural volume. Years of practice at lowering that volume deserted him, and Emma, ears ringing, didn't care.

"I can see it as well," Ally said. "Chase—"

Emma felt arms around her waist. Unfamiliar arms, in a very rough grip. Chase, she thought, surprised.

"What? I'm being careful."

She wanted to weep, but these tears were not tears of despair or fear. He was stronger than either Michael or Emma; he pulled Emma back while Emma held on. The arm gave way to shoulder, to elongated neck, to a face. A face.

Emma couldn't tell whether it was a boy's face or a girl's; it was a young face. Older than Helmi but not yet the age of Emma and her friends, long and thin with wide cheekbones and gaunt cheeks. Emma knew the worst was almost over; Michael's hands tightened—which shouldn't have been possible—as the dead person at last pulled free.

Her absence left an indent in the floor, not a hole, and she blinked rapidly, as if her eyes were real and she hadn't seen light for most of her life. Her lips, both thin and wide, trembled as she looked, at last, at Emma.

"Emma?" she whispered. Emma thought she was twelve or thirteen; she wasn't dressed the way the rest of them were, but Emma couldn't pinpoint her era from her clothing. Amy might have been able to, but Emma didn't ask her; it wasn't relevant.

"Yes," Emma told the girl. "I'm Emma. I'm sorry—I don't know your name."

"Furiyama Tsuki," the girl replied. "You speak my language."

Emma didn't. She spoke English with a smattering of French—French with questionable pronunciation.

"Dead is dead," Helmi said, speaking for the first time. "If she can see you, she can understand you—if you want to be understood." She glanced almost guiltily at Emma's hand—the one she herself was holding.

The girl stared at Helmi for a long, silent beat. "You . . . are dead?"

"So are you."

And Emma remembered that the dead—some of the dead—couldn't immediately see the others. She didn't understand how vision worked for the dead. Now was not the time to ask, and even if it had been, what could this girl tell her?

Helmi, to Emma's surprise, surrendered her hand, and drifted to the far side of the room—closest to the open window, the absence of the dead.

Emma, one hand free, began to shake. It was a mixture of rage and triumph and exhaustion—something had to give. But *not now*. Not now. She dropped her numb free hand to the top of her dog's head and glanced gratefully at Michael, whose fingers were probably stiff, they'd held hers so tightly for what felt like so long. "We did it," she told him. "Thank you."

Chase had released her waist the minute the girl had been pulled free. "No gratitude for me?" he asked, grinning.

Before she could answer, he added, "It's okay. I'll get it from Allison."

Her brows rose—but so did the corners of her lips; they twitched. It felt as though it had been years since she'd actually smiled. Allison punched his shoulder, and that fixed the smile in place, allowing it to grow. Chase said 'ouch' in a deadpan tone.

Emma thought: I love these people.

"We're going to need to eat," Ernest said, before she could actually embarrass herself by saying anything out loud. "There's water—drink that. If you feel tired or short of breath, it's the altitude."

"Or raw terror," Amy added, looking as if terror were as far from her as it was possible to get.

"Or that, yes." Ernest exhaled. "Margaret. Explain what just happened to someone who is too old and fixed in his ways to understand it."

Helmi snorted, but this time, Ernest couldn't hear her. Just as well.

"I'm not certain that I have an explanation. I think, judging by expression, Helmi does. But Emma looks exhausted, and I don't think it's a good idea for Helmi to talk to all of us at this time." She looked at Tsuki and at Tsuki's hand. Emma had not released it.

She was almost afraid to do so. What would happen to the girl if she did? Would she somehow go back to being part of the floor? She looked toward that floor and froze.

"Em?"

What had been solid and flat beneath her feet—beneath all of their feet—no longer looked like floor. "Ally—what—what does the floor look like, to you?"

Allison frowned. "The floor? It looks—it looks almost the same. I'd say there's a slight warping, but I wouldn't notice it if I hadn't been here when you pulled Tsuki through it."

"I didn't pull her through the floor," Emma said, voice almost a whisper. "I pulled her *out* of it. She was part of the floor."

"Em, what do *you* see? What are you looking at?"

"Hands," she said, voice faint. "Just . . . hands and arms. It's like they're reaching up out of a dark pit. I can't see anything else. No faces . . ." She closed her eyes. Swallowed.

Michael squeezed her hand, but he said nothing before he let her pull away. He then turned to look at the floor, and Emma, out of habit, let her gaze follow him.

The hands passed through Michael as he knelt; they grasped blindly at air. They were silent as they moved, the gestures of each individual and chaotic. Michael couldn't see them, which was a mercy. Emma couldn't *unsee* them, which wasn't.

But she hated it; she thought that Michael, of all people present, would grab each of the blindly grasping hands if he had the ability.

"Is the whole city like this?" Emma asked Helmi.

Helmi, like Emma, was looking at those hands; her own, she reflexively curled. "Probably. What you're seeing now — it's because of what you did. It's not the way the city looks, even to the dead. Not — not normally." She shook her head. "You want to help. But if you did — if you could — the entire structure would fray and disintegrate. While you — and your friends — are in it."

"But they—"

"We've been like this for a long time," Helmi continued. She wouldn't meet Emma's eyes.

"You haven't," Emma countered.

"... No. Not like this." Helmi looked up. "I don't love my sister," she whispered. "I did, once. Sometimes I remember her as she was before — before they came to kill us. Before Eric died. When we were alive, she could never have done this. Before she met Eric, she would never have tried." In a softer voice, she added, "That's why I hate Eric."

"Eric didn't ask her to do this," Emma replied. It wasn't a question.

Helmi shrugged. "Does it matter, to the dead? If it weren't for Eric, she wouldn't have done it. That's our truth." She then looked at Emma. "You loved Nathan."

It was a blow, but it wasn't the body blow it would have been a month ago. Or two. Emma said, clearly, "Yes. I loved Nathan."

"Would you have resurrected him if you knew how?"

"If resurrection meant bringing him *back*, yes. Yes, I would have." She expected Helmi to sneer, and was surprised when she didn't.

"And now?"

Emma exhaled. "Now? I know the dead can't come back to life. I don't want to drag a pretty corpse beside me from here to eternity." She turned away from the floor to the girl whose hand she still held. "I'm sorry," she said, without thought, because social apology came as naturally as breath.

"Your hand is warm." The girl glanced around the room, her eyes wide and unblinking.

"This is Michael. The girl near the window is Helmi; that's Amy, Allison, Ernest, and Chase. Oh, and Margaret. And this," Emma added, as her dog nudged her hand with his wet nose, "is Petal."

The girl was staring at Emma; her eyes were luminous. They were also uncomfortable to look at; there was a hunger in them that made Emma want to retrieve her hand permanently—even if she thought she understood it.

Help came from an unexpected quarter: Helmi. "You need to let go of her hand."

Tsuki's hand tightened in response.

"She's here to help us," Helmi continued. "But she needs to conserve her power." When the girl failed to respond, she added, in a much sharper tone, "Let go of her hand."

This time, the girl obeyed. She didn't fade from Emma's sight; she did disappear from anyone else's. Or anyone else who was alive.

Petal whined.

"I know," Emma said, scratching behind his ears. "I find it hard, too."

Helmi grimaced. "Try being dead," she snapped. When Emma failed to respond, she shook her head. "Sorry. You don't deserve that. I have to go. Wait here, or as close to here as is safe."

Emma was too shocked at receiving an actual apology from Helmi to reply.

"And I mean it—wait. Stay hidden." She looked at Emma's friends. "Tell them. Tell them what happens to people who don't." And she lifted a hand, and the hand was momentarily red with blood.

"Don't be too angry with her," Margaret said, when Helmi vanished.

"Do the dead not change at all?" Emma asked her.

"They change," Margaret replied. "But death, in some ways, defines them. They don't let go easily of the fears they felt at death. They learn to see them differently. They learn context. They have regrets—but those thoughts and feelings remain central to their existence on this side of death. Even if the way they view them shifts, the fact that they view them ... doesn't.

"Helmi is no different." Margaret smiled. Helmi rarely saw Margaret smile, and Emma wished, for just a moment, that the girl had remained. "She's seen you, Emma. She understands what you might mean to all of us. But she died because she did not hide. Hiding is second nature to her.

"She understands what your friends mean to you. She understands the event that *made* the Queen of the Dead. She is both fascinated and afraid of what you might become should you face the same losses. If the Queen finds you," she added, "you will." The smile saddened but did not leave her face. "You do not know what it means when you offer us your hand and we take it. It is costly—for you—but you do it, regardless."

Tsuki, who had not left, stared at Margaret and then at Emma. It was not entirely comfortable. She lifted her hand—the hand that Emma had clutched so desperately. "She is right," the girl said, in the softest of voices. "What will you do?"

"Eat," Emma replied. "We'll eat and we'll discuss our possible options. Margaret, you know the citadel. Tell the rest of us as much as you can?"

Margaret nodded.

Michael was not twitching; he was not walking in circles. But he might as well have been. His expression openly revealed what they were all feeling—but he had not yet shifted his focus. He was in an empty house that was built on—made *of*—the dead. He was afraid to sit on the floor; he felt guilty even standing on it.

Emma sympathized. There was, however, no alternative.

"I don't understand why she would do this," Michael said.

Allison—and Amy, who defined the word pragmatic in emergencies—had hit the backpacks; there was a brief and desperate search for a can opener while under the hopeful supervision of a rottweiler who clearly had never been fed in his Entire Life. Ernest eventually intervened, but Ernest was not yet one of Petal's people.

"You are a really, really stupid dog, you know that?" Chase said.

Petal wagged his tail.

"I don't understand it, either," Emma told Michael. "I understand that we have to stop her."

"How?"

"I don't know. But we're here, and there has to be something we can do. She's just one person."

"And her Necromancers."

"We've got Chase and Eric."

"Eric's not here."

"And Ernest. Michael—" Emma caught both of his hands. "We can do this."

Michael was silent.

"The Queen has never been able to find—and capture— Eric. Eric wouldn't be here if he hadn't made that choice. It doesn't matter how powerful the Queen or her Necromancers are. Eric doesn't have any special powers. He's normal, like we are."

"You mean, like the rest of us are?"

Emma did not grimace; she did bite her lip. "Yes. Yes, that's what I meant." She rose.

"Emma?" Michael rose as well, aware that he had said the wrong thing but unaware, at the moment, of why.

"No one wants to be seen as an outsider among their friends." It was Chase, unexpectedly, who intervened. Emma drew one sharp breath. "And no one wants to be seen as the only possible salvation—it's a lot of pressure. You're probably the only person here who won't—or can't—understand that Emma somehow thinks this is all her fault."

Michael frowned. It was the frown with which everyone in the room was most familiar. "How could it be Emma's fault?"

Chase rolled his eyes and ran one hand through his much shorter hair. To Emma's surprise—and growing concern— Chase tried to answer. "Try to see it the way I've seen it. Emma is a Necromancer. Emma—in theory, and given the rest of you, it's a pretty crap theory—could *be* the Queen of the Dead if she had the time. She could be taught. Or teach herself. She could do what the Queen has done." He held up a hand as Michael opened his mouth.

"I told you, it's a crap theory. I believed it when I first met her. But even I can't hold onto that belief. The Queen, however, will. She won't see anything else. The Necromancers will. They won't see Emma, and they don't know her as well as the rest of you do. Emma is thinking that the Necromancers wouldn't have come for her if she didn't have this power. And she's right.

"But neither Eric or I would be here, either. If we weren't here, you wouldn't be here. We wouldn't have the chance to somehow fix things or end things. I didn't see it that way when I met Emma, but I see it now. I've been fighting the Queen of the Dead—or her minions—for most of my adult life. This is the first time I've ever thought we actually have a chance."

"Why?"

"Because Emma *is* powerful. And Emma can do things that even the Necromancers would have said are impossible. She doesn't think the way they do. She doesn't—luckily for her—think the way Eric or I do. None of you do. And maybe that's what's needed. If we had the time, Emma could take the entire city apart without lifting a gun or shedding blood.

"And I think—I think she can open the door permanently. I think she can free the dead."

"Why?" Michael asked, again.

Amy, busy with food she would never have eaten unless she were camping, said, "Because she's already done it once. She almost died saving Andrew Copis. She didn't. Andrew Copis is wherever the dead are supposed to be. And frankly, I'm more than a little tired of all this, and we don't get to go back to real life if she doesn't." When Michael did not immediately nod, Amy added—with less patience than Chase had shown, "She's already proven that she can do it once—with just as little information or education on her part.

"I believe she can do it again, for real this time."

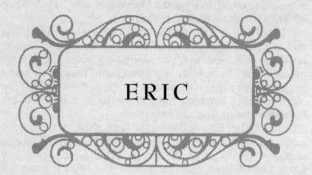

ERIC

LONGLAND CAN'T SWEAT. If he could, he would. The gun he carries appears welded to his hand. He is pale. Ernest and Chase don't trust Longland. They don't quite understand why Eric does. But neither of them are dead. Hurt, yes. Scarred, definitely. But they exist, persist, among the living.

Being dead has not inured Eric to the fact of death, the fact of loss. He does not want them to die. He has never wanted any of his comrades to die. But want or no, they all have.

Only Reyna is perpetual.

It has been so long since he's seen her. So long since he has dreamed of anything about her but her death, the death she avoided, the death that would free the dead, that would free Eric himself. He can't remember loving her, but he knows that he once did.

He stands in a small room composed of four walls and no windows. There is a door; it is closed. He faces it,

Longland by his side. He looks for Helmi. He has often looked for Helmi; she is a flag, a warning that death is coming—but not for Eric. Never for Eric.

He wishes—as he has wished for centuries—that he had never met Reyna. He wishes that she had never loved him. He might have loved her at a distance; he might have felt the pain of rejection, of things one-sided, unfinished. But that pain would be better than this pain.

Can you kill her?

Yes. Yes, Helmi. That belief has been the pillar of his existence for so long that life itself seems the greater dream. He has never questioned it. Here, in the world Reyna created by dint of will and terror, it is the only way he can atone.

But as the door opens, as he sees the angry, stiff faces of the Queen's knights, he wonders: atone for what? He was a young man, barely more than a boy. She was a young woman—young, slightly wild, always open. Her smile was radiant. Small things delighted her: sunlight on the lake, shadows beneath the boughs of the tree that served as their meeting place, wildflowers. Toads. She liked toads. He remembers because the first time he saw her involuntary smile, he said, *I see. This is why you like me*.

He remembers—only now—the sound of her laughter.

He loved her as the young love the young. She was the center of his world. He believed, had believed, that his family would accept her. He had wanted to spend his life by her side. He had wanted what young men want.

He cannot imagine that he could tell that young man not to love that young woman, not with any hope of success.

"Lord Eric," a young woman says. She curtsies, her back stiff, her expression wary. "Please, accompany us." Before he can speak, she continues. "You will want to change before you meet the Queen."

She is wearing the robes that the Necromancers wear in the Citadel. She rises. Her eyes are living eyes, but they, like Longland's, are heavy and bright with fear. And he has earned that fear.

Can you kill someone who loves you so much?

Yes. He has always said yes. But he is aware that "yes" is a simple word, an easy word; it encompasses broken desires and self-loathing and memory. He is not certain how he would answer that question if Helmi asked it now.

But he will know, when he sees Reyna.

He'll know.

NATHAN

IF NATHAN HAD HOPED that the Citadel would be empty enough he could find and search the kitchens, he realizes he has been naive. A story is unfolding in the Citadel's many halls; even the dead speak of it—those who can.

Eric, they say. *Eric has returned.*

Nathan knows Eric.

Nathan knows that Eric could not have returned alone—if Helmi is to be trusted. Emma is somewhere in the City of the Dead. But Emma's name is not mentioned. Emma's existence is not mentioned.

The dead who are free to travel—and they are few, and bound to the Necromancers or their Queen, as Nathan was—speak only of Eric. They speak of love, the Queen's love. They speak of the King, although they use that title in whispers. Eric is here.

If Nathan were comfortably dead again—if Nathan, like the disembodied, could move through walls and closed doors—he might confirm the gossip for himself. Then again, he might not. He has seen the illusion of Eric occupying the empty throne at the Queen's side in her audience chambers; he might, in his search for Eric, stumble across the Queen herself. He has no doubt just how pleased she would be to see him.

But he is not free to wander the halls. He is seen and noted. He is given orders to make himself fully presentable. He is not, however, given aid. Apparently the few living people who act as servants have been sent to tend Eric. The dead are perfectly capable of speaking to the Necromancers, and the Queen has sent them to deliver pretty much the same orders that Nathan received.

Emma.

Emma is here.

He swallows, out of habit. He drinks water and forces himself to eat something. He is trapped in his body. He is trapped in the Citadel. Even while the Queen is distracted, he cannot escape her. Not yet.

He dresses himself, which is awkward; the clothing is cumbersome. Before he was resurrected, he knew how to reach the audience chamber—the grand chamber—without the need for a map; he could take the direct route because he could *see* where the Queen was at any given moment. He cannot do that now.

He is terrified that he will be late. In that, he has company among both the living and the dead. The sense of dread permeates every conversation he can hear—although admittedly, there's little of that.

He knows the living need to eat.

He knows that Emma and the rest of his friends will need to eat. He doesn't know where they're coming from—and he only has a vague idea of how, because Helmi isn't exactly forthcoming with information. He wondered, at the time, if he could trust Helmi.

But Eric *is* here. And if Eric is here, the rest of it might be true. He can't take the risk of suspicion. No, he *can*, but he can't refuse to act because of it. And yet, he can't get to the kitchens. He can't figure out how to leave the Citadel. Not today. Not this afternoon—if it is afternoon.

He walks. He takes a wrong turn, or possibly more than one; the Citadel is a maze of large, decorated halls.

He is therefore relieved to see Helmi. She is not wearing the usual clothing; she is wearing something that looks fussier and more fairy-tale formal. Her hair is in loose ringlets at the front, but only the front; the back is a monstrosity of a setting into which something like a tiara has been placed.

She did this herself, of course, and looks him up and down quite critically. "What did you do?" she asks him.

"I tripped over a few standing suits of armor and shouted in shock. I was abjectly apologetic." He hadn't been certain he would survive, which is ironic, all things considered.

"And the other things?"

"I've spent the rest of the time getting dressed. I'm not sure the formal audience is meant to last; I think, if it goes well, there will be 'festivities' and celebration."

Helmi curses. She uses a very modern set of words, at odds with the rest of her presentation.

"Is—are they here?"

"Emma's in the city. She's not in the Citadel."

He doesn't ask where. He doesn't ask how. He is afraid that the knowledge will stand out, like a signboard with flashing neon lights. But he wants to know.

"Did you—" He stops. "I'm lost."

"I like her. I understand why you like her. What do you mean, you're lost?"

"I don't know how to get to the audience chamber by foot."

Helmi stares at him as if he's just said the most idiotic thing she's ever heard. It's the most ordinary expression he's seen on her face. "She's going to be very angry if you're late, given what she's done for you; it's a poor expression of gratitude on your part."

Nathan feels no gratitude at all. He has almost become used to the constant sense of loss and pain that's wrapped around him—he's only fully aware of it when he tries to sleep. But if death—well, if dying again—removed him from the layers of that external pain, he would be *grateful*.

"Follow me. Follow me *quickly*. I have other things I have to do."

Nathan doesn't ask.

But Helmi hasn't finished. "Did you know, when you first met her?"

He's confused.

Helmi recognizes this. She's impatient. "Emma. When you first met Emma, did you know that you loved her?"

"How could I know that I loved her? I'd just met her."

"Do you remember when you first met her?"

"Helmi—if I'm late, the Queen will be angry."

"Talk while we're walking. You're half-way across the Citadel, and you were going in the wrong direction. So, Emma."

This is a conversation Nathan has already avoided once—as if by avoiding it, he could protect something precious and rare. But Emma is here, and Helmi knows it. He can't tell what the queen's sister wants from him—he's certain she wants something. And he knows that for Emma's sake, he wants to give it to her. He begins to follow her drifting, slow lead.

"I remember when I first noticed Emma."

Helmi waits.

"It was because of Michael. Emma is—she's polite and she's social. She fits in. Michael . . . doesn't, really. I like Michael. He's direct and it doesn't often occur to him not to be honest. He doesn't always interpret questions the way the person asking them intended, though." Seeing her expression, Nathan moves on. "I'd expect that Michael wouldn't have a lot of friends. If he had friends, I wouldn't expect to find Emma Hall or her friends among them. I'm more than a little used to seeing a lot of judgement. Everyone's trying to fit in. Everyone's trying to be normal enough that they won't be the outsider.

"But Emma walked to school with Michael every morning. Emma and Allison. When there were changes in Michael's schedule, Emma was often the person who explained them—Michael doesn't always deal well with change. Emma even laughs at Michael's jokes, because she considers some of them funny." Glancing at Helmi, he sees that this has not really answered the question she thinks she's asking.

"I didn't love her for it. I *liked* her for it. I liked her more because it surprised me. Emma is capable of kindness. Not pity. Not condescension—kindness. She actually considers Michael to *be* a friend."

"But you didn't love her."

"Helmi—I told you, I barely *knew* her."

"My sister fell in love with Eric the minute she laid eyes on him. It was all Eric, Eric, Eric."

Nathan coughs. She sounds like an eight year old. An eight year old younger sister. "I don't believe in love at first sight," Nathan says.

"No?"

"No. I think love at first sight is a story. Don't get me wrong; I like stories. But I don't think stories—no matter how complicated—are things real people can actually live in. What I knew, when I noticed Emma, is that she could see Michael as he was. And if she could do that, and accept him in spite of the fact that other people couldn't, she could probably see *me*, and accept me, in the same way. Emma wasn't my first girlfriend. She was just my first non-disaster."

"I know what it's like to tell stories about love. I know what it's like to look for love as—as *purpose* or *salvation*. I know what it's like not to see the person in front of me because I'm too busy looking at what the person *should* be or do if they really love me. I'm not a saint. I like to think I learn from my mistakes."

"You probably just make new ones."

Nathan chuckles. "All the time. I just try to make sure they're different. I didn't love Emma at the very beginning. But I thought I could, in time. I always thought she was attractive."

"That's not really romantic, Nathan."

"No, not really. Sorry." He turns to the left as Helmi does. The halls here are not as empty as they were when Helmi found him. "If it's any better, at the end of the second month, I couldn't imagine life without her."

Helmi is silent for half a hall. "You loved her because she was kind?"

"It's not just that—but without it, in the end, I don't think I could have grown to love her."

"What did she love about you?"

"I don't know." At the sound of Helmi's impatient snort, he says, "No, I mean it. I honestly don't know. I'm responsible for how *I* feel, but in the end, I can't dictate how other people do. I don't understand why she was interested in me—and I probably didn't want to question it too deeply. I didn't want to break things."

"But you died."

He stumbles. "Yes. I died." Just like her father had. Of all the things that torment Nathan when he thinks of Emma, this is the worst. He knows what death means to her; he knows how much she feared it. He died, anyway. "I left her, permanently. I destroyed my mother."

Helmi has stopped moving. She drifts to hover in front of Nathan. "My mother said that the only good thing about dying when she did is she didn't have to see me die. I didn't understand it, when she said it. I couldn't see anything good about dying. And I always thought—" She grimaces. "I always thought my mom only had eyes for Reyna. Reyna the talented. Reyna the powerful. Reyna the next magar."

"She was your older sister. I had no siblings. Neither does Emma. Reyna was Emma's age when you died. You were eight. You might have developed talent or power—but power isn't always a good thing."

"No," is Helmi's dark reply. "Do you still love Emma?"

"Helmi, what is this obsession with my love life?"

"Eric loved my sister," Helmi replies, her voice lower and inexplicably deeper. "My sister loved Eric."

But Nathan shakes his head. The motion goes on that little bit too long. "I can't even sleep without hearing the wailing cries of the dead. Do you know what I'm wearing, Helmi? Not the clothing, but the body?" He stops himself. He knows, intellectually, that Helmi is ancient. He reacts as if she's eight. He's been trying to train himself out of that—but life has been hectic and disturbing and heartbreaking enough that he hasn't tried very hard. If Helmi doesn't know, he doesn't want to tell her. He wouldn't tell any eight year old about what was done to the dead.

Is still being done, to the dead.

"What she did to me, she did to Eric. To someone you say she loves. I don't know Eric well. But I think I know enough to say that it's not something Eric wanted. It's not something he wants now."

"Does Eric love my sister, do you think?"

Nathan wonders just how much pain he would feel if he

attempted to put his head through the nearest wall. "Helmi—"

"She did all this because of love."

"She *did not*."

"I think I *know* why she did things. I've known her for a long, long time."

Nathan exhales. "People tell themselves that they do things for love *all the time*. People *kill their wives* because they 'loved' them."

Helmi frowned. "What are you doing with your fingers?"

The wall continues to look very promising. Nathan is not up to explaining what air quotes actually mean, and gives up. ". . . Because they felt they loved them. But love doesn't destroy the person you love."

"Eric is not—"

"Helmi, if Emma had ever done this to me, it would break me. It's almost breaking me now. Having this done by the Queen of the Dead is like having it done by a—a demon or an enemy. You don't expect kindness from either. But if *Emma*, a Necromancer, had done this *to me*—how could I love her? How could I believe that she was still the person I noticed because of her kindness?

"I couldn't. Maybe—just maybe—I could convince myself that she was having some kind of breakdown. Maybe I could convince myself that my dying had driven her insane—and that if I held on for long enough, she would go back to being *my* Emma. The one I loved." He tosses his hands in the air. "But that's just me lying. I don't think I could hold on for long enough. If I couldn't talk to her, if she didn't *listen*, if she couldn't hear me and what it meant to me—I could never accept it." His shoulders slump. "You can never know all of what's in another person's mind.

"But I believe, I truly believe, that Emma loves me. She would never do this to someone she loved. Even if I *wanted it*, even if I *asked*, she could never, ever do what—what was done. And Helmi? I'm grateful for that.

"Your sister will tell you that Emma never loved me. Not truly. That Emma's love is too weak. Or that she's not committed enough. And that's a lie. What I loved about Emma was that she was capable of what I considered love. She loves her mother. She loves her friends—especially her best friend. She loves her half-deaf dog. And she loves me. But I'm part of that life. I'm not—I don't want to be—an excuse to abandon it."

Helmi stares at him as if he is trying to grow an extra head.

"Why are you even asking?"

"I told you—my sister loved Eric." Her frown deepens. "And Emma loves you. You don't understand what love means—has meant—to all of us. You don't understand why it's terrifying. Everything that has been built here—everything—comes down to love."

Helmi is wrong. Nathan has already explained that in the only way he can. He tries again, as the halls become more crowded. Unlike school, crowded halls aren't noisier; there's a tension in the gathering, a suspicion, a certainty of fear, that makes them far less lively. Then again, Nathan can see all of the dead people as well as the living—and he's fairly certain he'd like the dead better if they spoke to him at all.

"It isn't, Helmi. Maybe it's built on grief. Maybe it's just one giant cemetery, and all it's been waiting for is its guest of honor."

The doors to the audience chamber roll open. The Queen is not on her throne, and there are benches in tidy rows and columns across the majority of the floor. This is unusual; it makes the audience chamber seem like the nave of a church.

The benches are not empty; members of the Queen's court have been admitted early. Nathan is not among them, and he is grateful for it. They are wearing robes, not the more intricate—and uncomfortable—clothing demanded of the dead. Nathan can see their backs; they do not appear to be chatting. They appear to be rigid.

The Queen terrifies the living as well as the dead. The Necromancers do not feel that they have power over their own lives, in this Citadel. If they are careful, they will not join the ranks of the dead. That is possibly their only concern as they sit in the front rows.

The benches are old and finely carved, but they are otherwise unadorned; there are no flowers or ribbons on their ends—something Nathan has seen in churches, at weddings. The chamber feels funereal. A rug—a long, narrow rug—travels from the door to the dais upon which the empty thrones stand. This time, there is no image of Eric. The chair that the image usually occupies is empty.

Helmi leaves Nathan at the doors. She doesn't drift away; she vanishes. Nathan would vanish too, if he thought he could get away with it. He is momentarily frozen. The dead occupy the benches; to someone living, the chamber would appear to be almost empty. But Nathan is uncertain where he's to sit. There are no place-cards or ushers; no one to direct him to the seat the Queen has chosen.

He tells himself she won't care, but doesn't believe it. This is her moment of triumph. She will expect everything to be *perfect*, and lack of perfection might ruin her day. It will certainly ruin the day of the poor fool who doesn't know where to park his butt.

Emma is in the city, somewhere.

Nathan has seen some of that city—it is empty, a literal ghost-town. There are no stores, of course; there are no markets. There is no food; there is water—but that won't be enough, and Nathan isn't certain that Emma will have the freedom to explore. Not for long.

He should have asked Helmi who *else* was with Emma. He can't remember why he didn't.

He begins to walk down the blue carpet, looking at benches, thinking about invisibility. Only when the living outnumber the dead across those benches does he pause. Everything about the Court is about gaining, or keeping, the Queen's favor; the Queen's favor is given, predominantly, to those who have power. The people in the back benches don't.

They wear robes; they're Necromancers. But they're like Emma would have been; they've survived long enough to be 'rescued'. They've been told they're special. They've been told that if they learn enough and serve the Queen well, they'll be safe; they will survive everything that might kill them—even time. They probably didn't have Emma's home life; they didn't have her school life, either. School among the Necromancers is significantly more deadly. If the Queen wants to protect them from witch hunters, she doesn't much care about what happens to them afterward.

They know it. They also know that there is no strength in

numbers, here. They sit side-by-side; they might as well sit in different cells. They don't speak. They look straight ahead, at empty thrones.

There is no room for Nathan among them, because there is no room for Nathan among the living. He almost retreats, but one of the dead—a boy his own age, dressed very much like Helmi was dressed—saves him.

"You are expected," he says. "You will attend the Queen."

Nathan does not fall through the floor—but if he could, he would. Through the floor, through what lays beneath the floor, through the skies; he'd be happy to fall through the earth as well. He's never been wordy. In emergencies, words often desert him entirely.

He finally manages to say, "Attend the Queen?"

The young man purses his lips. "Yes. Please do not tell me you have no idea what this entails."

"I was told to—to get dressed. That's it. That's the sum total of what I know about attending the Queen."

"You are to help her with her train—the long back end of her skirts. You are to help her with her veil if there are difficulties."

Veil.

"The train will need to be arranged—to her left—when she is seated. You will, if it is required, attend Lord Eric as well. The Queen will sit before Lord Eric takes his seat—if he chooses to do so. After the Queen is seated, you will take her scepter. You will then return to Lord Eric's side, where you will stand behind him until he is summoned.

"You will not, of course, speak unless the Queen commands it. If she asks you a direct question, she will expect a *polite* and *respectful* answer. When she stands, you will return her scepter to her hands; you will take her train and you will carry it in such a way that she is allowed full mobility. You will then follow behind her."

Nathan nods.

"Go and stand by the doors; remain there until the Queen walks past you. An attendant will be with her; walk beside the attendant. The girl will join the other apprentices; you will take over her duties at that time."

Nathan wants a repeat, but it's too late. He glances down a carpet that seems, suddenly, to go on for miles and sees the Queen of the Dead in the distance.

She renders him speechless. No matter how much he fears her—no matter how much any of the dead do—she is, at this moment, incandescent. He knows that if she were kind, if she were compassionate, he wouldn't *care* about the closed door and the endless hell of unlife. She would be enough. He would be a moth, fluttering around her edges until she finally consumed him.

He wonders that he hasn't known, until this moment, that she is coming. How he could be so ignorant, so blind? She is limned with light, golden light. There are walls between them, but they might as well be made of the clearest of glass. She is wearing a dress with long, trailing sleeves and lace everywhere; he can see that it is almost the same color as the light she sheds. Her hair is gold. Her lips are red. Her eyes are a blaze of light that defy simple color.

But she *is* color, in this place. Everything else in the world is gray. Everything but Emma, who is not here.

Even the dead that are bound into the cage that contains him fall silent for a moment at her approach. She is the Queen of the Dead. In the end, she is the only afterlife they will know. Or so he feels, and it is so visceral a feeling that he is almost incapable of movement or thought. Fear, however, returns; it gives his legs strength. He walks—quickly— to the wall, and from there he traces the boundary of the room, to stand to the left of the doors.

There should be music.

There should be a triumphant processional.

There is silence. Only the sound of her steps—hers and Eric's—break it. But at the thought of Eric, Nathan closes his eyes. It doesn't help—he can see the Queen, although in theory she is not in his line of sight.

The Queen is walking down the long hall at Eric's side. Her people—the living and the dead—wait for her. It seems, for one long moment, that no one is breathing, and while the dead don't need oxygen, the living do. But the living can't *see* her.

The dead can't unsee her. She is burned into their vision, like a permanent sun spot, a permanent blindness. Nathan would be no different—but Nathan has Emma. Had Emma. Emma and the Queen are like the Sun and the Moon.

It is to the moon that Nathan is drawn, always; the light it sheds doesn't burn him, doesn't burn his vision; it doesn't create deserts. This castle, this citadel, this city of dreams and pain and love, is the only desert Nathan has ever seen.

Eric is part of it, owned by it; Nathan sees that now. Eric, like Nathan, is dead. Eric, like Nathan, is trapped in, built on, dead who are just as lost. There is no exit, no escape. Yes, they can get away from the Queen—but the world of the dead is not as large as the world of the living, and it contains vastly fewer possibilities.

The dead don't cry. Nathan doesn't. But if he could, he thinks he would. There is no joy in this reunion, and because there is no joy, there is no hope in it, either. No hope for the dead. No hope for the living trapped here.

CHAPTER
EIGHT

"CAN WE REALLY TRUST HELMI?" Amy asked as they ate the world's gloomiest dinner. Allison didn't have much of an appetite, and neither did Emma or Michael. Ernest and Chase ate. No one cared to answer Amy's question; they didn't like the answer. What choice did they have?

"You're used to this, aren't you?" Allison asked Chase, instead.

He shrugged. "Not really."

"No?"

"I'm used to eating when I have time. The breakfast we cooked at Emma's before we went to fetch Andrew Copis was so out of the ordinary it no longer feels real." Before she could speak again, he added, "I spend most of my life on the run. Running to something, running away from something. I don't expect to die peacefully of old age. I expect on some level that every meal I'm eating might be the last one.

"I don't sleep well. I *can* sleep standing up." He chewed

what looked like canned pear, swallowed, and added, "I never want my companions to die. But all of my companions— until now—have been like me. Any of the ones who weren't didn't last very long. None of you are like me."

Ernest coughed.

Chase ignored him. "It's easy for me to contemplate my own death. It's been kill or be killed for years now—it's the only way of life I know." He caught Allison's hand in his, entwining their fingers. "So I'm eating what might be my last meal with people I actually care about. Love makes you weak." As Michael opened his mouth, Chase grimaced and said, "Love makes *me* weak. When I care, I'm afraid. I'm afraid of losing the people who are important to me. Fear makes me stupid. When facing the enemies we've been facing, stupid gets us killed.

"But I want you to *be* what you are."

"Please," Amy said, waving a hand in front of Chase's face. "The rest of us are eating."

"Amy doesn't like public displays of affection," Michael added. "They make people uncomfortable."

Chase laughed. Amy, notably, did not. Allison squeezed the hand that held hers but said nothing. She'd always found Amy intimidating. Nothing had changed that.

Allison wanted to know if her brother Toby was still alive. She didn't want Emma's father to come anywhere near the city of the dead. Caught between these, she retreated—but absent her shelf of comfort books, the retreat was doomed to be incomplete.

"Emma?"

"Margaret's back." There was a pause. "And Helmi's with her." Emma reached out with her left hand, and the younger girl appeared. Margaret, however, materialized on her own.

They didn't have much in the way of paper. They didn't have chalk. Michael had his computer, but there was no source of electricity; Emma wondered if the city of the dead possessed any.

Margaret outlined the city, sans actual map. "The Queen is in her audience chamber. She has summoned her entire court. Even the dead who would normally serve as her spies are in the chamber."

"For how long?"

"Hours," Helmi said. "Think of it as a kind of anti-wedding." She glanced to her left, to a space that appeared to be empty.

"Shouldn't *you* be there?"

"Yes. I can't stay. But I wanted to tell you: Nathan is in the audience chamber as well. He's been assigned to Eric. They're both relatively safe. If you're going to move, now is the time to start. If things go well, she'll be parading in the streets — and you'll be looking down at her if you stay here."

Ernest opened his mouth.

Helmi glared and said, "It is *not* the time to ambush her. She'll have the entire court walking behind her. You've managed to survive her knights so far, but you've never faced their full assembly. Move to a building that's closer to the actual gates of the citadel. When she leaves the gates, I'll come back." She glanced at Emma. Or rather, at Emma's hand. She didn't want to let go.

"Helmi."

But she did. "My sister has never been happy," she said, her voice barely a whisper. She appeared to be staring at her feet; she could have been staring at her almost ridiculous skirts. "You love your friends." It wasn't a question. But the nonquestion was offered to Emma.

Emma's hand tightened, as if to offer brief, wordless comfort. "Yes."

Silence. Extended. Helmi broke it. "The Necromancers believe," she finally said, "that if the Queen dies, the city falls. Anyone living in it will fall as well. It's a long way down," she added, in case this wasn't obvious. "The dead can't die. We'll be fine." The twist of lips that accompanied the last word said many, many things; "fine" wasn't one of them. She fell silent for another long beat, and then her gaze drifted to Michael, who was watching her with some concern.

It wasn't the type of concern she was used to. In the ridiculous dress, she looked like an evil, spoiled princess, and her expression did nothing to dispel that impression. She looked at Michael as if he were a species of animal—or plant—that she couldn't quite place.

"In the history of the citadel, only one man came close to unseating my sister." She glanced at Emma before her gaze was once again dragged back to Michael.

"What happened to him?" Michael asked.

"He died."

Chase grimaced. Since the Queen was obviously alive, there could only be one outcome. Emma lifted a hand before he could put the thought into words. She watched Helmi.

"I think you're all stupid," Helmi told Michael.

"Ignorant," Michael corrected her.

Amy liked neither word and cleared her throat to indicate as much. She didn't follow with words. Like everyone else in the room, she was afraid enough that she wanted to hear the rest of what Helmi had to say—if she said anything more at all.

"His name was Scoros."

More silence.

"He was like a father to her. She trusted him."

"She killed him." Chase's voice was flat, uninflected.

Helmi hesitated again, her gaze upon either her feet or something beneath them.

"Could he be part of the floor?" Emma whispered.

"You don't understand my sister's anger," Helmi replied, her voice no louder. "The floors mean nothing to anyone."

"They mean something," Michael said, his voice much louder than hers.

She looked as if she would argue but not as if she *wanted* to. "They meant nothing to my sister by the time she built them. She doesn't see the dead the way you do." She looked for comprehension in Emma's expression, but it was slow to come. "He wouldn't be floor or wall or anything else that was supposed to look normal. It wouldn't be enough for my sister. She trusted him. He betrayed her."

"Would there be anything left of him at all?"

"I don't know. But when he attempted to overthrow my sister, he had his supporters. I don't think all of them would have been willing to throw their lives away, even to be rid of her. Scoros, by that point, would have. I don't think he valued his own life much by the end.

"You won't be the only person to look. You might be the only person to succeed."

"Your sister knows what happened to him."

"Yes. But she won't share. Not even with me. If I knew where he was, I'd tell you." Bitterly, she added, "If I knew where he was and someone was foolish enough to bind me, I'd tell *them*."

"Which means she thought there'd be something to tell," Amy said, voice rising slightly toward the end of the sentence.

Helmi's glance lost hesitance as she met Amy's eyes. Her lips turned up in a half smile. "I like you," she said. "And yes, that would be my guess." The smile dimmed. "If you have any hope of—of surviving what you came to do, he's your best chance. He might be your only chance." Her hair moved as if in a strong wind; her eyes were the clear, bright eyes of the dead. "You need to get out of the city before the parade starts."

She hesitated, looking down at Emma's hand; her lips thinned briefly, as if she were swallowing pain. Before Emma could speak, she faded from view, taking the cold with her.

Chase was rigid with silence. His arms shook; his knuckles were white. He exhaled only when Helmi disappeared. He then released Allison's hand and began to repack their precious, scant supplies. While he worked, he asked, "Margaret, where does the food come from?" The question made almost no sense to Emma, given Helmi's information.

Margaret, however, answered. "There's a portal in what was once considered a fae cave. The portal is a fixed structure; the passage is two-way. It is small, and it is well hidden. In the history of the citadel people on the ground have stumbled across it—by accident—perhaps a dozen times. For that reason, the citadel side is well guarded. The cave itself, however, is only intermittently watched. If we could reach the door in the citadel, we could escape." This made Chase's question make sense.

Emma exhaled. "If the Queen dies, how much time will we have before everything disintegrates?" As she spoke, she glanced at the floor—at the small indent which was, to her eyes, a field of waving arms.

"According to the Queen? None. It was one of several threats held over the heads of her court. She was our savior, and if we did not wish to commit suicide, we could not un-seat her. As attempts have been made regardless, I believe that some of the Necromancers thought she exaggerated for her own benefit; it would not be a first for her."

"How much do you know about those attempts?"

"Very, very little. I'm sorry."

Walking through the empty streets of a small, perfectly laid out city was almost surreal. There were no people except Emma and her friends. There was no traffic. The streets that existed between uniform and well-repaired buildings were wide enough for a large car but not for two, and, honestly, the driver of the large car would have had to be competent.

There were no birds, no trees, no grass—and no dump-sters, no recycling bins, no bushy rodents or rodent cousins. It was like walking through a professional photograph: everything sharp and crisp, everything evocative. As an im-age, the city invoked the *feel* of history, of things ancient.

That feel suited none of the people trapped in it. Even Margaret seemed withdrawn and tense.

Helmi was right. No one lived here. No one stayed here. If someone happened to look out from the vast reaches of the citadel's tower, they *might* see Emma and her friends—but only if they were looking. This didn't make Ernest or Chase relax, and neither of the two seemed impressed when everyone else did.

"We know what's at stake," Amy snapped.

Emma wondered whether they did. If the city streets seemed surreal, so did their mission. Not a single Emery student had ever killed a person. Or an animal, if it came down to that. Death was something that happened by accident—tragic accident. It was part of life. Murder was different: human beings interfering in the natural order. It implied many, many things: deliberation, malice, choice.

Emma had never lived in a war zone. Chase's entire life was one. But it didn't take Necromancers to create a war zone. Just people. In the end, Necromancers were people. The Queen of the Dead was a person.

And maybe there was a reason, some part of the intricate, messy, chaotic design of the world, that people—individuals—did not possess the powers of gods. Thinking this, she looked up to the sky; the air was thin and cold, but the sky was a clear sheet of blue that seemed to extend as far as the eye could see.

Emma wondered, then, what the Queen of the Dead was doing now. Eric had never been willing to speak about her much—but it was clear to Emma that the Queen of the Dead had been waiting for, searching for, hunting for, Eric. He was here now. What was the Queen of the Dead feeling? Was she happy?

If she had ever been happy, would this city and this citadel even exist?

Emma had not been born into a world that feared—and killed—witches. She hadn't been born into a world in which her family had been murdered before her eyes, in which the natural order was kill or be killed. She could forgive—not that forgiveness was hers to grant or withhold—the death of the villagers who had murdered Helmi, a helpless eight-year-old child. She was certain that had she been the Queen of the Dead in the exact same circumstances, with the exact same power, those villagers would still be dead.

What she couldn't understand was how Helmi's murder, Eric's death, could lead in a straight line to the death of Chase's family, among others. She couldn't follow the transformation of bereaved victim into callous mass murderer. Maybe if one killed, and killed enough—for any reason—life lost its value. All the good intentions, or at least the justified ones, couldn't preserve what life *meant*.

Emma shook her head to clear it. She paused, briefly, to talk to her traumatized dog. She felt a little like Michael at the moment: out of her element and very afraid to be so. She wanted the world to *make sense*. She wanted the world to be safe, or at least predictable. She didn't understand the Queen of the Dead, and because she didn't, she couldn't see the possible paths that led to a future in which they all survived.

It was the only path she wanted to see.

She lifted her face to Michael. "I think," she told him, "I understand a little bit better how you see the world. Nothing that's happening here makes any sense. And I hate it."

Michael met—and held—her gaze.

"Your mother is never going to trust me again."

The citadel was an impressively large and forbidding building. It looked like something taken out of a Lord of the Rings movie, but grimmer. And cleaner. There were no guards at the gates, although the gates were closed.

Margaret did not find this confounding. She took the lead, speaking quietly as she did. Ernest followed; Chase took the rear. Between them, Amy at their head, walked the rest of the Emery students. And Petal, who did not look any happier.

She should have left him.

She should have left him at home. She shouldn't have taken him to Mark's. She shouldn't have kept her promise to Michael. She shouldn't have—

Allison caught her left hand and held it tightly in her right, as if they were—briefly—five years old again, on a school trip. It steadied Emma.

Was it selfish to need people? Was it selfish to want their support and their friendship when things got unbearably hard? She wanted to reassure Allison. She wanted to tell Ally that she was fine. But the words wouldn't come.

Margaret walked around the gate; there was a peaked door to the left of the gate, so small in comparison it would have been easy to miss. "This," Margaret said quietly, "is how everyone but the Queen and her court leaves the citadel. Even when the gates are open, the apprentices and the novices are not allowed to use them; they exit before the Queen and move into their assigned positions in the streets.

"We'll need to move quickly; if she intends a parade, they'll be coming soon." She waited. After an awkward pause, she said, "I'll need someone to actually open the door for the rest of you."

The interior of the citadel was not, as Emma had half-expected, a grim, gothic dungeon. The first thing she noticed was the light. It came in from high ceilings and huge windows in spokes, the air so sterile no dust motes danced in its fall. The walls and the floors were a pale gray beneath carpets and runners and paintings; statues in small alcoves could be glimpsed at a distance.

She wondered if any of those statues were actual dead people, and the sense of evocative grandeur faded, the way safety sometimes did when sleeping dream turned sharply, without warning, into nightmare.

Her hand in Allison's to anchor her, Emma closed her eyes. She could still see the halls. The light, however, vanished. She couldn't see individual ghosts, but she understood that in aggregate, they were here. She opened her eyes again.

She wondered, not for the first time, where Nathan was and what he was doing—or being forced to do. He was, in the end, the reason that Emma had come. The thought—never spoken aloud—felt wrong and selfish. Less than an hour ago she had struggled to pull a total stranger out of a floor in an empty house; she had felt—in that moment—that it was the most important thing she could do.

Nathan.

Was love, in the end, just selfish? Nathan had loved Emma. Nathan still loved Emma—she was certain of that. But Nathan's love would not free the dead in the hundreds or thousands or tens of thousands. And Emma's love? Emma could remember a time when she hadn't loved Nathan because she could remember most of her life, when she hadn't known him. She knew that she hadn't fallen in love with him at first sight, but she didn't *feel* that, thinking of him now. He was—had been—Nathan. He had never been her whole world, but he had been her world whenever they were alone together.

And her love for Nathan wasn't going to save the world, either.

In truth, the world would continue even if Emma and her friends failed. The dead would live an eternity in servitude and slavery, but the world itself would barely register their pain or captivity. Emma had known nothing of what happened to the dead; she had known, deeply and personally, the cost of death to the living. The absence. The silence of the grave.

And the grave, she thought, would be silent again if they achieved their goal here. The dead—most of the dead—would leave. They would go on to whatever awaited them. Emma had no idea whether or not what waited was a giant scam, and until she joined the dead, she wouldn't. But she'd glimpsed it, and she understood why they wanted it. Why someone like Longland, who arguably didn't deserve it, could see almost nothing else.

"Margaret?"

Margaret had stopped; she was frowning. She turned to Ernest and said something that Emma could only barely hear. The actual words faded into the sense of syllables. Amy, being Amy, stepped in beside Ernest, folding her arms; Emma could only see the line of her back, but it was clear she was annoyed. Amy did not get left out.

Chase didn't move. "Margaret doesn't know where she's going," he said quietly, almost under his breath.

"Has the citadel been changed?"

Chase shrugged. "We can't stay in these halls. We're going to have to take a chance on a side hall or room and wait."

Allison and Emma were silent for a beat too long.

And Michael, in a fashion, rescued them. "Can't we just go down that hall?" He pointed to a stretch of wall, in the center of which was a small alcove.

Margaret said, "What hall, dear?" Ernest was only half a beat behind, but he dropped the "dear" at the end of his question.

The Emery students—and Chase, to Emma's surprise—turned instantly to look at Michael, following his gaze—and his slightly trembling hand—back to what appeared to be wall to their eyes.

"We don't see a hall," Allison told Michael. "We see a wall—with a small, curved alcove. There's a pedestal there for a statue—but there's no statue on it."

Michael said, "There's a hall." He looked momentarily confused, and then his eyes narrowed; he shed confusion as he gathered thought. He raised a hand, palm turned as if offering to shake the empty air in polite greeting.

Emma caught that hand. Michael walked, with obvious purpose, toward the pedestal and the alcove, Emma in tow. "What I don't understand," he said, "is why Margaret can't see it." He hesitated, and then he walked through the alcove's wall. Emma, trusting him, had to close her eyes. She wasn't surprised when she failed to hit stone, but only barely.

Michael released her hand and turned.

On the other side of what was, to all intents and purposes, a very secret door, she could see the hall and its occupants. It was like a one-way mirror. "Why would she do this?"

Michael shook his head. "I don't even understand *how* it works. Let me go get the others."

Margaret did not require Michael's help; she did require Emma's. But Margaret, like the rest of them, could see the grand halls of the citadel from this side.

This side, on the other hand, was vastly less impressive. Emma had read about servant's halls and servant's quarters—and had even been in a house that used those quarters as the nanny's living space—but she had never seen a hall like this one. It would have been at home in an ancient dungeon. It lacked the light and the sense of grandeur and open spaces that the citadel's grand hall had evoked; it was, in fact, exactly what she might have imagined the Queen of the Dead's citadel should be.

"I think we're more or less safe here," Chase said. "Margaret couldn't see the space; none of us could see it. Either the Queen created secret passages known only to her, or this was created by someone else. In the former case, the Queen's busy. In the latter . . ."

Petal whined.

Emma gently placed a hand on his head as a familiar pang of Hall guilt became a sharp pain. "I'm sorry, puppy," she told her dog.

Margaret seemed fascinated by the hall. She insisted on exiting it and trying to reach the corridor on her own. Emma, nervous, said nothing—it was Amy who granted necessary permission. Nor did Margaret react as if permission wasn't Amy's to grant.

"It might be useful," Amy told Chase, when Chase raised a red brow in her direction. "Helmi said the Queen uses the dead as spies. If even the dead can't find this place, we've got a base of operation for however long we've got food."

Ernest seemed to begrudge the fact that Amy's decision

had logic behind it. Chase, once again surprising Emma, didn't.

Margaret did not return immediately, and when she did, she looked both relieved and perplexed. "If I were not bound—in some fashion—to you, I would not be able to enter this hall. I could, of course, pass through the walls and the doors of the citadel, as one would expect the dead to be able to do; I could not pass into this hall. There are rooms beyond it; if I walk through the walls of the great hall, I enter those. I seem to bypass this hall—and possibly what it leads to—entirely.

"We will consider this good news," she added, in a very teacher-like way. "Shall we see where this hall leads?"

Seeing was a bit of an issue, which was resolved the practical way: with flashlights. Since the hall itself was so narrow, they walked single file; they had three flashlights, and they were of the emergency variety: small and portable.

The hall didn't branch; it curved. Michael was the first to notice this, but Chase wasn't far behind. Chase thought it also descended but was less certain about that; it was a very gradual descent, if true.

Margaret could pass through the floor and the walls to either side, but could not return the same way. "Helmi won't be able to find us."

"That's a bad thing?" Chase asked.

"In this case, quite probably. If she is in touch with Nathan—if she can speak to him without the Queen's knowledge—she won't be able to tell him where we are. Unless she knows about this space. It's possible. If the Queen created it, she'll know. If it was not created by the Queen, she might still have some idea. I think, at one time, she loved her sister."

"I think she still does," Emma said quietly. "She just doesn't trust her anymore."

"Why do you think that?" Michael asked.

"When she asked me what I meant to do with her sister." Michael waited. "It was the way she asked. I think she wants to stop her sister. I don't think she wants her sister to—to be dead and trapped the way Helmi has been."

"There's a room." Ernest's voice drifted back. After a moment, he said, "Or at least there's a door."

Some of the light changed direction, effectively dimming for anyone in the line who wasn't near the door in question.

"The door," Margaret said, after a brief pause, "is impassible. I cannot walk through it." She sounded slightly irritated and slightly surprised.

"It's also locked," Ernest added.

Chase said, "That's my cue." He began to bypass everyone else in the line; given the narrowness of the hall, people had to squeeze into the nearest wall to let him pass. He stopped for a bit longer in front of Allison, but Amy appeared to have stepped on his foot; he didn't linger.

He did kneel at the door; he did demand one of the two remaining flashlights, and he did curse—a lot. When he finally rose, he said, "I don't think it's that kind of door."

"You can't pick the lock?" Amy demanded.

"There are locks I can't pick. That type of lock is a little high tech for the Queen's citadel."

"Then what's the problem?"

"It's not a lock, per se."

"So the door should open."

"It's not a normal door." When Amy failed to reply, Chase glanced at her and said, "It's a Necromantic door."

"What is a Necromantic door?" Michael asked. To be fair, it was the question in everyone's mind, but Michael got there first.

"I'm guessing," Chase replied. "This door has a keyhole. It's missing tumblers or any other mechanisms—at all—that I can see. Michael, come take a look."

Michael obliged, although he made it clear as he knelt that he had no idea how to pick a lock.

"That's because they teach nothing useful in school," Chase snapped.

"He means," Allison followed up quickly, "that they teach nothing useful about dealing with Necromancers in school. School works out fine for most of the rest of us."

Michael, however, rose. "I don't think that's where the lock is," he told Chase.

"Fine. Are you willing to allow that this is Necromantic magic?"

Michael nodded, lifted his hand about two feet, and touched the door. It wasn't locked, for Michael.

The door itself was better suited to a closet than a room. Emma half expected what lay beyond it to be a dungeon cell.

Nothing about the dead, or the people who lived with them, worked as expected. She entered the room at the tail end of the group, Petal squeezing her into the left part of the frame. Chase was talking to Michael; Michael seemed naturally focused and far more at ease than he had since — since before they'd left the city.

The door had opened into a large room that contained chairs, two long couches, and a low table. Beyond this room was an arch, and beyond the arch what appeared to be a dining room; there was a small kitchen off to the side. Emma had doubts about the kitchen, but she said nothing. There was no fridge, and the oven was not a standard, modern appliance. It looked very much like a wood stove.

Chase and Ernest left the sitting room and headed toward the dining room and apparently beyond. Everyone else sat, heavily, as if the invisible strings keeping them upright had been cut.

Margaret spent some time testing the walls. To her surprise, they were impassible, just as the door had been. She could clearly see them, but she could not drift through them. Some of what must have been ferocious concentration when she had been alive took hold of her eyes and her face, transforming her expression; she no longer looked vaguely teacher-like.

Chase came back and sat beside Allison. This put him almost squarely in Amy's lap; a bit of shuffling and a lot of Amy glaring, which everyone pretended not to notice, ensued.

"There are two bedrooms," Chase said, "one small office space — there's a desk in it, three cupboards, and not a lot else — and a library. Guess where I left Ernest. The library is probably the largest room in the suite. It's down a very narrow set of stairs from the office. There don't seem to be any permanent magical traps; we've done a clear sweep. Ernest suggests you touch nothing but furniture until we've had a chance to be more complete."

"Does anyone look like they're moving?" Amy asked.

Chase shrugged and continued. "There's no food in the pantry." He slid an arm around Allison's shoulder; she tensed very slightly but didn't ask him to remove it. Emma thought it was mostly because the arm was a very public—and casual—display of affection, and as Allison had never had to deal with that before, it made her nervous. Then again, Chase alternately made Ally nervous and angry. "Margaret?"

Margaret turned at the sound of her name, half her thought clearly somewhere else. "Yes?"

"Is it possible that this is the Queen's version of an emergency bunker?"

Margaret's lips compressed into a single thin line before she finally answered. "It would make some kind of sense—but I don't think so. The citadel itself was the Queen's version of an emergency bunker. I think this must have been created entirely by someone else. It has to be old—I can't imagine it was created in an off-hour or two, and the Queen trusted none of the Court in my time."

"Do you know what it would take to create this?"

Margaret shook her head. "A few minutes of uninterrupted thought might afford better answers."

Chase laughed. "This is the first time," he said, continuing his obviously unwelcome interruption, "that I can see you and Ernest as a couple." His laughter faded as he glanced at Allison. His very theatrical sigh drew everyone's attention, even Michael's.

"What?" Amy demanded.

"Allison wants to see the library."

The office desk was large and unadorned; cupboards were mounted on the wall opposite the door, and between them were a very simple chair and a desk. The desk's drawers weren't locked; they opened smoothly, but with effort. Pens of the variety Emma was used to were absent, but ink wells—long since dried—suggested that whoever had used this desk had used it to write. There was no paper, though.

There were no books on the desk, no framed pictures, nothing to lend character or personality to the rooms' occupant. Or occupants.

"What we need is a history of the Necromancers," Allison said. To Margaret she added, "Was there some kind of official history or historian?"

Margaret shook her head. "History often disagreed with the Queen's personal memories, and she privileged her memories. She didn't intend to die; she therefore assumed that the only historical records she required, she contained. It's possible that other Necromancers left written accounts of their activities, but none would be official.

"In the case of traitors, none of those records would survive. I didn't keep records of anything but my lessons, personally. No opinion that was not the Queen's was safe to have. Shall we investigate the contents of the library? I admit a fairly sharp curiosity."

By the time they reached the library, they were talking in their normal tones. The tense, strained hush that had surrounded them all since their arrival in the city lifted, and with it, the harshest of their fear.

The library was, as Chase had claimed, the largest room here; it wasn't large, as far as libraries went. Emma's school had a larger library. Emma's *elementary* school had had a larger library.

"The Queen learned to read very late in her tenure. She could write—in a fashion—but the type of writing she had been taught was not to be found in the pages of books. She is not a woman who likes to acknowledge her ignorance, and if she couldn't acknowledge it, she had nothing to learn."

Emma nodded. "I can't read most of these."

"No. I can read perhaps a quarter. English was my mother tongue, but it was not the only language I learned. One of the few useful things taught to novices was languages. Emma? Emma, dear, what is wrong?"

CHAPTER
NINE

THERE WAS A GHOST in the library.
   She had the same weathered look that Allison's
grandfather had had, when he'd been alive; the same leath-
ery cast to wrinkled skin; the same slight stoop to shoulders
that would otherwise never bow. Allison's grandfather,
however, had had a warmth to the many, many lines of his
smile; if he had seen too much atrocity in his life, he had
also seen joy, and he had chosen to believe in it. This woman
had not.

   Her clothing was both simple and restrictive, but after
the first glance, awareness of it faded. It was the harsh, lined
planes of her face that caught—that demanded—attention.
Emma's attention.

   "Emma?" Margaret stepped toward her, her voice heavy
with concern. She frowned. "What are you staring at, dear?"

   The old woman's gaze didn't falter—but it didn't actually
move. She stood, casting no shadow, in the center of a carpet that had seen better decades; it might once have been
blue, and there was a faded pattern woven into it.

"I'm looking at a woman—a dead woman. She's old, and she's standing in the center of that rug. You can see the rug?"

Margaret's frown intensified. She turned, not to Ernest but to Chase.

"I can't see her, either."

"Can you see the rug?" Margaret demanded.

"I can. You can't?"

Margaret's silence was answer enough. Emma wasn't certain what her expression contained; she found it difficult to look away from the old woman.

Ernest said, quietly, "Chase."

Chase swore. "Emma's the Necromancer," he snapped, resisting the unspoken command. "If she sees a dead person, who am I to argue?"

Ally surprised no one who knew her; she stepped quietly between Chase and Ernest. It wasn't a declaration of love or attachment but a sign of friendship; she would have done the same for Emma or Michael. She wouldn't have done it for Amy—but Amy might find it offensive, and Ally always tried—hard—not to cause offense.

"If Emma sees a dead woman," she said, "There's a dead woman here. There." Emma finally turned away from the dead woman toward her friends.

"Margaret can't see her," Ernest replied. Although he was clearly accustomed to command and authority, Amy had laid ground rules: His chain of command didn't extend to the Emery mafia.

"Neither can Chase."

"Chase is unusual. If he works at it, he can see the dead. It is not entirely comfortable, and he does not do it the same way the Necromancers do. But, when necessary, he can. It is no doubt a large part of why he's survived as long as he has."

Chase snorted and stepped out from behind Allison. "The old man is too terrified of Amy to actually ask you any of the hard questions."

Allison turned, her hands falling to her hips. Chase grinned. But beneath that grin and the yellowing bruises, he'd lost a bit of color—and given his redhead's skin, he didn't have that much to lose.

"She doesn't seem to see me," Emma said, stepping into

the pause. "She's standing still, looking almost directly ahead. Oh, no, wait."

"She sees you now?"

"No, now she's looking around a bit. She doesn't seem to be seeing the same thing we see."

Margaret moved onto the carpet she didn't appear to see. "It's not uncommon for the newly dead not to see the dead," she said, but in a tone that implied that she didn't believe this was the case. She walked toward the center of the carpet and stopped a few inches in. Emma could no longer see Margaret's frown, but she was certain she could feel it.

"Margaret?" Ernest asked, using her name the way Margaret had used Emma's.

"I can't move forward," Margaret replied.

"Is it like the walls?" Michael—of course it was Michael—asked. "Like the hall and the hidden door?"

Margaret nodded slowly, turning back to offer him a rare smile of approval. "In fact, it is very like that."

Emma frowned. "Helmi said something earlier about circles." No one spoke. "I think the pattern on the rug is circular. Concentric circles. She seems to be standing in the center of it."

"I believe Helmi said the Necromancer was to sit in the circle, not the dead."

Emma nodded. "But it was supposed to protect the Necromancer from—from getting lost, I think? It was supposed to be a way of reaching the dead without actually physically walking to where they died." She exhaled. "I don't think the woman can see us because she's in the circle. I don't think you can see her because she's there."

"Be careful, Emma."

"I'm not afraid of the dead," Emma replied. "It's the living that scare me."

The circles embroidered into a carpet that was so worn were surprisingly sharply detailed. Although the edges of the weave were frayed and faded, the thread out of which the circle itself had been woven almost shone. It seemed to form a wall for Margaret; she could move around the circumference, but she could not move into the circle it transcribed.

Emma could and did.

The woman's eyes widened, changing the lines around the corners of her eyes; the way her mouth opened changed the rest. She could clearly see Emma, now.

"Who are you?" she demanded, her hands balling into fists. Emma had found Margaret prim and intimidating on first encounter. Intimidation was not fear; this woman reminded Emma of the magar, the start of this journey. She reminded Emma of death.

Ingrained Hall manners saved her. She drew one even breath. "I'm Emma. Emma Hall." Hall manners were clearly not reciprocated. The woman failed to introduce herself.

"Why are you here?" she demanded, instead.

Fair enough. Emma and her friends hadn't exactly waited for an invitation. "We're here to find our friend."

"Your friend?" The woman's lips thinned. "You've lost friends here?" Her eyes narrowed as well. "What on earth are you *wearing*?"

Since there was nothing remarkable about Emma's clothing—nothing terribly revealing, it being winter—Emma was momentarily at a loss for words. "Clothing. I mean, clothing from my country—and my time."

The woman was silent for one long, uncomfortable beat. "You're not dead."

"Not yet, no."

"Are you the new Queen?"

"God, no," was Emma's emphatic response.

"You remind me of her."

"Because you're dead."

The woman nodded. "Yes. Were you one of her supporters?"

"No. Until a few weeks ago, I'd never even heard of her. What I *have* heard—" Emma shook her head. "No."

"And the friend you're looking for?"

Emma hesitated. "She has him."

"Girl, you look soft. Young. I don't know how you came to be here, but this is not the place for you. Leave the way you came, and leave quickly." She hesitated. "Did my son bring you here?"

Emma shook her head.

The woman closed her eyes. If she had looked old before—and she had—she hadn't looked frail until this moment. "Then he is dead. He is lost."

"And you?"

"I am, as you see, safe. I am one of the few who are." She glanced at her hands and forced them to lose the shape of fists—fists that wouldn't be useful in any way. In a more conversational tone, she said, "Tell me, do the walls still scream?"

Emma decided then and there that she didn't like this woman. The question, casually asked, was barbed and pointed; it was meant to cut. And it did. She folded her arms tightly.

"Em?" Ally asked, the single syllable expressing all of her worry.

Emma focused on the dead woman. "Yes. And the floors. And probably the rest of the citadel too."

One gray brow rose, but so did the corners of her narrowed mouth. "You'll pardon an old woman," she told Emma. "I see there's some strength in you."

"Strength," Emma replied, "isn't measured by cruelty or anger."

"Here, it is."

"Maybe when you were alive."

A harsh bark of laughter followed. "When I was alive, girl? No. Had I been stronger from the beginning, there would be no Queen of the Dead. But that girl? She was kin."

"Her family died."

"Distant kin. Are you afraid, girl?"

Emma said nothing.

"This citadel was built on love and fear. Don't mix the two." Emma thought she meant to continue, but she fell silent. It was a haughty, bitter silence, from which Emma understood one thing: ferocious pride. Whatever her crime, she didn't want to expose it to a bunch of teenagers who were in no way kin.

"I cannot leave this place. I cannot leave the circle." The old woman closed her eyes. "I hear them, you know. I hear the dead. They shatter me with their accusations."

Emma shook her head. "They don't accuse."

"They would if they understood what I was in life."

"They don't accuse."

"Tell them what you know, and they will, girl. Death doesn't change the living—not when they're trapped here."

"It changes what they want." Emma's arms loosened; she dropped them to her sides. "You were taught what the Queen of the Dead was taught."

The woman inclined her chin stiffly. Everything about her was stiff. "Who was your teacher?"

"I haven't really had one. I haven't had the time."

"And you've come here to save your friend?" The obvious outrage in the woman's expression didn't quite reach her tone.

"Right now, there's no one else."

"You'll die."

"I'm going to do that anyway—hopefully much later. When I die, I'll be trapped just as you are. Even if I weren't, everyone I love, everyone I've ever loved or will love in the future, will be. I don't draw circles. I don't understand how they work. But honestly? You're safe from the Queen—but you're not any freer."

"In this city, safety is its own freedom." She looked down toward her feet. "It was not meant to last forever." Lifting her face, she said, "Is this now the eternity I face? It is the one I deserve."

"Maybe," Emma replied. "But I'm not qualified to judge that. And even if *you* deserve it, the rest of the dead don't. You said your son built these rooms?"

The woman nodded.

"Do you understand how? I mean—how he could make them impassible and invisible to the dead?"

The woman nodded again. Some of the steel had left her face, to be replaced by the weight of age.

"He didn't trust the Queen."

"He loved her, as a child; we do not trust our children to see wisdom when they are young."

"She's not young now."

"No? To me, she was only that, always that. But she had power beyond age and wisdom and nothing to prevent its use. I cannot teach you what you need to know; I am dead, and you will be dead soon."

"Then tell me about the circle," Emma said. "Tell me what it does and how it works. I've seen—I've touched— the dead before, but I've never done it from a circle."

"Then how?"

"I went to where they were." She hesitated and then said, "And I called them to where I was."

"Impossible."

Emma didn't argue. Helmi had mentioned circles, and there was clearly some safety in them. Unless the lesson took less than an hour, Emma wouldn't have the time to learn. But something about this circle, this private space, tugged at her. "What are the circles meant to do?"

"They are meant to protect us when we search for the lost dead. They bind us both to ourselves and to life. While within the confines of the circle, the living cannot be drained by the needs and the fury of the lost; they can approach the dead in safety.

"If the circle is broken or frayed, that safety is not guaranteed." The carpet on which the ghost stood had seen better days. "Yes," the woman said quietly, seeing the direction of Emma's gaze. "Nothing lasts forever except death."

"Is that why I could see you?"

Silence.

Emma reached out and offered her hand to the old woman. She couldn't say why, then or later; this woman was not the type of woman to whom one offered comfort. The old woman stared at that hand. She didn't take it.

"If you're here to bind me—"

"I'm not. I want you to talk to Margaret, but she can't enter the circle. And I don't think you can leave it, either. Not without help." When the woman failed to take Emma's hand, she lowered it. "I won't make you leave. I can't. I don't know how to bind you."

"Then you'll get no power from the dead."

"I don't want power—"

"You don't understand what you'll be facing. If you have no dead of your own, you have no chance."

Emma folded her arms again, disliking this woman. The woman was trapped—they were all trapped—*because* of the power the Queen had taken.

Emma believed she was a decent person on most days.

Maybe she wasn't the best daughter in the world. Maybe she wasn't the best friend. She lost her temper sometimes. She said things she regretted later. But *everyone* did that.

Before Mark, before Mark's mother, she had been certain of herself. Mark's mother—and the death of her son—had unsettled Emma. She was no longer completely certain that she would always *do* the right thing. She was only certain that she wanted to.

But when you had the power of life and death—literally—a bad day could have consequences that lasted forever. One day. One slip. One terrible temptation.

If Emma had had the power that the Queen of the Dead possessed, she wasn't certain that she could have let Nathan die. The grief of his loss, his constant absence, had blighted every day that had followed it. Yes, there were good days—but even those had thorns and barbs; there were always reminders of Nathan wherever she went. A stray song. A specific store. A restaurant dish. A piece of clothing.

He had promised that she could die first.

And some promises should never be made. Should never be asked of another person. She bowed her head. "Stay here, if here is where you prefer." She turned to leave the circle and felt the ice of a dead woman's hand touch the back of her own.

"You are a foolish, foolish girl," the woman said, tightening her grip.

"So I've been told."

"But warm," the woman continued, as if Emma hadn't spoken. "Warm. You reek of life, girl."

"So does the Queen of the Dead." Emma reached out—slowly—and caught the old woman's hand in her free hand, shifting her grip.

"Yes. Yes, she does. She had so much power, so much promise; she could find the lost far more easily than anyone I have ever taught or encountered. She wasn't—she wasn't an evil child."

"No child is evil," Emma replied. "I can understand what she did, if I try hard—but it doesn't matter *why* she did it, because she never stopped. The dead want to leave. It's the only thing they want. It doesn't matter what kind of life they lived." Emma's hand hurt. It wouldn't, in a half hour; it would be too numb. She turned to the woman and found herself being intently studied. "People who are hurt cause hurt."

The old woman nodded. Her eyes, the peculiar translucent color that Emma wanted to call gray, were shining as if with unshed tears. "Will you let go of me if I ask you?"

"Yes."

"Will you leave me here if I ask it?"

"Yes." But Emma knew then that she would never ask.

"What will you do if the Queen is dead?"

"Go home with my friends. Except for the dead one," she added, her throat tightening.

"And him?"

"If he can't find his way to the door, I'll walk him there." And try, desperately, not to weep while she was doing it.

Margaret's gaze sharpened when Emma stepped out of the circle. The hand that she held allowed the dead woman to cross the boundaries woven into an aged carpet with what appeared to be gold thread.

"The carpet is a circle," Emma told Margaret, half apologetically. "The living—Necromancers—would probably see her, as I did. But not the dead." Turning to the old woman, she said, "This is Margaret Henney." To Margaret, she said, "She didn't introduce herself, so I don't know her name."

"Names have power," the old woman said.

Emma didn't actually believe this, but Hall manners in a public space prevented any verbal disagreement. "She was hidden within the circle. I'm hoping she can tell us a little bit about the citadel or the Queen of the Dead."

"Or how these rooms were built?"

"Or that, yes."

The woman looked around the room, taking in all occupants at a glance. The fact that they returned her stare—some more politely than others—didn't seem to concern her at all. "This room, the rooms that surround it, are a circle."

"What *are* circles?" Amy seldom did something as trivial as asking where a demand would do.

"They are bindings," the woman replied. "Not chains,

but—reminders. When we leave our bodies, we meet the dead in their own domain. It is easy—far too easy—to become as they are. It is easy to lose ourselves and the sense of our own lives, and if we do that, we lose our lives. We're no good to the trapped and the lost if we become trapped and lost ourselves." She looked down an angular nose at Amy with very clear distaste before her glance returned to Emma and the hand that bound them. She seemed to be making a decision.

"The dead have no choice. But the living do. We leave our bodies tethered to the circles of the living world. Every circle is therefore slightly different, but at base, the principles are the same. We write or carve the ancient symbols of earth, fire, water, and air. We carve the runes of birth and death. We surround ourselves with those symbols, and into that mix, we choose one for ourselves. A name, if you will. A name to join the symbols that speak of life.

"From there, from behind those protections, we can seek the dead. It is not a trivial undertaking, to draw a circle. It is not trivial to learn the mechanics of creating one."

"I don't mean to be a killjoy," Amy interrupted, in a tone that heavily implied the opposite, "but these rooms aren't exactly circular."

"The circle is a metaphor," the woman snapped, her expression as cold as her hand. "There is a reason that the dead cannot drift into this space. The Queen could, but magics of her own devising prevent the finding of the rooms by the living. And perhaps those magics are finally failing—you are here, after all." She glanced at Emma. "Or perhaps your queen—"

"*So* not a queen."

"It is habit; forgive me. How did you find this room?"

Everyone in the room very carefully avoided looking at Michael. Michael was silent as well.

The woman didn't seem to find the silence offensive. "The rooms were constructed by my son over a period of years. The Queen trusted him, as she trusted very, very few. She taught him everything she had learned, and he taught her everything he had learned. Yes," she added, glancing toward the floor, "he became the first of her supporters, the first of her knights.

"He believed—*we* believed—that time would heal the pain she felt. We committed crimes in the short term while we waited for that healing. And we did so from a place of safety. We were free to speak about our vocation. We were free to exchange information about both our successes and our failures.

"You cannot understand what that was like—to be free to be true to ourselves. It was a powerful, heady gift. For the first time in our lives, we did not fear to be murdered in our beds by the terrified and the ignorant." Her voice had grown in strength as she spoke; Emma could see her features shift, the wrinkles sliding away from the corners of her lips and her mouth. Those wrinkles were not laugh lines or smile lines; they'd been carved there by grim frowns.

"She gathered us from the corners of the land; found us in our tents and our homes. She brought us to her village. And the village grew." She was definitely younger now in appearance; her hair was a wild, tangled spill down shoulders that were no longer stooped. She was, to Emma's surprise, striking—even beautiful.

"We offered safety and shelter to our distant kin. And they were grateful, just as we were. They felt free, just as we did. But some were troubled by the Queen's treatment of the dead and the use of their power. Some could justify it, of course. Some could not. The disagreement grew heated, and the division, bitter. It did not stop with words.

"It was perhaps the closest the Queen had come to death, beyond that first terrible day. She took control of those who were loyal to her and banished the survivors who were not." The woman hesitated, and then added, "There were very few survivors.

"But the conflict started from a very simple question: How long? How long were the dead to be trapped? How long would they exist in a state of servitude?" The woman fell silent. Emma thought she had stopped speaking. She was wrong.

"It's easy to say: just a little while longer. It's easy to speak of the primacy of the living. The dead do not age. They have time."

It was *not* easy for Emma. She said nothing.

"We had seen death. We had lived in fear. We were

drunk with the knowledge that we need not fear again." She shook her head. "But fear comes anyway. What we fear changes. I was not taught the arts of longevity. At that point, the Queen trusted very few, and I was not among them. I reminded her," she added, with a bitter grimace, "of her mother. And so, as all must, I died. But I died of old age. Of ill-health. Men did not come to murder me in my bed.

"And I existed thereafter as the dead exist. The enormity of what had been done—to the dead—became real to me only once I had joined them. I returned, not to the Queen but to my son. We spoke for some time. He asked me to wait. And what could I say to him?" She spread her hands, palm up. "Had I not decided the dead could wait when I was not myself among them?

"He would not listen to me, not immediately. I thought him cold and proud, and perhaps he was—but perhaps I was as well. He wished for the Queen to be safe."

"If he's dead," Margaret said, her voice oddly gentle, "He must have changed his mind."

The woman nodded; she wrapped one arm around herself, as if she could feel the cold. "Yes. The Queen required a legion of the dead to build her city, her citadel. She built a circle for herself, and she went out to gather them; she found them by the wall."

"The wall?"

"It is what I call what she has made of the only exit offered us.

"But it was not enough. Had the magar granted her daughter the one distinguishing item she possessed, it would have been much, much simpler. But if the magar loved her daughter, it was a harsh love, and it did not imply trust. She searched for her dead mother," the woman added. "For decades. For centuries, to listen to my son. She could not be found.

"And had I not come to my son, I would not have been found either. To the Queen, I was one of a legion of necessary tools. To my son? I was his mother. They argued, then. It was the first real argument they had had. In the end, the Queen relented, or appeared to relent; she agreed that I would not have the *honor* of becoming a necessary foundation for her future home."

"She didn't say that?"

"That is exactly what she said—to my son. My son did not agree. I make no excuse for him. He was willing to consign strangers—innocents, even—to the fate of being floor or wall for as long as the Queen reigned. He was unwilling to consign me to it. She acquiesced.

"But she was not happy to see his loyalty divided. The dead were dead. They did not have the primacy of the living. And even among the living, there was the Queen and everyone else. She did not wish me to continue to influence my son, and she attempted to bind me. I remember it. It was ... unpleasant."

Margaret nodded.

"He came in time to prevent this, and she apologized; she said I had insulted her, that she had lost her temper. That was her excuse."

Emma could well imagine it was true.

"But he kept me by him after that. I seldom left his side. It ... did not please her. She was always angered by lack of trust, even when the lack was deserved. My son proved not to be an utter fool; he had already built what he called a haven— this one. It was hard for him to come here in the latter days; they never completely recovered from the conflict. She was a child," the woman added. "And, as children do, she wished to be the most important—the only important—person. She wished to know that she, above all others, was cherished. He had given her that, for as long as he could.

"He created the circle you found me in. It is ... clever. It can be moved or placed where necessary, in a way that the Queen's circle cannot."

"What happened to him?"

"I don't know. He left me here." She lifted her chin. "I do not think he felt certain he would survive whatever it was he intended; he did not tell me. He did not ask my advice; he wished me to be safe and beyond her reach— something he could not, in the end, guarantee for himself.

"He intended, I think, to destroy her."

CHAPTER
TEN

"How?" Michael asked. The woman was so unfriendly, he didn't follow it with the usual barrage of subsequent questions.

"I don't know. He didn't tell me. If he failed—if we were discovered—I would have told her everything. There were things he did not want her to know. And that was wise. If he failed—and he must have, if you are here—he might have had hope that someone else would eventually succeed."

"He was taught the old ways?" Margaret asked, her voice still soft and shorn of all judgment.

"Of course," the woman replied, her voice harsh.

Amy folded her arms, tilting her hip to the right. "There's no 'of course.' If he'd been taught the old ways and he'd *stuck with them*, we wouldn't be in this mess in the first place." The woman's face aged as she turned to Amy, but age wasn't going to garner any respect from that quarter. "Don't even," she said, glaring. "The only reason you've got regrets is that you *personally* suffered."

If the hand Emma held had been cold before, it became

ice. Even the sense that she held something in the shape of a hand vanished. Time froze, in the same way her hand did; as if all warmth had been leeched from it, and warmth—like life—was required.

And yet, at the core of that implacable ice, there was heat—not warmth, it was too blistering, too unforgiving, for that. The sensation was both new and at the same time, familiar; Emma understood, just in time, what it meant. The fire wasn't meant for her. She was a conduit.

She had been a conduit for a dead child in just this way, and people had died. She'd had no regrets about those deaths; the people who had died had meant to murder Allison.

This was different. What she'd allowed a four-year-old child in her ignorance, she *could not* allow now; she knew who the power was aimed at. And if, on rare occasions, she'd strongly desired to kick Amy Snitman in the shins, that was the extent of her anger. Amy was, thorns and all, one of the best friends a person could have, especially when the chips were down.

After all, she was here, wasn't she?

Fire gathered in Emma's hands; she curled them into fists. That was simple; pain caused her to tense, to clench, to bite her own lip simply to endure. The only thing that was cold was her left hand. Without thinking, she reached for the cold—and to her surprise, it came, flowing up her arm and across her shoulders like a thin shell of sensation within which she could contain the rage of fire.

Her own rage was already contained because she was a Hall. She opened her eyes—when had she closed them?— to meet the older woman's and said, *No. I* will not *let you do this.*

The heat of the fire intensified, but Emma had cold, and as she applied it, the fire ceased to burn.

"Emma—" Margaret began.

Emma swiveled and Margaret fell silent—and not in the good way. The ghost took a step back, passing through Ernest before she stopped herself.

"Em," Allison said, at the same time. "Your hair is—"

"Standing on end," Chase finished. "What the hell are you doing?"

"Stopping a cranky old woman from turning Amy into an ash pile," Emma snapped back.

"That is not all you are doing," Margaret's voice was soft, almost a whisper, but it had an edge Emma had never heard there before.

Amy shrugged. Of course she did. "Emma's got my vote of confidence." She glared at Chase. "You asked a stupid question. She answered it, which is more than I would have done."

"Not noticing you're short of words right now," Chase replied.

"You asked her what she was doing. Rudely. She answered anyway. I personally don't care *how* she's doing it— I'm in favor of the end goal." She then turned to Emma. In a different tone of voice, she said, "Margaret's worried."

Since this was obvious, Emma nodded. "You remember what happened with Andrew Copis—the four-year-old trapped in the burning house?"

"Yes."

"She was trying to do what he did. She was going to lash out through *me*. I stopped her." Exhaling, she added, "I stopped me." Emma turned to the old woman. "Don't *ever* do that again."

The woman was utterly silent. What Emma had assumed was a glare because it was the woman's natural expression was something entirely different. She was staring *through* Emma, as though Emma was no longer visible. Or as though nothing was.

Emma had seen that look before. She yanked her hand back, and only when she did did she realize that she was no longer holding onto the woman's hand. She could still feel the cold, but it wasn't painful or numbing; it was almost pleasant.

She looked down at her hands. They hadn't changed. She was half afraid she'd see some sign of luminescence, of otherworldly energy; she didn't. She looked up, slowly this time.

"Em?"

"I think—I think she's bound. To me." She felt queasy, nauseated, even saying it.

"I think so too," Margaret replied. She had regained her composure.

"I didn't—I didn't have time to *think*," Emma said, voice dropping. "I recognized what she meant to do. I had to stop her."

"How did you recognize it?"

"It felt the same. I could feel fire. I could feel it in my hands. And I could feel ice, because I was still holding onto her hand. I used that. I used the ice to build a barrier between the fire and my fingertips."

"This is not the way it is normally done," Margaret said. "Normally, the binding process is much longer, much more onerous."

"Maybe they didn't have the incentive I did."

"No, dear, we probably didn't. We were concerned, of course, with our own survival—without power, it wasn't guaranteed. There are Necromancers who fail the many tests laid out for them. The Queen is not interested in failure."

Emma said, quietly, "I'm sorry."

The old woman stirred.

Emma faced her, uneasiness giving way to anger. "If the dead have power, it's meant to be used to *leave*. It's not meant to be used to kill the living—no matter *how* you feel about the living. You couldn't do it on your own—the only way you could do it is through me—and I'm not going to let you murder my friends because you happen to think they're too rude. I wouldn't let you do it if you were alive, either. Rude is not a death sentence in *this* world.

"And I think Amy's right. You think it's acceptable to kill someone because you don't like the way they talk to you? There's probably a reason that you were one of the Queen's early supporters. Or later, if it comes to that."

The woman's face lost the slack, distant look that had characterized the bound whom Emma had worked so hard to free. The fact that she was somehow bound to Emma—that it was because Emma had used her innate power when she had ceased to be aware of herself or anything else in the room—made it far, far worse: It was an accusation. It was proof that the power she had *was* the same power as the Queen's.

And she knew this. But the knowledge had, until this point, been entirely intellectual. Now it wasn't.

The woman's expression, however, was not one of

horror; it was almost . . . smug. "So you've will in you, girl. You're not as weak as you look." She frowned and added, "Children had better manners in my day."

"Not if they learned them from you," Amy shot back.

As she couldn't reduce Amy to ash, she chose the next best option; she pretended Amy didn't exist. "What will you do with me now? I have power." She said this with a certain amount of pride.

"It wasn't *your* power you were attempting to use," was Emma's quiet reply. "Can you just stay here?"

"You do not require my permission to leave me here."

"No, I guess I don't." Emma flexed her fingers, paused, and examined her hands. The chains that bound Margaret — or Nathan — had been visible *as* chains to her eye. There were no chains around her hand or her arm. There was no visible sign that she had enslaved this woman. She winced even thinking the word — but she forced herself to call it what it was. Anything else was a lie, meant for her own comfort.

She did not want to become comfortable with what she'd done.

"What do you mean to do?" Enslaved or not, the woman asked questions the way Amy did.

"I told you. We're here to find our friend."

"And I told you—"

"And free him."

"You will not free him—or any of the dead—while the Queen lives."

Chase said, "The Queen surviving isn't part of our plan." He was the only person speaking so far who could speak of death—of killing—so naturally.

"You are all fools."

Amy folded her arms.

"You do not have the power to kill the Queen. I am bound to Emma—she has whatever power I have. It *will not* be enough. Emma will need to gather the dead and hold them."

"You're not the only one that Emma holds," Margaret told her, as Emma said, "There has to be another way."

"Do you think you're the only one to try to kill the Queen?"

She knew she wasn't, and, oddly enough, this lent her argument some strength. "No. And every other person who did try tried it your way. It didn't work for them, and they *knew* what they were doing. It won't work this time, either." She turned away from the angry dead woman, to Amy and Allison.

The woman said, "You must find my son." Had her expression not been so cold, it might have been a mother's plea. "My son witnessed many attempts against the Queen. He understood intimately how each had failed. He was not a fool. He would not have made the attempt if he thought there was no possibility of success."

"Finding your son," Emma replied, "is easier said—by far—than done. But . . ." she exhaled. "The Queen trusted your son."

The woman nodded, sombre now. "He had no living children of his own. She was the child of his heart. When you have children of your own, you will understand."

Emma hoped that this would never be true. "Was his name Scoros?"

Silence. It was heavy with suspicion, anger, and the bitter tang of fear. The woman did not acknowledge the question, but it wasn't necessary. *Names have power.*

"We were told that a man named Scoros might be our only hope." Emma's gaze fell to the floor. "Scoros attempted to kill the Queen."

Silence.

"He failed. Helmi was certain that he wouldn't be part of a floor or a wall—his was the greatest betrayal the Queen faced. She thought something might be made of him, but she couldn't tell us what. She has no idea where he is—and Helmi spent a lot of time with her sister. There's not a lot she didn't see. Scoros, however, was hidden."

The old woman's grimace of distaste could probably be seen from orbit. *"Helmi?"* To Margaret, she said, "Are they *all* fools?"

Margaret's answer—and her lips did move—was lost to the sound of music. Amy's response was lost as well.

Organs rattled the floor beneath their feet. The notes were dolorous, almost funereal; Emma raised her hands to cover her ears. It didn't help. The song went on for what felt like hours, and even when it had finally paused, she could still hear it, could still feel it.

"We probably don't have much time before the organ starts up again," Amy said, into the blessed silence. "Where are we going?"

Everyone looked at Margaret, and when Margaret failed to speak, they looked at the grim-faced, bitter stranger. Even Emma.

"Did the Queen's sister tell you where my son might be found?" She asked the question as if everything about speech was distasteful.

"No, sadly." It was Amy who answered. She returned a youthful glare for the ancient, weathered one. "Do you have any ideas?"

Silence.

And then, surprising everyone who was actually looking at her face, the old woman said, "Yes." She met Amy's gaze, held it, looking down at the Emery student in every conceivable way.

Amy, however, had played this game before, and she won it more often than she lost. She waited.

Having watched Amy play, none of the other Emery students were stupid enough to break in; none of them, not even Michael, asked the old woman anything. Seconds stretched. Amy folded her arms. She didn't open her mouth.

The old woman moved first, turning away from Amy Snitman to gaze at the far wall. "The Queen's personal chambers. If some clue exists, it is almost certainly there."

The music resumed, like an aural earthquake.

NATHAN

NATHAN'S FIRST—AND ONLY—attendance at a wedding had occurred when he was six years old. Friends of his father were getting married; they had asked if Nathan wanted to be part of the wedding party. Parties, at age six, involved other children and loot bags, so of course he'd said yes.

He discovered that wedding parties were not like birthday parties. Either that, or adult parties were boring. The first night, he waited, playing with the flower girl under the watchful eyes of her mother while adults did their thing. And there was no cake.

But on the day of the wedding itself, it was different. He was required to wear a suit—and secretly felt that he had suddenly turned a corner into adulthood because of it—and to carry a small pillow that, on the *real* day, held a ring. It was his job—his single most important job—to make sure that ring did not get lost. Apparently the groom would be so nervous that he'd forget it somewhere or lose it if left to his own devices.

Nathan believed it, at six, but only because he trusted his mother to more or less tell him the truth.

He believes it in a different way now. He carries no ring. But he takes the position of attendant, and he stands beside Eric at the Queen's command. He stands one step behind as Eric is led to the thrones. He stands one step behind as Eric turns, at last, to face the audience.

They are mute for one second too long; they cheer and applaud on command. Nathan cannot see the Queen's face from his vantage. He can't see the expression she turns upon her subjects. He can guess.

So can Eric.

Nathan envied Eric, once. He envied Eric's ability to touch Emma without freezing her half to death, to interact with her, to *protect* her. It was stupid. It was stupid, and he regrets it now; he would apologize in a heartbeat if he could.

But he won't survive interrupting this moment, because it's the Queen's, and there's no room for anyone else in it. Not even Eric, who is theoretically the star of the show.

Nathan is not required to carry the crown. He's profoundly grateful.

Eric, however, is required to wear it, just as if it were a ring and this were a wedding, the end of a long romance in which obstacles to love have finally been vanquished. Nathan thought that the Queen loved Eric. That she loved him *so much*. And maybe, in her own mind, she does.

But the holographic image that once occupied the throne at her side was not Eric. It only looked like him. She had forced her Court, living and dead, to acknowledge his presence. She had cried at his absence, at his loss—although no one spoke of those tears. But that Eric, the Eric over whom she had grieved and for whom she had longed for centuries, was *not* Eric.

Nathan had not understood that until this moment.

He understands it now. He is terrified of the Queen, terrified for Eric, terrified, in the end, for himself. He told himself that the Queen loved Eric. He tells himself that Emma loves him. But if the words are the same, they mean entirely different things.

And the Queen of the Dead is not stupid. Malevolent, yes. Powerful. Delusional in her fear. But stupid? No. There is no love in Eric's stony expression. There is no joy, no relief, no desire. He is dead and not-dead, like Nathan—but Nathan has seen more expressive corpses.

She must know. He is certain, as she speaks, her voice carrying an edge of the fear that has informed her entire existence—he won't call it life—that she *does* know. But in her universe, she has given her *life* to Eric. She has built a world for him. She has done everything she can in the name of love.

And Eric had better appreciate it.

Nathan is afraid, for Eric, for himself. For Emma, who is in the City of the Dead. He doesn't know what the Queen will do when she finds out that Eric doesn't love her, but he is certain he is going to find out.

The Queen lets go of nothing. Her ancient fears and hatreds are her armor and her cage, and she bears them proudly and defiantly. It is defiance he sees in her face when she at last finishes speaking and turns—briefly—to nod in Nathan's direction. It is a signal. Nathan moves to stand behind Eric, and one of the Queen's knights—a title that seems far less ridiculous in this opulent, cold hall—comes forward, bearing a cushion upon which the crown rests.

Eric kneels. He kneels like a condemned man facing a guillotine instead of a noose or a firing squad. The Queen's knight holds the cushion to one side of his head and looks daggers at Nathan. Nathan's hands—which are not in any way his own—tremble as he lifts them.

The crown is cold.

The crown is cold even compared to Nathan's natural state. He is inexplicably afraid to touch it. It looks as if it's made of gold, gold and gems. Nathan was never into jewelry and can't tell glass from diamond. He doesn't need to. This crown is gold the way Nathan is alive. He can almost hear it screaming.

She can't.

It comes to Nathan that she can't hear anything. She can't see anything. If she could, she would know that Eric was killed, died, and *is dead*.

As the crown trembles in his hands, he remembers his mother. He remembers her shut in his undisturbed room, weeping in isolation. Changing his calendar. His mother won't do that forever. She won't. She's in pain because the loss was unexpected; there's no way to plan for the death of a son. If it were cancer, if it were some lingering, deadly disease, she might have had time. But a car accident in the middle of the day?

No.

The driver of that car didn't mean to kill Nathan. Oh, he killed him—he and his joyriding friends. But there was no intent. The men who killed Eric hadn't killed him by accident. His mother probably hates the kids who killed her son—but the hatred has walls. There was no malice. There was no intent. They didn't shoot him or stab him or—or hunt him.

He's no longer certain what would have become of his mother if her grief and her anger had a justifiable target. His mother was always the rational pragmatist. His father had the big, wide streak of sentimentality. It's possible his mother could have let it go. At this very moment, Nathan doesn't believe it.

The Queen saw her family murdered.

The Queen has never forgiven the murderers—or herself. She fashioned herself into a weapon, and in the end there was nothing else left for her to be.

Nathan sets the crown on Eric's brow. Eric looks up, their eyes meet. Nathan sees a reflection of himself in Eric's eyes. And a reflection of his belief; Eric shudders, in silence, as the crown descends. When he rises—as King of this graveyard—he almost staggers under its weight.

The doors roll open. Nathan steps in to catch—and rearrange—the Queen's train. Helmi is at his side, showing him, with actions, what he's expected to do. She doesn't speak. If the Queen won't, no one else can—that's understood, even by her younger sister.

She doesn't look young at the moment. She looks ancient—as burdened by death as Eric. She watches Eric's back with a mixture of profound resentment and a hint of pity. It's the pity that almost breaks Nathan. He hasn't had Helmi's centuries of experience. He doesn't envy them. But those centuries are the foundation that allow her to go gracefully through the motions in which everyone present—everyone—is trapped.

If he knew nothing, this would seem like a fairy-tale wedding, a happily-ever-after. The Queen is beautiful in her flowing dress, and the King is tall, handsome, dignified. At a regal signal from the Queen, the crowds—living and dead mingled to Nathan's eyes—raise their hands and voices in cheers that never quite destroy the solemnity of the occasion.

But not even a fairy tale could contain the sound of the music that starts the moment the Queen takes her first step—and how could it? Fairy tales are words. Words on paper. He starts to look for the organ that plays these notes; it must be a monstrosity, and he doesn't understand how he missed it. But his gaze glances off Helmi, and her swift, definitive shake of the head prevents his search.

He walks instead. He walks behind the Queen and her consort. The aisle stretches out to eternity, and he wonders if that's an artifact of mounting dread or if it's literal—if the Queen intends this walk to be significant enough that she has elongated the hall that contains it. Even this, he can't ask. Shouting at the top of what passes for his lungs these days, he's not certain he could make himself heard over the music.

He walks, and walks, and walks. In front of him, Eric does the same, but he pauses to offer the Queen his hand. It is the only deviation from her scripted coronation, and it is therefore the only time she hesitates.

For one moment Nathan can almost see the girl she might once have been in the widening of her eyes, the slight opening of her lips. He can see the ghost of youth in the corners of her mouth, the sudden, almost shy smile. It is possibly the most shocking thing he's seen today.

She sets her hand in Eric's, but as she does, the smile vanishes; for one moment—only one—she is utterly still, her skin as pale as her dress, her eyes narrowing. She searches Eric's face; she looks up at the crown. Nathan thinks she might snatch it from his head and throw it to the ground, her anger is so sudden and so intense.

She doesn't. The music is the only sound in the hall. Her gaze is dragged to the hand that she now holds, to something that binds his finger—ah, a ring. Eric is wearing a ring.

By her reaction, it is not a ring that came from her at any point in their life. It is simple, a plain band. Her fingers tighten around his; she forces the bitter rage from her expression. Nathan is reminded that the worst anger is always rooted in pain. Hurt or not, she will not let Eric go.

Nathan wonders, then, if this is Eric's test. It's not a kind thought. But this isn't a kind place; it is not a city in which joy is easily made, found, or held. The Queen begins to walk again, Eric by her side.

If Nathan were still alive, this would put him off weddings for the rest of his natural existence.

ERIC

GRAVES ARE SILENT because the dead do not occupy them. There has been no silence in Eric's existence. It is silence, in his darkest of moments, that he yearns for.

The crown is screaming as it is placed upon his head by Nathan's unsteady hands; it is a chill band of sound that resonates with his body. His hands shake, and his legs almost fail to hold him as he rises, consort to the Queen of the Dead. King, as she has often called him. He remembers, sharply—terribly—the ceremony of his resurrection.

He does not remember the facts of his own death so clearly; he remembers the pain, not of the injury that eventually killed him but of his father's bitter rage, his father's fear, his father's ugly disappointment. He had believed, although his father was a stern, harsh man, that he loved him. Love. It's a silly, thin word, and it has caused endless pain. Eric knows there is joy to be found in it—but he knows there's joy to be found in narcotics as well, and he's been around long enough to see the price both demand.

He remembers the dislocation of seeing his own corpse.

He remembers the first—and only—time he referred to his body that way in Reyna's hearing. The madness of her grief, her rage, her *pain* . . . it comes to him as if it were yesterday. The dead don't experience time the same way the living do. But they experience its passage nonetheless.

She ran to Scoros.

Scoros came to him. Scoros, twenty years older than Reyna, himself childless because of the witch hunts.

She is grieving, the old man said. Eric remembers his eyes: brown, lined with wind and sun and echoes of a similar grief. *Please, Eric. Give her time.*

What choice do I have? The words were bitter. He feels them as if they are solid, textured, as if they've remained in his mouth all these centuries. He sees Scoros flinch. Scoros, who is long gone.

You don't know what it's like to lose family, the old man said, his face inexplicably gentle, his hands so warm as they rest, briefly, against Eric's cheeks—as if Eric is a child, not a man.

I do. My father killed me. He had help, he adds. And even saying this, he knows that had his father not come to Reyna's home, had Reyna's family not been murdered there, she would be free. They would all be free.

Wait, Eric. I have no right to ask that of you. It is not what I was trained to do—but wait. She loved you, and when the madness of grief and fear abates, she will remember it.

And me? Eric asked. He did not say the rest. He had no need. Scoros understood the question. *Will I remember that I loved her? Will I remember it when her madness abates?*

Scoros said, *It is easy to judge. It is easy for all of us. We judge the hunters. We judge the villagers. We judge each other. It is up to you. I cannot keep you here.* Scoros' voice was gentle, then. He was gentle with Reyna and with the young. He was careful and respectful of the dead.

Scoros left the decision in Eric's hand, and Eric—whose arms could not enfold his shattered girl—made the only choice he felt he could.

He remained with Reyna. He remembers her face, reddened with tears, her eyes, the same; he remembers the damp streaks left through the dust on her cheeks. She did not wear a crown then. Did not wear this dress.

He cannot remember her smile. It is buried beneath too many other memories. It is buried—as deeply as he can possibly bury it—beneath the weight of the lives she has taken and the distant, dawning realization that Reyna will never feel safe. No matter how strong her fortress, how high her towers, no matter how much power she gathers, safety will always elude her.

And because it does, the dead remain, chained to their Queen and growing in number.

He knows that he has one duty, today. Only one. To distract the Queen of the Dead long enough for Emma and her friends to infiltrate the citadel. Helmi does not speak, but it isn't necessary; Eric knows who, among the many dead, Emma Hall must find.

He is not at all certain she will succeed because he is not certain he can hold the Queen's attention for long enough. He tries to smile. He fails. In this almost unimaginable perfection, he sees nothing of the girl he once thought he loved. He was young then. So was she. Life had not yet become clear enough, real enough, to interrupt the force of their feelings. They saw each other and only each other.

But they are neither of them young anymore.

Had he not been graced with a second body for centuries, the touch of the crown would destroy all thought, all concentration. But Eric is accustomed to screaming. He glances at the Queen and sees that she wears a crown that is twin to his; different in details, but not in size, in weight.

She means to honor him.

It is hard. It is the hardest thing he has ever done. Dying was easy, in comparison, and he would do it again in an instant if it meant he would be free.

He lowers his chin, draws his shoulders back, remembers distant, ancient manners. He remembers the weddings of his childhood—noisy, bawdy affairs so far removed from this solemn coronation he cannot think of it as a wedding at all. But he offers Reyna his hand, as he once offered it.

Her eyes widen. It is the first expression he has seen on her face that stirs memory. She hesitates. Her lips part slightly, their corners in motion.

For one long moment, he thinks he has done the right thing, and then her eyes narrow, like windows slamming shut in slow motion. There is a ring on his hand. It is not, of course, a ring that she gave him.

There is no explanation that will suffice if she demands one, but she doesn't. And that, somehow, is worse.

CHAPTER
ELEVEN

T HIS CITY, THIS CITADEL, was a prison.
    Emma wasn't certain if the Queen was the warden
or an inmate, and that was an odd thought. Ernest and
Chase were as silent and tense as Margaret; Michael's silence was different. He was afraid, but he wasn't terrified.
He walked beside Chase, scanning the walls, the floors, the
ceiling. In some ways, this wasn't new to him. Michael was
used to seeing things in a way that other people didn't.
Sometimes he could explain the difference, and sometimes
he couldn't.

Today there was no need for explanation.

Petal had been left behind in the safe rooms. He wasn't
happy about it, but he was skittish and on edge. If Helmi was
right, the citadel would be emptying, but the ceilings seemed
to echo even the smallest sound. A rottweiler at full bark
was not small. Chase had asked Allison to stay with the dog.
He pointed out—courageously, Emma felt—that she had
neither Emma's power nor Michael's unusual vision, she

couldn't fight, and Petal was comfortable with her. Allison refused. No one had asked Amy to remain behind.

The halls widened; the walls rose; the ceiling once again suggested light and air above the heights of those walls. The residences, historically sized and situated or not, fell away. These halls were the domain of the Queen of the Dead. Not for the Queen small closets and stone cages. No. The Queen's halls were colorful, if sparsely decorated; everything suggested majesty.

"Margaret?"

"Beyond this point, you must exercise caution."

Emma didn't ask how.

"The doors at the end of the hall—the large ones—lead to the Queen's suite."

"You've been in those rooms?"

"Twice. No one who did not aspire to replace the Queen had any desire—ever—to see what lay beyond those doors." She hesitated. "The rest of the citadel has been astonishingly empty, which was expected. I am not nearly so certain that the Queen's suite will be likewise stripped."

"You don't want to enter."

"No, dear. I don't. But if I understand anything that's happened today, what we seek will be somewhere in those rooms."

To Emma's surprise, the doors were actually locked, and the lock was mechanical. They were, Emma thought, real doors. They were wooden, and they were not in the pristine, likenew condition of every other door, rug, or stone the rest of the intimidating halls boasted.

Chase knelt, lockpicks in hand, and they huddled around him, looking down the hall and holding their breath. The hall remained empty.

Emma didn't hear the click that meant the doors were no longer locked; she heard the creak of hinges as Chase pushed one open. It wasn't a particularly quiet creak. Fear magnified it.

"Welcome," Chase said, "to the home of the Queen of the Dead." As they stared through the open door, he frowned. "Get in. Quickly."

Ernest and Margaret had already crossed over the doorjamb. Everyone else followed. Emma almost told Chase to leave the door open. She saw and sensed none of the dead; the halls were no colder than any other hall had been. There was no reason to leave the door open and plenty of reasons to close it. Chase, being sensible, closed it.

The halls behind these normal doors looked very much like the halls on the other side of it. They were grand, glorious, and almost sterile. Emma wasn't certain what she'd expected. She knew the Queen had made these rooms in the same way she'd made the citadel. Everything came from her.

All the same, she'd hoped for something different. She wasn't certain why. "Margaret? What are we looking for? Do you even know?"

Margaret nodded. She had drifted toward Ernest and stayed by his side, as if unconsciously seeking either protection or comfort. Emma shook her head. This was *Margaret*. Margaret Henney. She wasn't the type to seek either.

"Can you lead us there?" Emma asked softly.

"Can you lead us there today?" Amy demanded. Her arms were folded; she was no happier to be here than Margaret.

Margaret began to walk, the motion of legs and feet unnecessary but deliberate. "At the end of this hall is another suite of rooms. They are living quarters. When the Queen sleeps, it is there. Two rooms, meant to entertain more intimate friends, are behind those doors as well. I am not certain they are ever used.

"Down the hall to the right—and it is not a short hall— there is a library. I am not certain that the library has ever been used. The Necromancers knew of it; they knew that it contained books or journals that were not available anywhere else in the citadel. They assumed that the Queen's power resided in the knowledge therein."

"You didn't."

"The Queen learned to read late in life. Reading was neither required nor taught in her childhood. It was neither required nor taught when she began to gather her people. Most didn't read. The early Necromancers didn't either. It was only later that it became essential, as school and schooling spread. You all read, I assume."

Emma nodded.

"I'm not certain the Queen ever derived comfort—or knowledge—from the written word."

"Do you think we're looking for something in the library, if we're looking for forbidden knowledge?"

"No."

"What's down the left hall?"

"The resurrection room."

Nathan had been here.

Nathan had walked these halls.

Nathan had—if Helmi hadn't lied—been given a body.

Emma closed her eyes and inhaled the cool air. She opened her eyes. Everyone was watching her; no one had moved. She wanted to tell them that she wasn't leader material; Amy filled, and had always filled, that role, although sometimes the Emery mafia referred to her as the dictator. But even Amy was waiting on Emma. She wasn't waiting *patiently*, but no friend of Amy's expected patience.

Yet the expectation, the waiting, was a kind of support. Emma knew where they had to go. Margaret's expression, Margaret's tense silence, Margaret's almost obvious dread would have made that clear in any circumstance.

No one spoke as they approached the doors.

When Emma reached them, they rolled open.

REYNA

THE SKY IS CLEAR.

This is the day Reyna has dreamed of for so long now she only barely remembers the first time she made the wish. She can't remember the details; she is certain that details existed, in the long-ago village in which her life almost ended.

What did she dream of, then?

She frowns. Eric's arm is beneath her hand; it is stiff and cold. He walks by her side, but he stares straight ahead. He is wearing a ring on his hand. He is wearing a ring that she *did not give him*. Today, of all days. She wants to tell him to take it off. She wants him to understand how painful it is to see it there. She has crowned him. She has opened the heart of her citadel to him—as she always intended. He has never really *listened* to her. He has never understood what she was trying to build.

Oh, in the past he had questions.

She answered them. For some reason he refused to

accept those answers, twisting them into ugly things instead. He has always been better with words than Reyna.

Her hand tightens as they approached the gates. She remembers the stream and the tree against which she used to lean. She remembers the warmth of the sunlight; the shadows warm in a different way. She remembers, then, that her mother was alive. Her sister. She wanted to marry Eric.

She wanted to live in that village.

It was a small village. It was small, primitive, and ultimately savage.

What she has built for Eric—for the two of them—is so much better. There is knowledge here. There is *safety* here. They could love each other without fear of censure. Without fear of death.

But . . . for some inexplicable reason, she misses the trees.

She almost stumbles and casts a glare over her shoulder—but her train, her skirts, are perfectly placed. The stones beneath her feet are flat and smooth; there are no roots, no pebbles, nothing on which to trip.

This is not the dress she would have worn had she married Eric when her family was still alive. This is not the day she would have had. It's *better*. Surely it's better? This is something that Reyna has built for herself, with her own power.

But she remembers Eric's smile. Or perhaps the way his smile made her feel. She hasn't felt that way about anything in a long time. Not since Eric. Not since those days in the village when she fell in love and was loved.

She remembers sneaking out of her room when it was only barely dawn. She remembers the excitement, the giddiness, and the fear of her mother's anger, should she be caught. She remembers running all the way to the tree—but stopping a hundred yards away, because she didn't want to look pathetic to Eric.

But Eric was always there first. She would try to approach quietly, so as not to disturb him. She liked to look at his face, his expression, the half-closed eyes with their fan of lashes. He never seemed to be looking *at* something; he was alone with his thoughts. She liked that expression, but she loved best when he lifted his chin to look at her. No matter how quietly she walked, no matter which direction she approached him from, she could never surprise him.

She remembers the first time he held her hand.

The first time he hugged her.

The first time he kissed her.

So many firsts, to lead to this one. She almost lost him. Her most vivid memory of Eric—no matter how hard she tries to displace it—is his prone, bleeding body, his eyelids fluttering convulsively, blood spilling, without warning, from his mouth. He had no words for her. He had no words for anyone.

She had spent all her life interacting with the dead. She had cleaned and tended corpses in some villages. She had never, until that moment, come face to face with *death*. The dead, yes. She understood how they died; she understood why they were trapped, clinging to an isolated semblance of the lives they'd lived. But she had not *seen* them die. She had not experienced death itself.

Without thought, she shifts the position of her hand on Eric's arm. Instead, she reaches for his hand; it is so cold and so stiff when she touches it—

But he *wasn't* cold and stiff that day. She stumbles again, but this time when she does, Eric's hand tightens, his arm tightens, he offers Reyna support. It is silent. She wants to be grateful.

But he does not look at her. He doesn't meet her eyes. She has waited so long for the moment when he lifts his chin and meets her eyes and smiles. At this moment, on the day she dreamed of, almost everything is perfect.

But there are no trees. And Eric does not smile.

CHAPTER
TWELVE

THE FIRST THING EMMA NOTICED when she opened the doors was the shape of the resurrection room. It was circular. It appeared to be open to the sky, given the quality of the light, but there was a dome above them. Windows in the shape of petals let in the startling clarity of blue sky. The ladders used to reach Andrew Copis wouldn't have helped them reach the sky here—the ceiling was that far away.

Emma's gaze fell from the impossible heights to the ground.

In the center of the room, in the heart of it, carved into the largest single slab of stone Emma had ever seen, was a circle composed of symbols. It reminded Emma of the gold thread on the faded and worn carpet in the hidden rooms. She wished, for a moment, she'd thought to bring that carpet with her.

"I think—I think this is like the carpet. I think this is a circle."

"It is," a familiar voice said. The old woman she'd found

at the center of that carpet stood to Emma's left. Emma glanced at her face; it was puckered in something too intense to be a frown. "It is the Queen's circle."

"You were alive when she carved it?"

"No. No, by then I was dead. Tell me, Emma Hall, do you see anything unusual about this circle?"

Its existence, for one. Emma kept the words behind closed lips as she stared at the runes. She'd seen their like only once. They didn't look familiar. But where gold, in the hidden room, had glittered and caught light the way metal does, these runes were different: they had a light of their own.

It was a dull, glowing colorless light that she wanted to call gray. Even as she thought it, she froze, because if the shape of the runes wasn't familiar, the light they shed *was*. It was the color of the eyes of the dead.

"Margaret—can you see—"

"I see the circle," Margaret said. Emma glanced back at her; she stood beside Ernest—and Michael—against the far wall.

"Do you see anything unusual about it?"

The older woman, however, was the one who answered. "The dead are there. And you know it, girl. You can see them." Her tone was ice, but beneath that chill, there was fire; Emma could feel the heat of it, the pain of it.

"The circles," Emma said, her mouth too dry, "were meant to protect the living?"

"They were meant to allow the living to safely find the lost." Her tone implied that Emma should know this, because she'd already been told it once.

"But it's—"

"Yes, girl. Like everything else in the citadel, it's made of the dead." The woman's voice was lower, harsher.

Emma reached out with one shaking hand. She touched the nearest rune as if she expected it to burn. It didn't. She exhaled the breath she was holding. It felt like stone. But the floors in the empty townhouse had felt like floors until she had really touched them. Until she'd reached out and tried to pull them apart.

"Yes," the old woman said. "You could unmake this circle. You could unmake the citadel in exactly the same way, if you survived long enough to do it. And you won't—but it's possible. Say you succeed. How well can you fly?"

No one spoke. Michael stayed by the wall. But while everyone else was looking at the circle by which Emma crouched, Michael was staring ahead, a familiar frown puckering his forehead and narrowing his lips.

Emma rose. *We didn't come here to see this circle*, she told herself. She wasn't certain if this was cowardice. She didn't want to see a floor composed of clutching, frantic arms. She turned to Margaret, who was standing as far from the circle as the wall allowed. Margaret, prim, decisive, and unflinching, looked . . . afraid.

Fear made her look younger. And far more fragile.

Emma didn't want fragile, here. She had enough of her own to deal with. But fragile was better than broken. They'd come to the Queen's resurrection room for a reason. "Margaret."

Margaret met her eyes and nodded, staring just past Emma's shoulder at something that wasn't there. Or wasn't there *now*. "I see . . . nothing . . . out of the ordinary." The unspoken *for the Queen of the Dead* underscored her quiet words.

That was not what Emma wanted to hear, but Margaret wasn't the only person in the room who was focused on something she couldn't see. She turned. "Michael?"

He nodded; he didn't look at her. He appeared to be looking at a section of wall nestled between two ornate, standing shelves.

"What are you looking at? I can only see wall."

"A statue," he said, his voice very quiet. It was the wrong kind of quiet. He was stiff with tension, with concentration, and with apprehension. Apprehension was normal for Michael; it happened when he ran into something that made no sense to him.

"I don't think anyone else can see it." From Michael's expression, this was a comfort to everyone else. But it left Michael stranded. "It—I think it's supposed to be a man. A dead man."

She didn't want to ask him how he knew this. She didn't want to ask him anything else. She almost stepped in front of him to block his view, but he was taller than she was. He hadn't always been. And he wasn't a child. What he needed from her—what he'd probably always needed—was consistency and honesty.

And maybe, just maybe, working to give him what he'd needed had helped shape who Emma Hall had become. She didn't ask him to describe what he saw; given his expression, she wasn't certain she wanted to hear it.

"Margaret?"

"I see what you see," was the quiet response.

"I see a wall."

Margaret nodded. "The room is called the resurrection room. I was not here to be resurrected. I was not alone," she added. "Longland was here."

Ernest tried to put an arm around Margaret's shoulder. It passed through her without gaining any purchase, and Emma saw his expression shift, a brief, sharp bite of pain and regret, before he once again looked like a grim, older hunter.

Movement caught her attention; Allison's. She stepped into the narrow space between Emma and Michael, and reaching out, placed both of her hands beneath his, pulling them up.

And Michael said, "I don't think it's a statue."

"It's all right, Michael," Ally said. "We're here to help the dead."

"Not if you can't see them."

The old woman said, "It is something she would have done. She would not be abandoned by anyone else she loved." She exhaled ice; Emma could hear the air crackle around the single word that followed. "Scoros."

Emma approached the wall and touched it gingerly at first; what she felt mirrored what she could see: flat but gently curved stone. She grimaced; what she hadn't done to the circle, she now attempted to do here.

She listened for the voices of the dead.

The only one she heard was the old woman's; it was sharp and angry, but very thin. "What are you doing, girl?"

"If I'm right, I'm *trying* to reach what remains of your son." She regretted the words as soon as they left her mouth;

they were harsh, unkind, a funnel for her own anxiety and fear, her own resentment. No matter how much she disliked the woman, no parent deserved to hear that.

And regardless, Emma couldn't find him. She could touch only the wall.

She rose and turned back to her friends, shaking her head.

"Don't even think it," Amy said, before Emma could speak. "We're not leaving."

"I don't know what I'm doing. I don't know how long it will take."

Amy snorted. "Does it matter? If you're still here when the Queen comes back, we're all dead. The only hope we have of getting out of here alive is you."

Allison was trying not to glare at Amy. She was wise enough to leave it at that. But Emma was aware that everyone was watching her. Margaret knew about modern Necromancy; she didn't know anything about the older stuff.

But the old woman who had tried to kill Amy did. And Emma felt certain that there was only one way to reach the trapped man—the statue that Michael could see. She was aware that they were running out of the time Eric had borrowed for them. She was aware that learning something new took time.

And she was certain that she could not reach that statue in any other way.

Is it necessary? she asked; the room was cold and she had started to shiver. But the man trapped here had created the safe rooms *within* the citadel the Queen had built, and those rooms had not been found, until Michael. This man, this former Necromancer, understood the citadel and its construction in a way Emma never would—and if he had planned to finally kill his Queen, Emma guessed he'd left the metaphorical equivalent of parachutes *somewhere*.

She did not want to leave the dead trapped here.

She did not want her friends to die. Or herself, either, if it came to that.

"Tell me," Emma said, turning to the old woman with her narrowed eyes and pinched lips, "how to use the circle." Speaking, she began to walk away from Michael's theoretical statue, toward the engraved runes that formed the circle's circumference.

"It is not your circle," the old woman said. She had managed to tear her gaze away from the blank wall, but it kept returning.

"No, it's not. But it's *a* circle, and it's the only one we have. Tell me how to use it."

"You—" The woman clearly wanted to sneer, but she kept it out of her words. But she stopped speaking. Maybe she wouldn't start. Maybe she'd offer no advice, no guidance.

Emma was willing to take that risk. What else was there she could do?

She walked toward the heart of the room and hesitated only once, her toes an inch from the engraved circumference. This wasn't her circle. If what she'd been told was true, each Necromancer—or whatever they'd been called before the Queen of the Dead—drew their own.

And if what hadn't been put into words was also true, a circle had been the beginning of the Queen's power. If the circle was unnecessary, it wouldn't be here. It was the centerpiece of the resurrection room. It was much larger than the circle in which the old woman's ghost had been hidden, which meant that size didn't matter.

This was the heart of the Queen's power, made grand— like the rest of the citadel—and ostentatious.

Emma was not the Queen of the Dead. Nor did she ever wish to be that. And that was the reason she'd hesitated on the edge of the circle: because she felt that entering it was to don—for however short a time, and for whatever reason—the Queen's crown.

She looked back at her friends, inhaled, and squared her shoulders. She took a step, crossed the line, and continued, aware that it had started this way for that long-ago sixteen-year-old girl: the need to protect and preserve what she could of the world she'd loved in the face of certain death.

Nothing happened when she came to stand in the center of the circle. Looking out, she could see her friends. She could see the curving walls of the resurrection room, and the shelves and small tables that huddled awkwardly against it. She could see the edge of the circle.

"Do I look any different?" she asked.

216 ～ Michelle Sagara

Ally shook her head. Michael said, "No."

Amy said, "Do you feel any different?"

She didn't. She hesitated for another moment and then sat, crossing her legs rather than folding them. She took a deep breath, held it, and let it go; she did this three times. Nothing changed. The air was cold, the silence oppressive.

On the fourth inhale, Emma closed her eyes.

From the heart of the circle, Emma could see the walls, the shelves, and two tables. She could see the engravings around the circumference of the circle in which she sat. She could see the floor. She could, eyes shut tight, see her crossed legs, her boots, her clothing. She could see her hands. She could no longer hear her friends.

What she hadn't expected was the sidewalk. Actually, that was probably the wrong word. It was a path, it appeared to be made of stone, and it wasn't wide enough to be called a road. It led to one of the walls.

It led, she thought, to the section of wall that Michael had called a statue. But even ensconced in the heart of this circle, Emma couldn't see what Michael had seen.

Not yet, she told herself.

"Very good, Emma Hall."

She almost opened her eyes again at the sound of the familiar voice, which would have been pointless. She could *see* the magar while her eyes were closed. She could see the woman who had given birth to both Helmi and the Queen of the Dead.

"I don't know where you learned to draw a circle, but you are sitting in one now."

"I didn't draw it," Emma replied. "It was already here."

"Here?"

"In this room."

"Ah. I am not where you are. I am not in a room."

"Where are you?"

The magar's smile was lined and harsh. "Where the dead are. If you have not been taught the rudiments, you will not be able to make use of the circle."

"Can you teach me what I need to know in five minutes or less?"

This predictably caused annoyance in the magar. "I could teach you what you need to know in a decade. And yes, I know you don't have a decade—not yet. Most of my pupils started far younger than you are now; they understood their roles and their abilities as they grew into them.

"You have done the inverse; it cannot be changed. Come." The woman drifted toward where Emma sat. She wore age far less heavily than she had on the first occasion Emma had seen her. When she reached the edge of the circle, she stopped and bent over the runes, as if she could not pass above or through them.

She held out her right hand. "Do not move anything but your arm—not yet."

Emma lifted her left hand and bent to place it in the old woman's.

"Now, pay attention. I will help you to stand. No, I did not *tell you* to stand. I said I would help."

"I don't really need help standing."

"You do. I have never interfered in this fashion with any of my own—it is risky, and if it's required, it means the pupil has *not* been well taught. My daughter could do this on the day she turned sixteen."

"I have no ambition to ever become like your daughter."

"No," the magar replied, with a bitter, bitter smile, which made Emma feel as if a bucket of ugly guilt had just been thrown in her face.

Emma's grip on the old woman's hand tightened. To her surprise—and confusion—Emma didn't feel the usual, instantaneous ice that came from physical contact with the dead. She *did* feel the old woman's hand; it was wide, warm, and obviously far more callused than Emma's hands had ever been.

"I bore five children," the magar said, which came almost out of nowhere. "Three died before they reached the age of five. Two survived."

"That must have been hard," Emma replied, Hall manners kicking in automatically. She couldn't see why the magar's comment was relevant.

"Hard? Yes. But children, then and now, are born weak and helpless, and mine did not have the advantages that you, as infants, had. Death was no stranger to me. Even had

I not been magar, it would have been no stranger. It was no stranger to any of the villagers."

"The ones who killed you."

"Even so. They had no reason to fear us," she added, as if it were necessary. "But they feared. Fear is a very, very poor ruler—and its rule spans empires."

"You don't hate them for what they did."

"Why? Hate would change nothing. I wept when my children died. I wept when we buried them—and we did not bury them side by side. I knew that I *could* see them again, because I am magar. But I knew where they must go. I did not hope for them the torment and isolation of the trapped and the lost—and if they remained, that is all they would have had. I am grateful that they died when they did."

Emma was silent for one long beat. "Because they're not trapped?"

The magar nodded. "They are quit of the world. They went where the dead go and the living cannot. Helmi, my baby, has never had that peace; she understands that it waits and that she will never reach it. Not while her sister lives."

"Neither will you."

"No. But I carried the lantern for centuries, and its light kept me warm. It kept me safe."

"But—but you don't have it, now."

"No, Emma, I don't. You have it."

"Should I use it?"

"If you use it here, the Queen will know. She is living the moment of her greatest triumph; she is approaching the pinnacle of her dreams. But she has lived without that achievement for all of her existence; if she feels or sees the lantern, she will return. Are you ready to face my daughter now? No?" As she spoke, she helped Emma to her feet.

Emma stood.

Emma stood, turned, and saw herself seated, cross-legged, in the circle.

"You don't look surprised."

"I am, a little—but it's not the first time I've left my body. It's not because of the circle, is it?"

"No."

"It's you."

"Yes and no. It is your will, in the end."

Emma understood, then, why the containment circle allowed the magar and her kin to find the dead; they weren't constrained by what they could physically see and touch. What she hadn't understood until now was that she was almost effectively dead, which is why the magar's hand didn't hurt her. She frowned. "The dead pass through each other."

The magar nodded.

"How can you hold my hand?"

"Because you, Emma Hall, are not dead." The magar's lips thinned. "You are thinking of your boy."

She was. She was thinking that if she could find Nathan, she could touch him. He could touch her. They could hold each other and offer each other comfort in this world gone crazy. She was thinking of love, of what it meant, of why it meant different things to different people. She was thinking of the Queen of the Dead and Eric.

It was *easy* to think that she would never make the choices the Queen had made. But in truth, she wasn't certain. If she had *one chance* to save Nathan's life, one chance to save her own, would she truly have made a different choice?

The Queen hadn't saved Eric's life. If she *had*, if she *could*, things would have been different.

Nathan, she thought. *Wouldn't you have* wanted *to stay?*

The magar waited until Emma lifted her chin.

"Is there anything else you need to teach me?"

"For now, no. What I helped you to do, you should be able to do on your own. You did it once—foolishly, stupidly—without the grounding circle. You survived. Many, in our dim and distant history, did not. Do not leave your body if you are not confined; it is too easy to lose your way."

She inhaled—it was habit—and turned to face the wall. It was still all wall to her; leaving her body had not given her Michael's immunity to Necromantic illusion, if that was what it was.

"Can you see the statue?" Emma asked the magar.

Silence.

Emma turned; the old woman was gone. So much for help. No, she thought, that was unfair. The magar was at risk in this citadel. Mother or no, she was dead, and the Queen ruled the dead.

Emma listened. She couldn't close her eyes; her eyes weren't doing the seeing. She had hoped—somehow—that the circle would be her key to finding the door. And maybe it was; she just hadn't found the lock it fit. *Think, Emma.*

The only difference in the room now was the narrow path. It started at the edge of the engraved circle and led toward the wall. Emma thought that it led *past* it, but the wall obscured its final destination—if it had one.

She wanted—for one brief minute—to confer with Ally and Michael. Instead, she made a decision. She stepped onto the path and stood at the edge of the circle, listening. Silence. Either her friends weren't speaking at all or she had walked to a space that words and voices—living voices— couldn't reach. It wasn't a happy thought, and she glanced back at her body. She was still there.

And still here.

She began to follow the path.

The path did pass beneath the wall. Emma came to a halt in front of the curved stone surface, lifting a hand to touch it. And that was a mistake. The wall was not, as it looked, cool stone. It was warm. It was as warm as the magar's hand had been and as solid.

You already knew this, she told herself; her hand shook. The dead were here. If they took the form—unwillingly—of wall or floor or table, they were nonetheless *people*, far more trapped now than they had been in life.

She listened. After a brief pause, she spoke. "Hello?"

CHAPTER
THIRTEEN

SILENCE. The silence of held breath. Hers, of course. The dead didn't need to breathe.

She lowered her hands. The man trapped here—if the old woman was right—was only one of thousands. Or tens of thousands. He had stood beside the Queen. He had been a Necromancer in life.

Emma grimaced. Margaret had been one as well. If not for Eric and Chase, Emma would be a novice, imprisoned in a room that was, for all intents and purposes, a cell, trapped in a life that was designed and ruled over by the Queen of the Dead. Choice would be limited.

She wasn't here to judge. She was here to free the dead.

She was here to free Nathan.

She closed her eyes, which changed nothing. What she could see, now, had nothing to do with actual eyes. She couldn't free a man if she couldn't *see* him. Margaret, she had seen. The dead who had served as portable power generators for the Necromancers who had come to kill Eric and Chase, she had seen.

But . . . Andrew Copis she hadn't seen. She'd heard him. She'd heard him first. No, that wasn't right. She hadn't heard Andrew. She'd heard his mother shouting his name while a building burned, generating the smoke that would kill her young son.

She'd heard what *Andrew* heard. She'd walked into the fire that *Andrew* saw. He couldn't see anything other than the fire that had killed him. A four-year-old who had died in a terrible fire, he'd been jailed by his own fear and pain, trapped in the hour of his death.

Margaret wouldn't be here if the Queen of the Dead didn't exist. She would be wherever it was the dead were meant to go. Andrew would not.

He was gone now—but in truth, she *hadn't* freed him. He'd freed himself. She'd brought his living mother through fire and death and guilt. She'd provided a window through which he could see beyond flames and betrayal and abandonment.

The dead who were trapped by the Necromancers were trapped in an entirely different way. Chained, bound, taken out of their own lives, they were linked to the Necromancers who held their power.

She could break those chains.

She had.

But she hadn't seen them in time to save Nathan. She hadn't realized the truth.

In the other cases, she'd gone to the dead because she could see them. She could find the binding chains, grasp them, and yank them free. Those chains remained with Emma. She accepted that; Margaret didn't seem to mind so much.

But . . . she'd seen Margaret first.

She understood—barely—what the circle was meant to accomplish. Understanding the how was beyond her. And she had a queasy feeling that it was the *how* that would define everything that happened in this city of the dead.

How had she found Andrew Copis? How had she found Mark?

She'd heard them. She'd heard Andrew from halfway across the city, in a crowded classroom. The man she needed to free didn't have to be *here* to be found. But to be found, he had to be heard.

* * *

She almost asked him where he was, but she didn't. Nor did she ask the magar. She stood on the path that ended in wall, knelt, and examined the narrow, placed stones that seemed to continue beyond the wall itself.

Bowing her head, she listened.

She heard, first, the muted whispers that filled the room and realized that they were always present in the background — just as traffic noises were always present in Toronto. It was a terrible thought; in Toronto, cars were not sentient, and their owners were not trapped in walls or floors or furniture for eternity.

But those voices were not the voices she needed. If she survived, they would be. She swore they would be.

She rose, listening. Eyes closed, she retraced the path to the circle and watched herself, looking in. She was surprised by what she saw: Emma Hall, at rest. She felt separate from herself, enough so that she thought she looked young. Young, isolated, immobile. It wasn't a pleasant thought.

She opened her eyes — her real eyes.

She could see Michael, Amy, Allison. She could see Chase Loern, Ernest. Petal was in the hidden room, and she was both glad that he was safe, and afraid for him. But if he were here, the engraved circle wouldn't be much of a barrier for him; he'd lope across and dump his head in her lap and whine. He wanted to be home.

She wanted it as well. And there was only one way to get there.

She closed her eyes again. She listened.

Cemeteries were places the living gathered. It wasn't that people didn't feel grief anywhere else, as Emma well knew. Grief was sharp and unexpected; it could ambush her in the brightest and loudest of places. But in a graveyard, grief was expected, natural. It troubled no one else. It made no awkward pauses, no lurch in conversation. If there were tears, she could cry them.

Sometimes the tears were absent. Sometimes she felt anger instead — and guilt, because Nathan didn't deserve her anger. He hadn't committed suicide. He hadn't chosen to die. He'd intended to drive to her house to pick her up. To spend the afternoon with her.

The afternoon would never come. He was trapped in death—and she was trapped in *his* death, as well, because he'd been at the heart of her life. She was lucky. He hadn't been murdered. His death hadn't been an act of malice.

Lucky? She grimaced. She was lucky because his death had been an accident?

Her anger had no focus. On most days, she didn't want to find the boys responsible for his death. She didn't want to make them *pay*. Had they killed him on purpose, she would have. And she was a Hall. She wouldn't have *acted* on it, but the anger, the drive, would have been there.

Instead, she spent evenings in the cemetery with her dog. She could hear the familiar sounds of traffic, the occasional sounds of impatient drivers, the movement of leaves and long, weeping-willow branches. There were no people; she was almost in a world of her own.

The queen's city was a cemetery.

The walls, the floors, the vast windows, even the furniture—they were graves. But the living didn't come here for comfort. Not even the Queen. Perhaps especially not the Queen.

Emma wanted to speak to her father. Not Margaret, not the magar, the intimidating old woman who had started this journey. Not even Nathan. She wanted her father, because her father would know how to fix things. He always had.

And her father was in Toronto, in a hospital, watching Toby Simner's life bleed out.

She shook her head. Her father had been dead for half her life. He couldn't tell her how to fix things. He hadn't been able to fix things for her since she'd been just shy of nine. He hadn't been able to either hold her or offer her comfort.

She heard crying. For a moment, she thought it was her own—but Halls didn't weep in public, and she was, contained in a circle or no, in public. But the tears resonated with the ones she refused to shed, and instead of denying them, she let them in.

REYNA

THE STREETS ARE FULL. The old mingle with the young; she glimpses children between the full skirts of young women and old alike. Men bow their heads as she walks past. As they should, she reminds herself: She is the Queen.

Did she build these streets? They seem so long now, so full. They looked smaller, somehow, when they were empty. She thinks she would like to see them full, always full; she thinks she would like to glance out of her windows or down from her grand balconies and be surrounded by faces like these.

She glances at Eric, her hand on his arm. She expects his expression to be neutral, hooded. He is, however, looking at the crowd. He smiles at one or two of the people who catch his eye. She can't tell who those people are.

She can't tell if they're dead or alive.

Eric shouldn't be able to see the dead.

As she walks beside him, hand on his arm—and his arm is warm, her hand, cold—she thinks, clearly, *he shouldn't be able to see the dead.* And she wants, suddenly, to empty the streets of the dead. Because then, Eric won't see anything that he shouldn't be able to see.

Eric is not like Reyna. He never was. He didn't live her life. He hasn't lived her life for centuries. He couldn't see the dead. He didn't really understand them. He understood death—anyone alive in those days did—but he couldn't see what death sometimes left stranded, left behind.

She doesn't want to ruin this day.

She doesn't want to ruin this moment.

But this is not the first time since the day she lost almost everything that Eric has been by her side. She knows what love is. She has always known what love is. She has *waited* and *waited* for this day.

He does not look at her with reproach. He doesn't look at her with anger or disdain. The first time she saw him again, she expected both. She was so relieved to find neither. So relieved and so happy. But relief made her giddy. He is beside her now, yes.

But if he doesn't look at her with hatred or anger, he doesn't look at her *at all.* Instead, he gazes at the sea of faces to either side of this road. He hasn't aged—of course he hasn't aged. Neither has she. And it is because of her power that this is true. Their life together as it should have been was interrupted. It was interrupted by hatred and fear and ugly, angry men. She had never done anything wrong. She had never hurt anyone.

She had loved—had meant to love—Eric.

Why did he not understand that? That's what she thinks, her hand on his arm, the streets of a city she built for him, for *them*, surrounding them both. Why did he not understand that she loved him?

Does he not understand that she loves him, even now?

Does Eric not love her?

CHAPTER
FOURTEEN

IT WAS A GIRL'S VOICE. A girl's tears, made nasal because that's what tears did.

Emma wasn't searching for a girl, but this voice was the
clearest sound in the room. It wasn't attenuated or distant.
It wasn't stretched, thin, almost impossible to catch. The girl
might have been in the room with her, even beside her.

She looked; the sobbing quieted. The room—the Queen's
room—was empty. Emma could see herself. Only herself.
She could see her hands, her legs, the clothing she'd worn in
their run from Necromancers. She could see the path that
led from the circle and ended in wall.

She couldn't see the girl—but the path itself was laid
down in the wrong direction. She hesitated, but the hesitation was brief. She turned away from the wall, from the
path, and even, in the end, from the circle and went in
search of the voice.

She wasn't certain what she expected to find, but she
hadn't been certain what she'd find when she followed the
terrified, broken screams contained in Andrew Copis'

memories, either. She only knew that the visible path was not for her; it wasn't the right way. There was no path in the direction of the voice.

But there'd been no path the first time, either. Oh, there'd been streets—but they'd been the wrong streets; she'd tried to make Eric drive through a house or two in her rush to reach what she'd heard so clearly. Eric wasn't driving. He wasn't here. The protective shell of his car was absent. If Emma wanted to reach her unknown destination, there was only one way to do it.

She walked. The geography of the room began to fade, the walls receding as she approached them. No, not receding exactly; they were still there, immutable edifices of the architecture of death. She could reach out to touch them if she concentrated. But as she listened to the sound of weeping—the sound of grief—they became remote . . . while somehow standing in place.

She inhaled. Her chest rose and fell, a reminder that she was—for the moment—alive. Unlike the dead, she could leave this empty plane; the almost artistically sterile walls were not her prison or her resting place.

And if she encountered fire, it wouldn't kill her. In theory, nothing would. Only the living could now do that.

She was surprised to see trees form—trees, tall grass, the sporadic shapes of flowering weeds. She heard—although she couldn't see—birds; she heard the bark of a distant dog and thought of Petal. There was no road beneath her feet, but as she looked, she saw flattened weeds that implied a rough, unplanned footpath.

She felt sun as she walked. She heard the effect of wind through this memory of living things, because that's what it was: memory. She wondered, as she walked, if her own death would leave this snapshot, hanging in what she now thought of as ether, if someone searching for the ghost of Emma Hall would hear—or see—the things important to her. Would they find Nathan, smiling or listening or speaking? Would they see the father whose face she remembered now as photographs?

She shook herself. Whatever they might find, it wouldn't be this. There were no obvious buildings, but as she walked, the sound of moving water—more of a trickle than a roar—laid itself over every other sound. To someone, this had been familiar.

She wondered then if the weeping she heard came from the person she sought. It was high, soft, and very, very nasal—but it was a girl's voice. It grew louder as she walked, pushing herself through high stalks of dry grass and almost feeling their slap against her arms and legs.

The weeds formed a type of wall, a corner, but they opened up as she reached the bank of a river. No, not a river—a stream, a brook, something winding and narrow. The brook itself seem dominated by rocks of various sizes, but the water was clear.

And like the plants, the earth beneath her feet, the shade of a sky that seemed cloudless, it was gray. The world was, unoriginally she felt, black and white. So, to her own eyes, was she.

She saw the girl. On her knees, legs curled beneath the bulk of her body, arms wrapped around her as if they were the only thing supporting her weight, she had folded into a shape, a closed, furled tenseness, that Emma would ever after think of as the *shape* of grief.

And it cut her, because she knew it so well. There was no stream, no forest, no wilderness, in which she might have hidden her pain. Only the graveyard, and even there she had not wept. Not for Nathan. Not for her father. She stumbled, righted herself, and stopped moving.

Grief was, had always been, personal. Tears—the tears the Halls did not shed in public—had, in some ways, been more personal than sex. Done right, sex was joy and life, something that grief could never hope to achieve. No—grief was a black hole. If you were caught on the edge of its event horizon, you might never escape.

And she knew then who this girl was. She could armor herself against pity because pity was something she didn't want, and had never wanted, for herself. But crossing the boundary of privacy that grief demanded was much, much harder. She knew how she would have felt had someone—a total stranger—intruded in a moment like this. She did not want to do that to anyone else.

Not even the Queen of the Dead.

Perhaps especially not the Queen. *We want monsters*, she thought, frozen a moment by empathy and the bone-deep consideration that had been instilled in her by watching her parents over the years. *We want monsters because it means we're* not *them*.

Mark's mother had inadvertently killed Mark.

And in the end, in the face of her pain and her guilt, Emma Hall had taken her dead son home, and had left him there. It was what Mark wanted, and she could not, the moment she had seen his mother's face, do anything else.

But Mark's mother was not the Queen of the Dead. The Queen of the Dead *was* a monster. She had murdered Chase Loern's family. She had created the Necromancers, who were perfectly willing to threaten an infant with death. Emma had no doubt that they would have killed the child. No doubt that they would have murdered Allison. Or Amy or Michael.

All of it could be laid at the feet of this girl—if her feet could be found; they were invisible beneath her.

People do monstrous things. People, not monsters. Her father's words. Her father, who remained by Toby's bedside, unseen by the living, waiting to carry word to Emma.

She forced herself to walk; she approached the stream. Water splashed up her boots, dampening her legs. She cast a shadow in the fall of sunlight, and that shadow touched the weeping girl, who did not move. She didn't seem to notice Emma's presence at all.

And Emma couldn't see her face. She could see the crown of her head, her shaking body; she could hear her voice. And she thought she would never forget it; the sound stabbed her, tore at her, almost demanded that she, too, weep.

Her body responded. Her eyes. She felt tears gather, until vision was blurry. She couldn't force them to stop, and in the end, they rolled down her cheeks—and she let them.

She wasn't certain what she would have said or done—how did one interact with a memory, after all?—had the man not appeared.

She couldn't see him; she could see his shadow against the grass. Unlike Emma, the stream, or the weeping girl, he failed to cohere into something solid enough for her eyes to grasp, to interpret. She was certain of his presence because grass wavered as he passed through it.

He had moved through the same grass as Emma, and he had stood—as Emma had done—just behind the thinnest screen of remaining weeds, watching as Emma had watched, caught in the same turmoil: the desire to protect privacy, to protect boundaries, at war with the need to do something—anything—that might help and being uncertain what *would* help.

But he wasn't Emma Hall, a stranger who had every reason to hate and fear this pathetic, sobbing girl. He broke through the barrier nature had made for him.

Emma could hear his steps. She could *see* their impressions in the soft dirt of the dry bank. But she couldn't see *him*.

The girl on the banks could, although not immediately; it was hard to see anything with your forehead practically in your lap.

He put his arms around hers—around the clenched shoulders, around the hidden abdomen. This, too, Emma could see—in the line of the girl's clothing; in the way she tensed and redoubled her efforts to fold into invisibility. Her weeping did not cease; it redoubled, humiliation entering a tone that had, moments before, been pure loss. She struggled; he did not release her.

He didn't speak.

He held on.

He held her as if she were precious and fragile and her pain could somehow be enveloped; he held her as if, by holding her, he could vanquish all pain, all loss. He didn't ask permission; he didn't allow her to reject what he offered. He didn't make the offer of comfort contingent on her at all.

For one brief moment, Emma felt two things: anger.

And envy.

This human, tiny tableau went on and on; she was a mute witness to it. She had been uncertain upon sighting the weeping girl; she had hesitated. She was not uncertain now; now there was no place for Emma Hall. She almost left.

But the water of the stream in which she stood seemed to harden, becoming first ice and then something with even less give. She couldn't feel the cold; she could feel the insistence that she remain, that it was necessary *to* remain.

What she witnessed now had happened—if she understood anything—centuries ago. Nothing she could do could change it. But waiting couldn't change it, either. And any hope of survival lay in change.

Andrew Copis had been trapped by his memories; they had been the whole of his world. But he had trapped himself; nothing existed for Andrew except the fear, the desolate sense of betrayal, and the fire.

The man trapped here had not trapped himself. He had been trapped, bound, hidden. This had been his punishment. She was certain that it was *meant* to be his punishment.

But as the sobs finally quieted, Emma couldn't help but wonder how. This was, in the end, a memory in which he had taken a risk—she could feel the whole of the risk, still—and had been rewarded by success. He had offered a rough, complete comfort, and it had been accepted.

She needed to understand why. But understanding wouldn't come unless she could reach the man—and at the moment, she couldn't even see him; she could see only that he was present, somehow, and that he had had an effect.

"Emma's crying," Michael said.

Allison nodded. She looked with longing and dread at the circle that separated Emma from the rest of them.

"Don't," Margaret said, before she could take a step.

To Allison's surprise, Michael nodded. When she looked at him, the question transforming the shape of her eyes and her brows, Michael said, "Emma hates it when she cries." That was all.

Chase slid an arm around Allison's shoulder, and she leaned into him without thinking; the room was cold. Everything in the citadel was.

The landscape dissolved slowly; the crystal water around Emma's ankles dissolved as well. It was the last thing to go. Gone was the river, the bank, the black and white form of a huddled, weeping girl. Gone, too, the footprints, the disturbances caused by the man Emma could not see.

So, too, was the man. But the landscape did not reassert itself. She could not see the walls of the Queen's room. She could see the odd, translucent gray that reminded her so much of the eyes of the dead. She was standing in or on it. She listened.

It was harder now. She didn't know what to listen for or to. She could hear, as permanent background, the whispered pain of the dead—the dead who were trapped, as the man was trapped, by the machinations of their Queen.

She wondered, then, if the dead had ever heard the Queen cry.

The urge to reach out, to comfort the dead, was powerful; she took three steps, staggered, circling. There were *too many*. Too many. And they were not the right voices.

She felt lost, as the dead must feel lost; even knowing that she could return to herself and leave this place seemed such a distant possibility that she shuddered. She might have remained motionless except for that involuntary shuddering, but a sound caught her.

She flinched.

It was weeping. But the cries were different in tone and texture; grief didn't underlie them. Fear did. And as she listened, the fear grew stronger, the voice more powerful; it formed words that she did not understand. But the meaning was plain, regardless. She began, haltingly, to stumble in the direction of the voice.

She did not expect to see the Queen when she at last found features of landscape. She wasn't certain why, and in any case, she'd been wrong. The Queen was there.

She did not look particularly Queenlike, not as she had looked the one time Emma had actually seen her. It wasn't the absence of a grand, storybook throne, although that *was* absent. It wasn't even her clothing, which was remarkable only in that it had nothing at all in common with the clothing Emma and her Emery friends wore every day.

Her hair was drawn back in a single braid that traced the length of her spine, falling between shoulder blades so tense they could have cut. The floor beneath her was solid, worn wood. Before her, beneath two flat, stretched palms, was a table that was at least as worn. It was unadorned by carvings or flourishes.

She could not see Emma—and Emma was grateful. The

intensity of fury in her face made death seem inevitable. The grief that Emma had witnessed the first time was buried so deeply beneath icy rage it might never have existed at all.

She was not the source of the weeping, now.

Emma walked, gingerly, to stand by her side before the table. *This isn't happening now*, she told herself, squaring her shoulders. *This is just another memory*. She had nothing to fear.

But there was something vaguely terrifying about a grown man on his knees on the other side of the table weeping in terror. Men stood on either side of him; another man stood in front of a closed door. The room was scantly lit—the windows were glassless and small—but not even full sunlight would have banished the darkness in this room.

He was not, as it had first appeared, begging for his life. Not his own life. He was the only prisoner—there was no other word for it—in this room. The people he wanted to save—if they were still alive—were elsewhere. But his pleading made clear that that elsewhere was under the control of the woman—the girl—who stood before him. Emma held her breath. She knew, given her reaction to Mark's mother, that whatever anger she felt, whatever hatred, and there was no other word for it, would crack in the face of his terror.

The Queen did not.

She spoke the Queen's name, but the voice came out in a whisper—and it was not her voice that uttered it. "Reyna."

There was another man in the room—one Emma couldn't see. Just as there had been a man at the stream by which the Queen of the Dead had wept. It was his voice.

Reyna didn't appear to hear it. She didn't appear to hear anything; even the man before her seemed insignificant. But not so insignificant that she was unwilling to listen. And listen. And listen. She did not interrupt the flow of his broken words.

Nor did she look up at the sound of her name. Could not, Emma realized, take the risk of doing so. She was listening. She was measuring the man's pain against some invisible, internal pain of her own. And when he had quieted—and he did, briefly—his fate, or the fate of his loved ones entirely in her hands, she said, "We will show you the same mercy your kind have shown ours since the dawn of time.

"You wish us to spare your children? We will spare them in *exactly* the same fashion as you spared *ours*." She smiled, then.

He screamed. It was a blaze of sound, a last blossom before fear gave way to despair. He would die. He knew it. And perhaps he thought that death would bring him a measure of peace. And it hadn't. It wouldn't. Nor would it bring that peace to the children who would predecease him.

She spoke to the men at his side, and they slid hands under his armpits, lifting him to his feet—feet that would not carry him steadily. Emma thought one was broken.

She was, and felt, sick with dread and horror. She wanted to retreat. She almost did. But her body would not obey the visceral commands she gave it; she stood, as much captive to the memory as the man who owned it.

Stood, she realized, in the exact same place as he had stood. He was frozen there, by the Queen's side—the only man to be allowed that privilege—when the Queen turned, the steady, narrowed gaze of her eyes pinning him, trapping him, the anger flaring, and flaring again.

She did not dismiss the man at the door as she had dismissed the other jailers. She did not intend her words—or her response—to be private.

Breath held, Emma faced her. Breath held, Emma waited for the commands that she was queasily, sickly certain would follow.

"You know who he was," the Queen said, her voice burning ice, her eyes a darkness that made brown seem a shade of death. "You know what he did. You know what he *would do* if he were to survive."

"I do not counsel his survival," the man began.

She lifted a hand; it was shaking.

So, too, was the man's. Emma couldn't see his hand—he was no more visible here than he had been by the riverbank—but she could *feel* it. She could feel both of them; they were clasped behind his back. "The children have done you no harm. It hurts nothing to leave them; they're unlikely to survive on their own."

"Then consider it a kindness—a faster death than starvation."

"Reyna, whatever their father is, they are not him."

"It is the only thing," Reyna said, "that will hurt him. It is the only way to make him understand."

"The dead understand very little."

Reyna's laugh was wild, almost unhinged. "Is *that* what you truly believe?"

He flinched. Emma flinched.

"I want them dead," she said. "I want them dead before he is. He will watch. He will watch just as *I watched*." She turned away as the floor began to tilt beneath Emma's feet; she grabbed the tabletop to steady herself. "You will see to it."

Silence.

"Fire," Reyna said.

He tried only once more. "Your family was not killed by fire."

"Not mine, no. But some of yours *was*. And they will pay. They have to pay." She turned to the door, and then back. "Never try to interrupt me again. I am not a monster. I am justice—I cannot afford to be weak, to be *seen as* weak. You know what that cost me in the past." She closed her eyes. "Go. Do not start until I arrive."

It wasn't over. That was the worst of it. It *wasn't over*. This room, this darkness, the Queen's anger, was only the start of it. The door opened as Emma approached it; she felt it beneath the palm of her hand. Felt, as well, the look she was given by the remaining guard, the sole witness. The Queen ordered him out as well and remained standing by the table, in judgment.

Emma wanted to look back. She even tried. But the man she appeared to be inhabiting had not looked back, and this was his memory; he was captive to it. There was no freedom of movement, no way to effect any change. This had happened.

This was happening now.

She whimpered, moving. The sunlight was harsh, the sky cloudless; the whole of the horizon seemed to be one immoveable witness, and it watched. There were tents in the distance, a horse or two; she heard chickens—or birds, she couldn't see them. She saw, instead, the prisoner, and she saw the men to either side of him; she saw the beginnings of what might become a campfire—a bonfire—a thing by which she had sat or talked or listened to simple music, a place which typified the edge of adolescent parties.

But that wasn't what it would become. She knew.

She knew because she could hear the voice of a young child, shouting for her father. And she could see the father struggle now with his captors, with his injury, with the ultimate certainty of failure.

And she kept walking.

And as she walked, she summoned up reserves of bitter hatred, the dregs of a fear that would never quite leave, as if fear were a contagion, a plague, a thing that passed itself on, sinking itself into every corner of the mind and soul, thickening into something that was so dense, so loud, so much a part of you, it could *never* be escaped.

She called up images of laughing men. She called up memories of deaths—most often beating and bludgeoning, but once fire, much like this one. She remembered the audience, the ragtag gathering of men and women and their children, as if the event were some sort of celebration or fair. And, oh, she remembered the screams. The laughter couldn't kill them, couldn't mask them—and nothing could mask the *stench* of burning flesh.

And she remembered lurking in the crowd, pretending, dredging up some hideous reserve of will to voice something that might have sounded like laughter to the distracted. She remembered that she had abandoned friends in a desperate attempt not to join them on that pyre.

And those memories were so strong, they were enough to carry her to the piles of dry wood and the child belted to one standing log; the other waited beneath the heavy hands of guards, of men so much like those other men, a hundred miles or more away. She was silent, that child, dazed and uncomprehending, as if what must follow was so inconceivable it was simply impossible.

Emma approached the bier and paused there, the child's screams overlapping with the father's, adding a new color, a new layer, to memories of death. They were not her experiences; she understood this dimly, at a great remove. The understanding didn't save her. She was this man, now. She could not detach herself from him. She couldn't fight him—and, in truth, like the numb little girl whose life was going to end here, and horribly, some part of her felt it *must* be a nightmare. It must be. She would wake from it. She would wake and be safe and the world would be sane.

But she couldn't leave, couldn't wake; she was enmeshed in the memories of this nameless, faceless man.

He turned to Reyna, for even at this distance, he was aware of her; she cast a long slender shadow, more pillarlike than human. The sun was setting; it lengthened that shadow, until it touched the edge of the pile of wood. The child's sobbing had ceased some time past; she had given way to exhaustion and stood only because she was bound so tightly.

It was silent, for just a moment—one long stretched moment in which the man stood on the precipice of hell, teetering, uncertain. He reached, again, for the armor of bitter, bitter experience. He reached for that first moment in which he had realized, with utter finality, that justice was a lapstory, a lie told to children. Their prisoner, and men like him, had been the genesis of that. What right had they to end the lives of his kin?

They had killed women and children without cause and without mercy. He could still hear, echoing down the years, the ugly sound of their laughter. Why should they be spared what he himself had not been spared? Why? Because of his squeamishness? Because of his hesitation?

The thoughts were loud; the anger was real. It was real and it was *just*. And perhaps, perhaps if they saw this through, boys like he had once been, girls like Reyna had once been, would never be broken by the savagery of armed, human fear again.

It was worth the cost. He told himself it was worth the cost. He let anger burn, in the absence of fire—the fire would join it, soon enough.

Reyna's face, in the slow fall of night, was a mask so pale it might have been exquisitely carved ice.

But he knew her well enough to see what lay beneath it. She was afraid. She had lost family: mother, uncles, and a sister only slightly older than the girl on the unlit pyre. She intended to build a world in which she need never suffer that loss again. In which *none* of her people would suffer it a first time.

She would see this through.

And she would see it through by his side. She was committed; she demanded a like commitment from him. He could hear the cries of the dead that surrounded her; the cries of the living were brief and easily extinguished in comparison. He took the torch that was handed him; his hands were steady, his expression, as he turned to the bier, as remote as Reyna's.

He did not flinch when he set the fire to the logs; the man did that. And soon enough, the child joined him, her screams nearer and far, far harder to bear. He stepped back as the dry wood caught fire—it was not instant. Had it been in his power, it would have been; the wood would have taken the flames in an instant, and the blaze would have been so hot, so undeniable, death would come just as instantly.

It did not happen.

He did not step back. He did not flinch. He did not meet the screaming child's eyes. He simply waited. And waited. And waited.

And some time during that long, horrible wait, Reyna joined him, standing to his left, her toes even with his, fire reflected so strongly in her eyes that they were red and orange. He understood, then, why she had chosen the time of day she had chosen; he could see the tracks of her tears.

NATHAN

THE QUEEN OF THE DEAD IS RADIANT.

Her title is both absolute and somehow wrong. As she walks down the street, her Eric finally by her side, the street fills. It fills with her subjects. They are not the newly dead; they can change their appearance, including their clothing. They are different genders of many races, many ages. They appear to see each other—at least enough that they are standing in the same space they might were they alive: they don't overlap. They don't sink through stone.

They look like . . . a crowd. A crowd from a period movie, yes—but a genuine crowd. They're the extras, but their presence isn't insignificant. They watch their Queen. How much fear rests beneath the surface of their composed faces?

And is Nathan's expression nearly as composed as theirs? He is less worried about that than perhaps he should be; the Queen is unlikely to turn her back and look at her attendants. Either of them.

Helmi walks behind Eric at Nathan's side. She prompts

him when the long train of the Queen's dress needs adjusting; she can't—obviously—adjust it herself. But her expression is neutral, in the way stone is neutral. She glances at the dead without truly seeing them. Eric sees them.

Nathan sees them. But Nathan, seeing them, can understand Helmi's reaction. It is painful to know that they are nothing more than accoutrements, that they are accessories that will be put aside—or worse—without a second thought. He's not certain if that's because it's also the truth of his new existence, and they remind him of what he now is—but it doesn't matter why. It's uncomfortable.

Helmi has been dead for much, much longer than Nathan.

But then again, so has Eric.

Maybe it's because Eric has lived in the real world. He's met real people. He's lived as if he were still alive.

Nathan is watching both of their backs. The Queen turns to look—at Eric. Eric's gaze is elsewhere, moving and pausing. He doesn't notice the Queen's expression. He doesn't appear to notice the tightening of her hand.

But when she speaks, he hears her.

When she speaks, although her voice is so low it's barely more than a whisper, all of the dead hear her. The dead who are looking out the open windows. The dead who are in the streets. Nathan thinks—although he hopes and prays it is his imagination—the *street itself* hears her; it is rumbling slightly beneath the soles of his incredibly uncomfortable shoes.

Eric, do you not love me?

And Eric turns to meet her open, desperate gaze.

CHAPTER
FIFTEEN

"SOMETHING'S WRONG," Allison said. Emma's shoulders had curved toward the ground, her neck retracting; her arms trembled as she held them, stiff, at her sides. Her eyes were closed, but the tears hadn't stopped.

Allison made her way to the circle's edge; Amy's voice stopped her. Allison wasn't one of the Emery mafia. She wasn't one of Amy's inner circle. She was too stout and too unaware of fashion and style, which she'd assumed meant the same thing until Emma had disentangled the words for her.

But no one in Emery—at least no one in the same grade—ignored Amy Snitman when her voice took on that edge. And odd though it was, Allison trusted her. Here, at least. She turned back.

"She's in there for a reason," Amy said. To Allison's muted surprise, she appeared to be attempting to shift the tone of her words, to deprive them of—of whatever it was that made them so particularly *Amy*. "None of us know what she's doing. We know *why*."

"Emma doesn't know what she's doing either," Michael helpfully pointed out. He was as worried as Allison was.

Amy shrugged. "She got the kid out of the fire, right? And she knew even less then. Whatever she's doing now, she probably has to do it." She exhaled. "Look, I know you want to help," she said to Allison. "You've got 'Emma's little helper' written all over your face. But she's somewhere we can't go. I don't want our 'help' to pull her back before she's done what she needs to do."

"And you're sure she needs to do this?" It was Chase who answered. He came to stand beside Allison at the circle's edge—but not between her and Amy. Not even Chase was that stupid.

Amy's expression sharpened. What she wasn't willing to say to Allison, she was more than happy to say to Chase— and that came as a huge surprise to Allison. Amy wasn't known for either her tact or her consideration of other people's feelings. "I'm sure *she* thinks she does. I'm willing to hear rational arguments against," she added, in a tone that implied none of that rationality would come from Chase.

Chase swore under his breath. Clearly both Chase and Amy were struggling to be civil in their own unique ways. It wasn't Amy who responded—a glare from Amy didn't count—it was Margaret.

"I can't cross that circle," she said quietly. "Or I would. Anyone else in the room *can* cross the boundary—but it won't change what they see." Before anyone could respond she said, "I am not an expert in what Emma is now attempting. I have no advice or wisdom to offer. But, Allison, I'm also concerned."

It was confirmation, but it didn't make Allison feel any better. She turned back to Emma. "Will it *hurt* anything if I cross the circle?"

"I don't know, dear. I think it may disrupt things if you actually touch Emma—but again, I am not an expert. I do not know what she's attempting to do." She looked, again to Chase, as if it were against her better judgment. Or any judgment of any quality, anyway.

"There's no guarantee I'll see anything either," Chase said, the words pulled from him by an unseen force.

"No." Margaret waited. Ernest was watching Chase with

hooded eyes and the slightest hint of . . . pain. He said nothing when Chase turned to him. Not a single word.

Allison was aware that it was the silence, the lack of words, that stung Chase. Chase looked for all the world like a man who was determined to fight—but Ernest wasn't going to be his opponent. If anyone was, it was Margaret, and her usual prim and dour school-teacher demeanor was absent.

"She's a Necromancer," Chase said, but the words lacked the heated conviction that Allison found so very difficult.

Ernest said nothing. Margaret added a layer to the silence. She seemed content to wait.

Chase demonstrated his ability to swear without repeating a single word, which was impressive, given he hadn't paused for breath. Without thought, Allison put a gentle hand on his shoulder; he swung round, as if struck.

"I don't know what she did to you," Allison said, voice only barely above a whisper. "But you don't have to do this. Amy's right—we should trust Emma."

Chase's laughter was bitter, all edge. "Thanks to the Queen of the Dead," was his angry reply, "I'm the only one who *can*."

"You don't know what you're doing, either," Amy told him. "And this might not be the best time for your bull-in-the-china-shop routine."

He ignored her. Turning to face Allison, he said, "I don't like her."

Allison could have pretended to misunderstand; she didn't. She simply waited.

"I'm not doing this for her. Understand?"

"You don't have to do this for me, either. She's my best friend—but she doesn't have to be yours. Amy's right."

"On the other hand? I could live without ever hearing those two words side by side again." He grinned. It was a pale echo of his normal grin, but it was there, and it was real. In front of everyone in the room, he bent and kissed her. It was not a fast kiss. It said a lot about something that it was, for a moment, the most important sensation in the world.

And that was just wrong.

Chase pulled back before she could, the grin stronger and a little more lopsided. "Wish me luck," he whispered. He stepped away from her, squared his shoulders, checked—yes, his knives, as if they'd do any good—and headed toward the circumference of the circle.

Allison watched him go. She was standing less than a foot away from the engraved runes; it wasn't a great distance. But it felt as if it were miles. Emma had gone where Allison couldn't follow—and it was Chase who was joining her.

"I don't like her," he said, without turning back. "But I can't hate her. God knows I've tried. And without her in my life, there would be no *you* in my life."

Emma did not come back to herself. She did not come back to the circle in which she was sitting, in a grand, sterile room blessedly free of the terrible sounds of death. No. No that wasn't right. It was *full* of the sounds of the dead. But not— not the screams of the dying. Not the screams of men who had given up on life and who looked death in the face as if death were the only mercy left.

And it should have been.

She knew it wasn't. She was sitting on the dead. But it was *hard* to remember that fact while the charring corpse of a child occupied the whole of her vision no matter what she did. The first child, joined by the second. The two children joined by the man. And yes, by that time, he had wanted death—but the pain of it, the pain of *fire* . . .

She looked up, almost wild with the need to escape.

The need to escape inverted itself in the space of a single scream. It was not the terror and pain of children—it was the nameless, faceless man whose memories had once again absorbed Emma Hall. She wished that some of those memories could actually be useful: that they would be memories of how the powers of Necromancers were used *before* the Queen of the Dead had broken everything.

But no, this was not to be one of those memories either; the scream was joined by shouting, by one other scream, and by metal. Metal. Emma frowned. Metal.

Iron.

He had been running—desperation lent him speed, but only a little. She was, once again, in the passenger seat of his careening, painful memory. She saw what he saw. She felt what he felt. She could not look away, could not change the trajectory of what had already happened.

He saw salt across the ground and recognized the lines into which it had been placed; he kicked them, displaced them, and realized that iron shavings, under salt, now clung to his feet.

Iron and salt here.

Iron.

He knew before he reached the end of the hall what the iron presaged. He knew, as he removed his sweater and dragged it across the precise lines of salt, what it meant— but the knowledge was almost too large, too impossible to believe.

Men with bows or swords or axes, men with torches, men on horseback—these, they'd faced as they grew. They were a fact of life, an almost natural disaster.

But those men did not understand what iron *meant.* And even had they, they carried it as weapons. They did not draw it in lines across the floor. They did not—and he saw, destroying as much of the pattern as he could, in safety, destroy—inscribe ancient runes, invoking their protection and power.

Only his own kin could do that.

Another scream. A shout of betrayed rage. He didn't recognize the voice, and perhaps that was a mercy: There was only one voice he listened for, now. Only one. From half the building away, he heard it; he dropped the sweater, left it, avoided the rest of the salt and the iron shavings that would cling to too much of his boots. He paused briefly and removed those boots; he could not carry weakness with him. Not now.

Oh, they'd prepared.

They'd prepared for this. They'd chosen the meeting of the moon at nadir. Here, they gathered: men, women, and the youngsters who teetered on the edge of adulthood and their adult strength. He did not know—not yet—what numbers they'd come in. He did not know how many traitors there were in the midst of this village that Reyna had struggled to build.

That there was one was enough.

He paused at the wide doors to the long hall; they were open. Light and noise spilled into the natural darkness of the hall; the small torches were not enough to provide more than scant illumination. This close, he could hear voices more distinctly.

"You have broken all of the ancient codes. You have betrayed the gift you were given. You have betrayed and enslaved the lost."

He recognized the voice; had he not come to a quiet halt, he would have stumbled. As it was, he froze for one long beat, into which more words were spoken. Stavros' voice was fire and fury.

And there was only one person to whom he could be speaking. Reyna was silent.

He wondered, then, whether she was dead. But no—Stavros would not speak to a corpse, and if Reyna was not dead, there was time.

Time.

His hands were dry. His throat, drier. He opened his mouth to speak, but no words emerged; words were a bitter, broken jumble, a useless thing. He needed to see what was happening. He needed to see where Reyna was and how the room was arranged. More than that, he needed to know who had betrayed her. Stavros could not be acting alone in this room.

Reyna, he thought. *I did not understand you, until now.* He wished, bitterly, for that earlier ignorance, but he knew he would never have it again. Because he *had* the power. He had the power that Reyna had had on that fateful day that had changed everything.

It was forbidden power. It was the reason that she was surrounded by her own kin, facing exile. Facing, he thought, death. Because she'd had that power, and she'd used it, and she'd saved her own life.

Not just her own life. She'd saved *all* their lives. She had given them safety and harbor.

Emma was firmly ensconced in the memories of the unnamed man; she understood that this was not happening now; it had already happened. Nothing she said or did could change the past. But she tried, because the strongest memory she now had was that of murdered children.

That is not *all she did.*

It was for our safety!

Because young girls are so much *of a danger. They died horrible, horrible deaths. It wasn't about safety!*

It was.

You just tell yourself that, she thought, her fury far, far greater than his. Far greater, yes—and his own. She could not speak to an echo or a memory. She couldn't argue with one. She wasn't arguing with him now. He was arguing with himself. And he was winning—and losing.

He loved Reyna.

He loved Reyna as a child, not as the sovereign she would become. He loved her, saw her as an injured, scarred girl, in need of support. In need of, yes, the love that he felt for her. She was not his child; he knew that. But unlike his own children, she would survive.

He had had children.

Emma knew it was hard for parents to judge their child. To be angry, yes; that was natural. But to judge them? To exile them? To desert them? To let them be killed?

No.

But the scream she could hear building up behind his closed lips was almost her own. He held the dead, just as Reyna had shyly taught him to do. He held their chains, and he therefore held their power. He was not bound, as Reyna was bound; he was not yet captive—but he would be. No doubt, he would be. And he would then be as helpless as she must be now, for Stavros to speak so.

He had one chance, and he knew it. He had broken some of the confinement on his way to the hall; he had erased the patterns in which salt had been laid. None of these protections had ever been meant to be used against the living. Only against the raging dead.

And perhaps the dead were raging against Reyna now; they were certainly weeping.

He gathered their power, felt it infuse his hands with warmth; felt it lift him, although in truth he did not move from his silent crouch. He did not use the soul-fire; that would come later, much later. But he did summon fire.

He summoned death—because the dead knew death. He was limited by the knowledge of those that he had bound to himself. He was no longer limited by the promise he had made to them in that binding. They had given him the permission he required to use the power itself, and they had no choice now in how it was used.

He begged their forgiveness in silence. He gave them no voice and refused to listen to what remained—always—close to his own heart: the cries of the lost.

If you start this, you will never, ever stop.

He knew. But he could not live with the knowledge that he had stood mute, remained hidden, while she was murdered. It would kill him. He had the power to save her.

It's not your power!

But it was. He summoned fire, and it came, and it spread into the wooden slats of the open hall. It spread everywhere at his command, lapping with ease against the robes, dresses, tunics that it touched. As he entered, columns of fire rose; they were reflected in eyes that otherwise saw only one person.

She had turned toward the door; her legs were bound, as were her arms. She had been forced to kneel in the posture of the penitent. There was no penitence in her now; there was rage. Rage and gratitude. She struggled to stand, and he could not help her; he was too far away. Too far and too vulnerable.

He shouted her name. He could not break the barriers they had set up around her—not yet. But the fire would do that, and when it did, she would be free to act. Her face shone with tears.

They were the last tears she would shed in public.

He hesitated. He hesitated just once. Mira stood just behind Stavros. Mira, only a handful of years older than Reyna. Like Reyna, Mira had suffered for the crime of being born into the wrong family, the wrong *people*, and yet she stood in judgment.

And he did not want to kill her.

Did not want to light her ablaze. He was willing to do that to Stavros, for he was angry as well—but Mira was a girl. Barely older than child. Barely older than Reyna.

It almost cost him his life.

She stepped out from behind Stavros, she lifted a crossbow, and she pointed it—at him. She fired. He felt the bolt pierce his thigh. Her aim was not good—but the heat of fire was causing distortions in the air, and smoke rose in a quavering bloom. He ran—limped—to Reyna to cut her free.

"Do not approach me!"

He stopped. No, no, he wasn't thinking. She was right. Whatever power he had, whatever power their survival depended on, would not work if he was standing where she now stood. He had to trust that she would survive. The whole of the rough council could not be on Stavros' side.

He could hear shouts and screams—at his back, to his side—as the world dissolved in flame and noise. But he listened for Reyna, afraid to move, his leg throbbing as the world they had built ended.

She would survive. He was almost certain of it. But what she built in future would be different. What they built in future would have to be different. He had broken the only oath that had ever mattered in his long years of service to the shadows of death, and there was no restitution, no repentance, that would absolve him of that crime.

Reyna had to live, because if she died, nothing would remain to him.

The memory faded. The sickening lurch of guilt, rage, and fear remained in its wake. Emma struggled to breathe—as she'd struggled to breathe once before, in the fire that had killed a four-year-old boy in a distant Toronto townhouse.

His fear had been her fear for what felt like far too long. But it was not her fear, and she knew that were it not for his interference, the girl who would become the Queen of the Dead would have died in that long-ago hall. She knew— without knowing—that the men and women who had chosen to stand against her *had* died.

She didn't imagine that their deaths had been pleasant— and she was almost certain that she could see them all if she had any desire to examine them. And she didn't. She could see the screaming girl on the lit pyre. Had no one else died, ever, that would have been enough.

Enough? Enough for what?

She frowned. Lifting her head, she looked once again into formless, shapeless gray. Nothingness surrounded her, with a texture of its own; she could see no walls, but she felt them all around her: high, forbidding, thick.

Without thought, she reached for Margaret—something she had never done before. The faintest ripple of gray appeared. She could see it only out of the corner of eyes too sensitized to colorlessness to recognize the subtle shift in the air. Like everything in her surroundings, it was formless—but she could now see that something struggled to take form, to don shape.

And it wasn't Margaret.

She rose, aware that she had been kneeling. Aware, in some distant way, that she had always been seated and remained so. It was hard to wait, and in the end, she didn't bother. She walked toward whatever it was that was coalescing. She knew that she had managed to find the man whose memories she had inhabited. She had chosen to search for him. She couldn't blame him for that experience, but not even Emma Hall could manage to be fair all of the time. She did blame him.

She struggled with anger, with rage, with disgust, with—yes—hatred. On some visceral level, beneath the very justified reactions, she knew she was not here to judge him. To judge him was to fail.

But he *deserved* judgment.

He deserved to be trapped in whatever personal hell the Queen had created for him. The people trapped in the walls and floors and rooftops *didn't*. Her hands were fists. Never mind her hands—her whole body felt as if it were a fist. As if it were raised and shaking. She couldn't find the words that would convey the whole of what she felt—and she wanted them, as the swirls of translucence began to combine in a way that reminded her inexplicably of basket weaving.

Her father had done that once—as an experiment. She could remember it, hazy and distant, because she'd watched him in the act of this odd creation. Wet strips of something, carefully threaded through other wet strips. Emma couldn't believe that it would eventually be able to carry anything.

But it had. It had dried. Her mother still had it, somewhere in the heap of discarded kibble that characterized the Hall kitchen. She shook her head to clear it and then changed her mind. *She* was Emma Hall. She had had an easy life compared to this man. An easy life compared to his Reyna. An easy life compared to so many unknown lives. Certainly easier than Andrew Copis in his brief four years, easier than Mark, in his less than ten.

She was not here to judge him, no matter how much he deserved it. Lowering her hands, she took a deep breath and exhaled, and as if that were a sign, the ghost solidified in front of her, a yard from where she had chosen to stand.

There was no other landscape around him. No other sounds, no other light. There was no color to his clothing, which seemed to have been painted in broad gray brushstrokes. His face was similar; he looked like a storybook ghost. She couldn't see any hint of his feet. She hadn't spent all of her life seeing the dead, but she'd seen enough of them to know that they didn't look like this.

I do not recognize you, he said. His lips moved, but the words were more felt than heard.

"I don't recognize you either," Emma replied. "At least not from the outside." She hesitated as Hall manners struggled with reality—and won anyway. "My name is Emma Hall. I don't mean to be rude, but . . . most of the dead don't look like you do."

No. They would not.

"Is this because of something the Queen did?"

Yes, in part. It is also because of something that I did. He stared at her. One painted hand rose, fingers and palms clear. He lowered it. *You should not be here, child.*

"I don't have any choice."

There is always choice.

Emma shrugged. "Sometimes there's only one choice to make. I wouldn't have made the choices you've made."

You do not understand half of the choices I made.

"I wouldn't make the ones I know you did make." She exhaled again. "I'm not here to judge you."

And yet, you judge. It is the nature of mortality. Silence. It was cold, here. *It is dangerous to come here in judgment, child.* He drifted closer, but he made no attempt to raise a hand again.

Emma did. She reached out to touch him.

Do not—

Her slow scream was all the sound in the world.

CHAPTER
SIXTEEN

EMMA WEPT. For the first time in living memory, she didn't care who saw her. She wanted to throw up. To curl in on herself, sink through a floor made of the dead, and let them swallow her entirely. She was overwhelmed by Scoros. She had no doubt that was who the stranger had once been. It was who she was, now. Every step she took or attempted to take led her into another fragment of his past. He'd lived far longer than Emma; she could experience bits and pieces of his life until hers naturally ended.

She wasn't certain he was aware of her at all, and as she walked through the patchwork fabric of his life, she began to lose that awareness as well.

She struggled to remember that she was Emma Hall.

She could feel his anger, his sense of duty, his determination, as if they were her own. And she could feel his revulsion, his growing self-loathing, the lies that he invented and repeated to himself, over and over, in the vain hope that repetition would make them true.

She was good at those. They were already a part of the

Hall universe. That and guilt. And the guilt was too much. It was just too damn much. He had developed emotional calluses. He could almost will himself away from his own actions. He could wield knife or fire or soul-fire without so much as flinching—on the outside. But Emma was trapped on the inside, and she was no closer to the information she had wanted from him than when she had set out searching.

She could barely remember what it was.

Pivotal events in his life caught her as she attempted to extricate herself, deadly undertows that pulled her back, again and again. There were *so many* memories. There were so many atrocities. There was no light, no hope, no joy.

She could shelter, for moments at a time in his humiliation and pain—in his arguments with his mother, for instance, in his guilty sense of relief at his mother's passing. Relieved or not, he had begged leave to teach that woman the arts of longevity, as it was styled by the Queen, and he had been refused. The Queen had never cared for his mother.

Death had not freed him of maternal conflicts or anger. Short of binding her and silencing her that way, nothing would. An eternity of her regret, her anger, and her abiding contempt awaited him.

And he deserved it.

I did not choose Reyna over family, he said—to his mother, perhaps, or his memory of her—*Reyna was my family. She was all I was allowed to keep.*

And he'd kept her. He'd kept her safe. He'd offered her comfort. He'd tried to offer her unconditional love—the love of a parent for a very small child. But a small child was not the Queen of the Dead. He'd done everything he could for her and in her name. He had forced himself, had proven himself, over and over.

And she had never trusted love. Not his. Not anyone's. She'd required proof of love, and when she raged or cried, he offered what she needed. Her tears then stopped and her smile returned—but it never remained there. Her eyes would lose their width, her lips would narrow, her brow would crease; doubt would shadow everything she said or did until he came, once again, to prove that she was the most important thing in his life.

Emma had never been a parent.

She had once wondered—briefly—what it must be like to be the parent of a murderer. She knew now. She didn't doubt that Reyna was daughter to this nameless man. She couldn't fathom his love for her, his memories painted her so clearly. She believed that he had loved her, and she hated him for it.

As he hated himself for it.

She could not escape him. Instead, dragged back once again by this brief harmony of thought, she opened her eyes and began to walk toward every single reason the man had for self-loathing. The children had been the start of it but not the end—and not, oh, god, the worst.

Something pulled at Emma; something tugged her sleeve. She was so accustomed to the man's life, she thought it another event, another death, another loss, another betrayal— of self, of kin, of belief.

But . . . most of the people in the man's memories didn't *swear* so much. She looked down without thinking—and found that she *could* look down. For just a minute, her vision wasn't a captive passenger; her eyes could move in a different direction.

There was nothing tugging at her sleeve. There couldn't be. She was facing Reyna—the Queen now, to all but the man himself—to report. The Queen met with him alone, dismissing all of her living guards; those guards—Necromancers, but not yet knights—glared at him but obeyed their Queen; they retreated to familiar doors, opened them, and closed them when they had crossed the threshold.

The town hall had long since given way to the opulent heights of bright, domed ceilings that let in clear sky and daylight. Scoros knelt in a room with which Emma was familiar. It had been the last room she had studied so carefully before she had set out on her search.

Emma!

She recognized the voice. She turned again, turned toward the doors, and knew that this was impossible; she was in the man's memories, and the man, kneeling, could not turn. He did not dare to take any part of his attention from Reyna, the Queen.

So it was not through his eyes that Emma saw the closed door. Not with his ears that she heard her name being called. She tried to move toward the door and failed; she heard the Queen's voice at her back. She didn't turn, but she didn't have to; the memories reasserted themselves, and she was once again on her knees before her Queen.

EMMA!

Reaction was involuntary. Something in the voice that was calling her name was so raw with fear that she couldn't ignore it, couldn't turn away, couldn't do anything at all but move toward it. After all she'd seen, all she'd heard, all she'd *done*, she should have been too numb.

But this voice was not one of Scoros' voices; it wasn't a voice he knew or recognized. It was no part of the guilt or shame he carried. It was part of her life, Emma Hall's life. Chase Loern had come to Toronto, and he'd been pretty pissed off to find out that she wasn't dead. He wasn't above sharing that anger. And maybe, if that's all she knew of him, she wouldn't have responded.

But he had saved Allison's life. He loved Allison, and Allison was so much part of the fiber of Emma's existence, Emma couldn't remember life before Allison. No matter how much Chase hated Emma, he'd actually had the brains and the perception to see Allison clearly. Anyone who saw her clearly would have to love her.

And that's what Emma remembered as she turned toward the pain and the fear in Chase's voice.

She had been anchored in the stranger's memories, trapped in his viewpoint; she had been a murderer so many times over—even thinking it, she shuddered, twisting away from herself. And of course she couldn't. She *was* herself. There was no escape.

"EMMA!"

She did the next best thing. She ran to the closed door. The Queen's monologue didn't change; the Queen didn't move. And the man's voice, in the few words of reply he could wedge in, didn't shift either. But they grew distant, blessedly distant, as Chase's voice grew closer.

She was almost at the door when she felt the ground shift beneath her feet.

And will you abandon your duty?

She almost didn't recognize the voice; had she not spent subjective months listening to nothing but its shades, its textures, she wouldn't have. The door was a foot away from Emma's outstretched hand. In the eye blink before that hand made contact with its surface, the surface shifted shape; it widened, thickened. Grandeur gave way to ugly practicality, vaulted arches gave way to rectangular frame. This was no longer the door to the most important rooms in the citadel.

It was a door to the hidden rooms, to the darkness beneath the opulence. It was a jail door, a dungeon door. The wood was heavy, thick; it was scored and scratched, no doubt from useless attempts at escape.

But it had what the palatial doors lacked: bars. And bars meant space through which Emma could see out. She reached up, gripped the bars, pulled herself toward them. She opened her mouth to speak, but words jammed up behind her teeth, and her throat was already so raw it hurt to speak. She hoped—she *really* hoped—that she hadn't actually been screaming in the real world, because she could just imagine what that would do to her friends. To Michael.

And then she forgot the eddies of guilt as she looked between the bars. She'd recognized the voice. She didn't recognize the person on the other side of this door, and her hands faltered, their grip loosening.

The boy on the other side reached out and grabbed them, curling his hands around and over them. He was maybe fourteen years old; it was hard to tell. His hands were red with blood. Literally red with it. And his hair was that bright red-orange that was so striking. It was also much longer than Chase's.

"Don't you dare let go," he said, voice grim. Fourteen; his voice had already entered adult territory.

"Chase?"

"No, I'm the tooth fairy." A tooth fairy with a bruised face, a swollen lip. All of the blood—on his clothing, on his face—was scarlet and crimson, and his eyes were almost blue. "What are you staring at?"

"The tooth fairy, apparently." Her voice was thin and quavering, and she tried to bring it back under control. The words, at least, were the right words.

"And I've got something on my face?"

Blood, she thought. She didn't say it. She wondered, instead, what Chase could see. She didn't ask. She asked the other question, the bigger one. "Why are you here?"

"To make sure you come back."

And she remembered that it had been Chase who had pulled her free of a sea of hands and arms that would otherwise have devoured her.

"Fine. *How* are you here?"

His hands tightened involuntarily; Emma's tightened as well. She could feel bars, and they had the consistency of metal—but the metal was warm.

He smiled. It was the first time she understood just how much of a defense that smile was. This fourteen-year-old version of the Chase Loern she knew hadn't mastered it yet; the lips moved in exactly the right way, but the eyes were so bruised and so haunted, they didn't match. "You know that thing about crying you have?"

"What thing about crying? I don't mind if people cry—"

"Not other people. You. Allison says you're very definite on that. Emma Hall does not cry in public."

"Yes, but—"

"Emma Hall has nothing on Chase Loern in that regard."

"I'm not—"

"You are, Emma. Look—can you just wake up? You're scaring the crap out of your friends. Except Amy."

Emma laughed, or tried to. "Can you?"

"Can I?"

"Wake up, if that's what you want to call it. Can you?" Voice dipping, she said, "I've tried."

The very modern cursing that had first caught her attention went on for some time. "I'm not leaving without you."

"Can you?"

"I'm not trying. I'm assuming the answer is yes—but if I wake up, you're still going to be here, and from the sounds of it, here is not where you want to be."

Emma shook her head. She didn't always trust intuition—especially not her own—but she thought she understood why Chase was fourteen. She didn't understand why he alone seemed to radiate color—maybe it was because he was alive. "I don't think you can," she said softly. Certainly.

"Is this some weird Necromantic thing?"

"I don't know a lot about Necromantic things. No one taught me how to see the dead. No one taught me how to take their hands. Chase—I don't think you can wake up either. You shouldn't be here. You shouldn't have come." Emma was viscerally certain that Chase Loern was just as trapped as she was. Chase Loern, who'd argued for her death, who'd wanted her killed—and who, she was certain, would once have been happy to be the killer.

He shrugged. He didn't let go of her hands. "Wasn't my idea," he finally said. His voice was blurred, thick. But it was his voice.

"Please don't tell me it was Ally's."

He laughed. It was not a happy sound. "It wasn't Allison's. She told me I should trust you."

"She's always been an optimist."

He laughed again, and this laugh was less wild, less terrifying. "She'd have to be, wouldn't she? Can you see any way to open the damn door?"

Emma shook her head. Took a breath and felt it enter distant lungs. Chase had bought her space to think. He'd brought her back to Emma Hall, to her own thoughts, her own pale worries. He was holding her steady, but she wasn't certain it could last; behind his back, she could see fire. She could hear the sharp snap of something that might—or might not—be gunfire.

She was certain it was not Scoros' past she was seeing because she wasn't the one shooting the gun or setting the fire. For the moment, she was herself. She was not passenger—or captive—to experiences she could not change and would never have chosen.

Gunfire didn't make Chase flinch. She wasn't certain he could hear what she heard or even see what she saw. He could see her. She could see him. But she saw him as she saw the dead—and she was certain Chase wasn't dead.

"Emma—open your eyes. Your real eyes."

"My eyes are open."

He opened his mouth—his bruised, swollen mouth—and shut it again. "Then we are so screwed."

*   *   *

Chase looked at the door, which was difficult given the level of his hands. He was afraid to let Emma go. From this side the door didn't appear to have a lock. Or a door knob. Or a handle. It did not seem designed to allow anyone entry. "Do you remember how you got in?"

A hesitation. "I walked. You?"

"I'm not exactly in—but I walked as well. The citadel's doing a really fancy impression of Dante's Hell at the moment."

"Which level?"

"No fair."

Emma's brows rose. Her color—and she had color—was bad, but her expression was almost normal. "What?"

"That was an Allison question."

The corners of her lips twitched. Her hands were warm. They were the only thing in this grim place that was.

"Is there a handle of any kind on your side?"

"No."

"You didn't look."

Emma's forehead creased, but confusion—of a certain kind—was better than pain or fear or—he shied away from the last description before it had fully formed. "I didn't, did I?" Her gaze shifted. Chase tightened his grip on her hands. He wanted to reach between the bars and grab her wrists, but his hands wouldn't pass between them.

"I think there's a handle—you need to let go of my hands."

"No can do."

She grimaced. "Then you need to let go of one of them."

He couldn't say why, not then, not later, but his grip tightened. It was involuntary, and he saw Emma wince. *I can't let go of you*, he thought. There was a desperation in it, a frenzy of certainty—and it was informed in all ways by fear. He looked at his hands, tried to get them to obey his commands. They almost seemed to belong to someone else.

They were red, sticky, gloved in dried blood.

"Chase?"

"My hands—" He met her gaze. "My hands are—"

She nodded, as if not trusting herself to speak.

He stared at his hands, at her face, framed between them by bars, and last, at the hands he was gripping so tightly his knuckles were white beneath the darkened crimson. "Emma—Emma, your hands—"

"What about my hands?" Her voice was thinner.

They were as red as Chase's. The blood was newer, and it was slicker; it made her hands slippery. He knew. He was trying to hold on to them. "Emma, can you reach through the bars?"

She didn't answer. He could see her eyes widen, could see the shift in focus as she looked through him.

"What are you doing?" he demanded.

She didn't, or couldn't, answer. He was no longer certain she could hear him, or see him. Or perhaps she could. Perhaps she could see—in this land of the dead and the trapped and the damned—past the Chase Loern she knew.

His hands were red, they were sticky, and as he stared at them, he felt blood fill his mouth, where his teeth had cut his lip. He knew the sensation. It wasn't the first time it had happened. It wouldn't be the last.

He told himself this, clinging to her hands, struggling to remember why he'd come here in the first place. What he remembered instead—

No.

But his hands were the *wrong* hands. He hadn't noticed it before. They were his hands; they more or less obeyed his commands. But they were, blood regardless, too young. They had no calluses. They had no scars. They were the hands he'd once had when—

NO.

He was frozen in place, hunted, afraid. This fear was the first fear, the worst fear; this was the moment in which he had learned the meaning of the word. He turned, or would have turned; his hands were stuck, clenched in fists, bound.

He could hear the dog. He could hear the faint echoes of his mother's voice. *What's upsetting him this time?*

His father: *Probably a raccoon.*

No. No, Dad—not a raccoon. Run. *Run. RUN.*

How many times had he had this nightmare? It ended—it always ended—the same way. There was no hope. There was no chance. There was death, always death. And the only person to survive, the only person to be left behind, was Chase. No matter how hard he struggled. No matter how much he had learned. No matter how old he was or what weapons he carried. Nothing changed.

He could hear them scream. He could watch them die. He could be paralyzed by fear and the belief—the stupid, blind belief—that this *could not be happening*.

Emma saw the fire. It was small, but beneath it was kindling, and beneath that, logs piled high, in a rough pyre. Illuminated by its growing light, she could see the shape and outline of a woman. She recognized not the woman but the situation; she had experienced it so often.

The door with no handle, no knob, faded from view, except for the bars around which her hands—and Chase's—were wrapped. She looked at Chase and saw that he was fading as well, as if he had only been so much scenery, just another part of the nightmares of one dead man.

She tried to call Chase. Tried to shout his name. The name that left her throat was not his. She didn't recognize it and knew that the throat scraped raw by the force of those syllables was not her own.

Torches flickered, small whispers of flame; they were held by shadows, shades, their voices the only things that were clear and distinct. She could no longer see past them, could not approach them. But she *tried*.

Something hit her hard, caused her to double over. She had seen this fire before. But not these men, not these women. As the shadows grew sharper, she could see that there were children in the mix, their hands or shirt collars held by parents who otherwise paid them little mind.

"Do you *want* to die?" The words were a hiss of sound.

"My mother—I have to help my mother!" A hand was over her mouth, muffling most of the words, damping their volume. Were it not for the sound of the crowd, it wouldn't have worked—but the crowd was jubilant. Loud. Merry, even. It might have been a festival fire.

An old festival, a dark fire, a human sacrifice.

She struggled. She bit. Air rushed into her open mouth.

"Then go. Go and die. There is nothing you can do to save her."

She staggered. Her knees hit dirt, her hands following.

"Is that the death you want? Is that it? Do you think that's what your mother wants for you?" Again and again, the words hissed into his ear, his captor—who? Why?—unable to walk away, to let him go.

Her captor.

Her father. *No.* Not her father. Not Emma Hall's father. She was with Scoros again. This man was Scoros' father. She turned to look, to glare, to plead—and the look on his father's face killed all words. *You're just afraid. If we go—*

If we go, we'll die.

His father's arms found him again. "We can't save her."

He heard the fear in his father's voice. The helplessness that had never been there before. Against it, in the background, laughter. Laughter and the first scream. And he stood, no longer struggling, as his father lifted him, understanding this one thing about himself: He was a coward.

He valued his life, his survival, more than the life of the woman who had given him life. He would not do anything to save her. He would not lift voice or hand. He would not lift weapon. He would do nothing at all but walk away; he wouldn't even bury her.

He could not scream. Not out loud. But inside? The scream started then, and it never, *ever* stopped.

Emma was, and was not, the boy.

Emma could scream.

The sound shattered Chase.

There was no part of his body that didn't feel it as a literal, crushing blow; it drove him back in so many ways, staggering was the least of it. His mouth wasn't open. He could swear it wasn't open, but he could feel the reverberations of that scream on his lips. He could lift his head, open his mouth, and make the same sound, over and over.

He knew because it was the perfect harmony to his own scream. It was the same cry, the same wordless eruption of noise that had left his own lips at his mother's death. That was leaving it, even now.

It was not his voice.

He didn't hate Emma now. Chase Loern was tired, in this moment, of fear and hatred. "Emma!"

The screaming continued; the voice grew hoarse with it, and as it did, it became similar to the voice he recognized as Emma Hall's. Funny that the sobbing always sounded like her, even if he had never seen her cry.

His hands tightened; they still clutched her hands. He could see them—see *her*. And he could see the Queen of the Dead. He could see his mother's body. He could see his father's, to the left and in the corner. His father had died first.

And he knew, as he used Emma's scream as an anchor, that they couldn't be killed or tortured to death more than once. They were already dead. The Queen of the Dead could not kill them again. He struggled to find his own voice, to dislodge the past from it; his throat felt raw.

If he had screamed like that in the real world, Allison was going to kill him. Or kill herself with worry. It was, oddly, a good thought.

It was the only one. He couldn't save his parents. Emma Hall was not a substitute for them; there was no redemption for him here. But he had come to save Emma; she was not dead, and he did not intend to leave without her.

He wasn't the same Chase Loern. The naive, shallow boy of memory was dead.

"Don't take this personally, but if you die here—or worse—it'll break Allison. I am not leaving without you. Are you afraid that you're helpless, that you're powerless? That's been *my* life. Do you want to be me?"

Emma heard Chase. Heard him, turned toward him, struggling to hold on to the thread of his familiar voice amidst the volume of all the other sounds: laughter, screams, shrieks of a glee so obscene it was hard to believe they came from . . . people. Monsters, yes. She knew about monsters. She'd walked through the life of one, watching as he emerged. Seeing his choices, feeling his fear, feeling his love and his desire to protect what was loved.

She understood that he had watched people he cared about die; his thoughts had touched on it before. She had never seen it until now.

She had never seen the thing that had broken him.

But she understood. He was a monster because of

monsters. And monsters in this world started out as people, *were* people. It hadn't been all that he was, but that didn't matter; he couldn't escape the sum of his choices. Death had not freed him. It gave her no comfort to know how much they had tormented him, in life.

She could see the eddies of every monstrous action bleeding into the world, sinking roots in the hearts of other people and growing there.

"Emma! Emma, talk to me. Stop whimpering. It doesn't impress anyone, and it pisses Amy off."

She struggled against the imperative of death and death and death; struggled against the memories of the man she had come—she remembered this distantly—to save. To free. The thought of Amy Snitman helped enormously, because Chase was right: Amy would be angry. She did laugh, then. It was tremulous, shaky—it was too close to hysteria. But it wasn't a scream and it wasn't a whimper and it wasn't an endless litany of guilt and self-hatred.

"Tell me what you're doing."

She felt his hands once again; they were still locked around hers. Since neither of them were here, that was physically impossible—and she didn't care. Chase didn't look like he cared much either—because she could see him. Bruised, young, his eyes far too dark for the rest of his pale face.

She shook her head.

"Tell me," Chase said, his voice so soft it was more plea than command. Chase was not gentle. That was not part of his oeuvre. But he was trying.

And his voice was so much better than the voices of the crowd. The screaming had stopped—and that was worse for the man whose memories she still inhabited, although until the cries of pain and fear had ceased, he had wished so desperately that they would.

She didn't have an answer for him. She couldn't remember for one long, ugly moment. She couldn't remember because she was paralyzed by the death of her mother.

No. It was *not* her mother. Mercy Hall was alive, in Toronto, a world or two away. She had to remember that, because if she didn't, she would never leave this place. "I'm trying to find a man. A dead man."

"Which one?"

She struggled with the question. Chase knew. Chase should know. He had been there at the beginning. So had she. She tried again. "I'm sitting in the circle."

Yes.

"I'm in the Queen's circle. Where it was supposed to be safe."

"And it's not."

Emma grimaced. "Clearly." She fought, now. Her father did not restrain her; Brendan Hall was dead. She hadn't failed her mother. She hadn't walked away without even *trying*. This pain was not her pain.

And yet it was. It was, now. She could remember this stranger's life as well as she could remember her own. She took a deep breath, held it, exhaled. She could remember the *pain* and the *ugliness* of his life as well as she could remember her own. Her own life had not been painless—but it hadn't been joyless, either.

She was not the sum of her pain. She was—she had to be—more than that.

"I wasn't taught how to use the circle," Emma said.

It wouldn't have made a difference.

"Chase, your mouth isn't moving."

"Not the complaint I usually get."

Emma was silent for a long beat. She closed her eyes— or tried. It made no difference. "Let go of my hands."

"I don't think I can."

"I'm—I think I'll be okay."

"No, I mean I can barely feel my hands." He tensed.

"Chase?"

"Don't worry about me. There's nothing here I haven't seen before."

It was the way he said it. It was the fact that he was fourteen—or younger; that he was bleeding, that he was as yet unscarred. She heard a dog barking. From the sounds of it, it was an angry dog—the bark was territorial.

She couldn't see the dog. Neither could Chase; he was staring at her. But his fingers curled so tightly around Emma's they were painful. His shoulders tightened as if to ward off blows. His head snapped to the side; Emma couldn't see what hit him, but she had no doubt that Chase could.

Emma had never asked Chase about his life. She knew he'd lost his family at the hands of the Queen of the Dead; she knew he'd made his life choices because of that loss. And she knew, watching him, that he was just as trapped by those memories as she'd been by the memories of a dead man.

The difference—the big difference—was that these were clearly his own memories. Emma had some hope of separating herself from decisions she would never have made—if she managed to escape. She *had* a life, and if it wasn't nearly as long as Scoros', it was entirely her own.

Chase couldn't escape his own memories. Not that way.

"Chase. Chase!"

His eyes, unfocused, moved, widening until they were mostly whites. She tried to free one of her hands, but he hadn't lied—his grip was too tight. The dog's bark broke; it was loud and then it was nonexistent. No voice had ordered it to shut up.

And she knew, listening to the sudden silence, what would follow. She did not want to see it. She didn't want to be Chase Loern. She didn't want to watch her family die—again. But she didn't want to lose Chase here, either. He'd come to find her. He'd come to bring her back—and if back was to the heart of the Queen's stronghold, it made no difference.

"Don't make me do this, Chase. Don't. Please."

He didn't answer. Emma was afraid he wouldn't. She had no good choices here; no choice at all. And she didn't know *how* she was supposed to rifle through the memories of a living person. She heard a man's voice—adult. She heard a gunshot. Two. A scream, younger, female.

She wasn't seeing it through Chase's eyes—but Chase was.

Emma was, and remained, herself. The fear she felt was her own. The hatred—and it was momentary, visceral—was her own as well. Neither would help Chase. She could curse the Queen, curse Reyna. Or she could go back, curse the villagers who had killed Reyna's family and the man—no, boy—she had loved. She had no doubt, if she searched the citadel, that she would find other people to curse, other people to hate.

And again, it wouldn't help Chase.

Right here, right now, Chase was like Andrew Copis. He

was like Mark. He was trapped, reliving the events that had destroyed his life. And she was standing outside of them, with the desire and the need to help, and no certain way of doing so.

But she *had* found a way. Both times.

EMMA'S HANDS WERE CURLED TIGHTLY around the bars of the door's grille. Chase's hands were clenched over the top of them. She couldn't shake him loose, and at this point she no longer wanted to try. It wasn't his hands that were the problem—it was the so-called door, a thick, wooden wall with enough of a hole cut into it that she could see his face.

She was shaking. It wasn't fear so much as exhaustion. No, she thought, that was a lie. She *was* afraid. She was afraid for Chase, who mostly hated her but had come anyway. She was afraid for Allison, whose brother lay in a hospital somewhere in Toronto because Allison's best friend was a Necromancer. She was afraid that Allison, who had never, to her knowledge, had more than a passing crush on anyone, would suffer the same loss that she herself had suffered when Nathan had died.

Toby's life was not in Emma's hands.

Chase Loern's was.

She had let herself be pulled into memory after memory,

wandering almost aimlessly in the gray world of the dead,
searching when she didn't know what she was searching for.
She had been a passive witness to murder and torture. She'd
been too horrified to think; she'd lost all sense of herself in
the moment of each memory, struggling to reclaim it when
the memory shifted.

She didn't struggle now. She was Emma Hall.

Chase Loern was not dead. He wasn't lost and invisible.
Emma was not a Necromancer. But she'd been born with
the power of one. She accepted it now. The power was
meant to be used; she could feel the warmth of it, startling
and sudden, as it flowered in hands that had lost all circula-
tion.

The first thing she did was open the door. She didn't
reach for a handle that wasn't there, because she couldn't
free her hands. Instead, she refused to acknowledge the existence of the door. It wasn't solid. It wasn't a memory—or
if it was, it wasn't a memory in which she consented to remain trapped any longer.

The door itself dissolved. Last to go were the bars that
had become a kind of anchor; they weren't necessary. Chase
himself was attached to her hands; she didn't need anything
else. She looked at his face, his young face, at his eyes, at his
slack jaw, his odd hair. This boy would become the Chase
Loern she knew, but he wasn't there yet.

She couldn't prevent it happening. She understood that.
She hadn't been able to prevent Andrew Copis' death either, although she could see exactly how he could have
been saved. The fire had killed the four-year-old. The Queen
of the Dead had killed Chase's family. She wondered if the
Queen of the Dead had ever used the vast reservoir of her
power to attempt to change the past.

Wondered why she even thought it.

But she knew, and she tensed, squaring her shoulders.
She did not want to *be* Chase Loern. She didn't want to be
trapped in his animal fear and fury. But she didn't want him
to be trapped there either. Sometimes all choices were terrible.

Her hands still gripped in his, although they had been
lowered without the bars to anchor them in place, Emma
Hall stepped forward, into his life.

*   *   *

She knew, or thought she knew, what to expect. She had
traveled through a shattered map of Scoros' life, jolted from
memory to memory.

The sky above was dark; moonlight was clear and silver.
She saw the dog first and flinched; it was dead, half of its
head blown away. Gunshots. Its blood was too dark to be
seen as a color. Listening, she heard nothing; her breath was
sharp. Had she come too late? Was it over?

But no. No. She glanced down at her hands and saw
them, empty. But she could feel Chase's hands. Unlike the
hands of the dead, they were warm. Chase was here. He
didn't know that Emma was with him. As Emma had been,
he was trapped in memory—but it was worse. These memories were his.

And Emma was herself. She was not chained to Chase.
As if she were a grim tourist, she could move through the
landscape echoes his life had created.

She stepped over the poor dog's body and continued to
walk.

She found a house next; lights could be seen through glass
panes in the distance. But the house was not where she
needed to go. She moved to the left, to the gravel road that led
to the house itself, and she found what she was searching for.

She saw a man, lying face up, head pointing toward the
house. Like the dog, he'd been shot, but unlike the dog, a
bullet was not the only thing that had damaged him. She
knelt by his side, touched his wrist; her hand passed through
it. The death itself did not disturb her—not as it would have
done before she had entered the citadel. She had watched
two children burn to death.

She rose, continuing to walk.

Six people stood at the far end of the gravel path, and
three people knelt, arms bound. Chase's mother, she thought.
Mother, sister—and Chase himself. She understood, then,
why the Queen's knights had chosen to congregate on the
road; the house wasn't large, and she wasn't certain ten people would have fit in the living room or dining room.

Moonlight glinted off steel—not gun, but knife. The
knife had clearly been used. Of the standing figures, five
were men of varying ages; one was a woman. Emma

recognized her. She was dressed as the Queen and not the girl; she wore an ornate, complicated dress, and her hair was pulled severely above her face and neck. Her hands were gloved, her feet confined by pointed, polished boots. There was no blood on her.

No one moved as Emma approached. No one seemed capable of moving. No one spoke.

Emma reached, hesitantly, to touch the man farthest back—the man who had, no doubt, just killed Chase's father. Her hand passed through his elbow. This was a memory in the same way photographs were: a snapshot through which she had found a way to navigate.

More than that, she didn't try. Instead, she walked through the remaining figures, skirting only the Queen of the Dead. She headed straight for Chase, and when she reached him, she knelt. Tears were frozen in tracks along his face, smearing blood; Chase's cuts were superficial, but his eye had swollen.

"Chase," she said, raising hands to cup his face. "I'm sorry. It's over."

His eyes flickered, his expression shifted. He lifted the face she had cupped; his eyes met hers. "Emma."

She nodded. "There's nothing here. Just you. And me."

He jerked back, pulling his face from the cradle of her hands, his eyes widening as he struggled to turn. Toward his sister, Emma saw. Time did not begin to wind again; his sister and his mother remained motionless.

"Kaleigh."

The girl didn't answer.

"Mom?"

"They can't hear you. The only person who is actually here is you."

He struggled. He struggled with bound hands and forced himself to his feet. "Save them," he whispered.

She understood. And she thought she could; this was not actually happening now. It was very much like the door: a physical object that existed only because she had somehow consented to its existence—as had Chase. When she had consciously refused her consent, the door had dissolved into gray, vanishing as if it had never been real.

She thought the Queen and her men might be the same,

and she wanted—for one visceral moment—to do what he asked. To change the nature of nightmare. To give this boy, who was not yet the Chase she knew, a happier dream. He had done nothing to deserve this, and it was clear that some part of him lived *in* it, constantly.

But even thinking it, she knew she couldn't. He had not deserved it, but it had happened. The dream she could give him was the daydream she had given herself, day after day, week after week. What if Nathan had come by a different route? What if he'd never left home, at all—if she'd called him before he'd reached the door? What if she'd managed to get to the hospital before he was beyond all reach?

And none of those daydreams, not a single one, could change what had actually happened. Nathan had not deserved to die. Emma had not deserved to lose him. Chase had not deserved to lose his entire family in a single, long night. And all of these things had happened. They could not be made to unhappen.

"Please, save them," Chase whispered again.

And it killed her to hear it, to know that she could change what they both saw *here* but that it would change nothing.

Maybe, maybe it would give him the strength to break free. Maybe. She willed herself to believe it; she failed. Swallowing, she said, "I can't, Chase. They died years ago. You're not really here, and neither am I. But we have to go back. You have to leave this place."

He shook his head, mute. "Untie me."

That she could do and did, without ever touching his wrists.

He rose, pushed past her; she turned, still clinging, in some way, to hands she couldn't see. He leaped toward the Queen of the Dead, who stood beneath moonlight like the Faerie Queen herself. He passed through her, landed, rose, and charged again. And again.

Emma changed nothing. Instead, she stood, and she bore witness, and she knew he would hate her for it later. She couldn't stop herself from crying, but it didn't matter; no one here would notice. She waited. She didn't attempt to touch Chase in his youthful frenzy; she didn't attempt to speak to him, to talk him out of the attempts.

She had no idea how time passed in the realm of the dead, and even if she had, she wasn't certain it would have mattered.

Only when he had exhausted the reserves that drove him, only when he had collapsed on the ground at the knees of his mother and sister, did she attempt to remind him that she was here at all.

"Chase."

He didn't look up.

She wanted to apologize—that came naturally to a Hall. She didn't. Instead, quietly, she said, "The first time I went to the graveyard after the funeral was the hardest. Nathan wasn't there. I went at night because no one else would be there either. Just me." She hesitated, because Chase hadn't moved, and she felt that comparing the two losses was wrong.

She had no other way to reach him. "He wasn't there. Of course he wasn't. His body was, and that shouldn't have made a difference." Her voice dropped. "And it didn't, not then. Nathan wasn't there. My loss was. My grief. Maybe even a little anger. I spoke to him." She had never said this to anyone before. Not even Nathan. "I spoke. I wanted him to hear me. I wanted him to know that he would never be forgotten. That he had been loved.

"There was no answer. Of course there wasn't."

Chase was silent.

"I believed the dead don't care. Until Eric arrived, I believed it. I didn't want to believe it." She began to move as she spoke. She knelt, briefly, in front of the woman she assumed was his mother; she shifted her position to study the terrified, weeping face of his sister. Younger sister, clearly. Her hair wasn't the red that Chase's, even cropped so close to his skull, was. "I wanted to believe that the dead were there, that they were waiting, that they watched. That they would *know*."

She stood, raising her voice as she headed through the tableau of Queen and knights to the splayed body of Chase's father. She knelt by his side. Even captured like a 3D picture, the lack of life was pronounced, underlined. In this memory, Chase's father had already been killed. His face, slack and open-eyed, was broken, literally broken. She tried to imagine what he had looked like in life and failed.

She forced herself to try again. While she did, she kept speaking, although Chase had given no hint that he was listening.

"By the time I knew that that wish had been granted, I understood that even if the dead linger, they don't linger by their graves. Graveyards hold bodies or ashes but none of the life that defined the person. They're not meant for the dead. In a strange way, they're meant for the living. They're a place where loss is acknowledged, is meant to be acknowledged.

"Do you ever visit their graves?"

Chase was silent. But in silence he rose. Emma dared a glance at him, and her eyes remained on his hands, which were clenched fists. He shook his head. No.

Giving Chase advice was no part of whatever friendship they had. Emma had come as close as she could. She was surprised when Chase chose to join her.

Chase wondered what the dead saw when they looked at Emma Hall. She stood inches away from his father's corpse. He wouldn't have been surprised to find her weeping; she had a soft heart. A stupidly, enragingly soft heart.

There were no tears on her face when she turned toward him. She was pale, her lips were set, her eyes—her eyes almost reminded him of his own, not in color, but in expression. Was she angry?

Yes, he thought. But not at him. What she offered him was probably pity. He hated that. He didn't want it. He opened his mouth to say as much—with more words for color—but her words finally penetrated the miasma of his anger and, yes, his terror.

She was right. Of course she was right. They were dead and would remain dead. She couldn't save them—no one could. No one could. Thinking it, he turned again to where his mother and sister knelt. He both knew and refused to know; he believed and refused to believe.

He really had despised Emma. Oh, and feared her. Her life had been so easy, compared to his. Her loss had been pathetic. If his parents had died in a car accident and not like *this*, he'd be grateful. He had wanted her to see *his* life. He had wanted her to know it. He had wanted her to suffer his losses because then—

Then she wouldn't be Emma Hall, anymore. Maybe she'd be like Chase.

Death is death. He grimaced. He'd said that before, to himself. He'd said it to others. It was true. Dead was dead. But *dying* was not death.

Emma could content herself with the fact that Nathan's death was not on her hands. He turned to face her again and was surprised to see her hands behind her back. Her eyes were dry, her expression remote. He wasn't surprised when she began to speak, although everything about her implied a stiff silence.

"You didn't kill your family."

"You didn't kill Nathan."

She smiled. It was . . . not a happy smile. "No? Had you met the Queen of the Dead before she came here?" Her arm swept out to encompass the road, the house.

Here, at the heart of the destruction of his life, Chase was not going to offer Emma comfort. He was raw with death, with loss, with the curse of helplessness. He had nothing left for a teenage Necromancer. He shook his head. She waited. "No. No one in my family seemed to recognize her either."

"She would have come here no matter what you did?"

He nodded. Grudging it.

"Nothing you did would have changed that?"

"How the hell am I supposed to know?" This was not the direction his thoughts took when he was forced to relive these events.

She waited. She waited until he said," . . . No."

"The day Nathan died." She stopped. Blinked.

To his own surprise, Chase said, "You don't have to talk about it." He hadn't meant to say anything, but he was now afraid Emma *would* cry, and he'd never been good with tears.

"The day he died," she continued, not crying, "he was on his way to see me."

It was Chase's turn to fall silent.

"He was coming to my house. Coming to pick me up. I liked it when he drove." She looked down, to the wreckage of Chase's father, as if it would somehow steady her.

Death is death. But he couldn't bring himself to say it out loud because right now, he didn't believe it. He'd find belief again later. Maybe.

"I want to go back in time. I want to go back in time and cancel on him. I'd start a big argument if it'd help. I want to go back and tell him to stay home. He was coming *to see me*. And if he hadn't, he wouldn't be dead." She swallowed. She did not cry. "I know I didn't kill him. I know it. But I also know he died because he was coming to me.

"His death was so much better than this. And it was so much worse. Better, because he didn't have a lot of time to be terrified. Worse because—" She shook her head. "It was a lot of metal crushing a lot of metal, and he—"

"Emma, stop."

"Nothing you could have done—in reality, not in daydream—would have changed what happened here that night. Nothing. Even if you were the Chase Loern you are now, it wouldn't have changed a thing. There were five Necromancers *and* the Queen.

"Me? I could have made *one phone call*. And you know? I'm good at phone calls. My mother says I spend half my waking life on the phone. There is *nothing* about a phone call I couldn't handle. I don't have to be a Necromancer. I don't have to be the Queen of the Dead. Do you understand? There's *nothing* you could have done to save your family—and everything I could have done to save Nathan."

Chase stared at her as if he'd never seen her before. Or as if she had sprouted two extra heads.

The landscape in which they stood began to fade. It was a slow process. The Necromancers vanished first, leaving only their Queen behind, standing in the center of the bodies—dead and living—of Chase's family. The gravel road dropped out from beneath her feet; the grass, dark with night, sunk into the gray fog. In the distance, he could just make out the corpse of the dog before the fog rolled over it.

Chase changed as well. His face took on the subtle scars that she knew; his hair shortened into the tight crop he'd adopted after fire had burned patches in the greater length. His clothing changed as well; he wore the studded leather jacket that Amy despised volubly.

Without thought, he lifted both of his hands; with more thought, and more hesitation, she placed hers in them.

The land of the dead reasserted itself completely.

"You know you're being stupid, right?" Chase asked.

Emma smiled. Or tried to. "*I'm* being stupid?"

"I've never claimed to be smart." He tightened his grip on her hands. Exhaled. "There are no graves. Ernest found me. I didn't go back, didn't try to go back, for a year. When I did, I looked for graves. Believe that I looked. There were no graves. There *are* no graves. My entire family disappeared without a trace. The house was empty."

She didn't ask him if he had tried to go back to it. She doubted very much that he had. "You had friends?"

"Hard to believe?"

She shook her head.

"I guess not. You're friends with Amy."

The smile that pulled from her was more genuine. "She's a good friend. Just . . . harsh."

"She might be—she's never going to consider me a friend."

"Do any of your friends know you're still alive?"

Chase shook his head. "You've seen what happens to friends of potential Necromancers. Imagine how much worse it would be if they were friends of hunters."

"And you had no other family?"

He shrugged. She'd opened up. She'd given him her guilt—and inasmuch as guilt was a gift, he accepted it. Her hands tightened on his just before he withdrew them. "An aunt. Two uncles. Grandparents. Some cousins. And no, before you ask, none of them know I'm alive, either."

She didn't ask why. She thought she understood.

She was wrong.

He did not want to be here. Then again, he never did. "Even if I thought they'd be safe, what could I say? When they ask me why I'm still alive, what excuses do I make? How do I stand there and tell them that their children or their brother or their sister are dead when *I'm not*?" His voice had risen, which was strange given just how hard it had become to force air through his closing throat.

Chase, shaking with something that was like rage if you didn't look too closely, was rooted to the spot by the strength of Emma's grip. No, not Emma's. No matter how tightly she clung to his hands, it would be trivial to force her to let go.

He wasn't even trying.

More silence.

This time, when it was broken, it was not broken by Emma.

It was almost like hearing his own voice; for one moment, he thought it *was*. Most of what he'd just told Emma he'd *never* spoken out loud. He recognized his pain, his loss, his own hatred—and he understood then that if it had guided his life, if it had been aimed at Necromancers and the woman who had ruled them, it had also always been turned inward.

"It was not your fault. It was *not your fault*."

REYNA

THE PROCESSION COMES, instantly, to a halt.
The air is cold, the sky is clear and merciless. It sees what Reyna sees. She lifts an arm; the streets empty. The dead vanish almost instantly; the living—and there are few—take time. Reyna wanted an audience. She wanted witnesses.

This was to be her moment.

She looks at Eric's pale, pale face; he might be carved of alabaster as he stands in the center of the street. Her hand is on his arm; she withdraws it. She wonders—for one brief second—why she is here.

And then she wonders, instead, why *Eric* is here. Joy and hope and relief freeze; they hang suspended somewhere outside of Reyna as she studies his face. She *knows* his face. She has never forgotten it.

She has never let herself forget it. But this expression is not the expression that she has captured in a thousand different images. This street is not the edge of a forest; it is not the banks of a brook, run low in its bed by lack of rain.

There were more people here—until she dismissed them—than the entire village contained.

She made decisions. She made choices. She worked tirelessly. She has done everything, *everything*, for Eric.

Eric, who walked away from her once.

Eric, for whom she waited. And waited. And waited.

She looks at him now, and she is terrified, and she has never dealt well with fear. She can feel it rise like a wave, like bile, and she cannot will it away, although she does try. She has done *everything* for Eric. What has she not done?

You have never asked Eric what Eric wants or needs. You have almost destroyed yourself to give Eric what you believed he wanted.

And she hears the voice clearly, she *knows* the voice, although it has been centuries, literally centuries, since she last sought it out. Scoros. Scoros is speaking. He is not here. He will never be here again. She does not turn to look at him; she knows there is nothing to see.

She says, in anger, in despair, her voice as cold as she suddenly feels, "Eric, did you ever love me?"

But Eric is looking past Reyna. He is looking down the street, his eyes oddly shaped—not narrowed, not widened. Softly, softly, he asks, "Who was that?"

She realizes that Eric *heard*. He heard that voice from the dim and distant past; the voice that had promised love and understanding and in the end offered only judgment. And he *should not* be able to hear it. Wheeling, she turns to Nathan, to Emma's Nathan.

"Did *you* hear him?"

Nathan immediately folds into a bow that hides his face—and at the moment, shorn of disciples, she no longer wants that. She orders him, sharply, to rise—and he does. His face is the color of Eric's, his expression more strained. "He said, 'Who was that?' "

"And you heard nothing else?"

"You asked—you asked him a question." He does not repeat it.

Helmi says, "If you want, we can leave the two of you alone." Helmi rarely speaks anymore, although Reyna realizes this only because the sound of her voice is a shock. "You might want to talk about things too private for audiences."

Eric has not answered Reyna's question.

Or maybe he has. Maybe, over the passing centuries, he *has*. *Reyna, you are asking the wrong question.* The voice is gentle.

Reyna stiffens at the weight of it, the weight of familiarity, the pointed reminder of things missing, things gone. She has almost forgotten. It has been so long. She should have known that he would wake and be present today, of all days.

Today is the day that she could finally prove him wrong.

And Eric doesn't answer her question. She turns to her sister, standing beside her sole personal attendant. "You may leave. Nathan. Return to my quarters and wait." Nathan bows again.

"And me?" Helmi asks, in her little-girl, trying-too-hard-to-sound-bored voice.

"You may keep him company if that is what you desire — but, Helmi, for the moment, I need him. Do you understand?"

Helmi says, sharply, "Because he can do things, and I can't."

Today is not the day to deal with Helmi's resentment, but Reyna tries. "There are many things you can do. You've saved my life at least three times just by being careful and listening. I would never have made it this far without you. You are the only one who's stayed by my side." She watches Helmi carefully as she speaks, although she wishes Helmi were someplace else.

Helmi shrugs, sullen. "You just want to be alone with Eric," she says. It reminds the Queen, sharply and unexpectedly, of the life she led before the massacre. Before she almost lost Eric. She loved her sister.

But she wished — as she wishes now — that her sister would just *go away*. Without leaving guilt in her wake.

"Eric and I have things to talk about. I promise I will come and find you when we're done." She speaks without much hope; this never worked in the past, when Helmi was actually alive.

Helmi's frown sets. She looks — with disdain — at Nathan and says, "Fine. I'll be waiting. Nathan can keep me company." When Nathan fails to move, she glares at him, finding a different target for her sullen rage.

"Nathan," the Queen says. "Please accompany Helmi."

Nathan bows. He is not like Helmi; he is not sullen or resentful. He is a much quieter, much less brittle presence. Perhaps that is why she will keep him, in the end.

But Nathan is not her problem. She dismisses him, with far less work than she dismissed her sister. She dismisses *everyone*, and the crowds, the triumphal witnesses to the end of her long and bitter struggle, also disperse with far less resentment than Helmi did.

And when they are alone, she turns to Eric.

But there is one person she cannot dismiss. *You ask the wrong questions. You have always asked the wrong questions.*

"Shut up." Eric's eyes narrow—and why wouldn't they? "I—apologize, I wasn't speaking to you."

He says nothing, and this is troubling; she has *apologized*, and he has failed to respond. Perhaps he doesn't know how seldom she apologizes. It has been a long time, after all. Perhaps he thinks she is as powerless, as stupid, as she once was. And that thought angers her.

No—it revives dormant anger. It roots anger to pain. She wants—has always wanted—Eric. But she wants him *here*. Not standing at her side as if he were still half a world away, and hidden.

And what, she thinks bitterly, did she expect? That he would grovel, that he would beg her forgiveness? No. Pathos is not what she wants.

And yet, conversely, he *should* do all of these things, because he *left her*. He is not looking at the city. He is not looking at the buildings. He is not looking at *anything*. She did so much. She built so much. And for what, in the end?

"Eric."

Ask the right question, Reyna.

"Go away!"

If I could, I would. You know why I am here. You know why I am almost anywhere you choose to be. Child—

"I am *not a child!*"

Reyna, love, you are.

She turns then. Turns before she can stop herself. She storms toward the nearest wall—the wall of a townhouse—and slams her fists into it in fury. The wall shatters. If she stomped, the ground would shatter in the same way.

She turns again; the building's facade lies in shards, but the shards are not of stone or glass. She hears the distant wailing of living things in pain, and she realizes that some part of it is her own voice.

She does not look at Eric. She doesn't want to see his expression.

"Reyna."

She looks at her feet. At her magnificent skirts. At the stones she took so long to figure out how to make. At the fall of her own shadow.

"Reyna." Eric's voice is not harsh, not angry. She can't look up to meet his eyes. "Reyna." She doesn't look up until his fingers touch her chin, until he lifts her face. Until his thumbs wipe tears—inexplicable tears—away.

"Who are you shouting at?"

"It's not—it's not important."

He looks at the melting hole in what was once wall; at the shards that had once been all of a piece but now lie, becoming amorphous as the seconds pass, at her feet. He closes his eyes.

NATHAN

HELMI LEADS NATHAN out of the streets. She walks slowly, turning every so often to look over her shoulder. She even ditches the dress. Nathan wishes he could ditch the suit in the same way, but the suit isn't an integral part of what he is.

If the Queen notices, she says nothing—and Nathan is fairly certain she hasn't noticed. He is not Helmi. He is not the Queen's baby sister. He doesn't give much for his chances if he strips off his clothing, even in the ruins of her victory parade. Nor does he give much for his chances if he glances back and sees something he is not meant to see.

Helmi knows.

It's why she takes so damn long to clear the street.

He can't decide if her sullen resentment was put on or not. She isn't a child anymore—she just looks like one. He can't tell if she wants—as the dead do—to be ceaselessly near her sister's light and warmth, regardless of the fact that it burns to ash anything it touches. Given the Queen as the only choice, Nathan isn't certain himself.

But she isn't the only choice, not yet.

He suddenly wants to race down the streets. To race back to the citadel. Emma is here, somewhere. In life, Emma was his choice. In death, she is even more so. But he keeps pace with Helmi; it's a type of invisibility.

Helmi isn't in a rush. She doesn't appear to notice Nathan at all. Either she's the world's best actor, or things are complicated. Nathan goes with complicated.

"I can't help it," Helmi says, when they've turned a corner and put several solid walls between them and their Queen. "I hate Eric."

"Why?"

"If it weren't for Eric, none of this would have happened."

"Wrong. It had nothing to do with Eric, in the end."

"She loved Eric!"

"Is that what you call it? Love?" He lowers his voice, tries to still his hands. He is shaking with something like rage. "You can hate him—you're going to do what you want, anyway—but none of this is his fault. He didn't kill himself. You're blaming the wrong person."

"Really?" Sarcasm of the ages—all of them, ever—in that voice.

Nathan falls silent. He's been dead for weeks. Not years. Not centuries. To his knowledge, no one he loves and trusts has ever been guilty of murder, let alone Necromancy. He doesn't think it's Eric he'd hate, in Helmi's position—but how can he be certain?

"You didn't have sisters," Helmi says.

"Is it that obvious?"

"Yes. You want to ask me if I still love mine."

Nathan is silent.

"And the answer is no." It sounded like yes. "And yes." Which conversely sounded like no. "I don't remember what it's like to be alive. I *want* it," she adds, voice a burning kind of cold. "I *almost* remember when I'm with her. And that's irony, for you. I wish she had never fallen in love. I wish Eric had treated her the way most outsiders treated us: with suspicion and contempt.

"I never understood why we had to avoid people who

were kind. People who liked us." Her face, her expression, is uncomfortable; it is not a child's expression, but it is informed in all ways by a child's features.

Nathan doesn't know what to say. He wants to tell her that this is *wrong*, that it is not the kindness that has to be avoided. Or the love. But he understands—and he hasn't understood this so clearly before—that the kindness and the love, like the anger and the fear, are not divorced from the rest of the person. He doesn't doubt—he cannot doubt—that Eric once loved the Queen of the Dead.

"Sometimes," he says carefully, "people can turn anything to crap. Anything. It doesn't mean that it started out as crap."

"And some days," Helmi says, as if Nathan hadn't spoken, "I want what she *didn't* give me then. Or ever. I want her time, her attention, her affection. Even now." She exhales. "How stupid is that?"

He doesn't answer. Instead he says, "Do you know where Emma is?"

"No. I know where she was, but she's not there now."

"How can you tell?"

"I can't see her."

"Can you find her?"

Helmi says nothing. She closes her eyes. Nathan is aware that this is cosmetic for the disembodied dead. So is breathing. But he holds his breath, his constructed, artificial breath, until the moment her eyes widen in something akin to horror. "What is *she doing*?" she hisses.

Turning to Nathan she says, "The Queen told us to wait in her chambers. I'm going ahead." Turning, she marches—there's no other word for it—through the wall. Nathan, embodied, has to take the long way.

He runs.

CHAPTER
EIGHTEEN

EMMA'S HANDS FELT ALMOST NUMB, but not with cold. She turned first. She moved, subconsciously attempting to put herself between Chase and the stranger who had just spoken. Clutched hands made it almost impossible, but she wasn't certain she could let go of Chase's hands even if she wanted to.

And there he was: the man she'd stepped into a carved circle to find. He was older than Brendan Hall had been at the time of his death—if age meant anything to him; he was not newly dead and could change his appearance at will.

He was not looking at her. He was looking at Chase. Chase, who didn't appear to see him.

"Chase, you have to let go of my hands."

Chase's eyes found hers and narrowed; he shook his head, as if not trusting his voice.

"One of my hands, then."

He managed that, but it took time, and time had returned,

at least for Emma. What she wanted, right now, was home. Home, peace, and even her mother. She wanted her half-deaf rottweiler. She wanted safety.

She had no idea how to get home from here. In the quiet of her thoughts, she accepted the truth that she had shied away from. While the Queen of the Dead lived, there was no home that would be safe—not for her, and not for the friends who'd been dragged into the world of Necromancers because they refused, in the end, to be left behind.

Because they loved her, or needed her, or some combination of both.

Hall manners asserted themselves as Chase released her right hand. She turned to the man who had spoken—and who looked, to her eye, as shattered as Chase. She had lived through so many atrocities as a voiceless passenger—most committed by him. But the start of his path had been the same as the start of Chase's, and she wondered if that was the inevitable destination for anyone who was forced to walk it.

She held out her free hand.

The stranger stepped forward. He looked like a ghost, unlike the undead Emma was accustomed to seeing; he was entirely transparent. Even when he attempted to take her hand, his fingers passed through hers.

"I am Scoros," he said.

"I'm Emma Hall. This is Chase."

"Yes." It was at Chase he was looking. "It was not your fault." Chase blinked. Focused. He could *hear* the man and, with effort, could see him. "You didn't kill them."

"I didn't save them either."

"No. You couldn't. You didn't run."

"I couldn't. Why did she do it?"

"I do not know. I was not alive when it happened. You see me."

Chase nodded.

"And yet you are not one of the people."

"Neither is Emma."

Emma's eyes widened at the words. It was the first time Chase had said anything remotely like this. She wished that Allison could hear it.

"Why do you look like a ghost?" she asked.

The man turned to her. "Do I?"

"To me, yes—a storybook ghost. I can see right through you."

"With practice, Emma, you could see through anyone."

She grimaced. "Everyone else looks like a living person." When they weren't floors or walls.

"Ah." He looked past Emma and Chase, his eyes narrowing. Emma looked in the direction of his gaze and saw nothing. Nothing at all.

"I am not . . . all here."

"What do you mean?"

He smiled. "You are no part of the many, many memories it has been my task to keep. You are not the first person I have spoken to since my long confinement, but you are the first to hear my voice."

"I'm not," Emma replied. She didn't accuse him of lying.

His smile deepened; it was bitter. "But you are, Emma. My Reyna has not heard my voice for a very long time. I have heard hers." He lifted his head. "Eric is with her."

Emma nodded.

"I can see them."

"I can't."

"No. You are alive. You are not woven through the citadel. You are not embedded in its walls and towers and streets. You are not part of the bitter history of its creation."

"And you are?"

"Yes."

"Voluntarily?"

"No. No and yes. I knew what she would do. Reyna has always feared abandonment. I at least could never leave her."

"You tried to kill her." It wasn't a question.

"Yes. It is not one of the memories in which I've been imprisoned. She could not believe that the attempt would bring me nothing but pain, and she desired pain. Chase said you are not of the people."

Emma nodded.

"He was wrong. I can see it in you. You are very like Reyna."

"She's *nothing* like the Queen of the Dead."

"Is she not, boy? But I forget. You are not yet dead. You see the dead, but you do not see the living as the dead see them. To the eyes of the dead, she is no different."

"Not to the eyes, maybe," Chase said. "But what she does for the dead is different."

"Is it? I see that she has bound the dead. At least two; perhaps more. They are not with her, now."

Chase cursed. Stopped. "Can you see who she's bound?"

The man's expression rippled. If Emma could have, she would have kicked Chase; she was staring daggers at the side of his face. This man had tried to kill the Queen of the Dead *because* the Queen had attempted to bind his mother—and his mother was now bound to Emma. This could go bad very fast.

She stopped. How? How could it go bad? There was no longer anything this man could do to her. He was dead.

"The dead are not with her."

"Not here, no."

"Where are you, child?"

She resisted the urge to argue with the word 'child'. "I'm sitting in the center of a big circle that's been carved out of runes into stone floor. And I'm here with Chase—and you."

"And you found me through the circle?"

"I don't know. I was trying to find you—but you weren't where I expected you to be."

"When you say circle, what do you mean?"

Emma exhaled. "There's a big circle on the floor in the center of the Queen's—room." She could not bring herself to call it the resurrection room.

The ghost's eyes widened. "You are sitting in *her* circle?"

"I only had access to two, and we didn't think to bring the other one."

"It is not safe for you to use her circle."

"It's not safe for us to be anywhere near her rooms, let alone her citadel, no."

"That is not what I meant. Take me—take as much of me as you can—back to the circle."

Emma didn't tell him that she didn't know how to get back to the circle. She didn't want to tell him anything. She didn't want to take him to where her friends—her living friends—were waiting.

"Could I meet Reyna here, where we are?" she asked.

Silence. She met the man's gaze, seeing his eyes rather than the gray that lay beyond them, stretching out to eternity.

"You cannot harm her here. If you met here, it is you who would be in danger. She is not more powerful than you, but she is vastly more knowledgeable. Take me back to the circle." He looked down at the hand into which he had placed his own; his hadn't gained solidity. "There is, perhaps, something you can do—but you must act quickly. Reyna is aware of me, now."

"You said—"

"And she is not happy. I have perhaps spoiled her day." He tilted his face, as if he were listening. "Helmi is coming."

Emma opened her eyes. She saw gray; she saw Chase; she saw a ghost. She tried again.

"This will not do," the man said. "Have you forgotten?"

"Forgotten what?"

"That you are alive."

"No."

"Then remember what life *is*, child. Open your eyes."

She tried again. She failed again. What was life, exactly? She felt alive here. She had felt alive in the memories of the dead man. She had felt alive when wandering around the frozen tableau of the worst day of Chase Loern's life. She had felt alive—uselessly, pointlessly alive—in the cemetery to which she had retreated in the evenings with her dog.

She had no experience with death, except as an observer. Talking to the dead was almost exactly the same as talking to the living. This landscape wasn't life; she knew that. She had no idea how she was to leave it because opening her eyes changed nothing.

No.

She tried, after a long pause, to close her eyes instead. Closing her eyes, she could still see the man. And she could still see Chase. What she could no longer see was herself. She wasn't sure if this was better or worse—it was certainly different.

She kept her eyes closed, and she listened. The old man

had fallen silent. He was motionless, his gaze fixed on something beyond where Emma assumed she was sitting.

Sight hadn't helped. She chose to listen instead.

Listening was an art; she was an amateur. She had learned—with time—to hear the textures in spoken words; the words had meanings, but they were imprecise, and the voice in which they were spoken compensated for meanings words alone couldn't convey. The same sentence could have multiple meanings, depending on who spoke.

Silence was the same—but it was harder to understand. Sometimes it was a well, sometimes it was a barrier, and sometimes it was the only response one could offer.

Sometimes it needed to be broken.

"Michael?" The single word was rough, patchy; her throat felt raw.

"Emma?" Michael's voice.

She nodded, or hoped she nodded. "I'm having a little trouble opening my eyes. Can you keep talking?"

Pause. "About what?"

"Anything."

"Margaret says to tell you that the statue I saw before isn't there anymore."

"You can't see it anymore?"

"No. I—I think you did something. It . . . broke when you were . . . upset." She could hear Michael choosing his words with care.

"When I was crying?"

"When you were screaming," he corrected. "It's gone now. There's no statue. But there's a door, now."

"Can anyone else see the door?"

"No," Amy said, before Michael could answer.

To the man, Emma said, "Can you hear them?"

"If he can't," Chase replied, "I can."

"Can you see Michael?"

"No."

"Why can't you open *your* eyes?"

Chase exhaled. "Because I'm probably not conscious. I don't know how long we've been here. Look, I can see the dead—but it doesn't come naturally. The Queen did something to me—I thought it would kill me." He had probably hoped, at the time, that it would. "She left me alive as a message to Eric." Chase laughed. It sounded like a controlled scream.

"Why did you need to be able to see the dead to deliver a message?"

"I didn't think to ask."

Emma winced. "Sorry—that was a stupid question."

"Spending too much time with Michael?" He grinned.

"Margaret is worried," Michael said. "Allison is worried."

"Is Amy?"

"I think so. It's hard to tell with Amy."

"Amy," Amy said, "doesn't appreciate being talked about in the third person."

Chase muttered something under his breath.

Amy said, in a distinctly chillier voice, "I heard that."

And Emma opened her eyes.

Michael was standing outside of the circle; he was much closer than he had been. Then again, so was Allison. Margaret, Ernest, and Amy remained closer to the wall. Amy's eyes were narrowed in a very particular way, but their edges were largely aimed at Chase. And yes, Amy was worried.

Amy Snitman didn't do worry—or rather, if she did, she used it as a springboard for confrontation. She liked to face her fears. And stomp them flat. Unfortunately, if there was nothing immediately stompable, her foot sometimes came down anyway.

Chase was lying, cheek to stone, in a curl against the floor. Mindful of Ally, Emma reached out and poked his shoulder. He opened his eyes and pushed himself into a sitting position. On any other day, Emma would have told him not to bother. His complexion was almost gray, his lips the same color as the rest of his skin.

"Thanks," Emma said to Michael.

He blinked rapidly but nodded. "Did you find him?"

Emma unfolded her legs, stood, shook them out. "How long have I been sitting here?"

"Nineteen minutes," Ernest replied. "You have not been entirely silent."

"Amy? Care to explain that in normal English?"

"You've been screaming your lungs out or sobbing so much we were afraid you'd throw up. Better?"

Emma winced. "Sort of." She offered a Chase a hand; he glared and refused to take it. It took him longer to stand, and he didn't look particularly steady on his feet when he did. Allison also offered him an arm—but this time, his pride didn't get in the way of accepting aid.

Emma turned.

The man was standing behind her; she could see him if she concentrated. He was no longer transparent; he was so diaphanous she couldn't be certain he wasn't a trick of the light. And the light, in this room, was bright and endless.

She reached out to touch him and wasn't surprised when her hand passed through his arm. She had no idea how to make contact with him, beyond the visual.

"Scoros, can you hear me?"

She thought there was a ripple in the air. Chase left the circle, attached by arm to Allison. Emma hovered at its inner edge. She was afraid to lose Scoros. "Helmi's coming, by the way."

Margaret stiffened. "When?"

"Now," Helmi said.

"Now," Emma repeated. She wasn't touching Helmi, so no one but Margaret could see her. She doubted Chase was putting in the effort, given he was standing and his color had gone from gray to white.

Helmi looked like a bruised, underfed child. She wore a very simple shift, with a tunic hanging loosely from scrawny shoulders; her hair was long but not tidy. Helmi could choose her appearance.

Emma didn't think her current appearance was a conscious choice. Her expression was thunderous; she'd entered the light-filled, cold room, and she'd brought the storm with her. It flashed in the eyes she turned on Emma; they'd widened.

"What do you think you're *doing*?"

"Finding a man called Scoros—which is what you told me to do." She might have grown an extra head with less effect on Helmi than the words she'd just spoken.

The fact that the advice had come from Helmi was not

enough of an excuse. "Are you *insane*? Do you think my sister won't *know*?"

Emma had no answer.

"Leave him alone."

Helmi.

The child's eyes widened further. Emma heard Scoros' voice as an echo—something easily missed if one wasn't listening. Helmi, clearly, did not.

You saved the Queen's life the last time we met.

Helmi did not reply.

Will you save it again?

"There's nothing you can do, now. You're dead."

So are you. Do you feel there's no harm you can do because of it?

Helmi folded her arms.

"Can you *see* him?" Emma asked the girl.

Helmi didn't answer. Instead, she said, "You can't use another person's circle. Whatever you tried to do, it was just as dangerous as having no circle at all. You really don't know *anything*."

Emma nodded. "You said the circle—"

"You have to draw *your own*. You don't use someone else's. This is the Queen's. It'll keep her safe. It won't do squat for you."

Helmi is correct.

"If it was yours," Helmi continued, "you would never have found him."

"But . . ."

"But what?"

"The circles were meant to be used so we could find the dead safely, weren't they?"

Helmi snorted. "There's no safe way to find *him*. You need to let him go. Or make him go."

"Why?"

"Because you're alive. Most of your friends are alive. I'm assuming you'd all like to stay that way."

"He can't hurt us. He's dead."

"Outside of my sister and her stupid knights, he's the only person who *can*."

I cannot hurt any of them, Scoros said.

"She doesn't understand what was done to you. She doesn't understand how the citadel *rose*. Almost no one does."

You do.

"I was there." Helmi turned to face Amy and Margaret and Ernest. "Scoros attempted to kill my sister. He failed. His betrayal actually hurt her. It hurt almost as much as Eric's. Maybe more."

"She killed him."

"Yes."

"And then she bound him."

"I don't think it's as simple as that. What did he tell you?"

Emma said, after a thick pause, "He's told me almost nothing. What I know of his life, I . . . lived."

She wasn't certain what she expected Helmi's response to be—but it wasn't a derisive snort. "Of course you did. There's no other way to find the dead. But Emma, you need to understand something. Most of what was done to him was done *before* he died. It was done with his consent."

Emma turned to face the thin impression in the air; it hadn't moved. "Is she right?"

Yes. The dead are *dead, Emma Hall. But what remains of them when they no longer draw breath was in them before they ceased to breathe. It is how Chase Loern can see the dead. It is how you can see and touch the dead. There is part of you that is already dead. It is how the Queen can make bodies, how she could build a citadel that can house the living.*

We are what you are.

"What does Helmi mean?"

She was lonely, she was afraid. She understood that she was not valued by her knights. They did not love her. They did not revere her, although she had given them their power. They betrayed her and would have continued to betray her.

I see the citadel. I saw its streets before I attempted to kill her. I saw its halls, its rooms. There was only one room I could not—could never—see.

"This one."

Yes. She trusted me more than perhaps she trusted any

living person—but she was not given to trust. She needed a place in which she might rest, in which she did not need to worry that someone would see and disapprove of her. It made sense that it would be this room; this room was the heart of her power.

And now you are in it. She will come.

"What does Helmi mean? What is she afraid of?"

If I had to guess—and Helmi did not love me—she is afraid that you will die.

"And will I?"

If I am consumed, if I am recalled? Yes. But Emma, so will Reyna. She is like a god, but she is human.

Emma had her doubts.

She cannot fly. Disentangle me from the citadel, and the citadel will fall.

Emma turned toward her friends.

Yes. No one will survive.

"You're bound to the Queen of the Dead?"

I am bound to the citadel. He paused. *And yes, some part of me—the part that was not built into the foundation of her current life—is bound to the Queen. But one part of me is not. When I threaded myself through the citadel, I created one space which would be my own.*

"You left your mother there."

Silence.

"Emma, maybe this isn't the right time," Chase said. His voice sounded normal. His color, when Emma spared him a glance, was better. He probably wouldn't achieve good for a couple of hours, if then.

She inhaled and stepped out of the circle. Nothing had changed if you didn't include the presence of Helmi. The girl had traded the expression of outrage for a mask that denied emotion.

"Is the Queen on her way here?"

Helmi said nothing.

Scoros said, *No. Not yet. You have time to escape these chambers.*

"What did you do?" Helmi asked again. "Why did you come to *this* room?"

"I thought there was a man trapped here." She turned to Michael and added, "Can you still see the door?"

Michael nodded, lifting an arm to point at the frustratingly blank patch of slightly curved wall.

Helmi, following the direction of his arm, frowned. "There's no door there."

"There's no man there, either. Or if he is, that's not where I found him." She exhaled and added, "You might as well come out. I know you're there."

Another ghost materialized. She became far more solid than the almost invisible form of the man who had been her son.

Emma wasn't certain what reaction she'd expected from either Scoros or the older woman, and at least in Scoros' case, it didn't matter, as she could barely make out his face. The old woman, however, was dour and grim; she wasn't exactly welcoming.

"He was always a fool," she said, confirming the lack of joy. "But we all want to think well of our own sons. I could not imagine how *much* of a fool."

She felt, rather than saw, Scoros' surprise and almost shied away from it. Lifting her hand, she turned it and examined the palm she had offered to what remained of Scoros. It was empty, but she felt something—a texture, a subtle weight.

He was demonstrably capable of speech, but he said nothing.

"You'll help her, of course," the woman continued.

"She's talking about you," Helmi told Emma, her face expressionless.

Scoros did not answer.

"Yes," the old woman continued, as if he somehow had. "I'm bound to the foolish child. Did you know that? Did you suspect?"

Yes.

"I can't find my way back to my room. I've tried. For me, there is only one possible safety now. Reyna will not be happy to see me. How did the girl find what remains of you?" Nothing in her voice wobbled. She was as lifeless, as joyless, as vacuum.

She searched. This was clearly not enough of an answer, and Scoros knew it. *She searched the old way.*

"In a circle not meant or drawn for her use." Flat, almost disbelieving tone.

You must ask her, then.

"She couldn't answer. You can."

I was not in a position to observe her progress objectively. There was now a sliver of irritation in his reply.

"Even when you were, you were never objective," his mother snapped back.

Amy's brows rose; she looked to Emma. "I want to know who he's talking to."

"You can hear his voice, but not his mother's?"

"No."

"Be grateful," Helmi told her. Amy couldn't hear Helmi, either. The leader of the Emery mafia folded her arms; she looked about as friendly as Scoros' mother, but infinitely more attractive.

How did she find you?

"You'll have to ask her."

How did she bind you?

The old woman fell silent.

Emma.

"Don't you use that tone with the girl," his mother said, before Emma could even think of answering.

Silence. Surprise.

She is not controlling you. It was a statement with a hint of question at the end.

"What do *you* think?"

I think I do not understand Emma Hall. You are bound to her. There is at least one other.

Margaret said nothing.

"I told the girl she'll need more."

She will. But she does not have the time. I very much fear that Reyna will do to Eric what was done to me.

"At least then she'd finally have to admit that he's dead." Cold, harsh words.

Eric had been dead long before Reyna had become the Queen of the Dead. He'd been dead for centuries, possibly longer. She had built this place for Eric; it was to be their home. She knew this without examining any of Scoros' memories—or her memories of them.

How fitting, then, that this was built of the dead; it was built for the dead. Grief and loss and rage and helplessness had entombed a girl scarcely younger than Emma. All of those things, Emma thought, but also a bitter, terrible hope.

She understood it so well—and hated herself for the understanding—because the door opened and before anyone could think to panic, although both Chase and Ernest were suddenly armed, Nathan ran in.

NATHAN

HE TURNS TO SHUT THE DOOR BEHIND HIM. There are no bolts or he'd bolt it, for all the good that would do. If the Queen of the Dead seeks these chambers, nothing will prevent her entry. Nothing.

And he cares now because he sees Emma. She glows so brightly; she is the only thing he sees for one long breath. He is across the room, he is almost at her side, before thought catches up with action. He stops, then, lowering arms he had no intention of raising.

They're *all* here. Michael, Ally, Amy. The only thing that's missing is the dog. He almost asks. He doesn't. Emma has turned to face him. She is frozen but burning. He almost can't see her expression. But when she moves, he doesn't need to see it.

He has lowered his arms, and he keeps them by his sides. He wanted—wants—to hold her. But he can't. Not like this. Maybe she doesn't see what he is now. Maybe she doesn't understand. He knows he can touch her and she will not freeze. He will even feel the contact in some fashion.

But she can see the dead. She's sensitive to their presence. And he cannot believe that if she holds him, she won't see what now comprises his body. The dead, the weeping dead, are what she would be holding; he doubts that her actual touch can reach him at all. He wonders if it will help the four who are bound and trapped and almost voiceless.

She sees him pull up short. She moves.

He raises a hand, palm out, and she stops. Her eyes widen, her brows drawing briefly together in hurt surprise. He hates it.

"I can't touch you," he tells her, trying—and failing—to keep his voice steady.

"You have—"

"I have a body, yes. But Em—it's not mine. It's made of . . ." He really does want to hold her. He knows the look on her face. He watches it transform as she does what she always did: finishes the thought so he doesn't have to put it into words.

"It's made of the dead."

He nods. "I can control the body almost as if it were actually real. I'm told it even bleeds. But—" He inhales, exhales. "It wouldn't be me who'd be holding you."

"I don't suppose they volunteered, either."

He shudders. It was in this room that he watched the Queen create the cage that houses him. "Em—what are you _doing_ here? How did you _get_ here?" And then, before she can answer, he asks the only question that really matters. "Can you get back home?"

"Probably."

He doesn't believe her. He can't. Being dead doesn't change the fact that he knows her. It's only been a couple of months—and an eternity. If she's changed in that time, she hasn't changed enough to make her doubt invisible. "How?"

"That's Ernest's job," she replies. "We only have one job, now." But she looks at him.

And of course he knows what she doesn't say. He knows what that job is. He wants to tell her that it's impossible for her. He knows it's impossible. Power isn't knowledge. Knowledge is power. Emma lacks knowledge. But looking at her with the eyes of the dead—his own eyes now and forevermore—he can't believe it. She is a light, a fire, to equal the Queen's—the only such light in the citadel.

The only such light, Nathan suspects, in the world.

"Where is the Queen?"

"She's in the streets outside the citadel, with Eric. They may be arguing. She sent everyone away—dead or living."

"Will Eric kill her?" It is a harsh question; it is therefore not Emma's. Nathan's eyes glance off Chase's face. He's surprised. Ally is beside him, under his right arm, and the question didn't even make her flinch.

Nathan can't answer because he doesn't know. He knows that in Eric's position, he would falter—but he can't conceive of Emma *as* the Queen of the Dead. If she were?

If that's what she must become?

CHAPTER
NINETEEN

MICHAEL STARED AT NATHAN. So did Chase. Amy, never one for expressions of shock, nodded once, grimly, before her gaze moved on. It came to rest on Emma. No one did judgment as well as Amy Snitman. Amy Snitman could make a test out of anything—but it was easier for Amy; she never failed. She wasn't judging yet, but Emma knew this was a test.

Of course it was. Nathan was here. Nathan looked like *Nathan*. He was, to her eyes, alive. Even his eyes appeared almost brown. He was wearing very strange clothing, and his hair looked almost ridiculous, but none of that mattered.

She tried to see him as she saw the dead. She closed her eyes. Why had she never tried this with Eric?

"Em." Ally's voice. And Nathan's, overlapping it, maybe half a second behind. Emma had just spent a subjective lifetime trapped behind Scoros' eyes. She'd wondered, until Nathan opened that door, whether or not she would ever be just Emma Hall again.

The answer was yes.

Emma had loved Nathan, still loved him, still dreamed of spending her life in his company and the accepting warmth of his many silences. She wanted nothing as much as she wanted that. She wanted Nathan *back*.

It was a good dream. It had been the *best* dream. And it was time to wake up, to live—forever—without it. What was left was what-if, and she'd done that. She would probably continue to do that, in the quiet moments when she came face to face with her loneliness and the empty space where Nathan had once stood.

In the worst and the darkest of moments, she had wanted to die. Just ... die. She had never had the courage to kill herself, and, in truth, death and suicide were not the same. Even if they had been, she couldn't imagine deliberately doing to her mother, and the friends who needed her, what Nathan's accidental death had done to his.

But in daydream, death was different. It wasn't about the loss other people would feel or suffer. It wasn't about the pain she would cause.

It was about the pain she would no longer feel—because if she were dead, it would be *over*. She would never need to feel loss again. She would never have to confront the emptiness, the black hole, that had once been filled by Nathan.

She had been lucky, she realized, standing an arm's length away from him. She had been able to see him again, to speak with him again, to tell him all the things that she couldn't tell his corpse. His mother hadn't even had that.

She had been able to hear him tell her, again, that he loved her. But that was all she could have. It wasn't what she wanted. It wasn't *enough*. But it had to be. More was impossible.

Loving her, not loving her, wanting her, not wanting her—they were all in the past. They were etched in her heart and her mind. They turned joy into pain, over and over again. They turned *love* into pain. She wasn't certain she would ever love anyone again—not the way she loved Nathan.

She wanted love to last forever.

And this one could—but it could never grow and change. It could no longer sustain her. It could no longer sustain Nathan.

Nathan was dead.

She exhaled—she had been holding her breath. With her eyes closed, she could see Nathan clearly. He was wearing the clothing he'd been wearing the day he died—the day he was coming to see her. To pick her up. To take her away from the rest of her life. She'd loved, and still loved, that life—but it was the space they created when they were together that had given her the deepest joy.

And that was lost to death as well. Lost to Emma. She held out one hand.

He shook his head, but she didn't lower that hand.

"I see it," she told him. "I see it, now."

"See what?"

"The binding," she whispered. And she did. It was a slender, golden chain that pulsed with a faint light—as if it were a stretched, attenuated heart. It traveled away from Nathan, into the gray; she couldn't see the other end of it.

"Em—"

"Let me do this one thing." She couldn't tell herself that she was doing this for Nathan. She was doing it for herself. If she couldn't have Nathan back, if she couldn't have what had been irrevocably lost, she'd be damned if she'd let the Queen of the Dead have what was left.

He hesitated, his expression drawn; she realized she must be crying—and she didn't care. Just this once, it didn't matter. What were tears, after all, but the overflowing of pain when there was just too much of it for one person to contain?

"I don't want to touch you," he said.

"Yes, you do. You just don't want them to touch me in your place."

"Can you—can you see them?"

She couldn't. The only thing she could see with closed eyes was Nathan. She didn't understand the magic of the Queen's resurrection. But she was certain that she *could* reach the dead, if they were sentient, if they were somehow present.

She was certain of that if nothing else.

She smiled. She forced herself to smile. He knew, of course. He winced at her expression. "People tell you that love doesn't die as long as someone remembers," she said.

"I always thought that was bullshit."

She laughed, a blend of genuine amusement and endless loss. "Me too. Especially after you died. But it doesn't matter. It doesn't matter if it's bullshit. It doesn't matter if love dies with death or if it lasts for eternity. What we had was special, but it's *over*."

"Em—"

"And I don't want it to *be* over. I never, ever wanted that. But it is, Nathan. There's only one thing I can do for you." She opened her palm. Her arm was steady. "There's only one thing I can do for *me*."

He drifted closer, as if pulled by main force. Emma hadn't moved. "I don't want to let you go," she whispered.

He closed the distance, then. He placed his hand in hers. There, here, it didn't matter. She felt the warmth of his palm as it met hers—but she felt the ice, too. With her free hand, she reached for the golden filament, and as she'd done before, she snapped it.

It broke cleanly; there was no resistance at all.

She wanted to hold him. No, that was wrong. She wanted to be held. She wanted to lean into his chest, seek comfort and harbor inside the curve of his arms, rest her forehead against his shoulder. She'd done that before.

She'd never do it again, and never was almost too much. But too much didn't matter. Death *was*. It just was.

And she understood his hesitation. She could hear—or feel—something that was not quite Nathan in the curve of a palm that mimicked his hand almost perfectly. She understood *why* he hadn't opened his arms to her, or touched her at all until she'd practically begged.

She thought about Merrick Longland. If he had not told her that the body he'd been granted was not actual flesh, that the spirit it now contained was still, and always, dead, would she have believed it? It *felt* like life.

Without thought, she stepped into Nathan; without thought, he enclosed her in his arms. He said nothing. Neither did she.

"Em," Ally said, at a great remove.

Emma couldn't talk. Not while she listened, while she struggled to listen. In his arms, surrounded by him, she could hear attenuated voices more clearly—but not without effort; it took effort. Concentration. She had to *try* to hear them, and she thought she might never have tried at all if she hadn't known.

She wasn't in Nathan's arms, now. She knew it. But they *felt* like his arms. She was certain that if he kissed her now, his lips would feel like his lips. But they weren't, and wouldn't be, and she shivered, thinking about it.

She listened, as she had first listened when they had arrived in a deserted building. And she heard what she had heard then—but it was weaker, softer.

"Emma?"

She grimaced. "Michael, Ally—I need you to be quiet for now. I'm trying to hear the voices of the *very* quiet dead."

"Why?" Michael asked.

"Because Nathan's body *isn't* a body, not like ours. It's made—it's made of the dead, like the floor in the town-house."

"You want to free them?"

"Yes." One word. A single word.

"Nathan?"

"Yes," Nathan replied. "I want Emma to free them, too." The borrowed arms tightened, briefly, around Emma. "But— there's almost nothing left of them, and Emma can't hear them if there's any other voice."

Silence then.

NATHAN

H E HASN'T LIED TO EMMA. He won't.

But in his arms—in the arms that are not his but look exactly like the arms that once were—she feels like Emma Hall. He remembers the first time he kissed her. He remembers the first time he slid an arm around her shoulder; he remembers the first time he held her. He remembers the nervous desire, the elation, the quiet. He remembers his own heartbeat, and he can hear it now.

He can hold her. He could kiss her. He doesn't know what that would feel like, but he suspects it would feel the same.

He's no longer certain he would be aware of the cost of it, because in her arms, he can't hear the dead at all. Their voices are silent, mute; their weeping has banked. And maybe, he tells himself, this is what *they* want, as well. They want to touch Emma. They want to be with Emma. They want to bask in the warmth of her light, because in that light, they are no longer alone.

It's what he wants.

It's what he wants more than he's ever wanted anything.

If he could *ask* them, if he could be certain—but no. No. He *is* dead. He's dead, and this is not where he should be, because Emma will never live if he's with her. Emma will never forget.

He shakes his head and then kisses the top of hers. He's certain Emma will never forget him. He's certain his mother will never forget him. None of his friends will forget, either. He's not sure why that matters now. He's not, after a moment, certain that it *does*.

But he thinks he would give the gift of forgetfulness to his mother, at least, if he had the choice—because then her pain would stop.

"It's not just pain," she whispers. Her voice is so much a whisper it's hard to catch the aural edges of individual syllables.

"You haven't seen her."

"I've *been* her, though, in my own way. You gave me so much. You made me happy. And I was happy in a way I've never been happy before. I wanted it to last forever. I was— I am—greedy. I wouldn't feel this pain, and neither would your mother, if you'd never existed at all."

"And sometimes that would be the better option?"

She nods. She doesn't lie to him. "I know what happiness is now. I can't unknow it. I'm afraid I'll never be happy again."

He nods. He knows. But unhappiness is not what he wants for Emma. It's never been what he's wanted. It's not what he wants for himself, either. He looks past Emma, through the walls of the citadel, through the emptiness that must be sky beyond it, and he knows what he does want.

He wants to leave, because *there is no place for him here*. He knows—as the dead know—where home is. He knows that he cannot reach it. He knows that Emma is the next best thing—and that's a terrible thing to think.

But he feels the warmth of her, the warmth of her light— a light she can't see herself. And he feels it more strongly as the minutes pass; he feels it become heat but not fire. It does not burn. It does not consume.

And he understands why he feels it so clearly, so suddenly: Emma is unmaking his body even as she stands in his arms, pressed against his chest, her head bowed, crying. She is setting them free: the four who were called, the four who struggled, the four who were consumed. She is unraveling what was built.

Soon he will not be able to hold her. Or, he will, but he'll suck the warmth from her, numb her, freeze her skin.

He knows that the four didn't volunteer. He knows they had no choice. He knows, but he thanks them anyway. She untangles them all at once in a flurry of gray, the whole separating instantly into four distinct entities.

They see her, of course. Nathan can see them clearly: two girls, two boys; their mouths work, but their voices are so quiet even he can't hear them.

Emma can. He can see, from her expression, that their voices reach her. He can see that she's been crying, that she might still be crying, and that it doesn't matter, now.

But he hears what she says, and if he could close his eyes, he would. She thanks them. She apologizes for what was done to them—as if it were done for her or somehow at her request—and she thanks them.

And then she tells them to go. To go and to wait.

She intends to open the door.

CHAPTER
TWENTY

T HE FOUR DIDN'T LEAVE HER.
They remained, almost circling her, as Nathan's clothing—the clothing they'd collectively worn—drifted, empty, toward the ground.

Emma inhaled, wiped her eyes with the back of her hand, and paused; a golden chain was wrapped around her hand. Looking up to Nathan again, she said, "Margaret says she can appear in front of the rest of the living without holding my hand."

"I don't know how," he told her.

She turned to Michael. To Margaret. And to the old woman, who was standing just beyond the four, lips pursed in a frown that was probably etched there.

"You have my son," she said.

Emma could only barely see him. "He's not bound to me."

"No, I can see that. What did he do?"

Emma shook her head. "If you mean right now, he didn't do anything. If you mean in the past, or in his life, I think you already know the answer. And if you want to question him, you can probably hear his voice as well as I can. The two of you can talk. Michael."

Michael nodded; he was staring at the space that Nathan had occupied minutes before. "Is Nathan gone?"

"No. He's here. I have him." She lifted a hand again. "I need you to stand in front of the door."

"The door that you can't see?"

She nodded.

Helmi was staring at the dead that surrounded Emma. She transferred her gaze to Nathan, disembodied once again. Her expression was almost unreadable—always disturbing in a child of her apparent age. "He was dead," she said, voice as flat as her expression. "He was always dead."

Emma nodded.

"What are you doing?"

"Trying to find the rest of Scoros."

"Emma, you're talking to yourself again," Amy said.

"Yes, sorry." She held out a hand to Helmi. She had not been willing to do so for Scoros' mother, but she thought Helmi's input might be necessary, and thinking often went better in a group.

Helmi hesitated. "Are you sure?"

Emma nodded.

"My sister will come. You took Nathan from her. She'll know."

Emma nodded again; she did not lower her hand.

"Margaret says it drains your power."

"You know your sister better than anyone here except Scoros. I don't want to have to repeat everything you say— I'll probably get half of it wrong, which will annoy either you or Amy."

"But she's coming, and you'll need all the power you can get."

"Power alone won't be enough. I don't *know* how to do what she does, and I can't learn it in half an hour—or however long we have. Our only hope is to think of something that we haven't thought of yet. Take my hand."

Helmi obeyed. Her hand was cold.

Emma followed Michael to the wall, and Helmi drifted alongside. She was silent. "Scoros tried to kill your sister at the end of his life. He obviously failed."

"He was nowhere near as powerful as she was."

"No. But he knew her defenses. He didn't have to use Necromantic power to kill her, after all. He could poison her. He could stab her. I don't think guns were much in use when he tried—but she's *alive*. There are a lot of ways to kill a living person. The Hunters do it, and they don't use the power of the dead; they don't have it."

"How did he try?"

"I don't know. I didn't see that part of his life. And before you ask, I've seen enough of his life to last several lifetimes; I don't think I could bear the pain of looking at any more of it."

Michael put his hand on the wall at just above waist height. "It's here."

"Is that a door knob? I mean, is that where a door knob is?"

"It's locked," Michael replied, which was yes.

Emma saw wall. Even in the confines of the Queen's circle, she'd seen wall. There was nothing like a door where Michael said there was. She wondered if the Queen had learned the art of hiding things from Scoros, or if she'd developed it herself after Scoros' death. She certainly hadn't discovered his rooms.

"Helmi, can you see anything here?"

"Wall. You're certain *he* can?"

"He found rooms hidden in the citadel that we're fairly sure your sister has never discovered."

"Which rooms?"

"Scoros' rooms. That's where his mother was."

"And you figured out how to bind her?"

"Not deliberately, no. I'm not sure it's repeatable."

"How did you do it?"

"Can you just—" Emma grimaced. There had been a reason she wanted Helmi in the group. "She was holding my hand—the way you are. Amy said something that annoyed her, and she tried to use *me* as a conduit to turn Amy into ash. I stopped her."

"How?"

"It's my power," Emma replied, placing one of her hands flat against the wall where the door was. "I get to decide how it's used."

"And then you bound her?"

"And then she was bound, yes. It wasn't deliberate. I didn't think that's what I was doing."

Amy coughed. "Is that how binding normally works?" she asked Helmi.

"I don't think so," Helmi replied—more slowly. "I haven't been bound. I don't know."

"You've watched, though."

The child nodded. "It—takes longer." She was frowning. "You said she tried to use your power?"

"Or me, as a conduit. I knew what was about to happen. It's happened before."

"You let the dead use your power?"

Emma exhaled. The wall was chilly, but not in the way Helmi's hand was. "Not on purpose, and I'm not even sure it was my power that was used. A dead four-year-old boy wanted to save his living baby brother. I felt the surge of that intent leave my hands, and a Necromancer died because of it."

"That's not the way it's supposed to work."

"Maybe the Necromancers do more when they bind than just harness power; maybe they build in limitations."

"But—that means the dead could use you. I mean, the dead who *have* knowledge." She looked, then, to Margaret Henney, who hadn't said a word since Helmi's arrival. The child who was not a child seemed excited now. "You wouldn't *have to* learn how to use the power if the dead you've bound know how."

"Margaret?" Amy asked.

Emma closed her eyes. She could see the wall. Her own hand vanished, as did Michael. Helmi remained, of course, her eyes a translucent almost-gray that shone, faintly, as if with reflected light.

"What are you doing?" Helmi demanded.

"Taking down the wall," Emma replied.

"You don't have time for that."

"Then we'll die," Emma replied. "Our only hope of survival is Scoros—and some part of Scoros is here. It's hers—but I don't intend it to remain that way."

Helmi turned, still attached to Emma's hand. She looked at Scoros' mother—Emma still hadn't asked for her name and felt no particular guilt not knowing it. It was unfair, she supposed, but she couldn't forgive her for her attempt to kill Amy.

Longland, she reminded herself. She frowned. "Helmi, where is Longland?"

"I don't know. He was with the procession until she ordered everyone to leave. Maybe he thinks he can kill the Queen, with Eric's help."

"I don't know that Eric will help," Nathan said.

"No," Emma said softly, glancing at Nathan, who drifted toward the wall. "I don't know that he will either. He loved her once."

"Then again, so did Scoros," Helmi pointed out.

"I don't think Scoros really stopped."

"He tried to *kill* her."

Emma nodded. "It's complicated."

REYNA

YOU HAVE NEVER BEEN HAPPY.
Eric's eyes are narrowed in confusion; there are lines in his forehead; the shape of his brow has changed. Reyna, who knows every expression that's ever crossed his face, recognizes this one. He's worried.

He's worried *for* her.

He isn't armed. He has no guns, no knives. He has no iron, no salt. She loves him, yes. But love and trust are not the same. She's learned that bitter lesson, time and time again. Everyone she loves leaves her or betrays her. Sometimes, both.

It is not Eric's voice she hears. She struggles to ignore the words, but they come again.

You have never been happy.

But he's wrong. Scoros is wrong. She *has* been happy. She was happy with Eric, before the drought and the fear and the murders. She remembers it; how could she not? It was the only time in her life that she had ever been truly happy.

She had dreamed of the future, of love extending into forever, of Eric by her side.

Reyna, child, he wanted *to be by your side then.*

He is by her side *now*. He is here.

But Longland brought him. Longland and her knights. He did not come here on his own. He did not call her, did not return. He would not even speak to her for centuries, no matter how hard she struggled for even a glimpse of him. Instead, he picked up weapons and whittled away at her Court.

And it's true that she sent the troublesome and the difficult after the Hunters first, but not only, and not always.

"Eric," she says, voice thick. "You haven't answered my question."

She is afraid that he will pretend he didn't hear it. Or that he will look away. She is afraid, she realizes, that he will lie.

She hears Scoros again. She can almost see him, his voice conjures so many tangled memories. *You haven't asked him, Reyna. You have not asked the question aloud.*

"I will unmake you," she whispers, her fury so intense it swallows volume.

You have already done that, he says. His voice is gentle. *No, that is unfair. We have already done that, you and I. Eric was a child. He attempted to save you because he loved you, and he died.*

You were a child—

"ENOUGH!"

The ground shakes; the road undulates beneath their feet. The buildings, the facades of which she had worked on so carefully, ripple; for a moment, the world is liquid.

Eric catches her when she stumbles. Eric.

"Reyna." Her name again. Her name carried by his voice, so close to her ear. "Who are you talking to?"

"Scoros," she says.

Eric's gaze sweeps the streets. Cobbles and facades have reasserted their existence. Nothing moves—nothing but Eric and Reyna.

She is angry at Scoros. She intends—after today—that he *never* have a voice again. She can't remember why she left him one. She can't remember why she wanted to be able to hear him. Or why she wanted him to be able to hear her. But . . . that had happened before his death, hadn't it? That had happened before.

Before, when Scoros loved her as a father.

"Why did you come back?" she whispers. She pulls away from Eric before he can answer. She doesn't want to hear his lies. She is certain they will be lies. She almost removes his tongue, but to do that, she would have to touch him.

"Do you remember," he asks her, "the first time we met?"

It's not an answer. But it's not a lie, either. Reyna is tired. She is *so* tired. She nods, her back turned toward him, her hands clasped behind it. She knows that Eric can't hurt her. Even if that's what he wants.

She believes, in this desolate moment, that it *is* what he wants.

"You can make anything," he tells her. "Why this?"

Why this city? Why this citadel? "It is safe," she replies. "It is safe for us." She glances over her shoulder; he is not looking at her. He is looking at the empty streets. There are no trees here. There is no stream. There are cisterns for water, but no natural sources; there are no rivers. There can't be.

She can make water of the dead, of course, but it has never seemed desirable. Today she wishes she had tried. That's what she should have done. She should have created the world in the image of those early days.

Neither she nor Eric could have met in a city like this; Reyna's kin wouldn't have been allowed to walk these streets if they'd existed in her time. Reyna and her kin wouldn't have been allowed to stand as audience to such a wedding, such a procession.

No. The only celebration they could join involved their deaths—and the audience was jubilant at the ugliness, their own cruel triumph.

Why had she made this place?

Why had she thought that this is what *Eric* would want?

She shakes her head; she recognizes the thought, and it is *not hers*. She has hated no one in her life as much as she hates Scoros in this moment.

She wanted to make the world safe for love. Her love and Eric's. She would have been happy, before the villagers had come so many centuries ago, to live *anywhere* with Eric.

Anywhere. A hut. A wagon. Why should it matter, then, whether she has created a forest, a stream? Why is a *palace* worse than that?

Why does he not see her? Why does he not see only her?

Why, Scoros asks, *do you not see yourself?*

She ignores the old man. She cannot believe she has *ever* been happy to hear his voice. It is heavy with age and judgment. She thought of him, once, as a father—but now, she hears only her mother. The ground shifts beneath her feet, echoing her ancient anger.

She might destroy him, even now—but that would destroy the citadel. She has made each careful choice, has chosen each action, so that she might survive; she has no intention of committing suicide here. She opens her mouth to tell him as much—to shout it, to rage—but before the words leave her, something else does.

Nathan.

Nathan is no longer bound to her. Longland, she owns. She has lost none of the dead she's bound—none except Nathan. The streets are empty of everyone except Eric. Her knights have vanished, obeying her commands as if they were of the dead, and not sovereign over them.

If one of them has *dared*—

Eyes narrowing, she forgets Scoros, forgets weddings, forgets triumph. It is not as Reyna that she looks at Eric, but as the Queen of the Dead. It isn't even Eric's name that leaves her lips.

Emma.

CHAPTER
TWENTY-ONE

THIS WALL WAS NOT LIKE the floors of the town-house. Emma could hear nothing in it, no matter how intently she listened. She could feel the chill permeate her palm, but all of the walls in the palace were cold. She had no idea how to unmake this one—it might actually *be* stone.

But no—it couldn't be. She could still see the wall when she closed her eyes. This, like the floors of the townhouse, was made of the dead. Everything in the room was.

"You have done well, Emma Hall," a familiar voice said. "You have done well. Better than I expected when we first met."

Emma didn't turn to look at the magar.

"You will not find what you require—not this way. There are two things you must do first."

Emma lowered her palm. She had not released Helmi and was therefore forced to offer the magar her right hand.

The old woman shook her head. "I understand what you

are asking for. I *could* do what you desire; it is possible. But this is your fight. It is not mine—I am dead."

"That didn't stop Scoros' mother."

The magar nodded. "She and I have much in common; we might have been cut from the same tree. But even so, we were carved in different shapes, for different purposes. What she attempted, I will not attempt. You are alive. My child is alive."

"What must I do?"

"Draw a circle, Emma Hall."

"She doesn't have *time* to draw a circle!" Helmi shouted.

"No," her mother agreed. "Hush, Helmi. Hush. Emma understands."

For a long moment, the magar was wrong. She felt Helmi's frustration and fear as if they were her own—because they were. But she turned toward the Queen's circle, looked at the curved, precise runes that comprised the anchors of its circumference, and understood.

The floor was not stone.

The circle was permanent only until the dead that served as building blocks were finally free. Her hand tightened around Helmi's. In fifteen minutes, she wouldn't be able to control her grip, her hand would be so numb.

But Helmi looked up at her, seeing the question Emma didn't quite ask, and she nodded. "I know how to draw a circle," she told Emma, radiating, for a moment, the proud confidence of a girl who has suddenly learned that her knowledge is both superior and necessary. As if she were a child in anything more than appearance.

"I don't," Emma told her, as she approached the Queen's circle—a circle she had used in ignorance, assuming it would provide safety.

"No, I guess you wouldn't. Everyone who could teach you is dead." She looked over her shoulder at her mother, but the magar didn't move.

"Was your mother always like this?" Emma asked, lowering her voice.

"Like what?"

"I just—I feel like she's testing us."

"Oh. She is. Everything was always a test with my mother. The only person she didn't test was Reyna, and look how *that* turned out. She wasn't always like this, though. Sometimes she was worse." The grin she turned on Emma was bright and ageless. She started to move faster, toward the circle's edge, dragging Emma with her, although that was technically impossible.

They stopped when they reached the circle's edge. "Can you even cross this?" Emma asked.

"Yes and no. It's like the rest of the physical world—it doesn't exist for me if I don't want it to. I can walk over the circle. I can sink through the floor."

"Then how is it different at all?"

"I can't harm you."

"You kind of can't harm me now."

Helmi stared at Emma's hand, which was very, very cold. "Point taken. When you leave, when you go to search for the lost, the lost *can* harm you. Because you have to leave the living to find them. So, in theory, if you leave the land of the living, I *can* harm you. I wouldn't because I wouldn't know where—or when—you were. Death is confusing like that."

"And this is supposed to protect me?"

Helmi nodded. "If you lose your way, if you lose your time or your sense of who *you* are, you come *back* to yourself in the circle. You're probably going to faint or collapse—but you won't die, and you will recover."

Emma nodded. "That's why I tried to use this one."

"This one wouldn't have saved you, though. All circles are almost the same—but the difference between them is big." For the first time, she glanced over her shoulder toward the magar.

Emma's gaze followed Helmi's; the magar nodded at them. She said nothing. The nod was enough for Helmi.

"This symbol is earth." Helmi pointed with her toes. "It's the first one that's drawn, if you draw it with chalk or coal. It's the simplest—but it's hard to get exactly right, because wrong is so obvious.

"This one is air. The position is important," she added. "It's to the right of the earth, a quarter turn."

"Does the orientation of the symbol matter?"

Helmi's expression brightened. "Yes." As if Emma were a child, and had done something clever. "The symbol for fire is to the left, a quarter turn."

Emma nodded.

"Of the four, the last is the symbol for water. It's in opposition to earth. Water is birth and life, but it requires earth and air and fire. All circles have these four." She traced it with fingers that couldn't feel its carved edges; Emma traced it with fingers that could. Helmi moved on. Emma knew they needed to hurry—but she also felt, in this moment, that she needed what Helmi had to offer.

Or that Helmi needed to offer it.

"If those were the only things that mattered, it would be easy to draw a circle."

"What else is necessary? There seem to be a lot of other characters embedded in the stone here."

Helmi glanced over her shoulder again. The magar nodded, but this time she approached. "There are. They are the ways in which we anchor ourselves; they are runes that describe traits of life that are not always immediately visible. The circles we use change with time. But there are characters that are immutable and unchanging. Those," she added, "like the elements."

"And the others?"

"I think, child, the others are runes *you* can use. They are not so different from the ones I would counsel you to consider and write were I your master."

Emma turned to Helmi. "What do they say?"

"This one is sorrow," she said. "This one is hope. This one is love. This one is peace, I think. This one is strength."

"So, spiritual or emotional things?"

The magar snorted. "Perhaps. They are supposed to describe . . . yourself. They are meant to be honest, Emma Hall. They are meant to be the truth."

Emma hesitated.

"Yes?"

"I'm not sure anyone sees themselves clearly enough to write that kind of truth."

"No. Is what we see of ourselves a lie, then?"

"I don't think so," was Emma's slow answer. "But what others see of us isn't necessarily less true, either. And if I understand what Helmi is telling me, we don't draw the circles by committee."

"No. We write them in truth, Emma Hall. Do you understand why they change with time?"

"Because we change with time?"

"Yes. The words that might describe you at three are not these words, although some elements of them remain. The words that Helmi would have used are not applicable to you now."

Emma frowned. "Sorrow, hope, love?"

The magar nodded.

"Anyone of any age can understand those, surely?"

"Yes, of course. But at certain ages they are not prized, and in certain frames of mind, they are goals; they are not what you *are,* but perhaps what you desire."

"Sorrow?"

"There were stone circles," the magar continued, as if she had never stopped. "But only five characters were engraved there. The four for the elements, the fifth for *being.* This one," she added. "We tell our students that it means 'spirit' or even 'soul.' That is not exact. It is immutable as a character, but it is rooted in the shifting descriptions of self."

"Which ones are these?" Emma asked Helmi, pointing to the only runes that hadn't yet been explained.

"Those? They're her name."

Emma turned again to the magar. "If I understand what you're saying correctly, you think I *can* use this circle. The runes here that I don't know are runes you think I'd choose."

The magar nodded.

". . . Except strength. I don't think I'd ever describe myself as strong."

The magar pursed lips; she spoke, but the sound of her voice was lost to the loud rumble beneath Emma's feet. Beneath *all* of their feet. It sounded very much like they were standing on thunder. The old woman held out a hand.

Emma stared at it. She couldn't remember if she'd ever offered the magar her hand before. She hesitated.

"I think she wants you to take her hand," Helmi whispered. Helmi's expression, when Emma glanced down, was not heavy with sarcasm. Nor was her tone. She had existed for centuries. She could shift her appearance without apparent effort. But she was a child.

Emma placed her palm, almost gingerly, against the magar's.

The world vanished.

Gray gave way to black, the transition slow and seamless. But in the black, Emma could see stars. She held Helmi by one hand and the magar by the other—but she was no longer in the Queen's chambers.

No, that was untrue. She was undoubtedly still in those chambers. But she was here, as well.

"This," the magar said quietly, "is where I reside. It is all of the home left to me."

As homes went, it was impressive. But there was no house. There was no tenting. There was no landscape other than the distant stars. As Emma tilted her head skyward, she saw the faint outline of the low-hanging moon. She wondered why it hadn't been the first thing she'd seen.

Helmi did not look around. Her head, like Emma's, was tilted, and moonlight seemed to be reflected in her widened eyes.

"Your daughter couldn't find you here."

"No."

"Why?"

"She was taught how to search for the lost. She learned. But the lost exist in a world of their own creation—and it is a pale shadow of the world in which they lived. This is not. I am not lost. I am well aware that I am dead. I have never suffered the confusion that governs the lost."

"Why did you not go to her?"

"I could not take that risk," the magar replied.

Helmi, however, said, "She did. She tried to talk to my sister. My sister wanted to know where the lantern was; my mother wouldn't tell her. They argued. I hid."

The magar didn't acknowledge Helmi's statement. "She was a fragile child, in ways Helmi was not. And she knew, then and now, how to hold on to pain. You have come to the seat of her power, Emma Hall. What will you do?"

"Open the door," Emma said.

"And how, exactly, do you intend to achieve this?"

328 ~ Michelle Sagara

"I opened it once before."

"That is not an answer."

Emma nodded. It wasn't. "I intend to free the dead trapped here."

"Better. You avoid the question I have avoided asking. I cannot do what must be done." Having spoken, she waited, her eyes unnaturally bright and sharp.

"Could you do what Scoros' mother attempted?"

It was Helmi who answered. "No, she couldn't. Scoros—and his mother—learned the arts of Necromancy from the Queen. The magar didn't. None of the people had the knowledge or the power to stand against my sister. To do it, they would have had to do what she did."

"I can't."

Helmi nodded. "I'm not sure what she expects from you. She doesn't have time to teach you what you need to know."

"I have time here," the magar replied. "Time does not touch this realm."

"It touches the one I'm actually breathing in," Emma pointed out.

"Yes. It is why we are here. You walked for Scoros. It was a long walk, a harsh one—and very, very unsafe. I would say your own ignorance is likely to kill you—but you have not died yet. Perhaps you will not die today. Perhaps you will. I think it likely that you will, and I have brought you here because you must remember this place. It is to here you must travel—and in haste; she cannot follow."

"She can go wherever I can go," Emma said. It wasn't a question.

"Almost. You have one thing she lacks. You have the lantern. You are here because you carry it. And I am here because you are here, and you are carrying me. It is not so easy to find this place without it; the darkness is more . . . absolute."

"What, exactly, does the lantern *do*? Why does she want it so badly?"

The magar said nothing. It was Helmi who answered. "She thinks it should have been hers by right. She was the magar's daughter. She was supposed to be the successor—and the magar was dead. She expected my mother to give it to her when she was still alive—my mother, I mean. But she wouldn't. She kept saying my sister wasn't ready yet.

"My sister was always powerful. Always. She saw the dead on her own. She didn't even need the circle; they came to her, spoke to her. She could find the lost far more quickly than any other student. More quickly than our mother. She knew she was powerful. Our mother acknowledged her power."

Emma waited.

Helmi turned to face the magar. "She wouldn't acknowledge her *as* magar."

"I was not wrong," the magar said. "Look at what she has done since then. I had the raising of her. I had the training." Her lips twisted. "The failure is mine. Had I given her what she desired, that failure would be complete."

"Why did you give the lantern to Emma?" Helmi asked. "You didn't raise her. You didn't train her. The only thing you could know about her is that she's powerful. What was the difference?"

"You are thinking that if Reyna were happy, she would not have become what she has become."

Helmi shrugged.

"I gave the lantern to Emma because of Eric."

Helmi's expression tightened. "He told you to do it?"

"No, of course not. But he could not kill her. Or rather, he did not want to kill her. What he saw in her—"

"He didn't want to kill my sister either. He thought he loved her."

"Yes."

"Then what's the difference?"

"If Eric could, now, go back in time—and he cannot—he would kill my Reyna. I think he would be content to die with her. He would not argue with his friends and his colleagues to preserve her life. But he did, for Emma. He was not in love with her. He could see her clearly. And I could see him clearly."

"She hasn't been trained!"

"If you had trained the Queen of the Dead, would you be eager to train someone who has as much power, and as much potential? I failed the people. I failed *my daughter*. I could not take the risk of failing again. The cost would be too high."

"She can't go out there without—"

"She has found two of the lost, without training. One could have easily killed her; it is by the slimmest of margins that he did not. She has opened the closed door. The only dead to escape since your death—and mine—she freed. I did not train her. No one did. She accomplished these things on her own."

"I didn't," Emma said quietly. "I couldn't have opened the door—at all—without the lantern."

The magar shook her head. "You could not have done *any* of it without the lantern. You could have seen the dead and spoken with them. You could do as you are now doing for my youngest daughter. The lantern has power, whether or not you choose to evoke it consciously, as you did to truly set that child free. You have used its power.

"You are using its power now. Bring it out. Illuminate the darkness."

"I don't think we're ready to face the Queen yet."

"She will not see its light here. Raise it, if you can."

"But—"

"It is here that its light is strongest."

Emma didn't ask the magar what the purpose of that light was in this place. She didn't ask how it was that the lantern's light would be felt anywhere but here. She didn't even ask why the magar had brought her here, although she would have, had she been allowed one question.

Her hands were not cold here. They were still clasped by Helmi on the one side and the magar on the other, but they weren't cold. She could feel the palms and fingers pressed against her own as if they were flesh.

"I have to let your hand go," she said, to Helmi.

"No," the magar said, "you do not."

"The lantern—"

"The lantern is not a physical object. It becomes physical at your discretion. You think of it as an object that must be lifted—and in the end, that is true. But it does not need to be lifted in your hands." She paused. "Neither do the dead. You offer your hand because it is what is natural to you, but it is not necessary.

"Helmi is not yours; she accepts what you offer but is

wise enough to offer little of herself in return. That will have to stop."

Helmi frowned. Emma froze. "I don't want to use her. I don't want to use any of the dead."

"Oh? Did you not use the dead—as you put it—when you opened the door?"

"That—that was different."

"How?"

"For one, I had their permission. I had the permission of *every single* person there."

"Ah. Yes. Yes, you did. Do the bound dead not grant permission to their Queen?"

Did they? "I don't know."

"In a fashion, they do. It is the consent of the terrified, the consent of the terrorized, the consent of the lost. That is what she has created: a world in which *all* of the dead are lost." Her lined, weathered face compressed slightly. "The lantern, Emma Hall."

Nothing about the magar was comforting or encouraging. Emma, not used to being treated like an idiot, flinched and wished—not for the first time—that she were Amy.

"Helmi." The magar's use of the name was a command.

Helmi looked as rebellious as Emma felt. But she compromised; she transferred her grip on Emma's hand to Emma's elbow. In theory, this shouldn't have worked, because in theory, there was no contact between Helmi's skin and Emma's; the child was attached to sleeve. But she didn't disappear.

Emma lifted her hand.

She'd never really concentrated on summoning the lantern. When she wanted it, it appeared. She'd never stopped to think about how little sense this made; seeing the dead made little inconsistencies seem irrelevant.

The wire at the top of the lantern cut across her palm, tracing part of her lifeline as she lifted it. Its light was orange. Orange and blue. It was dense, much smaller than moonlight or the distant tickle of light at the corner of the eyes that implied pale stars. Her eyes acclimatized themselves to the brighter light as she looked around.

The magar remained by her side, as did Helmi.

They were not alone.

Emma wanted to ask the magar if she had made the lantern or if she had inherited it; the words did not come; she forgot them.

She wasn't standing in a field. She wasn't standing on a road or on a sidewalk. She wasn't standing anywhere; there was nothing beneath her feet. It was a solid nothing, like glass but without the texture. She didn't fall. Or rather, she hadn't fallen yet.

Neither had the people who lay arrayed around them. Some were curled on their sides, some flat on their backs, one or two rested on their stomachs, heads cradled in the crooks of folded arms. Some were entwined. They had no beds, but they didn't appear to need them; they slept. There was no rhyme or reason to their clothing, their ages, their appearances; there were both men and women, boys and girls.

Emma started to count, but gave up. There were too many.

"Why are they here?"

"They followed the lantern you now hold. I could not take them to freedom, as I might once have done while I lived. I could bring them to safety, of a kind. This is not a path that the circle can reach. Had it been—" She shook her head. "It was created by the lantern you bear."

Emma began to walk. There was room between the sleepers to place her feet, but she had to move with care. She didn't want to disturb them; they looked peaceful.

"There are no dreams or nightmares here," the old woman said, trailing behind Emma but above the forms of the sleepers. "They will wake only if you choose to wake them."

Emma continued to walk. The light that bobbed just ahead of her seemed, to her eyes, to brighten. "The lantern doesn't hurt them?"

"No, Emma Hall. It is one of the few things that brings them comfort when they wake. It is a sliver of the world to which the dead should belong. They can reach out for it, touch it, and find the promise of peace in its light."

Emma continued to walk; she wasn't even certain why. She trusted the magar's previous words—here, she had time. And maybe she should be using that time to learn what she could before she confronted the Queen. The internal voice that came to her courtesy of Amy Snitman was pretty much screaming that advice in her ear.

She wished that Amy had been the Necromancer. Amy would have been a better choice. Amy didn't dither. She was almost fearless, and the fear that did get past her natural self-confidence got stomped flat. She wouldn't be flailing here, terrified by her own uselessness. She wouldn't be wandering aimlessly through an almost endless field of sleeping people.

"What are you looking for?" Helmi demanded, and Emma smiled. She had thought Helmi very like a young Amy Snitman at one point.

Only people with a death wish lied to Amy. "I'm not sure."

"Maybe you should *be* sure."

"Helmi. Enough," the magar said, although her pinched expression implied strong agreement with her youngest daughter's sentiment.

"But she needs to know—"

"We don't know what she needs to know."

"We *do* know *some* of what she needs to know, and she's not going to learn it here!"

Emma, however, stopped walking. The lantern wobbled briefly, its light dimming as she knelt at the side of one of the sleepers.

"What are you looking at?" Helmi demanded. The magar said, or asked, nothing, but she released Emma's hand. She must have released it; Emma reached out with her left hand, and the magar didn't automatically come with it.

She recognized the child's face, although she had only seen it twisted in pain or fear. Just beyond the girl, another child slept; they were side-by-side, although the younger child had an arm flung across the chest of the older one. "How—how did you find these girls?"

The magar nodded. Emma couldn't see her and didn't look back, but she *felt* the nod. It should have been more disturbing than it was. "Scoros found them before the Queen did. He bound them, and he kept them."

Emma felt a sickening, visceral fury; not all of it was her own, but the part that wasn't was the weaker part.

"It is not what you think, child. Had he not killed them—
had he not murdered them—perhaps it would have been.
But he did. He set the fire. He watched them die. The death
of their father hardly troubled his sleep. The death of the
children broke something in him."

"He served for a long time after that."

"Yes. But he was aware that the children were blameless.
He had been that child, as I think you must be aware. Ven-
geance against the man had some rough symmetry, some justice. Burning the children to death did not. And again, you
know this. If you have found Scoros, you know.

"He found the children before the Queen did. I do not
know if she would have searched them out deliberately—
nor did he. But he wished to protect them in some small
measure. He wished to atone. It was the start of his discon-
tent, because he wanted absolution, and the only way he
could have given it to himself was to open the door and
usher the two children to what lay beyond it. And you are
aware of how impossible that would be."

"If they were bound to him, how are they here?"

"He died. Before he died, he called me."

"But I thought—"

"I can hear my daughter calling me, even now," the
magar said. "But I can choose my response. I could hear
Scoros, and I chose to take the risk; it was a small risk. He
did not and does not have my daughter's power. He has her
experience. He called, and he asked me to protect the children. I almost refused."

"Why? They were blameless."

"He was not. I am not a forgiving woman. But he con-
vinced me, in the end. He had kept the girls safe. He had
bound them, but he had only seldom called upon their
power; there were others he used in that fashion. He was
not—he was *never*—a kind man. I think he was, in his youth,
very like your Chase."

"Chase would never murder little girls."

"You are so certain that none of the Necromancers he
found and killed were children?" The question was sharp,
pointed.

Emma wasn't.

"He would have killed you if Eric had not intervened.

He would have done it without regret or pain. He would have killed you had you been twelve or thirteen, boy or girl. And Emma, Eric would have killed them as well. What you know of them *is* true, but it is not the whole of the truth.

"Scoros released the children into my keeping, and I brought them here, and here they slept. And sleep. *What* are you doing?"

Emma cupped the older child's cheek in her hand. She heard the magar's question as if it came at a great remove. She whispered a name. *Anne*.

Movement returned to the girl's face; her eyelids fluttered, as if she were dreaming. They opened before Emma could withdraw her hand—although she hadn't even tried. She heard the magar's consternation and even understood it, because part of her wondered the same thing. The child was at peace. She was safe.

But her eyes did open, and they met Emma's. Emma thought the girl might scream or flinch, but she did neither. Instead, she sat up, stretched—very much as if she were alive. She then turned to the younger girl beside her and shook her gently.

She didn't wake. Emma reached out and touched the arm that was still draped across the older sister. *Rose*. The younger girl's eyes opened in a squint. Where Anne had turned to her sister, Rose turned toward the light.

Emma wanted to set the lantern down, to offer a hand to each child.

Anne, however, stood, and Rose joined her; their faces were turned toward the lantern's light, and the light was brilliant, now. Warm. "Are we leaving?" the younger girl asked.

Emma didn't answer. The magar did.

"Yes."

Rose seemed terrified of the magar—which was just sensible, all things considered. Anne forced her eyes away from the lantern to the face of the person holding it. "Are we going with you?"

"Only if you want to. I think—I think you've been safe here. It's quiet. It's peaceful. Where I'm going, it's not."

Anne nodded, and Emma felt her throat constrict. She'd told them the choice was theirs, and she meant it—but she realized that for these two, there was no choice. Offering one was just a sop to her own conscience; it wouldn't change the outcome at all for either girl.

"Yes," the magar said. "But conscience is necessary. They have been waiting. It is time. You must return to the Queen's circle, now. There is one thing you must do if you are to have any hope of using it."

"I don't need to use it."

"Yes, child, you do. And there is only one way to use it safely."

CHAPTER
TWENTY-TWO

EMMA RETURNED to the Queen's resurrection chamber. She held two hands: Anne's and Rose's. The lantern was gone; the magar was gone. Helmi, however, remained. She wasn't attached at the elbow; Emma wasn't certain that she could still be seen by anyone else in the room.

The girls were silent; they seemed almost sleepy. Emma looked at them because she wanted a memory of their faces that was not pain and horrible, slow death. She'd never quite understood the idea of mercy killing before, although she'd heard all the arguments. She understood it now.

Had she had a gun, she would have shot them both to end a misery she couldn't otherwise prevent. But it wouldn't have mattered; they had died centuries ago. The deaths she had witnessed, she could do nothing to ease.

She stood on the edge of the Queen's engraved circle.

Michael approached her. Or rather, he approached the two girls. He stepped over the circle's boundary so he could face them, and he smiled. He had—he had always had—an open, unfettered smile, especially when dealing with children.

Anne stiffened. Rose, however, smiled back. It was a tentative expression that Emma caught in profile.

"I'm Michael," he said.

"I'm Rose. That's my sister. She's Anne. Your clothes are funny."

"They won't let me wear dresses," Michael replied.

Rose laughed at the idea of Michael in a dress. Anne hesitated, but her lips twitched in an involuntary smile. She didn't speak to Michael, though. She turned her head to look up at Emma.

"He's not like you." It wasn't a question, but there was a thread of doubt in the statement.

"He's not like me," Emma agreed. "There's nothing he can do to harm you."

Anne nodded. Her expression twisted briefly, but her face remained the same: a child's face. Emma's hand tightened around Anne's, a brief pressure, meant to comfort.

"Are you the new Queen?" the girl asked.

Emma inhaled slowly. "I really, really hope not."

"You look like her."

"Do I?"

Anne nodded.

"I don't think the dead need a Queen."

"But we have one, whether we want her or not." The last few words were lost to Rose's sudden laughter. "Why did you bring us here?"

Emma had no answer, and Anne seemed to expect one. "I don't know."

"You did bring us here?"

"Yes. I'm sorry. I—I saw you and your sister, and I woke you." She struggled with the rest of the truth but couldn't quite force it to leave her lips. She had wanted to see them, to touch them, to know that they were not trapped in fire for the rest of eternity. She had wanted to see them at peace, to quiet the memories she was certain would never leave her. She had recognized them instantly, had reached for them without thought.

It hadn't been for their sake.

Why, a familiar voice said, *did you bring them* here?

Ah, yes. Scoros.

*   *   *

Anne turned at the sound of his voice. Rose, absorbed in Michael's antics—he was on his knees in front of her making unfortunate noises—did not. The older girl didn't flinch or stiffen at the sound of his voice. She seemed—to Emma's eye—to relax. She didn't release Emma's hand.

For the first time since she had come back with whatever she could gather of Scoros, he seemed to emerge. He was not solid—Emma doubted he could achieve that—but he was clearly visible; he looked like a shadow, and as the seconds passed, the lines of that shadow hardened, as if the light casting it had grown sharper and brighter.

Emma felt his question as if she had asked it. She had no better answer than the one she'd offered Anne, but Scoros was not a child—and he wasn't the only one who demanded an answer.

"I need their help."

Anne glanced up at her. Rose did not. Michael was probably the most amusing thing she'd seen since she'd died. It hadn't occurred to Emma to do what Michael was now doing, and it wouldn't have; this was not the time for play.

Not for Emma.

She could feel Scoros staring at Michael and reminded herself forcefully that Scoros could do nothing to her friends. Nothing.

"You're dead," Anne surprised her by saying.

Yes.

"Did it hurt you too?"

Yes. But not as much as I deserved. Emma Hall, what do you intend to do with the children?

"Free them."

How?

Emma looked down at the circle's engraving. "Helmi?"

Helmi drifted toward her, passing through Rose; Rose didn't notice. Neither did Michael.

"It's these characters, right?"

Helmi nodded. "This is her name."

"What would my name be in this alphabet?"

Helmi snorted. There was no other word for the sound she made. "It doesn't matter. You don't have a name in our writing. But you do have a name in your own. If *you* wrote out the whole circle, you'd be using your own language. I think," she added, lowering her voice, "that the magar is wrong."

"Wrong?"

"I think the words my sister chose and the words that you would choose are different. She thinks you're both young girls—her words, not mine. She thinks young girls can be described in the same words because they lack experience." Helmi shrugged. "But I wasn't magar. These two are Reyna's name."

Emma nodded. "Anne, I'm going to have to let go of your hand."

"What about Rose?"

"I might need to let go of Rose, too." But not yet. Not quite yet.

"What are you going to do?"

"Erase the Queen's name."

Emma knelt. Scoros came to stand behind her, or possibly on top of her; she felt his shadow fall. It was cold. The other shadow that joined him was natural and belonged to Chase. Emma glanced up at him; he was watching Michael and shaking his head, his own lips tugging up at the corners.

"I wouldn't have believed he could exist if I hadn't seen him myself. Michael, you do realize the Queen of the Dead could be here at any second, right?"

Michael answered Chase without looking at him. "Yes. But I can't do anything about the Queen of the Dead. I don't have weapons, and even if I did, I wouldn't know how to use them. I can't do anything to help Emma, because Emma doesn't know how to do what she thinks has to be done. But I *can* talk to Rose."

"Fine. You talk to Rose. I'll help Emma. You ready?"

Emma nodded. "It'll be like the floor in the townhouse. I think."

The floor rumbled again. The dead didn't seem to notice it. The living did. Emma placed her free palm against the two runes, which steadied her until the floor was once again still.

"She's coming," Helmi said. Emma didn't ask who; she knew. She shook her head to clear it, although fear remained. She listened.

*   *   *

The voices she could hear were not, to her surprise, the distant and attenuated sobs she'd expected. They were clear, high voices that appeared to be lifted in . . . song. Two voices, one melody, one harmony. The song itself consisted of the same syllables, repeated over and over. A name.

"Anne, Rose, can you hear them?"

Rose ignored Emma in favor of Michael. Anne, however, whispered a yes. "Can you get them to change what they're singing?"

It would be the best option, in Emma's opinion. But before she could say so, the magar said, "No." Just that. Her single word was thunderous; it reverberated. Even Rose looked up.

"They would not hear you, Emma Hall. They would not hear your request." She glanced at Anne. "You hear singing?"

Anne nodded. "You don't?"

"No. I hear nothing. Margaret?"

Margaret's answer was wordless.

Emma surrendered the hope and concentrated instead on the voices. She could see the floor; she could see the engraved runes. When she closed her eyes, both were still clear. "I'm sorry, Rose," she said quietly. "I need my hand back."

Anne said something to her sister.

"Michael won't be able to see you for now. I'm sorry," she repeated. Rose was reluctant to surrender the hand—and why wouldn't she be?—but Anne made it clear that it was necessary. Older sister clearly trumped Necromancer in Rose's mind.

"Sorry, Michael."

She could hear the voices clearly. She couldn't see the singers. There were two; it would have made more sense to Emma if each name were held in place by a single ghost. That thought was followed, swiftly, by shame. These were *people*, not objects.

They were people, though, who couldn't hear her. She tried to break into their song, to introduce herself, to somehow catch the attention of people she couldn't see. She failed. There was no space between breaths, between notes. Her voice didn't interrupt them at all.

How had she pulled one girl out of the floor she'd been made part of?

She'd reached. No, it wasn't just that. The floor itself had become a sea of hands and arms when those trapped within had become aware of Emma. She needed to get the attention of these two singers. But this floor didn't change in composition. She could see nothing to touch, nothing to grab—no one who was reaching out for her. She could hear no sadness, no tears, no wails of despair: just the words themselves. The names.

All of existence, for these two, had been reduced to that. There was nothing at all that Emma could touch.

She placed her second palm beside the first; the stone was cold, but it felt like a natural cold, not the chill of the dead. And yet the dead were here, just beyond her reach. Her palms flattened as she spread them, pushing against stone as if to find purchase. Except for the indents engraved there, the floor offered none.

This wasn't working. Emma looked up and saw Michael and Chase. She thought she'd closed her eyes and couldn't remember opening them; she closed them again. She needed to see the dead if she was to have any hope of un-making what the Queen had made here.

And if she succeeded, what then?

She shook her head to clear it. She couldn't afford to be afraid of success. She looked down at hands seen through closed eyes. She knew that the path she had walked when she sat in the circle attempting to locate Scoros was not a literal path; she knew that her body hadn't moved. But she had nevertheless walked through so many landscapes and so many memories.

The floor here was not a floor in any normal sense of the word except one: It supported weight. It appeared to be stone. But if she had found Scoros—trapped in theory throughout the whole of the citadel, a complicated web that resembled nothing so much as echoes—it didn't matter. She was looking at it the wrong way.

She needed to look at it the right way.

Or she needed not to look at it at all. Nathan's body—the container into which he had been poured so that he might interact with the living—had not been difficult to unravel; she had done it while weeping. She had done it without thought. Intent? Yes, she'd had that. But she hadn't felt for arms or legs or the component parts of the bodies that were melted together. She had just . . . caught them, held them, let them go. They had dissolved.

She needed to be able to do the same, here. Her hands covered the majority of the carved runes, which was as close as she could come to achieving the same effect—but she could not penetrate it. She could *hear*.

She spoke. She raised her voice. Lowered it. She tried a different harmony; she tried to join her voice to theirs. Nothing.

And then, for one brief moment, she felt something smooth in a way that stone wasn't; smooth, cold—not ice, but . . . glass. Glass.

"Nathan," she whispered.

"I'm here. I won't leave you." He didn't say *I can't*, but they both knew it was true.

"When you look at the—the exit, you can see what's beyond?"

"Yes."

"But you can't reach it?"

"No. None of us can."

"I see—I saw—a door. I opened it. Until I did, I saw nothing of what waits. You saw it as a . . . window. A closed window."

"Yes. It's like there's a layer of unbreakable—"

"Glass."

"Yes."

Emma lifted her right hand and turned to Helmi. "You said your sister was coming?"

Helmi nodded. "You can't see her."

"No."

"She has to run the long way. She's not running yet. But she's moving. If you leave—"

"I can't." Emma turned then. To Michael, to Allison, to Amy. "But you can. I think you've got time."

Allison shook her head but said nothing.

"Michael, you have to go with them. You've got to take them back to the safe rooms."

"And you?"

"The Queen of the Dead is coming. I think she's coming to wherever it is she thinks I am. And she probably knows now. I'm not sure she knows about you yet—she probably will if I don't—" Emma exhaled.

"I'm going to do something that will grab all of her attention. I'm sure it'll hold all of her attention as well—and I think you guys can make it out of here. I'm worried about Petal," she added, which was actually true.

"If she finds you," Allison began.

It was Chase who cut her off. "Emma doesn't have what it takes to have you remain here. Before, when she didn't know what she was going to do—or how—she wanted advice. Support. She knows now."

"Care to share, Emma?" Amy asked. And it was a question, not the usual demand.

Emma shook her head. "I'm not sure it's a plan that stands up to scrutiny. You remember what I did after we got Andrew Copis out of the burned out building?"

Amy nodded.

"That, but—maybe bigger." She hesitated.

"And you want us gone because you don't want to have to worry about us."

"Pretty much," Chase said.

"Wasn't asking you," Amy replied. She pursed her lips, folded her arms, and met Emma's gaze head on. Emma had no idea what her face looked like; she had no idea whether desperation, fear, or exhaustion currently occupied her expression.

But whatever it was, Amy nodded. "You'd better make it out of here," she said—and that was the usual demand. "The rest of us probably won't survive if you don't."

"I think she knows that," Allison said. "Em—you're sure?"

"She's sure," Chase said. Allison wasn't Amy; she didn't demand the words come from Emma's mouth. She trusted Chase. She had never trusted his opinion of Emma before, but clearly, something had changed. She caught Michael by the arm.

Michael looked as if he would argue, but he didn't.

"It'll be over soon," Emma told him, trying—and failing—to be confident.

Michael nodded, and if the nod went on a bit too long, it didn't matter.

Emma hesitated. "Chase," she finally said. "Go with them."

It was Allison who said, "No."

And it was Margaret who said, "Ernest will go with the children." Amy didn't even bridle. To Emma's lasting surprise, Ernest nodded, grim-faced.

"You need me," Chase said. "I'm the only other person who can see what you can see."

"Yes, but you do it in a heap on the *floor*, Chase, and I'm not thinking that'll be useful. And if the Queen is on her way here, so is Eric."

"Unless she's imprisoned him. What does Helmi say?"

"Helmi says so is Eric," Helmi said. "She may well imprison him—or worse—when this is over, but she hasn't taken the time to do it yet. You guys need to *move*."

Emma repeated Helmi's last instruction. "I'll give you five minutes," she told them, staring at the floor.

The door opened and closed; the Emery crew were on the move, and they didn't take the time to move silently. Emma didn't watch them go; she turned to the wall that Michael had seen as a door. It hadn't changed. Neither had the floor. Chase moved briefly around the room, emptying his pockets as he did; he was silent, but it was the silence of intent. He armed himself only when he returned to Emma's side, and he watched the closed door.

Everything in this room was under glass. Metaphorical glass.

Emma turned to Chase. "Ready?"

He nodded. He didn't ask her what she was going to do. Neither did Nathan or any of the rest of the dead gathered here. Margaret, the magar, Anne, Rose, the remainder of Scoros. And his mother. They hadn't turned—as Chase had—toward the door; they were watching Emma.

Emma reached for the lantern. It came instantly to her hand.

Blue light radiated from its center. Not for the first time, she noted the words that were stacked in an even column. She had assumed they were Chinese letters because of the shape of the lantern. She'd been wrong.

"Helmi, do you recognize these words?"

Helmi failed to answer. The light grew brighter, and brighter still—but it wasn't harsh enough to cause Emma—or anyone present—to close their eyes.

"Helmi?"

". . . No." She was lying. She wasn't lying *well*, but only a small fraction of her attention was devoted to the attempt. The rest was drawn to, and held by, the lantern.

Emma said, "It's important."

It wasn't Helmi who answered. It was the magar. "She can't tell you, Emma Hall."

"Can you?"

"Yes. But it wouldn't help."

Emma frowned.

"It is the language of the dead. Anyone dead, from any culture, at any time, would recognize the words—even if they had not been taught to read or write or recognize writing. She could repeat them. I could. Margaret could. You would not hear them unless you yourself were dead."

"But I can—"

"You can visit, yes. You can occupy the memories of the dead who linger. You can act in the world they create. But you are not dead, and these words are not for the living."

"Even if they would help the dead?"

"Even so. I have made many mistakes in my life. Many. Making you the keeper of the lantern and its light might prove to be the biggest. But I will not do this. It would be murder." And the magar had enough on her conscience.

"What exactly are you trying to do?" Chase asked. Of course he did.

"You can't see it?"

"See what?"

She nodded, as if he'd answered, because he had. She guessed that the light growing steadily brighter as it dangled from her hands would be visible to Necromancers, but she didn't ask Margaret because it no longer mattered. Helmi had said the Queen was coming anyway.

And even that faded to insignificance as she studied the harsh, brilliant light. It cast no shadows. She turned toward Chase, the only other person who remained in the room who was also alive. The light revealed him in all his uncomfortable glory: shorn red hair, faded freckles, white scars, and yellowed bruises.

"Have I got something on my face?"

"Nose, mouth, eyes—the usual bits."

"Gallows humor is *my* job, thank you very much. Is it just me or is the floor vibrating?"

"It's been vibrating all along—"

"Not like this."

Emma frowned at him. "What do you mean?"

"If you were standing, barefoot, on the throat of a man, and he was speaking, this is what it would feel like."

To Emma it was a rumble like thunder, or the earthquakes of imagination, given she'd never experienced one in person. She didn't argue with Chase, though. If she couldn't feel the vibrations the way Chase did, she accepted that they were becoming constant.

"What are you trying to do?"

"Truthfully?"

"Let me get back to you."

She laughed, as he'd no doubt intended. It was a thin sound, but it was genuine. And it was miles better than whimpering or crying.

"But seriously, if you mean to dissolve the chamber, give me a bit of warning?"

"I'll try." She looked at the circle engraved in the stone of solid floor. To her eyes, the runes were now glowing, as if light had, like liquid, been upended into their grooves. "Oh."

"Oh?"

"I think I understand what you were saying, now."

"Is that good or bad?"

"Good," she said, although she wasn't certain. She could hear the words without apparent effort or concentration on her part. She could hear raised voices. It was hard to focus on one or two, because the entire chamber was beginning to fill with syllables.

What words could stone speak? What words could be uttered without throat or mouth?

These ones, she thought. She had touched a floor in this floating city, and she had *listened*. It had been a struggle to hear anything, and it had required the whole of her concentration. Now, she thought, the struggle would be the reverse.

In Toronto, the dead had come *to* her while she held the lamp aloft, drawn by its light. She had asked for permission to use the power they didn't even understand they had. She had asked their names. She had promised them that she would open the door. They had given everything that she'd asked them for. Maybe they'd given more.

The dead here were not free to move. They didn't roam city streets, trapped in memories of lives that steadily receded as people aged and died and the future became the present. They were trapped, instead, in one woman's dream.

Reyna had dreamed of safety. Of a place in which she would finally be free to love Eric. In which Eric would be free to love her. Emma knew this. She'd *heard* it, time and again, in Scoros' memories.

And she was aware that the dream of a girl in love had become a nightmare for countless others—some living, most dead. She didn't even wonder at it.

She had loved Nathan. Nathan had died. The dreams she had hoarded and guarded so carefully had been irrevocably shattered. She had tried to hold their shards when Nathan—dead—returned to her. She had been *so happy* to see him. So happy to finally be able to tell him all the things she'd wished she'd said before her words could never reach him again.

She could keep him here.

She knew she could do what the Queen had done. She could house his spirit in something that could pass for flesh. She could hold him, be held by him, be comforted by him. At heart, her *dream* had been the same as the Queen's. She had wanted forever, although she'd mostly kept that desire to herself because it was sentimental and sort of embarrassing.

She had wanted a love that never died and never changed.

As if he could hear the words, Nathan came to stand by her side. Guilt sat poorly on his face, but it occupied it nonetheless.

But she shook her head and smiled. She'd done her crying. She'd said her good-byes. If she could talk herself into being what the Queen was, she knew that Nathan would never forgive her. He loved her, yes. She saw that clearly; his eyes were almost shining with it. But he would stop loving her if she became like the Queen of the Dead.

Because he saw her clearly. He'd always seen her clearly. He'd seen her fears and her insecurities and her desire and her fear of that desire. He'd seen her anger, been exposed to her temper, and endured it all by her side, smiling or grave or angry himself. To do what had been done here she would have to be everything she wasn't, *except* wildly in love.

What he loved about her would die, just as surely as he had.

She would have taken his hand, but she couldn't. Even that, he understood.

The voices rose to a crescendo of sound, and Emma raised her voice above them, shouting to be heard. She couldn't hear her own voice over the din, but it must have been piercing, as all-encompassing to the masses of the dead as their combined voices felt to her. She reached out, one hand free, and touched the stone of floor, into which words had been carved *of* the dead.

Something shattered.

And just like that, the voices stopped, and there was an echoing silence.

CHAPTER
TWENTY-THREE

IN THE SILENCE, two words rose from the stone, leaving no grooves or marks in their wake. They left a gap in the circle's circumference as they came to hover in front of Emma. No, she thought, in front of the lantern. They fluttered there, like moths in a form too cumbersome for actual wings; she could almost feel them battering ineffectually against the lantern's body.

They spoke.

Emma listened.

The Queen's name reverberated in the air for a long, long minute, and then it died into silence and stillness. She reached out with a hand instead of the lantern, and the letter forms came to rest on her upturned palm. She didn't speak. She didn't have to. The forms of lines and curves melted around that palm, changing as light spread toward the floor, until she held the hands of two young women; they overlapped in her outstretched palm.

They were her age, maybe slightly younger—or slightly older. She was not surprised to find that they were beautiful, or at least that they had been beautiful in life, with wide, round eyes, long hair, regular, perfect features.

She was also not surprised to see tears.

"Isabella," one girl said, although Emma hadn't asked for her name. The other girl didn't speak. Or perhaps she did and Emma couldn't hear her; her hand rested over Isabella's.

"I'm Emma," Emma told them both.

They nodded. She meant to ask them if they could return to the circle, if they could speak—or sing—her name instead of the Queen's. She didn't; she knew, although she wasn't certain how, that they couldn't. But there was no name on this circle. Not yet. Not until she could remake what had been unmade.

"This," the magar said, "is why you found the two."

But Emma shook her head again, mute now. She turned to the girls, Anne and Rose, both silent. Their attention was focused on the Lantern, not Emma, and something in their expressions made her want to weep. Scoros had kept them safe. He had murdered them. He had been responsible for their horrible, agonizing deaths.

And then he had found what remained.

Even if they were willing to do what the two freed girls had done, she wasn't certain how to take advantage of that. She wasn't certain how to force them to be what the girls had been: words. Names that weren't their own.

"I'm sorry," she told the magar—and she meant it. "I can't draw a circle of my own. Not yet. Not in time. But this one can't be used safely by Reyna, either."

She lifted the lantern, her arm aching, her heart louder now than her own voice.

And Nathan said, "Let me."

She turned to him. "I can't—" and fell silent.

"Let me, Em. They were her name, right?"

It was the magar who nodded, because Emma was suddenly paralyzed.

"Just her name?"

"It is more complicated than that, but yes. Her name."

"And the others? The other words?"

Even as he asked, symbols began to rise, just as the two

girls had done. His fists tightened as these words also drifted toward the lantern, pulled, called by Emma Hall. Isabella and the silent, nameless girl withdrew their hands, turning to watch the same transformation they had undergone: words becoming people.

All of these were also Emma's age—the age she imagined Reyna had been when Eric had died. They were also beautiful. She wondered if Reyna had made that choice consciously or unconsciously; she wondered, as well, if the girls had all been dead when she had chosen them, or if she had simply ended their lives to preserve their deathly appearance.

It didn't matter.

"What are you doing?" someone asked, sharp-voiced and outraged. Scoros' mother.

"I'm not doing anything," Emma replied. "They are." She watched as the words that described who Reyna thought she was lifted themselves from the stone circle and vanished, one by one.

Only the elemental words remained. They were simple engraving. They did not appear to be written in the ghostly bodies of trapped, dead girls.

"They do not change," the magar told her. "They would never change. But the other words might, with time and experience. The words that might alter, in time, are the words that are rendered in the dead."

"It's not much of a circle, now."

"No, Emma Hall. And that was foolish of you. You have power, but you lack knowledge; this would have been one of your most effective shields." But she looked unruffled. Scoros' mother made up for it. She looked apoplectic.

And Emma didn't care. Because Nathan's sentence had finally cleared the fog of her thoughts and fears. *Let me, Em.*

She was horrified. The words became the loudest thing in the room. And he knew. Of course he knew. He'd known her better than anyone except maybe Allison.

"Those words—they're a description of who you are, right? And the first two—your name?" Nathan continued to speak.

She couldn't even answer. She had taken Nathan's chain—if that was even the right word, but she hadn't taken it to *use him*. To consume him. She hadn't—

"Em—give me the choice, okay? Don't make it for me. You know I always had problems with that."

She shook her head.

"You could talk yourself into the worst places. You could believe that a moment's anger described the whole of you forever and ever, that a random bad thought somehow made you a bad person. You could decide that you weren't good enough for me on the bad days. You might not remember them. I do.

"I remember all the days, Emma. I wouldn't let you decide that you weren't good enough for me on the hard days. Remember? Because that was my choice to make, not yours."

She shook her head again. Words failed her utterly, but she *did* remember. She remembered the insecurity and the excitement of the early, early days. The fear, and the jealousies that she tried so hard to banish. She'd forgotten them; it was easy to forget because the loss had been so profound.

"Don't choose for me. I'd give my life for you if I still had it. This is as close I come in the afterlife. Let *me* do this. I know you. I know who you are. And I know your name."

"I don't know *how*," she whispered. "I don't know how to turn you into—" something that looked nothing like Nathan.

He nodded and turned to the magar. The magar's pursed lips failed to move. But Emma heard her voice anyway. *You are not old enough, boy. You have not yet learned that form is habit and limitation.* She turned to look at her daughter.

Helmi snorted. She reached out with both hands for Nathan. Her hands should have passed through him. They didn't. Emma didn't understand why—but she realized that Helmi's hands were the same color as the light shed by the lantern.

"I know what to do," she told Nathan. "If you're stupid enough to do this on purpose."

His smile was crooked. "I don't want her to die." He stared at Helmi's hands. "Why can you touch me?"

"The lantern," Helmi replied. "And no, before you ask, it only works on the dead. You still can't touch her without freezing her. Are you going to ask stupid questions for the rest of her life? 'Cause if you are, that's going to be measured in minutes."

Nathan fell silent.

"You can stop him," the magar told Emma, watching her youngest daughter holding onto the only person Emma thought she would ever love.

She almost did. She had to struggle with her visceral re-action to do what he had asked: to give him the choice. To respect it. He wasn't Anne or Rose. He wasn't a child. He understood what would happen.

And he understood Emma. The magar had said the words that Reyna had chosen to describe herself were words that were also relevant to Emma. She had said it dis-missively, as if those words weren't actually important.

They were important to Nathan. He walked to the pe-riphery of the circle, knelt, and placed one hand on the rock beneath his ghostly feet. The rock began to absorb him. Helmi said, and did, nothing that Emma could see, but the light that was Nathan faded.

The dead didn't need to breathe; the living did. She for-got how.

Helmi turned to Emma and to her mother and shrugged. And then, to Emma's shock, Helmi also began to fade.

The magar said nothing. She simply watched. Emma glanced briefly at the closed door and then did the same.

Words began to emerge, recreating the circumference of the depleted circle. But they weren't like the words that had lifted themselves into the air in the lantern's light. They were English words. Words she recognized.

"It is not the form," the magar said, although Emma hadn't spoken. She couldn't. "It is never the form."

The first word was Love. The word that followed was Hope. The third word was Fear, and the fourth, Courage. The fifth—Loyalty—made her eyes tear. The sixth was not a word she would have chosen for herself—but she would have cho-sen none of them so far, except perhaps fear.

Responsible.

She smiled.

Kind.

The word that followed kind was Ignorant, which made her laugh out loud. That wasn't a Nathan word—clearly Helmi had opinions. And even if the word was unkind, it was true. Emma did not know what she was doing. She only knew the *why*.

The last word was Strength. She shook her head, denying it. She wasn't certain if Nathan was saying she was strong in his eyes, or if he was urging her to be stronger—but it didn't matter. This circle was like a love letter. Nathan hadn't been a big letter writer, but then again, neither had Emma. So, this was the first love letter.

She stepped over the circumference that was almost complete, and she folded her legs, sitting in the circle; she looked up at Chase and found that he was wavering in her vision in a dangerous way. But she didn't care.

He said nothing. He offered no sympathy, no advice. He shook his head. "Circle's not for me," he told her, drawing daggers.

The last two words to emerge were the words that completed the circle in which Emma sat. Her name. Emma Hall. She set the lantern in her lap and met the magar's steady gaze.

"Helmi," the old woman said, although no sign of her daughter remained. "I am proud of you. If you had lived, you would have become a better guardian, a better guide, than Reyna." Her lips twisted. "And perhaps better than your mother, as well."

The words were now grooves in flat stone. They had no ears, no faces, no way of receiving information, and no way of broadcasting it.

But a final word pushed itself into the circle, squeezed and cramped because it was not the shortest of English words. It was also misspelled.

GRATITUD.

Emma liked it. Death had made it hard to feel gratitude. Hard to feel grateful for what she had, the loss was so enormous, the pain of it permeating everything. But she still had her mother—who was not the magar. She had Allison. She had Michael and Amy and Petal. She had a school life she had once enjoyed and might enjoy again, given effort and time. She had a roof over her head, and food on the table, and a mother who made certain that both of those things kept happening.

She had so much more than Reyna had had on the day of Eric's death. None of it excused Reyna's choices or actions since that day, but maybe it explained some of it. Maybe. Broken people did broken things; it was an act of will to change the course that violence and death laid over a life. She'd seen it in Scoros, in his memories of Reyna, in Chase. Emma had been hurt. She hadn't been broken.

She looked toward the wall that Michael had seen as a door. She closed her eyes, although that changed very, very little in the room. But as she lifted her chin she saw, at last, what Michael meant. She remained in the circle, but she left it as well, just as she had done when she had gone in search of Scoros the first time.

She now went in search of him for the last time.

CHAPTER
TWENTY-FOUR

NONE OF THE DEAD tried to stop her. None of them moved. As she left the circle, she turned back to look at herself; she was seated, cross-legged, in the circle, the lantern in her crooked lap.

As Michael had said, there was a door where smooth, curved wall had been. As doors went, it looked like something that belonged to a closet; it was neither large nor particularly impressive. Emma walked toward it.

"You will not be able to open that door," a familiar voice said. The magar.

Emma grimaced. "You can see the door now?"

"No. You can see it now. But you are not particularly opaque."

Emma reached the door and placed a hand against it. Her hand passed through its surface.

"Maybe I don't need to open it." But she frowned. What she had assumed were scratches and wear were, on closer inspection, badly carved words. She couldn't read them, but she recognized the etching for what it was.

"Those words," she said to the magar. "The ones on the lantern. You said the living couldn't hear them."

The magar was silent. Emma took this as agreement.

"But we can see them."

More silence.

"Your daughter could see them. I think these words are meant to be the words on the lantern's sheath."

"They won't have the same power. They won't have the same meaning."

"This door can't be seen by the living. It can't be seen by the dead." Speaking, Emma lifted the lantern. She wasn't surprised when it came to her hand; it wasn't a physical artifact. "Reyna saw the lantern."

"When I held it, yes. She did not have it to study. If you are correct—and I allow the possibility—she wrote from memory. She had a very good memory for the things that hurt her."

"The lantern?"

"She wanted it. I refused to give it to her."

Ah. "The lantern *is* physical. You pushed it into my hands the first night we met." Frowning, she held it up to the door, to the less polished, less perfect words scratched into the surface, as if with a pen. "Magar—how was the lantern made?"

"We do not know."

Frowning, Emma turned to look over her shoulder. She saw Chase Loern, moving outside the periphery of her circle. She saw the dead; they had turned toward her—but of course they had. She held the light aloft.

Emma pressed the lantern into the door's surface. Light stretched and spread across wood that was far too irregular, far too blemished, to be anything but real. With her free hand, she touched the door again, and this time, her hand met resistance. It was not like the doors she'd opened—or tried to open, or beat her fists against—in Scoros' memory. It was solid, but it wasn't; it didn't feel like an actual door.

The handle—and it had one—didn't feel like a handle, either. Michael had been able to touch the door. He hadn't been able to open it. The only person in the room with a professed ability to pick locks hadn't been able to see it.

Emma gripped the handle. It was warm, which she hadn't

expected. She opened the door as the light across its surface faded. In the distance, she heard Chase curse.

The room behind the door was the size of a closet. It contained almost nothing that Emma could see. It was dark; there was a small table, a single stool. Emma wasn't certain what she had expected to find. Memories, maybe. That was how she had gathered the rest of Scoros.

Walking into his memories had been involuntary. She'd done nothing except walk out of the circle—a circle that guaranteed no safety from the dead. She faced this room in a circle that now did. Maybe that's why there was nothing here but silence and stillness in a cramped, tiny space.

She couldn't imagine the Queen ever sitting in that chair; she couldn't imagine the Queen sitting at this table.

"Scoros," she called. The lantern in her hand rose as she spoke his name.

She felt his presence as he walked through her. He was still mostly shade and shadow to her eye, although he had the outline and general features of an older man. He approached the table; she thought his head was bowed.

He took the single chair. As he sat, he placed his forearms on the tabletop, entwining his hands. For one long moment, he seemed to study the tabletop. The table itself, like the door, looked old, almost unfinished; it lacked the grandeur of every other piece of furniture in these chambers.

It was real.

"Scoros."

He lifted his head slowly. He looked old, to Emma— much older than he had looked in any other memory. He was bearded, but the beard was patchy; his brows were a crust of iron gray above the bridge of his prominent nose. His eyes were brown—but a brown that was dark enough she couldn't distinguish it from pupil. He wore robes that seemed threadbare. She might have mistaken him for a monk of the kind that wandered across historical flashbacks on television.

"Scoros," she said again.

His eyes focused slowly. "Reyna."

"No," she replied, her voice gentling without effort. "I'm Emma." She held out her right hand.

Her named confused him, which Emma hadn't expected. She glanced over her shoulder; the door was still open.

"The candle," he said quietly. "The candle is not lit." He looked at the center of the empty tabletop. So did Emma. What he saw, she didn't see; there was no candle here. Scoros' memory didn't cause a candle to materialize, either. This room was real. The candle that he expected was probably real as well, and she didn't have one.

"What is the candle meant to do?" she asked him.

His eyes flickered again, brushing across her face as if he couldn't actually see it.

"Burn," he replied.

She approached him, moving slowly as if afraid to startle him. His gaze brushed past her as she did, coming to rest at the table's center.

"Magar, what was the purpose of a candle?"

"We did not use candles," the old woman replied. "We did not hide rooms, or mark them in the fashion this one was marked. We did not bind and imprison the dead—they did that to themselves. It was our duty to release them from bindings, not to add to them."

Scoros frowned.

Emma walked around the chair, searching for the thin, golden line that meant he was bound to a Necromancer. There was no such line.

As Emma searched with growing concern, another woman entered the room—Scoros' mother. She looked very much as if she wanted to either slap her son or push him off his chair. Anger came easily to her expression, nestling into lines carved there by use and time.

She couldn't slap her son, though. It was the first thing she tried; her hand passed through his face. He frowned, blinked. She bent and shouted in his ear, which was even less successful.

"I don't think he can hear you," Emma told the woman.

"No." She looked at Emma, and beneath the anger, there was a hint of fear. "He hears Reyna. He only ever heard Reyna."

Emma understood why Scoros' mother thought it; she even understood the bitterness in the statement. But she knew it wasn't completely true. He *obeyed* Reyna. In a fashion, he loved her. He supported her. He had tried to make her feel safe—and that had been an utter failure.

Emma turned toward the part of the Queen's chambers she could see through the open, narrow door. She spoke two names, and two young girls walked toward her. Anne and Rose.

The mother glanced at them, frowning. She didn't recognize the girls. Scoros, however, did. They were the first thing to truly grab and hold his attention; he could see Emma, but not clearly enough to acknowledge her.

His eyes widened as the girls approached him. It was the first fear he'd shown since she'd opened this door.

"Do you hate him?" Emma asked Anne.

Anne glanced at her. "Do you?"

She almost said she didn't know him well enough to hate him, but that was untrue. She knew Scoros better than she knew most of the people she'd ever met or interacted with. "No. But he didn't kill me. He didn't kill my sister."

"No?" she asked, and Emma almost said, 'I don't have a sister'. But she realized that it was the hatred the girl was questioning.

"No. To find him the first time, I had to live through a lot of his life. *As* him. I'm not sure you can truly hate someone you've been."

"He tried to protect us."

After he'd murdered you both. Emma nodded.

Anne took his left hand. Rose took his right. What Scoros' mother couldn't accomplish, the children could. "The lantern," Anne said. She smiled, her expression at odds with her age. Or maybe not; it was gentle and even protective. "That's what the other girl said."

Emma blinked.

"You gave the girls—and Helmi—your hands. You did not release them."

"I did."

"No, Emma, you didn't. You didn't bind them; they were free to leave you. Come. My daughter will be here in minutes."

Scoros rose. He left the chair. The two girls—one on either hand—dragged him to his feet, looking for all the world like young daughters ganging up on a favorite uncle. His expression shifted as he left the chair, his eyes sharpening, their color lightening. He looked around the room—the closet—blinking rapidly. And then he looked at the lantern, and he froze.

"Magar," he whispered.

Emma turned to her right, but the magar wasn't there. A voice from her left said, gently, "He is speaking to you, girl."

Emma shook her head. "I'm not your magar. I'm Emma. We've met before."

Anne reached Emma first. She held out her free hand, and Emma took it. Then Anne passed Scoros' hand into hers. Her eyes were shining. They were the eyes of the dead, but they were brimming with light, and the light looked, for a moment, like tears.

Emma realized then what was wrong with Scoros: His eyes were brown. Or black. Or some color-in between. They were not the eyes of the dead. This Scoros was like a memory.

Yes.

"Scoros," Emma said—to the brown-eyed man. "I need your help." She held the hand; it felt weathered, old—but not cold. She wondered, then, whether this was a side-effect of the lantern.

"To do what?" the older man asked, eyes narrowing as he glanced past Emma to the doorway.

"To save the citadel," Emma replied.

"If the citadel's safety is your concern, magar, leave me."

She swallowed. "It's not. I don't care what happens to the citadel." That was also a lie. She tried again. "I do care what happens to the citadel. I want to unmake it. I want to free the dead. But I can't do that until the living are safe. If I try to destroy what the Queen has built now, we're all going to die."

He frowned.

"The citadel is flying."

"Impossible."

"No. Maybe it was impossible when you were actually alive."

Again he frowned, glancing at Anne and Rose, at the open door, and at the table. "I am not dead."

Emma grimaced. She had no time to argue with him, and she had no choice. But she didn't, couldn't, understand how he could be here, trapped in this semblance of life, and be *there*, everywhere, trapped as the dead were trapped.

"Magar."

Emma exhaled. "If that's what the lantern means, then yes. I need your help. I need it now. Will you give it to me?"

"Will you free the dead? Will you shepherd them to their final destination?"

"Yes," she told him. "Yes, even you."

"Will you save my child?"

What?

He tried to reach out across the table, but his hands were occupied. "Will you save my child?"

Emma stared at him. She met his gaze and held it. His eyes were brown. The lines of his face had shifted in place, deepening across the brow. He seemed old, tired, frail. And he seemed alive. But the girls could see him; they could touch him. She didn't understand.

And now was not the time for confusion.

No, magar, it is not.

"You're dead," she whispered, to the disembodied voice.

She felt his bitter, bitter smile—a smile that didn't touch the face of the man seated in front of her. *Yes. Yes and no. Death is complicated in this place.*

"So is life."

No, Emma—life is not. But she felt his attention shift to the man seated in the chair, as if he were an entirely different person. *Life is simply a struggle not to become one of the dead.* He stood by the seated Scoros, as if he were a shadow—his shadow.

"Anne?"

The girl nodded.

"Why can you touch him? Why—"

She looked confused. "I can touch you," she finally said.

"Yes, but I'm—" She stopped, shook her head, and turned toward the open door. "I think," she told Scoros, "it's time for you to leave this room."

"Why?"

"Because Reyna is coming."

He looked confused—far more confused than Anne had. "Of course she is." He glanced at the two girls and said, gently, "You must let go of my hands. She will see you."

Emma stood at the threshold of this tiny prison. The very vague plan she'd made—and calling it a plan was a gross overstatement—was gone. She had intended to open Michael's invisible door, to find what remained of Scoros— and to take over the bindings that held him here.

The memories, the gathered bits of Scoros, had said or implied that Scoros was woven throughout the citadel, that it was his essence and his power that somehow kept it together, kept it afloat. He had implied, again, that if she found the element of himself that was hidden and bound, Emma would gain control of enough of the citadel that her friends wouldn't plunge instantly to their deaths.

He hadn't, however, told her that he was *alive*.

She had no idea how to bind someone who was still living. She had no idea how she had found *any* of Scoros if he wasn't dead.

"Leave him," the magar said quietly.

"I can't—"

"You have two options. Kill him or leave him. He is of no use to you if he is alive."

"He's of no use to me if he's dead, either." She exhaled. "But he's not—he can't be—bound to the Queen."

But the old woman shook her head. "He is bound," she said, grimly. As Emma opened her mouth, the old woman continued. "I thought he was dead. No wonder I could never find him. Do you understand what was done?"

Emma shook her head. She approached the old man, and held out her free hand. "I don't know if I can save your daughter," she told him. "I hope to save everyone else."

He stared at her hand.

"I'm sorry, Scoros, but you must leave this room."

"It is my room," he said, with a soft smile. "It is hidden, defended; it is here that Reyna can flee if there is danger. It is here she comes when she requires comfort or guidance. I cannot leave."

"Are you bound to this room?" she asked him. "Do you come to life *only* when this door is opened?"

Yes, the shadow Scoros, the gathered Scoros, replied. *When the door is open and only then. It is a prison.*

But Emma shook her head. She thought she understood some part of what had been done. Parts of Scoros were dead, but he himself was—barely—alive.

"Which one of you," she asked, her voice clearer and harder, "attempted to kill the Queen of the Dead?"

Do not do this.

She couldn't meet the eyes of the parts of Scoros that were dead. The parts, Emma thought, that must be killed, bound, and hidden if the man seated in front of her was to love and comfort the Queen.

"You did this to yourself."

No. But we were not enemies, then. I had given her all of my life that mattered, and it was not enough. I was not the first to attempt to kill her. I will not be the last. Perhaps you will be—because the attempts will not end while she lives. Perhaps they will become infrequent. Perhaps they will all be ineffective. When I suggested what was done to me, I wished to protect her.

I know what was done to the dead to build this place. This was my penance: to suffer what the dead suffer—and for just as long as they suffer it.

But I chose. I chose what to surrender. I chose what to bury. And I watched. I watch her now, he added. *She is almost here. She has not stopped to gather her knights. Tell him—tell me—that Eric is with her.*

She realized that Scoros couldn't hear his own voice. He could see the dead. He could see the lantern. But he was of the people.

"If the Queen kills you, what happens?"

Silence.

"Scoros, I'm sorry, but you must leave this room. It doesn't matter now that the room is defended and protected against attack. Attack comes." She lifted the lantern, understanding what it meant to him. Understanding what it made her, in his eyes.

He rose. "Magar," he said, and this time he bowed to her. "We have waited. We have waited a long, long time."

She left the closet-sized room, and Scoros followed, trailed by a shadow that didn't conform to the fall of light.

The room was no longer empty. Men and women of all ages, shapes, races, had gathered there; they were silent. The voices of the dead—those without form, without mobility— were not.

They fell silent only when the doors at the other end of the chamber rolled—slammed—open.

REYNA

THE QUEEN'S KNIGHTS do not reappear. She is too angry to call them. The mobile dead have vanished. Nothing stands between Reyna and the citadel except Eric.

"You will wait here," she tells him. Her voice is the Queen's voice, not the girl's, and there is death in it. Of course there is. Who disobeys the Queen? She storms through the empty, silent streets; the only thing she can hear is her breathing and the rustle of her train.

Eric does not obey. Were he anyone else, he would be dead, now. He almost dies anyway, so potent is her rage. Everything in her is angry. Everything rages, although she does not speak.

She thinks she has never been so angry. She thinks she will never be so angry again.

She is wrong.

She reaches the great doors of the citadel; they are open. They were opened for the procession, and they will not be closed until the ceremony is finished—if it is *ever* finished.

She enters. The halls are as empty as the streets. Beneath the high, vaulted ceilings, her footsteps echo. Her hands have curved into shaking fists; she cannot loosen them.

She is certain that Emma is here. It is a sick certainty, an angry one. She meant, once, to bring Emma here as a novice. Later, she intended to bring her here for other reasons. She kept Nathan, resurrected him, with that in mind. She wanted to have something to offer Emma.

Why?

She almost can't remember.

But Nathan is *Reyna's* to offer. He is meant to be a gift, a magnanimous act. She will not allow him to be *stolen*.

She walks toward her chambers; her anger cools. Emma is an untrained girl. She is less, much less, than Reyna was at the same age. She has been taught nothing. She has no skill. How has she taken Nathan? How has she broken that binding?

She slows. *Longland*. She will speak with Longland. She takes a deep breath. Another. She needs to think. Turning, she sees Eric. He is watching her. He does not smile.

She is not smiling either. The day is ruined. The event, destroyed. But Eric is here, and there will be another day. A better day. Maybe she was foolish to begin immediately. Maybe she was too impulsive. Things hurried are seldom perfect.

But she remembers hurrying to the tree by the stream in the early, early hours of the morning. She remembers Eric, standing beneath its boughs, watching her approach. She remembers the urgency, the joy—both hers and his. She knows there is no joy in him today.

But is there joy in her?

She opens her mouth, closes it, waits for the right words to form. She isn't certain what to say. She doesn't want to appear weak. Even if Eric is here, she remains the Queen of the Dead, and weakness is not allowed.

She is never certain, later, what she would have said. She knows her mouth is open, and his, closed. She knows that he is standing a yard away. She can close that distance or preserve it; he has given the choice to her.

It is not what she wants—the choice, the responsibility of

choice. What she wants is his joy and his desire and his love. Her love has never died; she knows that love can last forever. She means to say this—even if this is the wrong time, the wrong place.

But a sudden, brilliant light cuts across her vision, blinding her; it permeates the walls, the floors, rises to the heights of the vaulted ceiling—and beyond. Reyna knows that light. There is only one thing that can cast it.

She turns toward the lantern. She can see its shape; there are walls between the light and her eyes, but they are made of the dead, and even if they weren't, the light would still be visible; it is close.

It is too close.

She sees the shape of Eric's eyes change; she knows he sees what she sees. She feels the rumble of the floor beneath her feet; imagines she can see the tremor in the walls and the ceiling they support. The whole of her world seems to strain toward the lantern's light.

And of course it does.

Emma.

"Tell me," Reyna says. "Tell me about Emma." She walks. Eric shadows her. "What is she like? Is she beautiful?"

Eric doesn't answer immediately.

"Does she look like I look?"

"No. She looks almost nothing like you."

"Is she powerful?"

"How could she be?"

"She has the lantern." Her voice cracks on the last word. Cracks and lifts. "Tell me, Eric. What is she like?" She walks, dragging him in her wake. She cannot see where the lantern is, but she knows it is close.

"How did she find my mother? How did she convince my mother to give her the lantern?"

Eric says, after a long pause, "Emma is kind."

It is not what Reyna wants to hear. It is not, in truth, what she *expected* to hear. She laughs; it is a bitter, incredulous sound. "The magar gave the lantern to a child because *she's kind*?" She is shaking, almost in time with the floor and the walls, as if they echo her fury—and the longing and the rage and the disappointment—always, always, the disappointment.

"What does that *even mean*? My mother was never *kind*!" It is true. The magar was bitter and harsh. She despised weakness. She despised her oldest daughter. Every bit of approval she gave was grudging and qualified—and there was little enough of it. So little.

Reyna did everything her mother asked. Learned everything her mother wanted her to learn. Lived with the dead, because that was what her mother wanted. She learned *everything*. She learned *quickly*. She was more powerful than any of her cousins. She was more powerful than her mother. She did what she was told to do, time and again, even when it meant that she would lose the day with Eric.

She has never understood what the magar wanted from her. Even Scoros couldn't explain it. She has never understood why she was not, why she was *never*, good enough. Her mother doesn't know Emma. Her mother didn't raise her. Her mother didn't live with her.

But her mother gave the lantern to *Emma*. Emma is her mother's choice of magar.

Reyna coughs around words and gives up on them.

She will kill Emma Hall. She will take the lantern. She doesn't need her mother's permission or approval. And then, when she has it, she will find her mother, and her mother will answer every question Reyna has.

She lifts her skirts, hating the train, hating the confinement, hating everything. She doesn't know where Emma is—but she knows Emma is in the citadel.

It is Scoros who tells her, indirectly.

What is kindness? What does it mean?

She will banish him, too. She will kill him. She doesn't need Scoros anymore. Maybe she never did.

It means vision, little one. Emma Hall sees what is laid before her. She sees—or tries to see—clearly. She does not judge.

"And I *do*?" Reyna shouts.

Scoros doesn't answer. It doesn't matter. Reyna knows where Emma is. She knows where Emma must be. A bitter, bitter anger fills her, spills over; the floor beneath her feet almost unravels with the potency of her rage.

Eric tries to take her arm, and she pushes him away—without touching him at all. It is Scoros she wants to kill. Emma. But if she is not very careful, Eric will also be caught in the cauldron of her rage, her loss, her endless, endless sorrow.

For just a moment, she wants that. She wants to immolate everything. She wants to give up on love, because love has always, always betrayed her. She is tired of pain. She is tired of trying. She is tired of everything.

And angry.

CHAPTER
TWENTY-FIVE

THE QUEEN OF THE DEAD stood beneath the arched frame of the open door.

She was, in a fashion, beautiful; in the light from the skylight, she glittered in a way that suggested sequins—or diamonds. Her dress was white, the skirts full and rustling behind her; Emma thought there was, or would be, a train. There were no attendants to carry it.

Her crown was gold, a shade warmer and darker than her hair, which had been pulled back off her face.

She looked beautiful, perfect. She looked like a bride. A bride made of living ice and rage. Her eyes, brown, glittered as Emma met her gaze. She stared at Emma, seated in the center of her own circle.

The royal gaze swept the room and came to rest not on Chase or Emma, but on the old man who was seated within the periphery of the circle. Emma's circle. From what she understood, the circle would afford him no protection.

But she wasn't certain that the circle would afford anyone in the room any protection from the Queen's rage. She trembled with it, swelled with it, embodied it; it seemed larger in all ways than she was.

"How *dare* you?" Her voice was thin—like the edge of a blade—her eyes, narrowed. Emma found her so compelling that she almost missed Eric as he entered the room behind her. It was Eric who closed the doors; the Queen didn't appear to be aware of them.

It was Eric who bent and carefully straightened the Queen's train. It was such an unexpected gesture, Emma stared at him. He failed to meet her gaze. But he failed to look at the Queen herself, either. He simply stood behind her, as if he were a guard or an attendant.

Maybe, she thought, love didn't die. Maybe it couldn't be killed. Or maybe it was just Emma's love that was so conditional. If she had ever loved Reyna, she would have stopped centuries ago; there would be nothing in the woman she had become that would keep the love alive and much that would kill it.

If Nathan had been the King of the Dead, if he had changed so much from the Nathan she'd fallen in love with, she wouldn't have been able to continue to love him. Love— Emma's love—needed some small embers to continue to burn. She wondered what that said about her, because she had believed—not intellectually, but emotionally, viscerally— that love was forever.

She accepted that love was not fixed. It wasn't diamond. It was organic. It grew. Like a tree it required soil, sunlight, water, and deprived of those things for long enough, it died.

Reyna's had not.

But Eric's?

"Scoros. Why have you left your room?" Rage lent a killing frost to her tone.

Scoros' expression was drawn, reserved; his shoulders drooped, his spine turned gently down. He was not a young man, but he had aged a decade or two since the doors had opened. A bitter mix of yearning, grief, and disgust twisted his lips, narrowed his eyes. He glanced briefly at Emma; the expression didn't change.

"Reyna."

If the Queen narrowed her eyes any farther, they'd be

closed. "Your Majesty," she said, correcting him. "You will *never* use my name again."

But the old man shook his head. "You are Reyna," he said. "To me, you will always be Reyna. I failed you."

Reyna stared at the lantern's light. She was silent for a long moment.

"Get ready," Chase let the two words escape the corner of his mouth. Emma heard them but didn't respond. She looked at the cast of the Queen's face in the lantern light. The Queen seemed to be drawn to it, just as the dead were.

"You might redeem yourself," Reyna told the old man.

"I have failed every attempt to do so," Scoros replied. Even as he spoke, Emma heard echoes and harmonies fold around each syllable. But she saw his expression shift, and she realized that even now, knowing everything he knew, Scoros—*this* Scoros—wanted redemption.

Reyna saw this too. "Take the lantern from her hands."

His chin dropped. He moved his hands—slowly—and folded them in his lap. When he raised his face again, he smiled. It was not a happy expression. "Have you forgotten so much?"

Silence.

"If you want the lantern, you must now prove yourself worthy of its light and its burden."

"I *am* worthy of it! I always was!" She seemed shocked by the words that had escaped her. She couldn't retrieve them; she could control anything else that left her mouth.

"We don't get to decide our own worth," Scoros replied, his voice gentle. But beneath the surface of those almost fatherly words, Emma felt the slow movement of glaciers. "Emma did not decide that she was worthy of the lantern. The magar did."

Silence.

"And you will not decide you are worthy of it, either. Emma will. The lantern and its burden is now hers, to carry or to pass on."

It was clear that Reyna had no desire to prove herself worthy to Emma Hall. It was clear, as well, that she wanted the lantern—and that she could not simply take it. Her lips folded in what was meant to be a smile; it did nothing to gentle her ferocity.

"I would have trained you," the Queen told Emma, her voice quieter but no softer. "I sent my Knights to save you from the hunters. You repaid them with death."

Emma, stung, said, "They would have killed a *baby*. They would have killed Eric and Chase."

"They would not have dared to kill Eric. Even had they, I would have resurrected him."

"They tried to kill my best friend. Even after I said I would go with them if they released her. They tried to kill my best friend's family. They may have succeeded with the youngest. Nothing you could have offered me was worth that. Nothing."

"Is that what you were taught? Poor child. You have lived in ignorance of the gift to which you were born. Do you know how old I am?"

"Not to the day, no. I don't see how it matters."

The cold smile almost fractured; the Queen held it in place with obvious effort. "Perhaps not. But, Emma, I resurrected Nathan for you. I did, for you, what I did for myself. He loved you. He wanted to be with you. It is only me who could make that possible."

"By binding him to you?"

Do not argue with her.

"Yes."

"But you didn't have to bind Eric. Have you become less powerful with time?"

Reyna raised a hand—a fist—and part of the wall melted. "I would have returned him to you," she finally said. The wall didn't reform. "If you proved worthy of his love, I would have given him into your keeping. I resurrected him because I know what it is to lose the man you love. I expected—"

"Gratitude?" Emma asked, her voice much softer, much fuller, than the Queen's.

"I would have given anything to have Eric back," the Queen replied. "And I *did*. Where is Nathan?"

Emma kept her gaze on the Queen. It wasn't as difficult as it should have been. "He's dead," she replied. At this very moment, it didn't even hurt to say it, which was a first. "Nathan is dead."

Eric turned to Emma, his expression almost unreadable.

It was the first time since straightening the train of a very beautiful, very impractical dress that he had moved. It was the first time since he'd entered the room that he looked *at* Emma.

"You killed him?" the Queen demanded.

"No. A drunk driver did that." Emma tried to return her attention to the Queen—the most dangerous thing in the room. But Eric's expression caught her and held her—there was pain in it. Pain and hope—but hope was so often painful.

"Don't play games. What have you done with him?"

"He's dead," Emma said again. Eric nodded. She turned toward the Queen, and as she did so, she rose. The lantern came with her, part of her right hand.

Scoros attempted to rise as well, and Emma glanced back at him, shaking her head. "You don't need to stand," she told him quietly. "This isn't about you anymore."

"If it weren't," he replied, accepting Chase's aid, "I wouldn't be here. I, too, would be dead."

But Emma shook her head. "It affected you. It affected Eric. It affected the dead. But it wasn't *about* any of you."

"It is not," he said, his voice gentle and thin, "about you, either."

At that, Emma nodded.

Reyna had lost the thread of words; they were buried beneath accusation, anger, and the familiar sting of betrayal. Her eyes were fixed on the lantern as Emma raised it. "Eric," Emma said. She extended her left hand.

The Queen mirrored the gesture as Eric moved; she extended that arm into his chest, restraining him. "Eric is *alive*," she said, voice low. "You have no power over him."

Chase laughed. It was an ugly, harsh sound. He said nothing, but the laughter was accusation enough.

"Reyna," Scoros said, speaking the most forbidden words in the citadel, "the boy is dead. He's been dead for centuries."

Fire erupted from the floor, scorching and blackening it. The fire was green, bright, wild; it seemed to require no wood, no spark. Chase flinched but held his ground; the fire didn't enter the circle that enclosed the three of them.

Emma could feel it and was surprised: There was no heat in it. It was a wild, lapping green ice.

"You will destroy the citadel," Scoros told her gently. "Before you can destroy me."

Reyna cursed. And it came to Emma, listening to the rising fury of the Queen, that she could understand every word the Queen spoke. That she had always understood every word—even in memory.

Surely that was wrong. The language Reyna had learned from birth wasn't modern English. The Necromancers that she had plucked from their homes across North America couldn't be the only Necromancers born. Had Reyna chosen the language of her inferiors? Had she chosen to adopt a tongue that wasn't her own?

Emma would have. If it eased communication, if it helped to build—and hold—a community, a family, together, she would.

She stared at eyes that were markedly brown in a pale, white face. She stared at the contours of lips and cheek and jaw, at the color of hair that could be seen above the rise of a crown, at the perfect, smooth skin of her throat. And she remembered Reyna as Scoros had first seen her.

This woman was not that child. Not the girl that Scoros had vowed to protect. Her eyes were the same, but very little else was; her build was different, her nose a different shape, the curve of her forehead less pronounced, the point of her chin too delicate. In other people, some of the differences would be produced by age.

But the Queen had not allowed herself to age. She had maintained the semblance of youth because Eric was young.

Eric, dead, would be forever young. Unless the Queen chose to change his body, the form that she'd made for him, he would never age.

The dead couldn't. The dead didn't. They were trapped and held forever in memories that could no longer be added to.

Eric was dead.

But, Emma thought, so was the Queen. Dead enough that her words were clear to Emma, no matter what language she spoke. All of the dead spoke in a language that

Emma could understand—because they weren't actually speaking. And when Emma answered them, neither was she. Speech was a function of an actual body.

Reyna had that.

But how much of what she now had was built—as Nathan's body had been built—of the dead? How much of her living self remained beneath the shell of the perfect form, made and remade, massaged and changed, over the passage of centuries?

Something must remain; her eyes were living eyes. But the rest of her? Emma lifted the lantern, extending her arm to its full height. The light weighed nothing.

"Scoros," she whispered.

The old man seated beside her didn't reply. But she wasn't talking to him.

"Preserve them. Please." She didn't mention her friends by name. If she failed, she didn't want to tell the Queen who'd been here. Stairs—familiar stairs—appeared in the circle, the lowest step an inch from her foot.

I will, he replied. *But preservation has never been my strength.*

No, it really hadn't. But Scoros was not yet dead. Living, parts of himself had been scattered through the citadel, underpinning it, forming a structure beneath the whole, like a spider's web.

You understand what was done? he asked her.

"No. But I think you keep the citadel in the air. Bring it to ground," she whispered. "Quickly. Safely."

It was the living man who answered. "Yes. I did not intend to kill her. I hoped to separate her from the power that destroyed her."

"Destroyed me? *Destroyed me*?" Green fire leaped and sizzled in the air around the circle; it consumed the walls of the resurrection room. "It *saved* me! It saved us!"

"Is this salvation?" he asked her, raising one arm in a slow, steady sweep. "Is this life? It is a *tomb,* Reyna. It does not return you to the earth; it doesn't offer peace to the living. It is not a place where memory brings joy. It is not a place that offers comfort—to either the living or the dead."

"It is *not* a grave. It is home!"

"It is not a grave, no," the living Scoros replied gently. "It is a tomb. It is a gentle tomb. A monument of stone and unnatural grandeur. A thing made of—and for—man. Emma has spent much time beside graves. She knows the difference." He looked beyond Reyna. "Eric."

Eric was staring at him.

"It is time," Scoros said. "It is past time. I do not ask you to harm her. You can't without her permission. I regret what was done to you and your kin."

"It's not on your head," Eric replied, his voice rough and low.

"I regret what was done to mine."

Eric shook his head again.

"The magar will grant you the freedom you have never had, if you ask it. But she will, I think, grant you that freedom even if you don't."

"Scoros!" Reyna shouted.

The old man winced. "I loved you, child. Not wisely and not well. I love you still. But I can see it, Reyna. I can see what waits. And, child, I am tired." His expression gentled. "Aren't you?"

Chunks of the floor fell away, in answer to the question. Parts of the wall eroded, thinning and becoming porous.

Emma took this in before she squared her shoulders and set one foot on the stairs. She looked across the room at Eric, who stood, empty hands by his sides.

"Where is Nathan?" he asked her.

She shook her head. "Here," she whispered. She began to climb.

How many of the dead did Reyna hold? How many had she bound? How many had she drained? With each step she took, Emma wondered. She didn't ask. She wasn't certain that the Queen of the Dead was capable of answering that question—not now. She raged against Scoros, against her absent mother, against Eric. Emma was barely mentioned.

Emma began her ascent alone, but as she walked, people joined her. They poured through—or from—the broken walls, the crumbling floor, and they followed her, almost unseeing. No, she thought, they saw. They saw the light she carried. They saw what waited at the top of the spiral stairs.

And they wanted it. Of course they did.

She didn't ask them their names; nor did she ask for permission to use whatever remained of their power. She did note that some of these dead appeared as ghosts and some as living people. It didn't matter. They streamed toward the door above Emma's head, and when it failed to open, they retreated, standing in the glow of the lantern.

They didn't reach for it, not as they reached for the closed door. But it didn't matter. The lantern's handle was cold, and it grew colder as she climbed.

Emma wasn't certain what the Queen saw. Did she see stairs as Emma did? Did she see the dead that the walls and the floor had released? Or did she see Emma Hall sitting in the circle?

The circle itself didn't fray. It didn't shatter. The Queen of the Dead stormed toward it, toward Emma, and only when she reached the circumference did she stop. Emma couldn't see her expression; she could hear the sudden silence. It was the silence of slowly drawn breath. She looked down, over the slender rail on which her left hand rested.

The Queen's face was raised. Silence was broken. "Do you think you have any hope of destroying what I've built?" Hysteria, anger, grief, were gone. Icy contempt remained.

Emma shook her head. She glanced at Eric, whose face was white and still. "No."

"I see you've attempted to remake my circle in your own image. Clever." The Queen knelt, her skirts an impediment; their hems brushed against the words she attempted to study, obscuring them. Impatient, she pushed them aside. "But if my mother is your adviser, you don't have the knowledge to defend what you've built."

"I am not her adviser," the old woman said.

Reyna rose, the circle momentarily forgotten. "You gave her the lantern." Her voice was ice; her eyes almost glittered with it. "You gave *her* the lantern. An outsider. How could you?"

"She is of the people, Reyna. She has power to rival yours. To eclipse it."

"She does not!"

"And power was never the issue. You knew this. You know it now. Emma Hall has walked through the fires of the dead to free the lost—without training, without a circle to protect her. She thought she was risking her life, but she took that risk. I did not guide her. I did not advise her. She had nothing from me."

Reyna's lips were white. "And without lessons she learned how to draw *this* circle?"

"No. Most of what she knows of circles," the magar continued, "I did not tell her."

Reyna threw Scoros a murderous glare.

"Reyna," he said, his voice softer than the magar's. "It is time. It is past time. The dead have been weeping for centuries. The gift we were given—"

"It was *not* a gift," Reyna said, her voice low. The heat that seemed to drain from her was contained in those words. "You think this is a tomb?"

"It is a place of death, of the dead. There is almost no life in it."

She laughed. It was not a pretty sound. "What do you expect me to know of *life*? All of *my* life was given to the dead. To death. I wasn't allowed friends. I wasn't allowed daylight. I wasn't allowed *love*. The only thing that mattered to my mother—to my family—was death and the dead. There was nothing of *me* in it, and none of you cared.

"You think I should have built something else? How?"

Scoros closed his eyes.

"You never cared about living. Only survival. And Scoros? *I survived.* I don't intend to stop now." She reached out and placed her hand against the gentle curve of letters. Emma looked down, halting her climb. She shook herself and started to move again. Reyna was right. Emma had no knowledge and no weapon that would prove effective against her. She had no defenses, and Chase hadn't had time to prepare any.

Chase.

He was watching the Queen of the dead; Emma couldn't see his expression. She wasn't certain what he would, or could, do; she was almost certain he would try something. But the fire that lapped at the edge of the circle hadn't reached him yet. Both he and Scoros seemed safe.

That safety wouldn't last when the Queen unmade the circle. Emma had no doubt that she could—and she could remake it once again in her own image. While it lasted, Emma climbed.

She reached the door.

REYNA

REYNA RECOGNIZES THE WORDS. They are English. They are not the old tongue, with its compact runes; they are not the hidden language. The circle shouldn't work, written as it is, a mishmash of the words that remain unchanging and pure and words that should not be written in a circle at all.

She is shaking with fury, burning with it. Ice melts, cold fades. These words are not carved in stone; they are carved in the bedrock of death. Death is Reyna's domain. Her rule over the dead is undisputed.

And yet they stream past her as if she has become invisible. Those that can, all but fly; they do not stop. They offer no obeisance and no power; they do not recognize their Queen. Nor does the circle that Emma Hall has fashioned prevent their passage. They come at will, as if nothing is preventing them.

Did Emma learn nothing?

Perhaps not. Perhaps it is only the lantern that gives her

the strength to defy Reyna. It doesn't matter. Emma *will* learn. Starting now.

Reyna breaks the first word, changing the shape of the offensive, foreign letters. She is not sure that she has chosen the right word to start with, but it doesn't matter; they are all wrong, the wrongness so obvious it practically burns.

As if anything could burn her now.

But the word struggles against her, as if it had will; its shape breaks and then reverts, resisting her commands. She is shocked for one long moment; she assumes there is a greater treachery here—and that should not surprise her.

It doesn't surprise her when the doors burst open. It doesn't surprise her that the steps she hears are heavy, audible. It has been a long, long time since she has been vulnerable to physical attack, and she is not concerned.

Not until Merrick Longland brushes past her, leaping into the circle she cannot instantly remake. Her heart rises at the sight; she believes, for the briefest of instants, that he intends to kill Emma Hall—and she knows that Emma Hall is vulnerable to all manner of physical attack; she is not what Reyna has become.

But he does not kill her. The whole of his attention is riveted by what she holds in her hand.

Emma looks up at him—but everything in the gesture implies that she's looking down, as if from a height. Her eyes are glowing faintly, but it is not her eyes that catch the attention—it's her smile. There's something in it as she looks at Longland; some hint of recognition, of connection. Of warmth.

Was it Longland? Did *Longland* teach her?

But no, no; he couldn't have. Reyna never taught Longland this. And Reyna knows that Emma Hall is indirectly responsible for Longland's death. She's heard the report. She's seen the injuries, writ in the memory of the dead.

Longland kneels, or begins to kneel; she stops him, catching his arm. Reyna can no longer see Longland's face, but he bows his head, and Emma Hall lifts a hand to touch his forehead. She is still smiling.

"Merrick," Reyna says, weighting his name with the whole of her command.

His body stiffens; he turns to look over his shoulder, to

meet the eyes of the woman to whom he *should* kneel. He is hers. He is bound to her. She cannot force him to return the way the dead do—but once he is in her orbit, he belongs to her. His eyes widen, and Reyna realizes that he has run here—he has run past her—without even *seeing* her. He has looked at, and for, Emma.

Emma, who has the lantern, which she could never have obtained without the consent of Reyna's mother. Emma is a stranger. She is not of the people. And yet somehow, she has obtained the approval and trust that Reyna was always denied.

The love, she thinks, hating Merrick Longland, hating Scoros, hating everything. Why? Why does it always work this way?

Merrick Longland kneels at her silent command. He kneels, facing Reyna. What Emma will not accept, Reyna demands. He bows to Reyna.

"Kill her."

He rises. She can feel him strain against the command, against the binding placed upon him. But he is powerless before the Queen of the Dead. He removes a gun from its holster, his hand shaking with the effort.

Even Longland, Reyna thinks. Even Longland, who died because of Emma, would choose Emma if he could. She almost destroys him, then. She will, later. But without a body, he cannot do what needs to be done. He levels the gun and turns to face Emma.

Eric moves then. He moves. Reyna lifts an arm; his chest hits it. She sees that he wants to go—as Longland did—to Emma. And, oh, the anger that rises, then.

EMMA DIDN'T HESITATE.

She didn't love Merrick Longland. She didn't even like him. But she understood that when he turned, he would do as the Queen commanded. He didn't have a choice. Lantern in hand, Emma could see the filaments that stretched from his core to the Queen's; it was bright, vivid, golden. And it was a chain.

What she had done for Nathan, she now did for Longland—and she did it without hesitation, without terror. She reached for him before he could turn from the Queen; he was standing in her circle. The height of the stairs did not prevent this. The paradigm of stairs faded. She didn't have to ascend. What the dead needed was not at a lofty, forbidden height. It was here.

The Queen was not.

The circle was proof against death and the way the living could lose themselves in the memories, the fears, and the dying, but Emma was certain it wasn't proof against knives or bullets. It was ironic that she had spent nights longing for death to sneak in and take her too. It was visceral and terrible, but she understood that it wasn't death she wanted. It was peace. It was an end to loss and pain.

And she wanted to live.

She wanted life. The only hope of joy in this world was in life; death was endless privation. And she wanted that to change, too. Because everyone she loved now—everyone she would *ever* love—would die eventually. She would die as well. And this could not be all that waited. This could not be eternity.

She wouldn't let it be.

She placed her free hand on the back of Longland's neck, feeling the taut cords of muscles that strained with effort. She could even guess what caused him to make that effort.

"Do it," he said, his voice the product of clenched jaw and minimal movement of lips.

She nodded.

His body came apart beneath her hands. She felt it unravel, but this time, she paid attention to how; she saw the moment his body became its disparate elements—not flesh and blood and internal organs, as her own would have been, but the dead. They were older than the victims chosen to house Nathan; almost of an age with Longland's physical appearance now. They were also two women, two men—their forms so transparent they could be lost in the light.

Or they could have been had the source of that light been anything other than this lantern. She heard their whispers; she knew that was all she would ever hear. But they looked beyond Emma. They looked up, transfixed.

The gun held in their collective, single hand clattered to the floor, forgotten.

She held them. She broke the chains that bound them to the Queen of the Dead, reaching for Longland in the same way. She wasn't surprised at the tensile strength of his binding; the woman who had created it was here, and she knew more about binding the dead than Emma Hall would ever willingly know.

But it didn't matter. Emma had closed a hand around Longland, and if the hand no longer held his neck, it held him. She felt a grim amusement at the idea that she and the Queen of the Dead were playing tug-of-war over a former Necromancer. She was probably the only person present who did.

The Queen's eyes rounded, her brow rising into the momentary folds of her forehead.

"Chase," Eric said. The Queen's arm was still level with his midriff, as if this could stop him from leaving her side. She was smaller, finer boned, less well-muscled; all she had was power. She had not bound Eric except in one way: She had left him nowhere to go.

Chase bent and picked up the gun Merrick Longland had dropped.

Emma didn't turn to look at him; she was watching the Queen of the Dead. She knew, before Chase fired the first shot, that the bullet wouldn't hurt her.

Given Chase's lack of verbal response—and the lack of follow-up shots—he'd known, too. He watched as the bullet was absorbed by her body. She hadn't even stumbled.

"Do you honestly think you can kill me—any of you?" the Queen demanded. Fire burned at the edges of the room, but it no longer raged in the center. "Do you think I would have left myself vulnerable to you?"

"Scoros," Emma's ears hurt.

"I make no guarantees," he replied, as if she'd actually asked a question. He rose on shaking legs. No surprise there; Emma's were shaking as well. "Do what must be done," he added softly.

Emma nodded and turned to face what she called a door. It was the only door in the room that mattered to the dead; it was the only one that now mattered to Emma. The dead watched Emma, pressing against it in urgent silence.

Chase drew two daggers.

"Chase," she said softly. "You don't think those will make a difference?"

He didn't reply.

"Don't leave the circle," she whispered. More than that, she couldn't say. She turned her attention to the door.

It was thick, heavy wood; it seemed scratched and scarred, but only superficially. It was a solid door.

It was a door the dead couldn't see. What she saw now was invisible to them, except in one way: it was closed. They approached it as if it were a window against which they could find no purchase.

Emma had opened that door once. She had no idea for how long, although *not long enough* was the only relevant fact. She had strained and struggled to hold it long enough for one four-year-old boy to escape an eternity of afterlife. To do that, she had called the dead, and they had come, in hundreds. In thousands. She had borrowed their power, and she had used it, struggling to give them what she had promised.

Freedom.

"Emma," Longland said.

And in the giving, she had—for one brief moment—seen *peace*. She had seen an end to loss and suffering and self-hate and guilt and emptiness. She could not describe it in words. She couldn't even recall how it had looked to her. But she knew how it had felt.

And she knew, as she struggled, that that was what she needed to feel. She needed to see as the dead saw, as if she were one of them. Opening the door wasn't what needed to be done—that was the wrong paradigm. There was a window, a thick, plate of impenetrable glass, laid across the only freedom the dead were promised—and it couldn't be opened.

She needed to shatter it.

"Emma, dear," Margaret said, her voice startling in its urgent clarity. "The Queen is unmaking your circle."

"She's trying," Emma countered. "Margaret—I need to concentrate. I'm sorry."

Silence. Emma thought of warmth.

"Emma."

She looked at Margaret because Margaret appeared to have stepped in front of her. And Margaret Henney was clearer than the rest of the dead who had also gathered there—clearer, brighter, much more *solid*.

"Not that way, dear."

"The door—"

"Yes. It's here. It's everywhere. But you cannot approach it that way."

390 ～ Michelle Sagara

"How do you even know what I'm doing?"

"I can see it."

"What is she trying to do?" Chase demanded.

"She is trying to die."

Emma was offended. "I am *trying*," she said, through gritted teeth, "to see what the dead see."

"Yes, dear. And there is only one way for you to do that. Whatever you feel you must do, this is *not* the way."

"I need to see what the dead see to free them."

"No. You need to see what they saw *when they were alive* to free them, if I understand everything I've heard correctly. And the circle?"

Emma shook her head. "I trust them."

"Trust who?"

"Helmi," she replied. "And Nathan."

The Queen's dress shifted in place, wedding white—and complicated train—becoming something metallic, ornate. The crown remained, as did the tight pull of her hair; her eyes glittered.

Chase, knives in hand, stepped between the Queen of the Dead and Emma, placing his back against the latter while she worked. He glared at Eric. Eric, his partner. Eric, his rival. Eric, the *reason* the Queen of the Dead existed.

He had hated Eric when they'd first met. Of course he had. He'd been sent to deliver a message to Eric. All the pain, the death, the torture—all of it—a message for Eric. Eric was the reason his family had died.

He wanted to kill the Queen. He had dreamed, and day-dreamed, about this moment for years. The blades of these knives were a bitch to keep sharp; they were silver. But sharp didn't matter. What the bullet couldn't pierce, these blades could.

He was willing to bet his life on it. He'd been waiting so long to make that bet. But Emma had said only one thing: Don't leave the circle.

He tried not to care. He'd done suicidal things so many times since his family had died, it was practically all his life amounted to. If he killed the Queen, Emma would be able to finish whatever it was she'd started in safety.

No.

Allison would be safe. Michael. Amy. The Old Man. Eric? In some fashion, Eric would be safe. All of the dead would be. His mother. His sister. His father. He didn't know if dogs counted, but in his opinion, they should.

He could see the dead, with effort. But he had never seen *his* dead. He had never seen his family. He was certain that they would see Emma. They would see what Emma was doing. They would leave.

And he was fine with that. In every other way that counted, nothing could hurt them anymore.

Things could still hurt Chase. That was the problem with love and affection—once you had it, it was yours to lose. Life could hurt you without ever touching you. If Allison died now, it would kill him. It would do more damage than guns or knives when they didn't end life.

He wasn't certain what his death would do to Allison. It had been forever since he'd worried about the effect his death would have on someone else. In fact, this might be a first, because he'd never really thought about death as something that could happen to him or his family, when he'd had one.

"Chase."

He looked away from the Queen's rigid face, her newly formed armor, her ringed, cold hands. He met Eric's eyes.

"Don't step away from the circle while it still holds."

"I can—"

"I've seen that fire level small villages," Eric continued, his eyes strangely translucent. "It hasn't immolated you—or Emma—because of that circle. It's a power that's built on the dead."

"The dead—according to Emma—are already standing on top of her head."

"Yes. The dead she allows, the dead she welcomes. But she won't let the fire touch you. And there's nothing to extend that circle. There's no way to preserve your life. There's no point in throwing it away."

"Eric," the Queen of the Dead said, her voice like a blade's flat. "Do you not love me?"

Eric was silent.

"Why did you return?"

"Reyna."

She didn't turn. Her eyes would have frozen whole lakes.

If her tone implied pain or tears, those eyes were never going to shed them. She flinched when he placed a hand on her shoulder, although given the armor, she shouldn't have felt it.

"Why?" she demanded, as she looked at Emma.

"Because I want you to leave this place," he said, voice low. "I want you to leave it with me."

She looked, again, at Emma. And then she shook her head. "I will never leave this place." But there was something in her expression—bitter, dark, yearning, and loathing—that spoke to Emma. Because Emma, looking at the door, could nonetheless see the Queen clearly.

She wasn't carved into it; she wasn't part of it; the door itself was simple, dark wood. But she was more than a superimposition.

"Scoros," Emma whispered, "What is this door?"

Chase shifted the grips on his knives.

They cannot hurt her, boy. He recognized the voice and glanced at the old man. The old man wasn't speaking. He wasn't looking at Chase, or even Emma. His whole attention was focused on the Queen of the Dead. His lined, weathered cheeks seemed to glisten with tears. There was no fear in him. No aggression. He sat as if bearing witness. Again. *Wait. Trust the magar.*

"The magar's dead," he muttered. "No one dead stands a chance against her."

She is not dead; she is new, and she is too young. He spoke of Emma.

"She'll die."

Trust the magar.

"Because that worked out so well for you last time."

The Queen gestured, and Eric flew—almost literally—from her side. Chase saw him strike the far wall and slide. He wondered whether anything was broken. He knew that it didn't matter. Eric's body was exceptionally good at healing itself.

He even thought he understood why, and for the first time—ever—he pitied Eric. Plotting against the insane version of the woman you had once loved at a distance wasn't the same as personally stabbing or shooting her.

Green fire enveloped the room, scorching every square

inch of floor except the ones she occupied. He looked across to Eric and then away. The fire was too intense to see through. If she had decided to destroy him, it didn't matter. She *couldn't* destroy Emma yet, and Emma was the only responsibility Chase had now.

"None of you," the Queen said, "will escape."

She didn't bend to the circle, this time. In that armor, bending was probably impossible.

Instead, she lifted her arms slowly and deliberately. She seemed to struggle with the motion, her arms trembling as if she carried weight in her hands. The weight was invisible to Chase, at least to start, but as the movement continued he could see it clearly.

The words that defined the circle in which he was standing were rising. They were golden; they reflected soul-fire. Some of the words, he recognized; some he didn't. They trembled as they were dislodged.

Given that they'd been carved into stone, it should have been impossible to lift them; their shapes were the absence of matter. But they rose. They rose in concert, each word legible. Even the misspelled one.

The Queen's face was stone; if her arms felt weight, she didn't acknowledge it. Her eyes were the color of the fire that surrounded her. The words rose to the height of her chest in a ring. She brought her hands down in one swift, sudden motion, as if they were blades.

Chase expected the words to break.

They didn't. They hovered almost gently in the air, Emma Hall at their absolute center.

The Queen's brows rose, her eyes rounding in astonishment. When they narrowed, they became blade's edge— glittering with sharpness and the promise of death. She brought her hands down again; the circle rippled, the letters rising and falling as if they were buoyant. But the words they comprised held.

The air was hot with fire, but it chilled as the Queen of the Dead summoned her army: the dead. She had made a citadel, a home, of the dead—but not all of the stones and planks and windows were bound to her. They remained where they had been laid, but their voices grew in strength as the minutes passed.

The bound dead came through the walls. They came through the floors. They flowed like the coldest of winter air. Chase could see them. He could see them without losing his grip on the rest of life.

They circled their Queen, making obeisance in the lap of green flames as if the flames were wildflowers or stalks of densely packed corn. They rose at her regal nod—even armored and armed and in combat, respect clearly had to be received—and turned at once toward the circle of gold and words.

Emma had said that she trusted Helmi and Nathan. Chase had only half understood what that meant until he watched those liminal words. The dead approached them in a wave of motion, reaching for individual letters with a sea of arms, a sea of hands.

They shouldn't have had any effect on the words, but the words wavered as more and more of the hands of the dead reached them. The letter forms began to sag, to shift; what had been perfectly engraved all caps began to resemble writing, and not the careful, deliberate work of chisels.

"Emma."

She nodded.

"The words—she's going to change them. She's trying to remake them in the old image."

Emma stared at the Queen, although her back was, in theory, turned toward her. She could see the fires that raged around the Queen's chamber. She heard Chase's voice. It had none of Margaret's pinched gravity or careful urgency. But she knew what the Queen was attempting.

And she knew it would, eventually, succeed. Helmi and Nathan could hold out for some time—but not against the power the Queen now brought to bear. Once the circle ruptured, the fire would blaze in, killing them all.

And the door wouldn't open. Emma strained against it, pushing, pulling, but nothing worked. And why would it? She'd been across an ocean the last time she'd tried. She was now standing in the seat of the Queen's power.

Margaret was talking, her voice lost to the rising crackle of burning flame.

"I'm going to try to distract her," Chase said.

Emma turned away from the door, away from the stairs and the thought of ascension. She shook her head.

"Emma—"

Because she understood why the image of the Queen was so clear when she looked at the door. She understood what powered the barrier. She understood what had to be done to destroy it.

Yes.

"Not yet, Chase," she told him, touching his shoulder. He was tense—of course he was tense. "I can't throw your life away."

"You aren't." He was frowning. Something in her voice made him turn to her. His eyes widened. Emma wasn't certain what he saw in her expression, because she wasn't certain what her expression was. "You can't." His voice was flat.

"Throw your life away? No. No, I can't." She was deliberately misunderstanding him.

He didn't want to allow it. She couldn't think how this red-haired, angry, violent person had come to mean so much to her. Maybe it was because she'd seen some of his past and understood how it had opened up the path he walked. Maybe it was because Ally loved him, or maybe it was because he loved Allison.

Or maybe it was just because he was here, and even disliking her, he was willing to throw his life—and possible future happiness—away to buy her time. And it wouldn't be enough time.

He looked annoyed. "You can't kill her."

She said nothing.

"You've never killed anyone. In your life. You won't be able to kill her."

She felt calm. "I have to kill her," she said quietly. "She's the barrier, Chase. She's the door. She's the reason the dead can't leave. And they'll never be able to leave while she lives."

"In case you haven't noticed, there's soul-fire across every square inch of floor. You step outside of this circle and you're ash. Less than ash. You *won't be able* to kill her. You'll just die."

Emma shook her head. "Look at the circle. Look at the circle, Chase."

He did. Emma knew he would have grabbed her arm or shoulder if he'd had a free hand, but he didn't. He had two hands full of knife, and he didn't intend to surrender them while the Queen lived.

The circle that the Queen had pulled up from the ground remained. But it wouldn't remain for long, not against the concerted effort of the Queen and her army of undead.

"Just a little bit longer," she whispered. "Just hold it a little bit longer." To Chase, she said, "You'd better help Scoros."

"Help him what?"

"Stand, Chase. I'm moving, and the circle will come with me." She wasn't certain what Chase did. She wasn't certain what Scoros did. She looked at the Queen and only at the Queen. The army of the dead and the fire it produced wouldn't kill Emma yet. A simple knife would if the Queen carried one. A gun would.

The only gun in the room was on the floor beneath Emma's feet. The man who had carried it would never pick up a gun again. It didn't matter.

Reyna's eyes were clear and cold and almost green as they met Emma's. She looked faintly confused. "What are you doing?" Her eyes fell on the lantern that Emma carried. Emma held it out to her, as if offering it. She reached for it slowly.

But Emma shook her head. "You gave me a few days with Nathan," she said. "I thought I would never see him again except in dreams. Memories. I got to say everything I thought I'd never get to say again—and he could actually hear it.

"I got to hold him." She swallowed.

Reyna was watching her, arrested, although the fires didn't diminish, and the thinning of the words that held the circle together—the circle that moved now, with Emma—continued.

"I spent a lot of time sitting in the cemetery. I spent a lot of evenings sitting beside what was left of him. Probably as much time as I got to spend with him, in the end." She inhaled. Exhaled. She was an arm's length away from Reyna.

In one hand, she held the lantern; the other was empty.

"I thought the world ended the day he died. I had plans, Reyna. *We* had plans. It was easier for me. His parents don't get to choose what he does, and mine don't get to choose what I do. When his mother found out about me, she didn't come to kill me. She wouldn't. Even if she hated me, she wouldn't. It would have killed Nathan." She swallowed, smiled. There were no tears left. "I wanted to go to university with Nathan. I wanted to spend years with him. Live with him. I wanted to get married, find a home, have children—I wanted that life."

Reyna was still, in the light of the lamp.

"I *still* want it. I want it so much, sometimes I can't breathe. I look at every other man, and I can only see the ways in which they aren't Nathan."

"Why—why are you telling me this?"

"Because you'll understand it," Emma replied. "Because you'll understand it better than my friends or my mother or my teachers."

"But I *gave him back to you*," Reyna said, voice low—but not loud.

"No. You didn't. Nothing can give him back to me. He's dead."

"I resurrected him!"

"You made him a body of the dead. He's as much alive as the floor is. He's *dead*. And I can stay here, and grieve, and want, and let it destroy me. But, Reyna, it's not what he wants. It's not what Nathan has ever wanted for me." She swallowed. "The only thing he wants—the only thing I can give him—is peace. He wants what waits for the dead. He can't want me anymore—and I hate it. I hate that I can't—" She shook her head. "Eric's dead, Reyna."

"He is *not* dead—"

"But because of the choices you've made, so are you."

"Do you think you can—"

Emma shook her head. "Right now, Reyna, you are more dead than alive. You've never stepped out of the shadows. You are as trapped in Eric's death as—as Eric is. There's peace, there is joy, there's something beyond pain."

"You don't even believe that!" Reyna's eyes narrowed. Helmi had said she wasn't stupid.

"I believe it. I don't *feel* it. I don't *know* it the way I know how to breathe. But I do believe it. There's peace and joy and belonging and love—that's what Merrick Longland said. And that's what I've seen. You must have seen it yourself."

"I *hate* death," Reyna said. Bitter, angry, and bewildered. "All my life. *All of it.* Nothing but death. The dead. Always." She shook her head. "Only Eric—only Eric was about life. He made me want to live. To be alive."

"It's what I wanted as well," Eric said. Even in her rage, she had preserved him. "It was all I wanted. When I was working in the forge, it almost killed me—I'd get so distracted. I wanted to go to the stream. I wanted to stand beneath our tree. I wanted to watch until you arrived—you were always so breathless. I wanted to watch you look up and realize I was there, waiting, because your smile—" He touched her frozen lips, his hand so gentle Emma was certain that he could never have forced himself to kill her. "This isn't where I wanted to live. This isn't how I wanted to live. There's no stream, no tree—and no joy, Reyna.

"You haven't smiled at me that way since I died. Even this time."

"But *I'm* here," she whispered.

"Are you, love?" He bent down, kissed her forehead gently. "Emma?"

Emma held out her arms, lantern dangling from one hand, stepped forward, and hugged the Queen of the Dead. She hugged the Queen as if the Queen were another teenage girl, new to gut-wrenching loss and wandering the halls of an empty school, weeping. She hugged her knowing that in seconds the circle that protected her would dissolve, and she would die in the fires of that girl's wrath.

And she hugged her knowing that her body was mostly composed of the dead, the way Nathan's had been. The way Eric's was. Immortality, of a sort, had been made just as a new body had been made. And it could be undone the same way.

It would kill the Queen. It would kill Reyna. It would free the dead. And because the last thing was true, Emma unraveled the dead bound to the Queen's physical form, releasing them as she did. She knew what would happen, or thought she knew: Age would rush in, and the semblance of youth—with nothing to support it—would vanish.

In an odd rush of something like sympathy, she would have spared Reyna that. Because no one wanted to look like that in the eyes of the man they loved. And it was stupid, and she knew it. And she hated the choices the Queen had made, the damage she'd done, and she knew that if there was any justice, this wasn't it.

But she no longer believed in Hell. And even had she, she never wanted to be Hell's ruler. It wasn't, in the end, up to Emma to mete out punishment or judgment. It was simply to find the lost and lead them . . . home.

And it happened as she had expected it would; the health and vigor of this pseudo-youth drained away from Reyna's living body as Eric held it, held her; the armor melted, and the heat of the fire slowly banked. Eric's arms tightened as he smiled down into a face that was sinking into age and ruin and decay, smiled as he gathered her tighter, as if he could hold her to him forever—as if he *wanted* to.

Reyna whispered his name. She lifted a withered, bony hand, skin draped over its sunken flesh, its atrophied muscle, and she touched his face and said, "Eric, you're crying." And she didn't seem to notice that her own hand was so old, that her arm was spotted and white, that her hair had fallen out and away. She was smiling.

She was smiling as she died.

CHAPTER
TWENTY-SEVEN

THE GREEN FIRE DIED when the Queen did, winking out of existence in the cold, high air so suddenly it left nothing behind. The floor wasn't scorched; nothing was burned. But the holes in the wall and floor remained. They weren't sharp-edged or jagged; they were rounded and smoothed, as if portions of the rock had melted.

Except it wasn't rock.

Emma looked at Chase, briefly, before she turned to Eric. "Your turn?" she asked, voice soft.

He shook his bowed head, his arms tightening around a wizened corpse. She was glad that she couldn't see his face, which made her feel guilty. But it was Hall guilt, it was small and normal, and she almost welcomed it.

Chase had sheathed his knives. "That's it?" he asked.

Emma shook her head. She heard the cries of joy, of jubilation; she saw the dead—those who could move—shiver in place. She had thought they would stream to the exit, because the door that was locked had been opened, and it would never close again.

But they didn't. They looked—they looked up—and they raised arms or hands, as if something were reaching for them. As if something were gently gathering them. She watched them vanish, their expressions etched in her memory. The joy and the tears and the relief were bright. They gave her hope.

She even recognized one of them. Merrick Longland. She was surprised when he turned—arms still lifted—to look over his shoulder. She had never seen him look like this: younger, stronger. Happy.

She knew he didn't deserve happiness. But in that moment, she didn't care. Because the people he had killed, the people he had trapped, the people he had used, wouldn't care either. Like Merrick, they would pass beyond all pain, and she knew that they would deny Merrick Longland none of the joy they themselves felt. Even if he didn't deserve it. It was not the type of happiness that depended on the unhappiness of others to shine more brightly.

He didn't speak. Neither did Emma. But she smiled at him and nodded.

And when she looked down, Eric was watching them. But he gently—gently—set Reyna's body aside.

"Where is she?"

"She's only just died," he whispered. "She won't be here yet." He stood. His legs shook.

"Can I—"

"Not yet. I know what it means for the dead who contain me. But they know, Emma. They've seen."

"But you could leave. *They* could leave."

He nodded. "We will. But there's work to do here—for me, for Ernest, for Chase—that you can't do. There's not much of it left, but the Queen of the Dead taught her Necromancers well."

"I can do what I did to—or for—the Queen."

"If it's all the same to you," Chase cut in, "no. Allison would kill me if anything happened to you. We know how to fight Necromancers—and now they have no Queen. We'll do what we've always done. Let us finish this."

"I want you to come home," she told him softly.

"Emma, this *is* home for me." He walked over to Eric's side. Eric met his gaze, and to Emma's surprise, it was Eric who looked away. "But I want a different home. And I won't trust it until the last of the Necromancers is dead. They'll come back. Allison's baby brother may already be dead. Who's next? Her parents? Michael's? Yours?

"I don't want that life for any of you. Even Amy. And I won't be able to believe in home until I believe that it won't happen again. You get that, right? There's no damage this hunt can do to me. Not anymore."

She hesitated, and Eric watched her. "Chase can see the dead," she finally told him. "I don't want to leave the rest of your dead trapped the way they've been trapped for so long. It's not right, Eric."

"Emma—"

"If I do it—if I do it for a good reason, I'll eventually do it for a bad reason. Good, bad—it seems so much of it is subjective. I know what you intend to do. I think it has to be done. But I don't think it has to be done by you."

Eric exhaled. "Magar," he said. It was what Scoros had called her. Eric's gaze, however, traveled to the left of her face.

The old woman, Reyna's mother, was standing beside Emma, her arms folded, her lips pursed. She no longer looked like a shambling, ancient, undead creature. She looked like a joyless, severe taskmaster. "It is not up to me," she told Eric. "It's not my decision."

"But you would allow it."

The magar said nothing, refusing to offer anything Emma might use as guidance. Refusing, Emma thought, to take any of the responsibility of decision off Emma's shoulders.

It was Margaret who said, "Ask them."

"Ask?"

"Ask the dead."

"They'll want—"

"I am still here, Emma. I believe your father will wait for your return. Nathan and Helmi are both here—because the circle is still, barely, coherent. You will need it," she added softly. "They had the choice; you gave it to them. I admit Helmi surprised me. Ask them."

"I can't do what she did. Even if I could find dead who were *willing*, I couldn't rebuild a body for him." And she didn't want to, either.

"No. But I believe Scoros could. If it is necessary, I will volunteer."

Emma was silent. "I think we need four."

They both looked at Scoros. Scoros shook his head. "Emma has the lantern," he told them both. "If Margaret is willing, and you are willing to use its power, Margaret will be enough. More than enough. She already draws sustenance directly from you, magar."

"I don't understand."

"No. Do you doubt me?"

Emma shook her head. To Eric she said, "Margaret won't be voiceless. Not the way—"

"They aren't voiceless," he said softly. "They weep constantly. Or they used to."

Scoros approached Eric. "Then come," he said quietly. "I understand what you intend, and I would stay to aid you— but it is my time as well. Past time, and for the same reason. Emma will free the dead bound to me, and I will vanish. Before I do, I will do this one thing. Understand that it is contingent upon Emma's survival. If she dies, it will unravel."

Eric nodded. "Ernest won't be happy about it."

Scoros said nothing.

"Ernest will not be happy," Margaret agreed. "But I'll deal with that if I'm still left a voice. There is no other way. Emma will not let you leave as you are—and Eric, I don't think she's wrong."

Scoros came to stand by Eric. He held out his hands, palm out; Eric placed his in them. "This isn't the way—"

"I do not wish you to leave if you do not wish it. And I have never attempted this—not without some element of living flesh. Mostly my own. The containment that the Queen created must be preserved, and I cannot do it from a distance. Reyna was the most gifted, the most powerful, of our number. What she could achieve, we could not achieve on our own." He smiled almost apologetically. "It is possible that your body will not be quite as functional as it currently is."

Eric shook his head. "I'd like to be able to sleep at night. It's been hard since—"

"Since your resurrection. Margaret."

Margaret came to stand beside Eric, and then, after a

moment, she stepped into him, occupying the same space that he occupied, although they weren't the same height or general shape. Emma turned to the magar.

"Do not ask me for approval. Do not ask me for permission. Your guilt or your pride are things you must come to on your own. And, child—my daughter became the nightmare of the people, made flesh. If I were infallible or wise, none of this would have happened. You must make the choices that seem wise to you. And you must understand that no choice is without fear or doubt."

"It was forbidden to use the power—"

"Yes." She glanced at the circle, pale and luminous, that still floated around Emma. "My choices were not your choices. But it is not you who is using their power, Emma Hall. Helmi chose. Nathan chose. You are a conduit that allows them to express their desire in a way that affects the world of the living. You did not decide; *they* did. Now, I must go. But I will return. Scoros is finished."

Scoros was no longer holding Eric's hands when Emma turned away from the magar. Eric's hands were at his sides. He didn't look significantly different to Emma. Before she could ask, the old man said, "Brace yourselves."

Chase, however, said, "Lie down on a solid patch of floor. Now."

Since he was following his own advice—and at speed— Emma did the same. The floor was cold. Emma absorbed its chill. "Will the citadel dissolve?" she asked, voice shaking.

He answered the question she hadn't asked. "No. Not yet. Large parts of what remains will require your intervention. But your friends are as safe as they can be."

"The other Necromancers?"

"Some are dead; the Queen's fire was not contained to this room."

"The others?"

"They will not find your friends. It is the only thing I can guarantee. They may find *you*, but I do not think they will come looking. They will be concerned with their own escape. They will know that the Queen is dead."

"Will they find her?"

Scoros shook his head. "Not without both time and effort. And yes, Emma, they may look. She knew much, and she did not share all of it. But they will not find her yet. She is too new to death—as I will be."

Anything more Emma could ask was lost as the floor shook. She expected it to crack, to break, the vibrations were so strong. But the floors only looked as if they were made of stone; they weren't. They were made of the dead, just as the walls and the ceilings were.

When the shaking stopped, she pushed herself from the floor to her feet. She could see the words of the circle around her; they moved as she did. She wasn't certain anyone else could see them, but it didn't matter. She understood why Helmi and Nathan remained.

She was going to have to free the dead that were trapped here, not by their own memories or their inability to walk away from the lives that had ended, but by the will of their deceased Queen.

This was a temple, a cathedral, to grief and loss. It was vast and it was fortified and it was, in a fashion, starkly beautiful—but it was a grave. It was a grave that Reyna had dug, had lain down in, and had occupied for all but seventeen years of her existence, adding to it, enlarging it, but never emerging.

And Emma understood it. And understood that grief was not respect, in the end. It wasn't a testament to love, to how much Nathan had deserved love. It just was. And she had survived it—would survive it—because she had Allison and Michael and actual responsibilities. There were whole gray, empty days that waited—and she would fill them as she could bear to fill them.

But she would not be Reyna. She would not create the same space, albeit with vastly different decor, and attempt to remain in it, forever frozen, waiting for something that could never come.

She lifted the lantern again, and, circled by Helmi and Nathan, she turned to Scoros.

Scoros nodded. "It is done. The citadel is upon the ground, as you requested. Your friends have survived its landing, although I believe your dog is very upset. And loud."

She placed a hand very gently on the old man's chest,

and she undid the bindings that kept his body functioning, freeing the trapped, mute dead, who streamed away from him, arms raised, faces upturned.

And she watched as elements of Scoros came together, as if rushing in to fill the space that the dead had occupied, and she realized that Scoros had been both alive and dead, and he was becoming whole. She didn't ask him how it had been done. It was enough that it would be undone.

She began to walk through the Queen's resurrection room, and as she moved, the floors became liquid; she could see arms raised, a sea of waving, frenzied limbs. This time, it didn't disturb her. She reached for a hand, and instead of being pulled under, she had the strength, the balance, to lift, to pull the dead man—it was a man—free. As if he were a tightly compressed piece jammed into a very strained, intricate puzzle, the rest of the dead began to follow; there was nothing to hold them in place.

She knew where they would go. She could hear their voices raised—a whisper of sound, but so sharp, so sweet, words would have been superfluous.

She didn't know if the ease of this dissolution was due to the lantern or the Queen's passing, and she didn't care. The radiant joy of the dead was enough to move her to tears, and she let them fall as she walked. She didn't need the circle. The dead trapped here couldn't trap her. But she felt Nathan's presence as a comfort and Helmi's as a sharp encouragement to continue until every last one of the dead was free to leave.

She found Allison and Michael near the end of that journey; they were pale and drawn, but they lost the look of shuttered tension the minute they saw her. They stood on overgrown wild grass, and as they moved, a black blur streaked past them heading for her legs and whining in that high-pitched, overexcited way of happy dogs everywhere.

She knelt into a faceful of tongue and dog breath and was grateful for it, and when she rose, she said, "Where's Amy?"

"Marshaling the rest of the living," Allison said. "And Chase?"

"Chase is doing something similar with the Necromancers."

"I doubt it; Amy is only terrifying the maids."

"Maids?"

Allison nodded. "Some of the living weren't novices. They were just regular prisoners. They did the cooking and the cleaning, things like that. Ernest is with them as well."

"He should be with Eric and Chase."

"And leave the rest of them to Amy?"

Emma laughed.

"He's trying to arrange for a safe exit for all of us. Some of us aren't on the right continent, and we have no passports, among other things." She didn't mention clothing or food, although that was in short supply as well. At the moment, they had their lives. "He's also trying to come up with some sort of cover story for how we got here—and an international slavery ring isn't going to cut it. Even if the rest of us were good liars, Michael isn't."

The rest of them were, sadly, not good liars—they only looked good in comparison to Michael. Allison glanced at Michael and added, "Michael called his mother."

Emma nodded.

"With Amy's phone. He told her that we were all safe, just—not really close to home. And that we'd be home as soon as we could. Is it over?"

"I'm not sure it's entirely over—but I think the worst of it is." She hugged her best friend, and held on tightly while Petal, feeling left out, whined and jumped.

But Michael said, "Where's Nathan?"

Emma released Allison. "He's here," she said. And he was: the thread-thin words of a circle still floated around Emma at chest level.

"Is he going to stay?"

She reached out, touched a word—the badly spelled "gratitud"—and shook her head. "No. He can't. He's dead." The word was cold in her hand, but she expected that. She wasn't even surprised when it began to dissolve, the letters fully fading as the words gave way for peace, in a way they hadn't for war and death.

Standing in front of Emma, when the words had vanished completely, were Nathan and Helmi. She felt a surge of gratitude at the sight of them. Gratitude and grief. But she accepted the grief.

"Thank you," she said—mostly to Helmi.

The child snorted. "You were never going to get it done on your own. Neither was he."

Nathan grimaced—safely beyond Helmi's line of sight. "She argues more than Amy when Amy's on a roll." But there was affection in his words—affection Helmi could see when she pivoted to face him, frowning.

"Can you—can you see it?" Emma asked them both.

Helmi nodded, eyes shining. "You would have made a terrible Queen."

"Thank you," Emma replied, meaning it. "I can barely manage my own life. I don't think I want to be responsible for anyone else's right now." Petal whined. "Except my dog's."

Helmi settled small fists on her hips and surveyed the landscape. Emma wasn't certain what she was looking at; the dead, as she well knew, saw things differently. "Hey," Helmi said, staring off into the distance. She frowned when Emma failed to answer and turned to glare at her.

"Sorry—I wasn't sure who you were talking to."

"You. I thought my mother was an idiot. I mean, I *still* think she's mostly an idiot."

"I have days like that."

"I had centuries. Don't interrupt me."

Nathan was grinning as Emma nodded silently.

"You did a good job. You did the *right* job. Thanks." Her urchin smile deepened around the corner of her lips, her eyes almost sparkling with mischief. She looked young, to Emma. Maybe because joy was youthful. "My sister was really broken."

Emma nodded.

"Don't hate her. I mean, if it's possible. Don't hate her."

Emma said, quietly, "She's dead. There's no reason to hate her now."

Helmi shook her head.

"... I'll try, Helmi. I'll try hard. I think—" But she shook her head. Held out a hand. Without hesitation, Helmi placed hers across it, and beside Emma, Michael's eyes shifted.

"Helmi wants to say good-bye. And thank you." And to Emma's surprise, Helmi did, smiling up at Michael with unfettered, uncomplicated joy. When she released Emma's hand, she looked up at Nathan, waved, and walked away. Well, *bounced* away, really.

She inhaled, turned to Nathan, and held out a hand. Nathan shook his head, and looped both of his hands behind his back. "I have a favor to ask."

Emma hesitated.

"I want to talk to my mother."

"She's not here."

"I know. I want you to keep me by your side until you get home. I don't know what you're going to tell the parents—all of the parents—and I don't have good advice. I imagine Michael will tell the truth, Allison will say almost nothing, and Amy will lie. I don't know what you're going to tell Mercy."

"A lot of 'I'm so sorry, Mom.' "

He laughed. It was the most wonderful sound in the world. His laugh was one of the first things she'd noticed about him. "I know the dead and the living aren't supposed to meet. I know there are rules—but, Em, I want to talk to my mother. Once. Just once."

"She'll want—"

"No. She'll understand why it can only be once. Unless you keep me here, I can't stay."

Emma understood. Chains of grief had bound Eric for centuries. She felt that grief tighten. She wanted—for just a moment—to be loved so completely that she would be the only thing Nathan wanted. She wanted him to *want* to stay.

And she wanted to let him leave. She was not ready to die yet. She knew she would let him go. She would smile. And part of her would mean it. Part of her would grieve—but she accepted that, too. She had loved Nathan, had anchored her dreams in him. It was okay to feel pain at the loss. It was what the living did.

"I want her to know I'm okay. I want her to know where I'm going and what's waiting for me. And that I'll be waiting. Just that. I think—I think that'll be enough."

"If you're bound to me the way Margaret was," she told him, "you should be able to make yourself visible without touching me. I don't know if it works at a distance."

Nathan nodded.

"I—I don't want to be there when you talk to your mother. I don't want to do that to her."

He smiled. Nodded. "She'll cry."

"I know. I would."

EMMA

THERE AREN'T A LOT OF SURFACES on which
Emma can draw a circle in her house. Her room—all of
the bedrooms—are carpeted. The dining room has hard-
wood floors, but the floors are heavily laminated, and they
don't take chalk well. She knows from experience that they
would take paint or marker, but she's not three anymore,
and even when she was, that hadn't gone over well.

In the end, she settles for the garage. She bundles herself
in heavy winter clothing although it's spring, and she heads
out, a box of chalk in her hand. She's had some practice in
circle drawing in the past two years. It's been interrupted by
the usual things—end of school, graduation, searching in
panic for a university that both wants her and that she
wants to attend.

Allison has started to complain about her annoying baby
brother again; apparently he was still stealing pens and paper from her room. For nine months, she didn't offer a single word of complaint; his lungs were damaged by the

gun—almost everything was. He needed physiotherapy and time to recover, and he lost almost an entire school year.

But he didn't lose his life.

The first time Allison stormed into his room to retrieve her stolen supplies and threaten to kill him with one of them, he laughed. That was normal. And then he cried, which was not.

Allison's mother got teary. "Allison's been trying so hard," she said, with a fond, but watery, smile. "But he needs to know that he can annoy her. He needs to know that she thinks he's strong enough—safe enough—to threaten."

Emma privately agreed. But she didn't think that Toby was the only one who needed it.

She thinks of this, smiling, as she writes. The magar wanted her to learn the old runic forms but finally surrendered—gracelessly—when Emma had insisted on English. "It was fine for Helmi," she pointed out. "And it worked."

She'd been surprised to see the magar, two months after they'd returned to Toronto. The old woman had walked through her closed bedroom door while she was conversing with her father about her university choices.

Her father, of course, had stayed.

He was almost ready to leave, he said, because Mercy was *almost* happy. He didn't mind Jon. In fact, he seemed to approve of him. Emma wanted him to go—but while he remained, she was happy to have his company. Happy and a bit chilly.

She was less happy to have the magar's company—but she was not at all surprised to see her. She turned to the old woman as her father tactfully faded from sight. "Did you come for the lantern?"

"The lantern," the magar said, "is yours. It's up to you to pass it on." Her frown practically became a canyon. "What are you going to do, girl?"

Emma could have pretended to misunderstand. She didn't. She wasn't a Necromancer. She was, however, Emma Hall. She thought about Andrew Copis a lot in the quiet hours of night. Andrew Copis was a ghost who would have been trapped in the moment of his death for decades or centuries, regardless of the Queen of the Dead.

It had been so important to her to free him from that.

"I'll learn," she'd told the magar.

Emma doesn't misspell "gratitude," although she considers it every time she draws the circle. It's the one word she's certain she won't give up, no matter how much living her life changes her.

She writes in careful chalk and she waits. She doesn't have to wait for long. The garage door is open to the evening sky. She can see street and trees in the boulevard just beyond the sidewalk.

And she can see Eric walking up the drive. He almost heads to the house, but some instinct causes him to jog a bit. He approaches the garage.

"You knew I was coming?" he asks, as he looks at the circle that's nearing completion.

"The magar dropped by." Like a Sisyphean boulder. She looks up to see his expression; dusk hides most of it. Or it would, if he were alive.

"I don't envy you," he replies, with a grin.

"You've got Margaret."

"She heard that. She's trying not to be amused." He takes a seat, leaning against the only bare wall he can find; he stretches his left leg, folds his right, and rests his elbows on his bent knee. He then lowers his head.

"Where's Chase?" she asks.

"I left him at Allison's. If I know Chase, he's standing on the sidewalk out of line of sight of her house trying not to look as terrified as he feels."

Emma laughs. She fumbles in her pocket for her phone.

"That's cheating," Eric says, but he's smiling broadly as well.

Emma texts her best friend. *Chase is outside on the sidewalk. He's too nervous to knock on the door.* "I'll blame you. Besides, Ally doesn't always check her text messages."

Apparently, she's checking them tonight. *OMG.* She doesn't even ask Emma how she knows.

Emma looks at the source of the information. "You're ready?" she asks him quietly.

Eric nods. Emma doesn't ask about Necromancers; Eric

doesn't volunteer the death count. She is grateful that it's not her job. But she has a job to do. Emma carefully steps over the perimeter of her circle. She holds out a hand to Eric. There's no hesitation when he takes it.

But he says, "Margaret first."

Emma nods. She doesn't pull out the lantern, but she doesn't need it. In some fashion, Margaret is still bound to Emma. It's far, far easier to unravel her current shape than it would be to create it. In a matter of minutes, Margaret Henney is standing before her, smiling.

They exchange a few words, and Margaret says, "I'm going to go speak with your father."

"Don't waste breath. I've already tried. He says he's not ready to leave."

"I'm not wasting breath, dear. The dead don't. And I think he'll be ready to leave when he understands—and believes—that the threat Necromancers pose to you is over." She turns to Eric, her smile diminishing.

"Eric."

He nods. He's never been demonstrative.

"Good-bye, dear."

"Don't waste good-byes on me. We'll be seeing each other soon enough. Go talk to the Old Man."

"He's a little far—"

"He's in the car."

Margaret nods and leaves him alone with Emma. To Emma's eye, Eric looks the same as he did when he entered the garage. No one else will see him that way. He's dead. But he's been dead for as long as Emma has known him. It seems a lifetime. It's been just over two years.

"Are you sure you can do this?" he asks.

She nods but decides on honesty as she answers. "If there were anyone else who could, I wouldn't." She doesn't tell him why; there are so many reasons to choose from. But her biggest is Chase. She has nightmares about what happened to Chase's family. She understands why it's hard to let go of hatred or judgment.

She's surprised when the magar appears.

"You don't intend to help me, do you?" she asks.

The magar's glare is withering, but Emma's built up a tolerance to it. "That is not the way the circle works."

* * *

Emma sits at the rough center of the circle. She closes her eyes. She listens. This is the peaceful part of her task. She is never certain what she's listening for. The dead aren't always loud. They don't always cry or scream or plead. Andrew Copis didn't. But his memories were so vivid she could hear his mother's screaming in place of his voice.

Tonight is a bit different from the usual searching: she knows who she's searching for, and she has no doubt that she'll find her.

When she steps outside of her circle—and outside of her body—she touches down in a landscape she refers to as gray. It's an inexact description of a washed out nothingness. It has no character, no features, nothing to give it form or shape.

Or at least that's what usually happens. Today, however, the landscape has one distinctive feature. Eric. His hands are by his sides, his expression too complicated to place. But his lips turn up in a small smile as she appears.

She doesn't offer him her hand; he doesn't attempt to take it. "You know where you're going?" he asks.

She nods. She begins to walk, and Eric falls in beside her.

As they walk, Eric speaks. Eric, who never talks about anything personal. Eric, who is the foil to Chase Loern's gregarious anger.

She's never asked Eric if he still loves Reyna. She doesn't ask him now. She doesn't ask him if he stayed for Reyna's sake because she knows the answer is No. He stayed to finish the job.

But she sees his restlessness so clearly now, she wonders if that's all of the truth. She's come to understand that truth, like the people who believe it, is complicated; it's never entirely one thing.

She notes the moment the landscape changes, gray becoming stalks of dry, wild grass and the trunks of distant trees; she sees the sky become blue with a hint of clouds. She hears the rush of water and thinks of rivers or streams. The shadow of birds cross the ground as it solidifies beneath her feet, their wingspans large and open.

Vultures.

She has seen so much death on these walks. So much pain. So much fear. She glances at Eric; he is grim now. He knows exactly where they are. She almost offers him a hand because she's not certain he will be able to remain here. He shakes his head with a rueful smile, and she understands.

She concentrates.

She can hear a girl scream. It stops her in her tracks, and for one long moment the scenery loses color. It threatens to lose stability, she is so overwhelmed by what she hears. It is not Emma's voice, but it might as well be; her throat aches, and her chest; her hands are shaking fists.

She fights for control, fights to push the feelings aside just enough that she can navigate. She's had practice by now. She's lost evenings—and even weeks—to the lives the dead lived. She doesn't want to lose this one, because Eric is with her. He provides incentive to master her reactions.

It's been two years. More. She hasn't seen Nathan except in photographs—and she will never see him again. It hasn't hurt as much as this for a while, and she knows why. The girl's loss is new. She is looking at death. She is looking at Eric's corpse.

She glances at Eric; he is looking at her, his lips slightly thinned. "I'm sorry you had to do this."

"I didn't have to do it," she replies.

"It was you or no one."

She smiles, meaning it. "Is this where you expected me to find her?"

He is silent as the roof of a small house comes into view. He pauses there. "I wasn't certain. Were you?"

Emma nods. "I was certain. I don't know that she would have been happy with you, in the end. I don't know that you would have been happy with her." She has her doubts, but they're irrelevant. What she knows is that Reyna never had the chance to live that dream, and Reyna was fragile enough—young enough—that it destroyed her.

It destroyed so many people.

"Are you ready?" Emma asks.

"I don't know." His smile is apologetic, and his hands are tight. He is watching vultures and hearing the ugly laughter of villagers. Emma doesn't know if they actually laughed; memory, she has discovered, is subjective.

And irrelevant. This is the past. This is the cage that traps the dead. They don't see it, can't leave it, without help. She knows that Reyna deserves this cage.

But she knows that Reyna did not, on the day Eric died, deserve this pain. She didn't deserve to lose her mother, her sister, her uncle, and the only man she would ever love. She didn't deserve the murderous cruelty of villagers goaded by fear into an act of madness. If she hadn't suffered, if she hadn't been victim to things *she* didn't deserve, there would never have been a Queen of the Dead.

And it is here that the Queen of the Dead was born. It's here that she will, finally, die.

Eric makes—has made—no excuses for her. Emma is certain that centuries of almost-life have killed the love he once felt. But maybe love survives, in some fashion.

Or maybe Eric is as trapped by death as Reyna has been. Maybe some part of Eric is still the boy that loved her, in this village, centuries ago—the person he was when he was killed. And he was killed, Emma knows, attempting to protect Reyna. He was willing to give his life for her.

He did.

Emma can see the body. She can see Reyna. The gown and the tiara that characterized her later reign are no-where in sight, and her hands are covered in blood. Eric's head is cradled in her lap; she is bent over his face, the edge of her hair matted red and sticky. Emma can't hear what she's saying, but she can guess, and she's grateful for the distance.

Eric, however, shakes off uncertainty and fear as he sees her there, cradling his head. He walks—almost runs—to her side, and stands in front of her, looking down at her bent head. He kneels.

"Reyna," he says, as Emma approaches them both, moving slowly. *"Reyna."*

Reyna doesn't look up. She's not aware of Eric's presence. Emma feels a pang of disappointment on Eric's behalf, but she shakes it off quickly and smiles at Eric as he looks up at her.

She feels her clothing shift as she becomes firmly rooted in this memory place. She knows her hair changes. She's not certain whether or not she retains her own face because she's not certain her face would be relevant to village life — or life on its outer edge.

But she says, as she approaches, "I've called for a healer."

Reyna looks up at the words. She doesn't see Eric. She sees his injured body.

"We need to get blankets," Emma continues. "And we need to build a fire. We need to keep him warm." She doesn't look at Eric's chest, at the gaping wound that appears to cover the whole of it. She looks, instead, at Reyna.

Reyna is frozen for one long moment. She looks at Eric's body and looks at Emma, and then she very, very gently lowers the memory of Eric to the ground. She stands, facing Emma, and as she does, the scenery fades.

The look on Reyna's face is one of recognition. Emma is surprised. She's not afraid. She knows the circle will protect her, if protection is needed. The dead she has guided to freedom never recognize her for what she is until they are almost at the exit.

But Reyna recognizes Emma.

"I didn't think you would come," she says.

"If you could think that I wouldn't," Emma replies, "you shouldn't be here at all. You shouldn't be trapped here."

Reyna shakes her head. Her appearance remains as it was on the day Eric died and her world ended. There is a quiet dignity in her now that Emma never saw in the Queen. And there's pain — but it's an honest pain, not a pain transformed into anger or rage or hatred.

"I was always trapped here," Reyna says. "I can't escape it on my own. I know — I know it's not real. Who better than me, to know it? But it holds me anyway. I — I didn't think you'd come. Why did you?"

Emma says, truthfully, "Because there's no one else."

"I would have left you here."

"I know. But I'm not you."

"Because you're better than me?" There is no rancor in the question. No accusation. No fear.

"Because," Emma says, surprised at the tightening in her own throat, "I was *safer* than you." She smiles and adds, "And because I was asked, as a favor."

"My mother?"

Emma shakes her head. "Your mother doesn't ask for favors. In fact, your mother doesn't *ask* for anything."

Reyna winces, but she laughs, and her laugh is surprisingly warm. "You've spent some time with my mother, I see." The laughter fades slowly. "Who asked you?"

Emma reaches out for Eric.

Eric hesitates and then places a hand in hers.

It's clear that Reyna can see him the instant their hands connect. Her eyes are wide and luminous—with death, and possibly with the tears the dead don't shed. And her smile steals breath, it's so radiant. To Emma's surprise, Eric appears to *blush*.

"Eric?"

"I told you," he says, voice rough and low, "I want you to leave this place. I want you to leave it with me." He looks down at her—he has to, she's not tall—and he says, "There's my smile."

And he smiles back.

"I'm proud of you, Sprout."

Although the garage is chilly, the words are warm. Emma's not a child; she doesn't *need* to hear them. But some part of her is still her father's daughter and always will be. Even if he's dead.

She is silent as she leaves the circle; she doesn't scuff it or obliterate the binding words beneath her feet. She doesn't know the precise moment when Margaret leaves, but she knows when she's gone. Eric is gone. Nathan is gone.

Memories are a poor substitute for life—but regardless, they're precious. The memories are Emma's to hold on to for as long as she wants, and they cost no one.

"Thinking?" Brendan Hall asks, as she leaves the garage, falling in beside her.

"Mostly that I have to take Petal for a walk."

"Want company?"

She nods.

Petal is older and deafer, but he has the heart of a puppy. A puppy that no one has fed, ever. She takes dog treats, picks up his lead, pops her head into the family room to let her mother and Jon know they'll have to do without a begging rottweiler for a while, and heads out.

Her father keeps her company, although he stays out of the family room. The only thing Emma resents Jon for these days—and it's a tiny, tiny resentment—is her father's stiff reserve. But Jon makes her mother happy, and Mercy Hall deserves some happiness out of life.

And, if Emma is honest, she likes Jon. Jon can pull a smile out of her on days when that's harder than pulling teeth. There are still bad days, after all. But they're fewer.

She walks to Nathan's grave. The fact of the grave once felt like the end of her life, and for a while, it had been. Things that had been so important became, instantly, trivial. She had gone through all of the right motions, with no sense that they meant anything.

But if this marked an end, it marked a beginning as well. It was here that she first met Eric and the magar. It was through Eric that she met Chase. In the past two years, Chase has become as important to her as friends she has known since she was five, which is good, because now that he has returned to Toronto to stay, she is going to be seeing a lot of him. He wants to marry Allison.

She glances at her father.

"You're okay, Sprout?"

"I am. I'll miss Eric—but it was time." Saying that, she runs the back of her hand across her eyes.

The tears are not for Eric. Her father knows. But she doesn't speak until she finally reaches the cemetery, and even then, it's hard.

"The worst thing about being dead," her father says, starting the conversation, "is the helplessness. I wanted to pick you up when you fell. I wanted to hold your mother when she cried. I wanted to be able to duck out to the store and buy the groceries I knew she'd forgotten."

"I did that."

He smiles fondly. "Responsibility is for the living, to the living. I wanted to know you were both okay. I wanted to know that you were doing well." He shakes his head. "Every bad day either of you had wracked me with guilt, because there was nothing I could do about it.

"And then you met Eric and the magar. I am not—I will never be—grateful to the Queen of the Dead. But the consolation was that I could speak with you again. I could offer you comfort. Cold comfort," he adds, with a slight smile. "I watched you for years."

Emma turns, then. "I'll be all right, Dad." She wills herself not to cry but fails.

"Yes. Yes, you will. Thank you." When she doesn't respond, he reaches out with his cold, dead hands and touches her cheek. The tears should freeze, but they don't. "The best gift any child could give their dying—or dead—parents is that: the certainty that they'll be okay. You'll be more than okay, Emma." His smile deepens; hints of pain change the shape of his eyes. "Part of me doesn't want to leave. Part of me wants to stay and watch what you choose to do, how much you'll achieve, from here on in."

Emma holds her breath. Exhales. "But no pressure."

He laughs.

Emma smiles. She understands the part of him that wants to stay. She was his daughter. He loved her. But she understands, as well, that he is tired. He is exhausted. The only thing that ties him to the world of the living is the daughter he loved—but they both know he can no longer be part of her life.

Life is hard, sometimes. But it continues. Having seen the result of one desperate woman's attempt to create an eternity of love, it's best that way.

Emma opens her arms, and her father hugs her. "Can I walk you there?" she asks.

"I'm not sure it's a good idea."

"I've seen where you're going. I've never followed any of the dead."

"You've had no incentive."

"The magar has been teaching me for two years, Dad."

He laughs again. And he doesn't say no.

"I want for you what you want for us," Emma says, before he can. "That's all. I want to know that you're safe, that you're happy, that there's some peace for you."

"You don't know what actually lies on the other side of that door."

"No. But no one living does. If I can see you off happy,

that's enough. That's enough." She takes his hand; it's cold. Of course it is. "Thank you."

"For what?"

"Everything. Giving me life. Loving me while you were part of it. Watching me when you couldn't be. The usual." She stops speaking and waits until the tears are under control before she leads her father away.

He's smiling. She'll remember that later.

ABOUT THE AUTHOR

Michelle Sagara lives in Toronto with her husband and her two sons, where she writes a lot, reads far less than she would like, and wonders how it is that everything can pile up around her when she's not paying attention. Raising her older son taught her a lot about ASD, the school system, and the way kids are not as unkind as we, as parents, are always terrified they will be.

Having a teenage son—two, in fact—gives her hope for the future and has taught her not to shout, "Get off my lawn" in moments of frustration. She also gets a lot more sleep than she did when they were younger.